City of gods
Hellenica

By Jon Maas

Copyright © 2013 Jon Maas

All rights reserved.

ISBN: 1490366326

ISBN-13: 978-1490366326

WgaW Reg #1632294

Library of Congress Reg# TXu 1-851-080

DEDICATION

I dedicate this to NG, MM and JJ. Think big and don't let anyone tell you it's silly to do so.

CONTENTS

Introduction	7
Part I - Recruitment	
Death	13
War	23
The White Knight	33
Pestilence	51
Part II – The Academy	
Hellenica	63
Training	85
The Pledge	109
The Banshee	125
The First Class	131
The Legged Snake	149
The Amazon Demon	165
The Manitou	185
Kross	195
The Norseman's Banquet	219
The Cure	233
Part III – Dagon and the Mermaid	
The Trial	265
The Bomb	291
The Return	321

The gods are back, and they are tearing this world apart

Zeus, Dagon, Loki, Lugh and countless other deities have come back to this earth and rule over their individual districts with no goal other than satiating their own petty desires.

The sole remaining functional province, *Hellenica*, decides to act. They build the *Academy* and are about to recruit 16 young gods with the hopes of training them to police this world.

The Horsemen

Of these 16 young gods, four have strange powers that the Academy might not be able to control. Kayana Marx, Gunnar Redstone, Tommy Alderon and Saoirse Frost aren't like normal gods, and their abilities stem from the Monotheistic times.

But if Hellenica has any hope of holding this world together, they will have to teach these four to exercise their powers to their fullest extent, even if it might bring everything to an apocalyptic end.

CITY OF GODS - HELLENICA

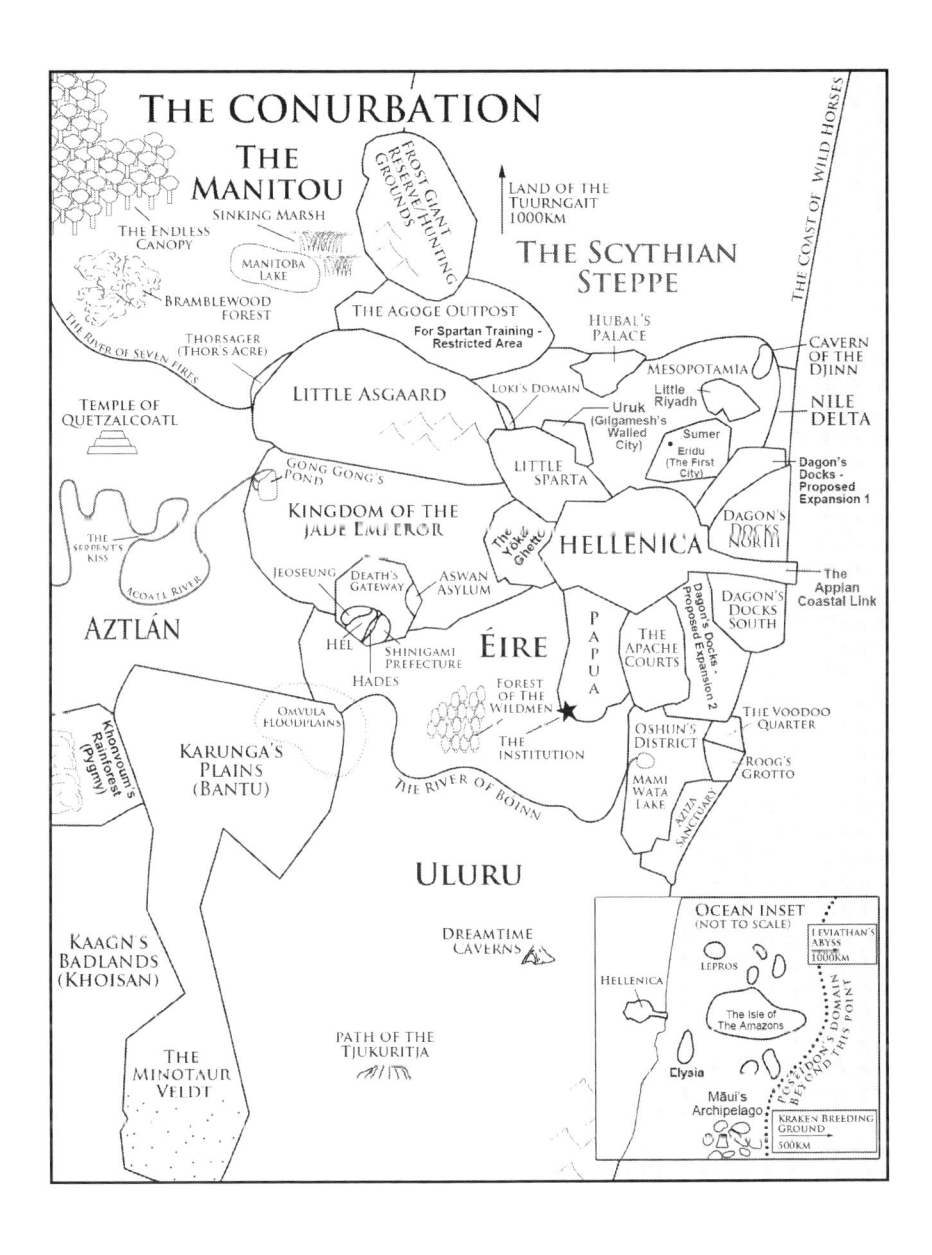

JON MAAS

PART I
RECRUITMENT

DEATH

Kayana Marx woke up to the sound of a high-pitched laugh, the laugh of a dullard. She flipped a switch and twenty bulbs turned on at once, flooding the room with light. This was one of her requests: *complete light or complete darkness, nothing in between.* Kayana caused no trouble, so the doctors were happy to oblige her demands, no matter how strange.

She peeked through her viewing hole to see who was laughing. Her heart sank when she saw a doughy, hairless Celtic boy, perhaps seventeen years of age, perhaps thirteen or twenty-four. It didn't matter; he could no longer speak. All he could do now was *laugh*.

This was the handiwork of Loki, and it caused Kayana great despair; the boy should have died years ago.

Another one of Kayana's requests was that under no circumstances should others come within two meters of her. She regretted that request now; if she were free to roam, she could simply lay her hands on the boy and he would die with a bit of dignity. Perhaps others would be hurt, but she could help him. She knew this boy and his dull laugh *should not be.*

/***/

It all started five years ago, when a group of drunken Celts from Éire stumbled into the Apache Courts and beheaded a young man. This was done without Lugh's permission, of course. Lugh was the Éire district's leader and didn't believe in violence without an absolutely noble goal. But the drunken Celts had started a war, and Lugh was bound to end it. The war between Éire and the Apache Courts lasted a year.

The Apaches were humiliated with each skirmish. The Celts' style of fighting was brutally effective: fast, haphazard, chaotic and unexpected. No plan, no official battle, just cross the line into the Apache Courts and start beheading.

The Apache god, Usen the Creator, did everything he could to fight back. He bestowed his warriors with courage and quickness and even cast a spell to allow them to see in the dark. But it was no use; the Apache Courts were small and peaceful, and they could not mount an effective defense against the overwhelming numbers of the drunken Celts.

So Usen played his last card, the card that most small districts played when they faced annihilation. He went over to Little Asgaard and had a secret meeting with Loki. Loki, of course, agreed to help.

"I will help you defeat the Celts," Loki had said, "but you must fight dirty."

Usen blanched at the plan but had no other option; it was Loki's way or have the Apache Courts wiped off the map.

"We're about to do ignoble things," the Apache god Usen had said to his people. "Depart now and you'll still be in my constituency."

The next evening, with Loki's help, only two Apaches launched their raid into Éire. They captured the first son of one of the Celtic leaders and brought him back to a hidden underground cell. The boy's name was Caratacus.

The Celts were disheartened, but not devastated; Celtic tradition prepared every boy for kidnapping, torture and death. If the Apaches tortured him, the boy would not scream, and the Celts would sing songs about Caratacus in the pubs for centuries to come.

But the Apaches did not torture Caratacus; they *deformed* him, with Loki's help. They fed him a diet of lard and little else; within three months, Caratacus was a drooling simpleton. The Apaches kidnapped twenty other first-born Celtic children and did the same to them.

At the end of the year, the Apaches kept some of these boys as fools for their noble houses and delivered the rest to the boys' original doorsteps in Éire.

This move was devastating to the Celtic psyche. The Celts feared neither death nor pain, but having their sons turned into simpletons was more than they could bear. Lugh himself offered unconditional surrender.

"Kill our sons, or raise them as your own and train them to defeat us," Lugh had said, "but do not do this thing."

So there was an uneasy peace between the two districts, negotiated by Loki, with the condition that both districts build a temple to him. The kidnappings stopped and the Apaches returned all the kidnapped boys to Éire, but the pain remained. The Celts were not prepared to take these boys in, so they sent some to be killed in foreign wars. Many, like the laughing boy in front of Kayana, ended up wandering the streets of the conurbation until they made their way to the institution.

/***/

Kayana looked at this boy; he was almost two meters tall and a hundred and fifty kilograms in weight. She closed her eyes and thought of what his life *should be*.

15

His name is Aiden, she thought. *He was supposed to be a father of four, an engineer, and a poet. He was supposed to die in a boat crash soon after his fifty-fourth birthday. One hundred and fifty people from twenty different districts would have attended his funeral, which would have been led by Lugh himself.*

Kayana's eyes went into the back of her head and she meditated upon what Aiden's life would be like now.

He will live sixty more years and will never utter another word; he will only laugh. Ten years from now he will become enraged and kill a nurse. They will give him medication, and he will spend the next half century in bed.

Kayana knew his life would be an abomination, and should not be. She meditated deeply about what she could do to make it right. *I will get out,* she thought. *I will take my gloves off and lay them on him at my first chance, and he will die that night.*

But she had requested that the guards keep her isolated, and the institution had made arrangements so that she wouldn't be allowed amongst the general populace. She was thinking about how to bypass this when a guard came to her door.

"Kayana Marx?"

"Yes."

"The lead physician would like to see you," said the guard.

Kayana felt that her plan to help the laughing boy could wait; if nothing else, she had time here.

"I will see the physician, provided he keeps his distance," replied Kayana. "And make sure his office is completely lit or completely dark. No shadows."

/***/

Dr. Julius Shaw sat three meters away from Kayana in a brightly illuminated meeting room. He was reading a computerized tablet detailing Kayana's history. She saw the reflection of her biography in Dr. Shaw's thick glasses:

> Subject's hair is black and grows thickly but does not grow on the sides of the subject's head. She has a fine bone structure, small stature, and does not smile. Her skin is devoid of pigment, yet it does not burn in the sun. Her home district and lineage are both unknown. She shows no malevolent intent but should be considered extremely dangerous. She prefers an environment of complete light or complete darkness because she claims that shadows cause her to disappear. Her vision, hearing and sense of smell are all preternaturally acute, placing her in the 99.99th percentile of all groups and—

"Orphaned since birth," said Dr. Shaw. "Your parents are listed as *unknown*. Rare in this day and age, don't you think?"

Kayana didn't respond, but averted her focus from her profile and stared at Dr. Shaw through the strands of dark hair that fell over her pale face.

"Fifteen years old, three different foster families before you committed yourself here. You state in your initial interview that you were responsible for deaths in these foster families. Why do you think that?"

"When I touch people," said Kayana, "they die soon thereafter."

"Don't you think that's a bit dramatic?" asked Dr. Shaw. "Someone of your ... *remarkable* intelligence should understand that causation and correlation—"

"Would you like me to touch you?" asked Kayana, removing her gloves. "If you survive the night, I'll admit there's neither causation nor correlation."

Dr. Shaw thought for a moment, smiled, and put away his computerized tablet.

"Let's say you are to blame," asked Dr. Shaw. "Your touch causes death. Do you feel remorse at your family members' passing?"

"None," said Kayana.

"None? Yet you turned yourself in so that you could do no further harm."

"Their deaths were not supposed to be *now*," said Kayana. "My presence brought their ends early, and that *should not be*."

"Your profile indicates intelligence so high that it can't be measured," said Dr. Shaw. "It also suggests that you're a complete sociopath."

"I agree with both assessments," said Kayana.

"I disagree with the sociopath part," said Dr. Shaw. "I think you have a profound sense of justice, of fairness. I think you have an enormous amount of compassion; it just can't be measured according to our standards."

"I am a sociopath," said Kayana. "We are all sociopaths."

"Now, that's not true—" said Dr. Shaw, but Kayana interrupted.

"Sub-Saharan Africa, 873 A.D.," she said, "there was a battle between the Owambo and the neighboring Himba, the seventeenth of twenty-one battles that century. The Owambo won. They slaughtered ten thousand Himba warriors, took the women as slaves, and slaughtered a thousand infants in cold blood afterwards."

Kayana looked Dr. Shaw right in the eyes. Her own irises were jet-black and merged with her pupils to form two dark circles, but her eyes flashed completely white for a moment before narrowing and turning black again.

"Dr. Shaw, do you feel sad because of this occurrence?"

Dr. Shaw replied truthfully.

"No."

"But you recognize the abomination that occurred that day?" said Kayana.

"Yes," said Dr. Shaw.

"I feel the same pity for my dead parents as you do for the ninth-century African woman who was killed in front of her own child. Though I cannot shed a tear for them, I recognize what *should and should not be*. So I came here so that I would do no further harm."

Dr. Shaw smiled, then got up and looked out the window.

"I see your point," he said, "but I still believe in mine; you aren't a sociopath. In fact, your sense of morality and compassion *far supersedes* what the average human can feel. I feel your sense of right and wrong is more adept than mine or anyone else's."

Kayana thought for a moment and then smiled.

"Perhaps," she said.

"You see the world through a very specific and simple moral lens," said Dr. Shaw. "What *should be*, and what *should not be*; is that correct?"

"Perhaps," said Kayana.

"So I ask you this," said Dr. Julius Shaw. "How do you feel about the world now, specifically the conurbation? How do you feel about this world we live in?"

Kayana thought for a moment. She thought about the laughing boy, her family and the conurbation.

"Is the world as it *should be*?" asked Dr. Shaw.

"No," said Kayana.

Dr. Shaw smiled, picked up his tablet and pressed some buttons.

"That answer alone is good enough reason to kick you out of the institution," said Dr. Shaw with a smile. "Above all else, you're completely *sane*."

"Sanity is an arbitrary construct," said Kayana, "a relative standard of brain chemistry that has no bearing on reality and—"

"You're meant for something more, Kayana," interrupted Dr. Shaw, "something more than rotting away in a cell, wearing thick gloves and switching lights on and off."

"Perhaps," said Kayana, "but if you want to send me back to another foster family …"

"I will do no such thing," said Dr. Shaw. "Your touch causes death; I admit this. I'm releasing you to another group that has asked for you specifically. It's a school for your kind."

"My kind?" asked Kayana.

"You have powers," said Dr. Shaw.

"A lot of people have powers," said Kayana. "New gods show up every day."

"And unlike you, they use their abilities for personal gain," said Dr.

Shaw. "This school asked for you specifically. They want to train you and others like yourself so that the conurbation can be brought under control again, so that society is once again as it *should be*."

"No school can contain me," said Kayana.

"This one would like to try," said Dr. Shaw. "It's called *the Academy*."

JON MAAS

WAR

Gunnar Redstone had three men and a spirit on the fight schedule tonight. The three men would be easy, and Gunnar made a note to give them a quick knockout to conserve his energy. There was a Nubian slave with a net and fork, a trained mercenary from Little Asgaard and an overconfident fishmonger from Dagon's docks. Gunnar had faced worse than them when he was twelve.

The fourth warrior was a spirit, and it intrigued him a bit. Gunnar was to fight some sort of animal sprite from the Yōkai ghetto. Yōkai were always interesting. The spirit would probably be some small and unassuming forest creature that turned into something big and menacing at the last second. Still, the Yōkai didn't worry Gunnar too much; these Japanese creatures were not equipped for one-on-one combat. Yōkai were built to enchant and to take you to another world, but they were not built to fight in a pit against the likes of Gunnar Redstone.

Gunnar looked through the cage and listened to the bettors take their final wagers. He heard the Nubian barking insults at him from across the pit, screaming that Gunnar would soon be in his net, being skewered like meat. Gunnar looked around at the crowd calling for the next match and wanted to leave. *This is all a waste*, he thought. *Fighting for money is the corruption of something beautiful.*

But he had to make a living, and fighting was the only thing he was able to do. Still, he felt a deep sense of melancholy. Pit-fighting put food on his table and gave him a place in society, but it made him feel dirty, perhaps like a prostitute would feel. But Gunnar was a Spartan, or rather an *ex-Spartan*, and their training taught them little else.

If only I'd stayed in Sparta, thought Gunnar. *If only I'd killed the Helot, I wouldn't be here. I'd be a guard on some tower, perhaps a mercenary decimating a village, but I wouldn't be here fighting Nubians and Yōkai spirits.*

Gunnar knew the concept of *Little Sparta* was a farce; it only existed to train mercenaries to protect *Hellenica*. Like the Sparta of old, each male was educated through the deadly training known as the *Agoge*. Gunnar was sent to the Agoge at age five; before that time, he had no memory.

The Agoge is a farce that breeds killers and nothing else, thought Gunnar, *but I excelled there, and at least I had a place. If only I'd killed the Helot...*

But Gunnar was no longer a Spartan; he was no longer *anything*. He had no district to claim as his own, no family and no skills other than warfare. So he fought in the pit.

And one day I'll die here, thought Gunnar. *One day, someone will get lucky and drive me through with a lance.*

He'd dispatched a score of men in combat, but what had he *done*? He'd not yet seen the world; he'd not even kissed a girl. With his tall, muscular physique, dark hair and ice-blue eyes, girls had always noticed Gunnar and often cat-called him from the audience while he fought for their amusement. But the girls he'd grown up with in the Agoge were taught to humiliate and belittle their male counterparts, and after Gunnar left Little Sparta he had no idea how to even start a conversation with a female. He had no mother, no father, no brothers or sisters, and now that he had left his troop, he had no friends and was going to die alone.

Gunnar shook off his sadness and made short work of the Nubian in the first match. The dark-skinned warrior was highly skilled, but Gunnar knew the net held a glaring weakness; in close distances it was neither a shield nor a weapon. So Gunnar dodged several of the Nubian's feints, went in tight, disarmed his fork, and that was that. The Nubian pleaded for mercy as Gunnar put him in a chokehold, and the crowd screamed for blood. Gunnar put the Nubian down with a gentle tap to the back of the head, leaving him humiliated but alive.

Gunnar refused to kill in the pit. *A pit-fighter is like a prostitute*, thought Gunnar, *and asking a pit fighter to kill is like asking a prostitute to fall in love. I'll fight anyone they put in front of me, but I will not kill.*

The crowd booed, but only slightly; they had come to expect this behavior. The bettors went to the moneychangers' booths to collect their small winnings; Gunnar had won his last twenty-three bouts in the first round, so the payouts for a victory like this were small.

The second warrior, the mercenary from Little Asgaard, was a little tougher. He was undefeated, like Gunnar, and to match Gunnar he'd gone into the pit without a weapon. Before the match started, Gunnar noticed the mercenary was reading a poem aloud to a member of the audience. Gunnar couldn't see whom the mercenary was speaking to, nor could he understand the mercenary's Old Norse dialect.

But as soon as the poem ended, a change happened in the mercenary. His muscular arms seemed to fill with blood and adrenaline, and he began gnashing his teeth and whirling about in a bizarre convulsion. It wasn't a show; Gunnar's opponent was possessed.

Gunnar looked up into the crowds and could make out glowing eyes looking down upon them. Gunnar understood immediately; the mercenary had prayed to *Óðr*, the Norse god of poetry and frenzy. Óðr was a minor god, but it was becoming common for citizens to pray to gods such as these. *Odin is powerful, but wouldn't even hear this fighter's prayers,* thought Gunnar. *Óõr probably brought this fighter into his office and promised him power in exchange for eternal loyalty.*

At the bell, the mercenary charged with reckless abandon. Gunnar noticed the mercenary's eyes were focused with a dull, impersonal rage, like those of an animal. The mercenary barreled into Gunnar, and though Gunnar was able to avoid most of the attack, the mercenary caught just enough of him to send Gunnar against the cage.

He's preternaturally strong, thought Gunnar. *Who knows what other powers Óõr has given him?*

Gunnar pushed himself from the cage's edge, and then shoved the mercenary away to create some space. The mercenary ran at Gunnar once more, and Gunnar dodged this attack completely. The mercenary slammed against the cage and opened a cut on his forehead. It caused him no pain, but it was deep, and Gunnar decided to exploit it. Gunnar dodged another rush from the mercenary and shoved his face into the cage again, splitting the cut wide open.

The mercenary was blinded by his blood but continued to fight. He kept up his brave, clumsy charges and after his third charge, Gunnar put a knee to his forehead and it was done. Gunnar put him in a lock to submit, but the Norseman wouldn't submit; Óõr had taken away the mercenary's ability to feel pain and fear.

Gunnar put the mercenary in a prostrate position and then stared into the crowd at the glowing eyes. He wanted Óõr to know that he should never again do what he did. Minor gods like Óõr could send anyone they wanted into the pit, but if they sent him to Gunnar, Gunnar would send him back in pieces. Gunnar gave the mercenary one more blow to the back of the head, and the Norseman was unconscious.

"Please congratulate Mr. Redstone on his *second* victory of the evening!" said the announcer to light applause. "For his third opponent, before the showdown with the Yōkai, we have a man straight from Councilman Dagon's district! He's a hundred-to-one long shot, but that's a *big* payout! Please welcome *Alcides!*"

The applause came slowly and Gunnar sized up his opponent. The fighter was a clean-shaven, powerfully built man wearing odd, baggy clothes. He was almost Gunnar's height, but twice as wide. *This Alcides does not look like a fisherman from Dagon's docks*, thought Gunnar, *he looks like a warrior.*

The bell rang and Gunnar stayed at the periphery, jabbing into the man's thick midsection. Gunnar recognized that this Alcides showed no fear and was quite skilled in his movement. He dodged Gunnar's punches quite easily, and the punches that landed appeared to do no damage. As Gunnar fought the man, he noticed that underneath the baggy clothes was a perfect physique, perhaps a hundred and fifty kilograms of pure muscle.

This man isn't from the docks, thought Gunnar. *One can't get that physique by tossing fish.*

Gunnar dodged a few of the man's punches, just barely. Each of the missed punches sent a rush of air that concerned Gunnar. *If just one of these connects*, he thought, *it could be trouble*.

Gunnar continued his jab, pushing his fist into the man's midsection. The man was clearly leaving his torso open, as if he knew it was invulnerable. Gunnar decided to focus his jab on the man's face. He connected with a punch, but the man's jaw was like iron, and his whiskers grated against Gunnar's skin. He dodged a bull rush from the man and then created some space between them. Gunnar looked at his hands; they were bleeding. The man's whiskers were so rough that they had cut his skin open.

The man's whiskers cut my flesh, thought Gunnar, *and when he entered the ring he was clean-shaven. Who is he?*

Gunnar dodged another rush, but it was a mere feint. The man was toying with him now; it made little sense. *This man is a fishmonger from the docks and worships Dagon,* thought Gunnar. *There are no fighters from Dagon's docks, let alone a man like this with a jaw of iron, who sprouts skin-cutting whiskers!*

Gunnar put some distance between them and formulated a new strategy.

"*Erēqu gadalŭ kelkēn?*" asked Gunnar in the Babylonian language of Dagon's district. *Who are you, fishmonger?*

The man seemed not to comprehend; Gunnar knew he was a fake. Dagon demanded loyalty above all else, and first and foremost all Dagon's constituents spoke Babylonian.

While Gunnar was pondering this, Alcides the fishmonger was on him in a flash. The warrior grabbed Gunnar by the neck and held him up; for the first time in his life Gunnar knew what it was like to be perfectly at the mercy of another human being. If the fishmonger wanted to end Gunnar's life, all he had to do was squeeze. But the man slammed Gunnar down onto the mat with such force that Gunnar was numb.

"Who are you?" asked Gunnar with a choked whisper.

"Who am I?" responded the fishmonger. "*Who are you, Gunnar Redstone? Who are you?*"

And just like that, the man put his fist in Gunnar's face, and Gunnar was out.

/***/

Gunnar woke up in his dressing room to see the fishmonger in front of him. The fishmonger had a full beard now, and was holding a small nettle.

"This is from the Yōkai warrior that you were to face after me," said the man. "Don't touch it; it's poisonous."

Gunnar's head was throbbing. But he could see the man was correct; the nettle was from a poisonous Yōkai. It was an illegal practice of course, but happened whenever someone wanted to eliminate a pit-fighter. Gunnar would have won the match and the Yōkai would have turned into a spider to give him one more sting. Gunnar would have most likely died a few weeks later.

"You're not merely a pit-fighter, Gunnar. You're a General," said the man, holding up the nettle. "And the best way to kill a General is through an assassin."

The man held up the nettle as proof.

"Thank you for saving my life," said Gunnar.

"I also tried to kill you, Gunnar; don't you remember?" said the man with a smile.

"Whoever you are, I sense you could have killed me but chose not to."

"Hardly. I didn't pull my punches, and that brings an interesting question. That final punch I gave you would have killed any mortal ten times over," said the man, "yet here you sit, broken but alive. Why do you think that is?"

Gunnar couldn't think of an appropriate response.

"I'm a *nobody*, fishmonger," said Gunnar. "I'm a failed Spartan, nothing more."

"I disagree, Gunnar," said the man, "and whoever sent this nettle disagrees as well. Perhaps a powerful man fears you, Gunnar. Perhaps a powerful *god*?"

"The powerful don't fear the powerless," said Gunnar, "and I'm powerless."

"In my day, a king would assassinate an infant to save facing him as an adult," said the man. "And who is more powerless than an infant, Redstone? So whoever sent this nettle must see great potential in you.

Do you not agree?"

"I don't care to partake in this war of words," said Gunnar. "If you choose to say something, state it. Take that nettle and shove it in my neck if you so desire, but don't continue this rhetoric."

The man laughed heartily.

"And they said *I* was a brute," he said, "but compared to you, Gunnar, I'm *Calliope*, Muse of Eloquence herself! So I'll no longer engage you in rhetoric. I'll tell you that you're special, that you don't belong in Sparta, you don't belong in the Agoge, and you *don't* belong in the pit."

"I agree with you in terms of the Agoge and Sparta; I have no place there," said Gunnar, "but society has given me a place here in the pit. So perhaps I *do* belong here."

"They tolerate you for now," said the man. "You're a novelty, but you don't win anyone any money. Sooner or later they'll send another nettle, probably before you turn sixteen."

"That's my problem," said Gunnar.

"No," said the fishmonger, "it's mine too. I see the powers you have and can't bear to see them wasted."

"If you think I have *powers*, you're mistaken," said Gunnar. "I'm just a kid who can fight, nothing more. I'm not a god …"

"You're *better* than the gods, and that's why I'm here," said the man. "We have a special Academy for those with powers like you. We want … we *need* … you to attend. And those behind this nettle want the opposite."

The man had Gunnar's full attention.

"Your days of fighting in the pit are over," he said. "You'll retire, and no one will miss you; no one ever misses those who are violent. You've always *loathed* the petty brutality around you, Gunnar, and the Academy will allow you to do something about it. Would you like to come?"

Gunnar looked at the man's bearded face; he wasn't lying.

"I'll go," said Gunnar, "but I need to see this place before I commit; I've had my troubles with warrior schools."

"Great," said the man. "We can go tonight."

The man got up to leave and then turned around.

"I noticed you speak Babylonian," he said. "Although I'm not proficient in it myself, they do know me in Dagon's docks. They call me *Ērklŭ*."

Ērklŭ was the Babylonian name for *Heracles*.

THE WHITE KNIGHT

Emetor Kain was particularly active this morning. He was teaching Saoirse Frost and her clutch of *Hetaerae* emotional bonding.

"The common man wants two things from a common prostitute. Second in importance is release, in any way, shape or form. First in importance is for the prostitute to disappear when he is done—the sooner the better. The prostitute must be like a meal at a restaurant: easy, predictable and leaving nothing afterwards to clean up."

Emetor Kain looked over the clutch of girls, and his gaze lingered long on Saoirse. She was the oldest of her clutch at fifteen years of age, and the only girl that had begun to develop; many of the other girls had no hips to speak of. The Emetor's eyes always focused on Saoirse more than the others, but he made it clear that he had no lascivious thoughts for her. He also made it clear that, with her flawless, chocolate-colored skin, soft blonde hair and gently curving frame, she'd earn him a lot of money one day.

"You aren't prostitutes; you're *Hetaerae*," continued the Emetor. "You're not there for men's carnal pleasure, and you don't disappear afterwards. The prostitute has a john; Hetaerae have *Danna*, councilmen, district leaders, and occasionally *gods*.

"The common prostitute pleases her client to make a living. Hetaerae are not concerned with *making a living*; you please your

Danna because you love them, because pleasing your Danna is part of *who you are.* You provide more than just your body, an empty vessel to be filled. You have a heart, a mind, a soul, a personality. They all belong to the one who purchases your services of course, but you are each unique.

"This is why you've spent your life up to this point learning skills. Music, voice, poetry, gymnastics, literature. You are to be your Danna's partner, your Danna's love, your Danna's muse. They will ask for you by name and it will give you a thrill. When they visit you, they will fill that void inside you; your Danna will be the missing piece, without which you have no purpose.

"You will be your Danna's confidant and friend. *Elysian* poets will write about the love between you and your Danna, and this poetry will be sung for centuries to come. You'll be with them throughout their lives, and when they are no more, you'll attend their funeral, in secret, so as not to disturb their family. You will love and understand their needs *so much* that you'll do this."

Kain looked across the room and saw Elsephela Grex come in from the other end of the studio bedchamber, her pet striped hyaena trotting behind her. Saoirse noticed that she was carrying a small glowing box but couldn't quite tell what it was. The Elsephela was clearly angry at something and wanted to speak with Emetor Kain immediately.

"At times you may feel unable to love," said the Emetor. "Your Danna may be unsightly, malodorous or simply unlovable. Truly loving the unlovable is a difficult task. For this we have many drugs that will help induce feelings of closeness and …"

The Emetor couldn't continue; Elsephela Grex's striped hyaena was growling.

"Emetor, I've a complaint against one of your girls," she said.

"Which one, and what for?" he said.

He's protective of us, thought Saoirse, *but in the way the shepherd is protective of his lambs on the way to the smokehouse.*

"My issue is with the dark-skinned one," said the Elsephela. "The one with blonde hair."

Saoirse's heart sank. What could the Elsephela possibly want with her? She'd done nothing out of the ordinary. *They told me the Elsephela can read a girl's mind*, thought Saoirse, *and I've had some dark thoughts lately. Am I in trouble for my thoughts?*

"If your issue is with Saoirse," said the Emetor, "I can assure you that you're mistaken. She's never given one spot of trouble in all her fifteen years and—"

"Don't lecture me on the spotlessness of a Hetaera's soul, Emetor. They have trained their whole lives to be liars; I above all else would know this. Give me Ms. Frost for a little bit of time so that I may ask her some questions. That's all I ask."

"If you abuse her—" said the Emetor, before being interrupted again.

"I don't abuse your precious golden geese, Emetor, not physically, not emotionally. All I want is answers. Saoirse, come with me now."

The Emetor nodded at Saoirse to go. Saoirse walked by her clutch of girls towards the Elsephela and her hyaena. They all bowed their heads, not daring to make eye contact. Saoirse walked down until she was close enough to smell the old woman. The hyaena inspected Saoirse curiously and then started to whine.

"Come, child," said the Elsephela, holding her glowing box, "we have only one thing to discuss."

/***/

Saoirse Frost sat with the Elsephela in a dark interrogation room three floors below. Saoirse felt quite uncomfortable; this was the first time she'd ever been in a room with hard, cold edges, and the first time she'd sat on anything besides velvet.

The Elsephela reeked of rotten sulfur. Retired Hetaerae used a noxious herb called "Devil's dung" to provide a scent that stated they were no longer for sale. Few would want the Elsephela even if she smelled like roses; like most retired Hetaerae, she had her face powdered white and her teeth dyed black.

"I was like you once, child," said the woman. "I put in my ten years; that's all they ask of our kind. Most slaves are given a life of servitude, but our kind, we're only required to give our youth. No labor, no hot sun, no starvation. You'll even be given two servants of your own. They're waiting outside to cater to your every need right now.

"So I ask you, child, why would you destroy everything you have?"

Saoirse didn't know what to say.

"Short of words?" said the Elsephela. "Or more likely you're short of mind? Girls who are given your gifts—bright hair, dark skin and sweet breath—need not develop thoughts to have value. Is this it? Is this why you would choose to disfigure yourself? To disfigure every other Hetaerae in your clutch? To ruin their features so that you may win your own freedom?"

Saoirse was on the verge of tears. She had learned the arts of love, music and poetry, but not the art of conflict.

"Speak, child. The brainless silence of beauty may work with the Emetor, but not with me. Not here, not now."

There was an uncomfortable silence, and then it was broken by the hyaena making a high-pitched laughing sound at Saoirse. It snapped Saoirse into action.

"Forgive me, Elsephela, but I know not of what you speak."

The Elsephela looked over Saoirse for a few moments, and then spoke.

"My striped hyaena has an excellent sense of smell, you know. Certain pheromones tend to be given off in fear; certain pheromones only come from lying. He knows which is which."

The Elsephela gave the hyaena a look, and in a flash the animal bounced up on the table. He was now unhooked, and went over to Saoirse. He gave off a growl, but Saoirse didn't flinch. He peered at her, sniffed, and peered some more. Finally he rubbed his scent glands on her, lay down and groomed himself.

"It appears you're telling the truth," said the Elsephela, "but this doesn't mean you're without guilt. I believe that you've caused this without your knowledge, because you're *too stupid* to realize what you've done. You were given many gifts but brains were not—"

The hyaena barked his high-pitched chirp and interrupted the Elsephela. Saoirse sensed something strange underneath the hyaena's voice, as if he were pleading with the old woman to stop.

"Forgive me, Elsephela, if I do not have the ability to understand," said Saoirse. "But if you could just tell me what troubles you, I would be able to help you. All I ask is that you be clear."

The Elsephela peered at Saoirse and narrowed her eyes.

"It appears the Emetor has trained you well," she said, "but I am not some hen-pecked Alderman to be assuaged by silken words coming from someone who is not his wife. Here is what angers me."

The Elsephela brought out her box and put it on the table. She opened it to reveal a glowing golden disc with some strange symbols on it. It seemed to pulsate as it glowed. There were some bloodied teeth by it, but still, Saoirse found it attractive.

"I know not what this is, Elsephela."

"You do," said the old woman. "This is the handiwork of your goddess, Oshun."

Oshun. This was Saoirse's personal goddess, the Yoruban goddess of beauty. Saoirse had never known her parents but had resembled Oshun from an early age, so she worshipped her. That was it though; she'd never sent Oshun a malicious prayer, and knew not what this strange glowing disc was.

Saoirse immediately went on the defensive. *Sometimes your*

Danna is clearly wrong, the Emetor had taught her, *but you're not here to win arguments. Never go on the offensive, and never escalate the argument. Defend yourself passively and appear to join the side of the one attacking you.*

"We're only allowed to worship goddesses of beauty in our clutch," said Saoirse, appearing genuinely inquisitive. "This is so that we may do no harm. Please, Elsephela, educate me upon what harm Oshun may have done so that I may rectify it, or clear it up if it's a simple misunderstanding."

"I know what game you're playing, child," said the Elsephela, grinding her black teeth. "I played it myself for a decade."

Saoirse's heart began to race; the Elsephela was truly angry. *When in doubt, fall back on innocence,* Emetor Kain would say, *fall back on passivity. The world is a cold, cruel place, but you are neither. Your integrity will always win in the end.*

"Please, Elsephela," said Saoirse, "I know not what this object is. Please tell me what it is so I can soothe what ails you."

"This is a lip plate, child," said the Elsephela. "It makes even the most beautiful woman hideous. It's worn by Africans to prevent being taken as slaves."

Saoirse had no idea what the woman was talking about, but the Elsephela continued to explain it like a prosecutor might condescendingly describe a weapon to the accused. She crept up to Saoirse and put the glowing plate close to Saoirse's mouth.

"This one isn't simply a plate worn by a Nubian peasant girl. This one is infused with Oshun's magic; it seems to work automatically. First, it knocks out your four bottom teeth. Then it wedges in between your chin and lip until they're torn in two. Then it grows and spreads scars all over your body. Then it changes you into a different creature altogether."

Saoirse could not help getting a bit defensive.

"Elsephela, I know *nothing of what you speak*," she said, "but please tell me what this has to do with Oshun. Failing that, please tell me what this has to do with *me* so that I may rectify my actions."

The Elsephela crept closer to Saoirse. Saoirse tried to breathe through her mouth to avoid the smell, but the old woman's odor was unavoidable.

"This is one of five plates found over the grounds in the past three days. There are more popping up each day. Two girls have used them already, and one now looks like Medusa herself. I took this plate to Apothecary Qelex, and he stated that it was made by Oshun, *your* Yoruban goddess of beauty. You are the only one who worships her, so *you* must have brought this upon us, intentionally or—"

"Why would *a goddess of beauty* create a relic that causes disfigurement?" asked Saoirse. "It doesn't make sense. Oshun would never—"

The Elsephela slapped Saoirse across the face and Saoirse's nose started to bleed.

"Don't contradict me, child," said the Elsephela. "The Apothecary knows of what he speaks. You are the only one on this island who worships Oshun. And one evening in your prayers, your ungrateful little mind must have called out to Oshun *for a way out of your situation*. And Oshun delivered; she controls beauty, so surely she can make a relic that takes all beauty *away*."

Saoirse started to cry, but then controlled herself. *Let a few tears fall to show your love*, the Emetor would say, *but do not lose yourself. Your Danna does not come for tears.*

The Elsephela calmed down a bit and offered Saoirse a piece of cloth. The hyaena whined in sympathy.

"Truth be told, child, these plates are intriguing," said the old woman. "Not even *Aspesia*, mistress of Pericles, would have chosen the fate of a Hetaera. Aspesia was given both mansions and gold, and songs are sung about her still. But every woman yearns to be free; even if the only way out is to turn herself into a monstrosity."

Saoirse bit her lip; she knew the Elsephela's sympathy might just be a ruse.

"I do not know about these plates, Elsephela," said Saoirse. "Should I warn my clutch not to use them?"

"It's no use," said the Elsephela. "Oshun has deposited these plates in too many places. Soon each Hetaera will pick them up and use them, or perhaps threaten to do so. And the Hetaerae are the primary source of income in Elysia.

"We have a year here at most before that money runs dry, all because your goddess Oshun decided to free you. What will you do, Saoirse?"

Saoirse had never considered that notion. *To do?* She'd done as she was told all her life. Perhaps someone else would come in and tell her what to do; someone always did.

"And what am *I* to do, child?" asked the old woman, her anger rising again. "Like Aspesia, I have houses, land, but they aren't mine. They belong to the island and are lent to me as pension for my youth, for a single decade earning them extraordinarily high profits."

Saoirse didn't answer, thinking the question rhetorical, but the old woman pressed on.

"What am *I* to do, Saoirse? Your prayers have ended my existence here, so now you must answer me. When this island crumbles, what am I to do, and where am I to go?"

All the years of rhetoric, poetry and training failed Saoirse now. There was no place for this old, foul-smelling woman to go. If Elysia vanished, the Elsephela could re-enter the conurbation as a low-paid prostitute, or perhaps a beggar. *She could also die*, thought Saoirse, but she kept her thoughts to herself.

"All I need is a little money to live out the rest of my days, Saoirse, and I think that you owe me this, wouldn't you say so? Don't give me coyness or passive diversion; answer me *yes* or *no*. After destroying my only means of support, do you believe that you owe me a way to spend the rest of my days without penury?"

"Yes," said Saoirse, more out of reflex than meaning.

"Good," said the Elsephela, "then I have found your Danna. He will come to take you away tonight."

Saoirse's heart skipped a beat yet again, and then sank. This was both her destiny and the day that she dreaded, and it was coming tonight! There was no time to prepare and no time to say good-bye. And the one thing she always kept at the back of her mind was now gone: *there was no time to run away.*

"I don't think Emetor Kain will approve of—"

"Emetor Kain won't know of this. I've already received the initial payment and will receive the rest of it upon your arrival outside this island."

"Arrival? Where?"

"I don't know. But this is the way it will be done."

Saoirse started to cry, and unlike any other time in her life, she couldn't stop. The striped hyaena came up close and rubbed his head against her leg until the Elsephela shooed him away. The old woman got up close to Saoirse, and her stench was so overpowering that Saoirse's nose began to bleed again.

"You'd better stop crying, child," said the Elsephela, "for if your Danna rejects you, there will be consequences. I have another man who is willing to pay for your services, not as much as the Danna, but he will pay enough to sustain me for a few years. He owns the Mines of Capua and he will use you as he sees fit. I believe only prisoners work those mines, isn't that true? Would you like to go to the Mines of Capua?"

"No, Elsephela," said Saoirse.

"Then get yourself together for your Danna, and smile," said the old woman, "because this will be the happiest night of your life."

/***/

Saoirse was in her room alone without a clue what to do. Could she escape? She would surely be caught. What if her Danna was *"unsightly, malodorous or simply unlovable,"* like the Emetor warned? What if he was cruel?

And why was he taking her away? Only on the rarest occasions would Danna take their Hetaera away, and that was after a decade of courtship. *Something feels wrong*, thought Saoirse, *and not just with me. This night feels different; it feels like the world's going to end.*

Saoirse had not given up on the idea of escape, but had no idea what to do. She'd never been off the island in her life, and boatmen in the area are told not to pick up girls like her. Could she stow away? Surely there was some ship carrying supplies that wouldn't notice her presence. *There are no ships carrying supplies at this time of night*, thought Saoirse. *All the ships here are the ships of Dannas, and they're built for wealth and pleasure, not for cargo and stowing away.*

It was then that Saoirse saw something glowing on her windowsill. She looked closer and picked it up. It was one of Oshun's lip plates.

I prayed to Oshun for a way out, she thought. *Is this my destiny?*

The lip plate was beautiful and felt warm. *Just put it close to your mouth,* she thought, *and Oshun will do the rest. Oshun will take care of you.*

She thought of how it would be. She'd lose her beauty, but what had her beauty done for her at this point? All it had done was to keep her in this cage and headed her towards tonight, the night she dreaded. If she would take the lip plate, what would she do? Where would she go?

Saoirse heard a scream outside from the courtyard. She went to the window and saw another clutch of younger Hetaerae running away. She noticed they were running from a girl in the middle who was on the ground, convulsing. The girl seemed to be changing into some sort of small, hairy creature, and she was making a strange sound, like bleating.

She had a glowing plate wedged in her lower lip.

It was then that Saoirse saw that the girls were not running from their fallen sister; they were running from what was nearer to the walls. A group of more developed creatures was approaching the fallen girl, and they all had lip plates as well. They were covered with thin fur and moved with a quiet agility; Saoirse could barely see them in the darkness. They fell across the prostrate girl and made several chirping noises, which seemed to soothe her.

The creatures helped her up, looked around and made a few barking sounds, and then started babbling in a high-pitched language Saoirse could not quite hear. *But I can sense what they're trying to say,* thought Saoirse. *I can't make out the words, but I can understand them.*

The creatures seemed to be talking about freedom and how the island wouldn't survive the night. One girl looked up at the moon and then barked instructions to the rest of the pack. In an instant they went scurrying in four directions with great speed and agility. They climbed the walls of the courtyard with the greatest of ease, and in a flash they'd gone over the wall.

What were they? thought Saoirse. *What has Oshun done?*

Saoirse looked at her lip plate. It glowed and tempted her to wear it, to become one of these animals, to flee the courtyard and live in darkness the rest of her days. She turned to look out the window again, and saw that one of the creatures was just outside her balcony.

She went up to meet the creature. Its face was cute; something like a monkey's but smoother and with less definition. The creature had sharp teeth, but it was apparent this creature was built for climbing, not fighting, so Saoirse approached easily. The creature sniffed her and then chirped its odd tongue again. Once again, Saoirse didn't know the language, but *she understood.*

Oshun's magic is not for you, the creature said. *You've something far greater in store. Now leave this place immediately or you'll burn with it.*

In a moment, the creature was gone. Saoirse stuck her head out the window and could see nothing but the moon. She was trying to locate the creature when she heard a knock at her door.

"Yes?" she asked.

"It's me," said a husky voice. "Your Danna."

/***/

"Where are we going?" asked Saoirse.

The man didn't answer. He was tall, athletically built, clean-shaven, and young-looking. He didn't seem like the gruff, grey Danna Saoirse usually saw and didn't seem particularly interested in her; he focused entirely on driving the boat. Saoirse saw her island drop into the background and started to panic.

"Where are we going?" she asked the man. "And who are you?"

"Please," he said, "be quiet, and all will be explained."

"I need to know who you are," demanded Saoirse.

The man looked at her and stopped the boat. He pointed in the direction of the island. Saoirse could see that flames were coming from the center and spreading out towards the beach.

"Your Isle of Elysia is no more," he said. "Now, please *be quiet*. All will be explained later."

Saoirse sensed that he was telling the truth but noticed that he wasn't headed inland; he was headed out towards the ocean. She could see a small island in the distance, about an hour away.

"Just tell me, are we going there?" she asked.

The man nodded and increased the speed on the boat. Saoirse looked back; the flames had spread to most of Elysia, and looked like they were going to engulf the whole island soon. She turned around and saw something dangling from her Danna's neck. She looked closer and found that it was a glowing lip plate.

/***/

An hour later, the boat came to a dock in the second island. It was manned by two tall women who grabbed the rope and moored the boat quickly.

"Bring the girl to the President right away," said one. "Interrupt her if need be."

The guards beckoned Saoirse forth and together they traveled forward. They walked for ten minutes on paved roads and came to a city at the center of the island. Saoirse noticed that every single person she met seemed to have a crisp, soldierly look to them. She also noticed that every single person here was a woman. This wasn't Elysia though, and these women were not Hetaerae. These women, even the young girls, were *warriors*.

The group approached a building. They were moving at a brisk pace, but they were not forcing Saoirse to walk with them; it was clear that she wasn't a prisoner. The building they approached was grand, broad and gilded, and its edges were very square. They went inside and immediately came to a security checkpoint. Two guards asked them to surrender all their arms, and the women around Saoirse handed over at least twenty weapons. They went through some sort of electronic detector. After a few moments it beeped, and the security guards waved them forward.

The inside of the building was sterile, holding long hallways and endless office suites. As they walked past, Saoirse realized that once again, this building was almost exclusively female. Occasionally Saoirse would notice a man attending a meeting, but this building clearly belonged to women.

They came to another security checkpoint and they were frisked by two more female guards. One guard found Saoirse's lip plate and took both it and the Danna's lip plate.

"These will be returned to you after you leave," said the guard.

They went through several detectors and entered a different-looking zone of the building; it was cleaner, whiter and held less rooms. They were heading down to an office at the end of the hallway with a strange regal seal. They stopped at the doorway, and one of the guards pressed a button.

"Do as we do, Saoirse," said one of the females next to her. Saoirse's Danna was now in the back of their group, following as well.

The door opened automatically to reveal a grand office with a large chair that faced the other way. Next to the chair was a dark-skinned woman with glowing eyes. This woman appeared to be in conversation with whoever was in the chair.

"President Hippolyta," said the guard, "may I present Saoirse Frost, of the former Isle of Elysia."

The chair turned around to show a woman who looked to be seventy years old, clearly once beautiful, but now grey and wrinkled with age. The whole group, including Saoirse's Danna, knelt in the President's presence. Saoirse knelt with them.

The dark-skinned woman with the glowing eyes nodded at President Hippolyta and walked towards Saoirse.

"Rise, child," said the woman. Her eyes glowed the same color as the lip plates.

"I am Oshun, goddess of beauty," she said, "and you are in the office of President Hippolyta of the Amazons."

Saoirse wanted to maintain her composure, but found it difficult. *Emetor Kain has only prepared me for pleasing a Danna*, thought Saoirse. *No one has prepared me for this.*

"We have been watching you since the day you were born," said Oshun, "and we're so happy to get you here, to this point."

There was a brief moment of exhilaration, and then President Hippolyta broke in.

"Phoebe, you've done excellent work. You may reveal yourself, and then be excused," said President Hippolyta.

Saoirse's Danna took off her hat to reveal long, flowing hair and then took off some of her outer clothes to reveal that she was clearly a woman.

"Good luck, Saoirse," said Phoebe, and she quickly departed.

"Now, all sit," said Hippolyta. "We have much to discuss."

Hippolyta nodded at one of Saoirse's guards, and the guard snapped her fingers. Three women came in with several chairs and soon they were all sitting down.

"This must all be a shock to you, Saoirse," said Hippolyta. "Indeed, being ripped from all you've ever known, no matter how abominable the situation, is terrifying. However, your previous home was a stain on this earth, and now it is no more.

"You are one of us. You have been since the day we placed you on that island, knowing full well that your connection to Oshun would serve as a 'time bomb' which would eventually destroy the place. Does this make any sense to you?"

Saoirse couldn't speak; there was just too much to take in.

"You'll understand all of this in time," said Hippolyta.

"Am I an Amazon?" asked Saoirse.

"Not quite; you weren't born here," said Hippolyta. "In fact, we know not from where you came. And though you'll always be linked to the Amazons, your destiny does not lie with us."

"Understood," said Saoirse. "What shall I do to please you?"

President Hippolyta cast a knowing smile at Oshun.

"You've been trained to be a Hetaera, and unfortunately, this has become part of who you are," said Oshun, "but your days of servitude are over. You have duties, yes. You have honor, yes. But you must cast aside your desire to please others. You now serve the Amazons, humanity and yourself. You'll put no stock in the pleasure of a single person, be it Danna or even President Hippolyta.

"You've already done humanity a great service by destroying the concept of the Hetaerae. My connection to you allowed me to place these plates everywhere, and the plates turned the wearers into *Aziza*."

Saoirse had heard of Aziza; they were African fairy creatures with arcane powers. It wasn't uncommon for them to set fire to an entire island.

"Indeed," said President Hipployta, "you've done a great thing, but at the expense of your soul. Instead of learning warfare and camaraderie like a girl should, you've learned softness and servitude on the Isle of Elysia. It is time for us to make amends.

"But your training won't continue here; it cannot. Once again, your destiny lies beyond the Isle of the Amazons."

After a pause, Saoirse spoke.

"President Hippolyta, goddess Oshun, what am I?"

"We don't know," said Oshun. "I sense great power within you, but I don't quite know what you are."

"There is an Academy on Hellenica that's calling for your kind," said President Hippolyta. "I think you'll find your answers there."

"An Academy?" asked Saoirse.

"Yes," said President Hippolyta. "We've inspected it and they're nothing like your Isle of Elysia. Their goals are noble, and the skills they'll teach you will surpass anything you can learn here as an Amazon."

Saoirse didn't know whether to trust these two or not, even though one was Oshun, a goddess to whom she had prayed every night of her life. It was true, the Amazons had saved her from a world of servitude under Emetor Kain, the Elsephela and a Danna, but she'd never been able to trust anyone completely before. Those with power might give her a place in this world, but it always came at a price. Ultimately, authority figures always seemed to sell girls like Saoirse for a profit, and now President Hippolyta was delivering her to an "Academy" that wanted to use Saoirse's skills for their own ends. Whether those ends were noble or not, Saoirse was paralyzed with fear; after a moment of indecision, she subconsciously fell back on Emetor Kain's training and became deferential.

"Thank you, President."

President Hippolyta smiled.

"Yes, indeed, and one more thing. We spent quite a bit of time scouring Elysia for survivors and found something for you. Oshun can understand it and said that it was calling your name specifically."

President Hippolyta snapped her fingers, and two more guards came in.

They had a long chain, and attached to it was the Elsephela's striped hyaena.

PESTILENCE

Tommy Alderon woke up to the smell of burning leaves, or perhaps a Norseman's funeral pyre.

"It's the Isle of Elysia, right over there," said Brother Kojo, who had come to wake Tommy up. "Someone burned it last night. It's no more."

Tommy looked out the window and it was true; there were a hundred boats salvaging people and goods, but the island itself was now ashes.

"My father told me of the Island," said Kojo. "It ran twenty-four hours a day, *every* day, war time and peace time. Open constantly for two centuries. They claimed they held only Hetaerae there, but you could get anything you wanted there for a price. *Anything*.

"Their only rule was absolute privacy; no photographs, no paintings, no reporters. But now look at it. In a few days it will be as if it had never existed."

Kojo always spoke so beautifully, rationally. He was a soft-spoken, thoughtful young man, and Tommy liked him. He had come to Lepros a year ago as a young Samaritan training to be a nurse, and within a year he had contracted smallpox. His Yoruban skin, once unbroken and new, looked like someone had dragged him over coals.

But he didn't seem to mind; the Samaritans never seemed to mind when they contracted a disease from their denizens. The Samaritans considered scars a badge of honor and pointed at them whenever they used sacred words like *humility*, *faith* and *penance*.

Kojo joked that his scars inoculated him against other infections; indeed, he was one of the few people that dared stay around Tommy.

"Will there be another island?" asked Tommy.

"Most definitely," said Kojo. "Vice is part of humanity. There will always be those who'll go to any length to acquire more than is allowed. And there will always be those who'll *sell* more than is allowed. Vice isn't a function of morality; it's a function of opportunity.

"But that's for Elysia, or whatever island will take its place," said Kojo with a smile. "We are different on Lepros, or at least try to be. Speaking of which, some new denizens came in last night. Plague, I believe. I'd like them to see your suit at morning bells; it will give them hope."

The sun was just beginning to come up, and Tommy saw Low Priest Aaron ambling across the courtyard towards the bell tower. The Samaritans always rang the bells at 5:00 a.m. No one was required to wake at the hour; some had sleep disorders and couldn't wake at all. But most Leprosians attended the event; it gave them structure to their day and a sense of community.

Kojo helped Tommy into his mechanical suit; he loved the suit that Tommy had built. Tommy had originally created it as a hermetically sealed outfit that would keep others from catching his diseases, but he soon modified it to augment his crippled legs. He worked on it every day, and he'd given it night vision, the ability to go under water, and a belt full of tools. *It does more than protect others from your condition*, Tommy remembered Kojo saying, *it gives you the power of a god.*

They walked out of their room into the hallway. A Samaritan was rubbing down the floors with bleach; the chemicals quashed the smell of smoke from Elysia. That was common in Lepros; there would be an odd smell, an odd noise, an odd feeling, but it would only last for a moment. It would be the smell of someone's burst pustules or the groan of a dying man, but there would always be cleanliness and quiet soon thereafter. *You all have value,* Tommy remembered High Priest Elazar telling the Leprosians. *Though society has forsaken you, each and every one of you has value. And in order to realize your value, we must have calm, quiet, cleanliness and consistency.*

Tommy snapped the facemask in place to hermetically seal himself into his suit, and he and Kojo ambled out into the hallway. Even with the added inches of his suit, Tommy seemed to be half the height of Kojo. But he was getting used to its features and was almost as able-bodied as Kojo. *We'll improve the suit*, Elazar would say, *and soon you'll be faster, stronger, quicker. You'll have value. Perhaps you may one day re-enter society.*

Tommy walked alongside Kojo like a pet, and traveled down the hallway to the outdoors. He passed the wing for violent patients and noticed the thick doors barring escape. That wing had filled up recently due to the new strain of syphilis that was spreading throughout the world. *Antibiotic-resistant, develops quietly, and doesn't kill you for twenty years*, Kojo would say. *It's the perfect disease.* Patients with the new syphilis became violent, yet retained much of their faculties. They could act normally, reason, and even hold elected office if left unnoticed. But they were dangerous.

"If those doors would open," said Kojo, "we'd be burning like Elysia within the hour."

"I understand," said Tommy, "but we must have compassion."

"True," said Kojo. "Above all else, we must have compassion."

They walked down to the main courtyard and stood in front of High Priest Elazar and all Lepros's able inhabitants. *One thousand patients, the contagious of the contagious, the sickest of the sick,* thought Tommy, *and ten healthy Samaritan priests to tend them all.*

There were twenty new faces at the front of the crowd. Most were dressed in black cloaks; Tommy listened to the soft, sibilant tones they spoke amongst themselves, and guessed they were from the

Mesopotamian quarter. High Priest Elazar confirmed it when he spoke to them.

"Where is your *Gilgamesh* now? Your *Djinn*?" he asked, half-rhetorically.

Not one of the new arrivals spoke. Low Priest Aaron began to translate, but still, not one of them took the bait. One boy was shirtless and was scratching a pulsating boil under his arm. A cloaked woman on the other side of the group came to him and made him stop scratching it, but the boy continued and then started to cry.

Elazar was a kind, rotund older man with a soft face and a graying mustache. Tommy had heard him give this "tough love" speech before, and he knew that Elazar didn't enjoy giving it. Though it was necessary to rid the new denizens of their previous prejudices, Elazar didn't relish giving immigrants the cold, hard truth: that the gods to whom they had prayed every night of their lives didn't care for them.

"Your heroes and genies are not here," said Elazar, pointing towards the mainland. "They are *over there*. They're busy running around, working for their worshippers' personal interests, but *you*? They have abandoned you. I've lived here all my life, and never have I seen a god take one of his people back from Lepros."

The boy stopped crying. After Aaron began to translate the group stood still, rapt in attention.

"Look to your left, and look to your right," said Elazar. "*This* is your family now. *We* will not forsake you. Continue to pray to Zeus, make a sacrifice to Ba'al, and tell your children the tales of noble Lugh. But if you need something, depend on your neighbors. All blood feuds, hatred, and linguistic barriers mean nothing here.

"The Celts and Apaches may be at war in the city, but they are *family* here. That's the only rule here, *that we are all with each other*. No division. Do you understand?"

Again, there was only silence from the Mesopotamians. High Priest Elazar noticed it and began to smile.

"If you don't believe me just yet, I understand. Lifelong habits are hard to break," said Elazar. "But tell me, who are your mortal enemies on land?"

Again, silence after Aaron translated. The boy giggled and then spoke up.

"Yoruba!" he said. The woman tried to hush him, but he cried and started yelling, "Yoruba! Yoruba!"

High Priest Elazar smiled and took no offense.

"The boy only speaks what he's been taught," continued the High Priest. "And over *there*, you've been taught—"

Just then, the boy keeled over and started convulsing. The boil under his arm had burst and he was foaming at the mouth. The Mesopotamians exploded into a million bits of chatter, and High Priest Elazar calmly walked up to the boy and put his hand on the boy's head. Priest Aaron spoke up.

"Shall I get the care specialist?" he asked.

"Yes, have Brother Zebulon bring an anticonvulsant, whichever appropriate. But I want Kojo here to administer it."

Kojo nodded. The Mesopotamians began to chatter as he came near, but Brother Aaron seemed to say some words that calmed them down. Within seconds, Zebulon came with a needle. He prepped the skin and let Kojo perform the injection. The woman eyed Kojo warily, but allowed him to do his work. After the injection, the boy relaxed and Kojo smiled. Kojo wiped some stray fluids that had wound up on his arm, and then shared some words with the Mesopotamians in their own dialect.

"Nurse Kojo is a Yoruban, your mortal enemy in the conurbation," said Elazar, "but here he is your friend."

Elazar got up and then patted Kojo on the back. He told Sister Keziah to lead the group in song, making sure that the truly infirm could hear it from their beds. After the song and the daily announcements, he dismissed the group, but approached Tommy soon thereafter.

"In my office," said Elazar with a smile. "We have something very important to discuss."

/***/

Elazar caught Tommy looking at his strange Samaritan Torah placed against the wall.

"It's okay," he said with a laugh. "I understand you must think our religion strange."

Tommy couldn't help but respond.

"You have but one God," said Tommy, "one God you cannot see or touch, one God who doesn't respond; you just believe he's there. It's hard to fathom."

"Our God is mysterious indeed," said Elazar, "but tell me; who is *your* personal god?"

"Hephaestus."

"Ahhh, Greek Hephaestus. He went by *Vulcan* when I was a child. One of my favorites too, he of the clubbed foot, he of the humble, he who likes to *build things*," said Elazar, winking at Tommy. "But back to my God. It's a good question, how to *worship something that doesn't answer back.* Though the gods in the city may have forgotten the Isle of Lepros, they are visible, they are tangible; they forget us, but they are *there* to forget us.

"But I ask you: to what end is our society headed towards? What's the natural conclusion of our polytheistic, polyreligious society?"

Tommy thought about this for a moment.

"Either one religion gains permanent domination, or we eventually reach a state of constant equilibrium," said Tommy.

"Genocide or constant war," said Elazar. "Do you like these

options, Tommy?"

Tommy had no response.

"I want to ask you another question," said Elazar. "What has our society produced in the last century? I'm not talking about a new temple or some shiny amulet, but what have we *produced*?"

"I made this suit," said Tommy.

"Precisely. But you made it *here*, outside of the district's constant feuds."

"Perhaps."

"The members of the conurbation are at a standstill, Tommy; they're in crisis," said Elazar. "They do nothing but appease their own personal deities at the expense of others.

"What little progress that's made is made out *here*. Suits, medicines, electronics are all made *here* by a small fraction of the population—by the grievously ill, no less! You should be happy to know that Hephaestus himself has seen the prototype of your suit and is quite impressed."

Tommy's heart skipped a beat.

"Hephaestus is reasonable," said Elazar, "as is Hellenica. They have their share of petty gods and infighting to be sure, but Hellenica depends on reason to survive. And they recognize that though Lepros brings in the sick of body, we are pure of soul. The same can't be said for the conurbation.

"And so this comes to you, Tommy; what are *you* going to do about it? How are you going to clean up our city?"

"Me?"

"Yes, you."

"With all due respect, sir, I've never set foot outside this island in my life. I fear I wouldn't survive if I left."

"Poppycock. You've survived more than a phalanx of warriors face in their lifetime. Every disease on earth tried to kill you, but couldn't. You built a suit to protect *us* from you."

"Are you sending me there? To the mainland?"

"Only if you want to go. This island is nothing if not a society of choice. But if you go it's not because I've sent you, it's because you've been called. Hellenica has asked for those with *your abilities* to join a special school, an *Academy*. They'll train you to fight the corruption, *the pettiness* of our gods."

"But why me?"

"They're not just asking for you," said Elazar with a laugh, "they're bringing in a group of young beings with powers. Gods, if you will. But these are not *entrenched* gods like Dagon and Lugh. Hellenica wants the young, the unjaded. They want those that still care more for society than themselves."

"I'm not a god," said Tommy. "I can't even walk without assistance."

"Do you remember your early youth, your parents, Tommy?"

"No."

"Nor do I. You may be a god, or something very much like it; there's a character similar to you in a book based on my Torah."

"If I'm in the Torah then I can't be a god," said Tommy. "Your religion is monotheistic."

"*Vehemently* monotheistic," said Elazar, "but both the Torah and this book, which we call *The Bible*, have certain grey areas when it comes to supernatural beings. If not a god, you'd be considered a demigod, or perhaps an *angel*. The book calls your kind *Horsemen*."

"I still don't follow."

"You won't need to, Tommy," said Elazar, "but I'll tell you that your talents are wasted on this island. My question to you is this: do you want to further your studies at the Academy, or stay here building toys?"

Tommy thought for a moment. The prospect excited him to be sure, but he was happy here. This place needed him, and he knew no other home.

"I've worked my whole life to make a perfect society, Tommy, one based on compassion and harmony, not strife," said Elazar. "But I've only succeeded in an unseen microcosm here. No one cares for Lepros, and no one ever will. But if you go inland, you'll show them what we can do. Will you go?"

"Yes."

"Good," said Elazar. "You report this evening. So listen to what they teach you, and be careful. The *Academy* is trustworthy, but the rest of the world is not. Though you may have supernatural powers, I fear you can still be killed. And there are those in the conurbation who'll seek to do just that."

PART II

THE ACADEMY

HELLENICA

The Spartan mercenary picked up Kayana two hours before dawn. He was prepared for her; he wore thick gloves and he kept his windowless van flooded with light. They stole off quietly into the morning and together they traversed the conurbation in a zigzag fashion, avoiding the dangerous districts like Éire, Papua, and the Apache Courts. Soon Kayana lost track of where they were. *The safe areas in this city are rare*, she thought, *and are getting rarer still.*

Still, she felt protected in the van they had sent. The van appeared to be run-down from the outside, but the mercenary explained that the exterior was run-down on purpose, to blend in with the city and to prevent kidnappings. Inside, the van held the latest technology. It showed a holographic map of the conurbation, potential threats ahead and the best streets to take, updated in real time. She also had quite a bit of space in the back seat and could turn the lights completely on or off with a switch. The driver, a Spartan mercenary named Cassander, told her he could drive in complete darkness if need be; he had night-vision goggles.

"We don't have an escort," said Cassander. "Strength and numbers are no substitute for stealth nowadays; kidnappers have been getting bold. It's a shame."

"Kidnapping is a function of ransom, which is a function of economic disparity," said Kayana. "It's not a shame. It just *is*."

"You've been in that cage too long," said Cassander. "It's not just money nowadays. A god gets bored, asks a follower to kidnap some high-ranking official or Druid priest, and that starts it. You think a Celtic god is gonna pay an Apache *ransom* to get that Druid back? No, he'll round up ten Gallic Warriors, have them attack at dawn. They'll come back with the priest and ten Apache heads. They'll sing a song about the rescue and wait for the Apache counterattack. It's a sport to these gods."

Kayana nodded her head in understanding. She sensed that the violence outside was different than when she had entered the institution. *Bad things should happen as a matter of nature, of time or even bad luck,* she thought, *but not for sport.*

"We're taking a detour," said Cassander. "Turn the lights off."

Cassander drove the van into a tunnel and they were underground. Right before she turned off the lights, Cassander turned to look back at her and smiled. He had a Hellenic name and pale skin, but by his accent Kayana guessed he was born a Sumerian. When he turned to smile, she noticed that he was young but had a seasoned look in his eyes and a deep scar on his neck. *He's old beyond his years and truly familiar with kidnapping*, she thought, *and he knows Celtic headhunters all too well.*

Kayana looked outside and found that they were deep in the bowels beneath the conurbation. She'd heard of this place and liked it; though it was dangerous, it felt untouched by the city above. There were monsters and diseases down here to be sure, but monsters and diseases kill out of instinct, not out of sport, and Kayana felt safe.

Kayana looked into the darkness and could see the faint images of creatures scurrying about. Many of the creatures were natural but some were not. *How many unnoticed battles have gone on under the ground between these creatures?* she thought. *How much blood has been spilt over territory lost, won and lost again?*

They traveled through the tunnels for more than an hour. Cassander's front window illuminated the surroundings with night vision, and Kayana could see that he was clearly on a road. They even passed several cars going in the opposite direction, and Cassander waved each time. *I'm not the only one who feels safe in the darkness,* thought Kayana. *Hellenica must use this as their main thoroughfare.*

"Kidnappers, thieves, they can go anywhere now," said Cassander, "any district, at any time. The key is traveling where they don't *want to* go. Too much effort to get down here, nothing to steal. So we're safe, *more or less.*"

Cassander pumped the brakes and they came to a complete stop. He backed the van up a few meters, and then parked around a corner. He motioned Kayana to be quiet and pressed a few buttons on the dashboard. A small camera extended from the front of the van and displayed what was around the corner. Two creatures twice the size of bears seemed to be locked in a desperate fight. Kayana heard the grunts and growls, but couldn't quite make out their shapes. After five minutes, the slightly smaller one bit the larger one. Kayana heard a squeal, and the larger one collapsed to the ground.

"Don't worry," said Cassander, "they eat fast down here."

Three minutes later, Cassander drove past the larger creature's remains and they were going through the tunnels again. He picked up speed, and Kayana could see several smaller creatures getting out of the way of the tires as they moved forward. They came to what looked like an underground river, but from its smell Kayana could tell that it was sewage. Cassander pressed another button, and a protective layer came from the roof and covered the windows. Cassander waited for the layer to snap shut and then proceeded to drive straight into the muck.

"Kidnappers don't want to go here," he repeated with a smile. "Breathe through your mouth."

They traveled like this for half an hour. Cassander was navigating the van with sonar now, moving slowly around the corners. They came up for air and stopped on a bank. Cassander pressed another button and a spray from the roof washed all the detritus from the van. Kayana noticed there was daylight at the end of the tunnel, and Cassander began to drive towards it.

"This is the only good part of this trip," he said with a smile. "Arrival back in Hellenica."

They came up through the opening and were surrounded by four thick walls, 100 meters high, with gunmen in the towers pointing at the van. *It looks like an Ishtar gate,* thought Kayana. *The Hellenica I knew never needed gates, let alone an Ishtar gate with gunmen.*

Four Spartan mercenaries came up to meet the van. They were four different races, and had probably had been born in four different districts. But they carried all the markings of Spartan guards: wiry, muscular bodies covered in battle scars, scowling faces and untrusting eyes. A guard commanded Cassander to open the window, and Kayana realized how different Cassander looked in comparison to the average Spartan. The man outside the van window was a seasoned warrior who would kill anyone or anything if ordered, but Cassander's face showed empathy, and he had a soft smile.

"License?"

Cassander held out his hand; they scanned his palm lines until their machine beeped.

"Business?"

"I'm transporting this young woman on orders of Charon," he said. "We're taking her to the Academy."

"Mind if we take her out and ask a few questions?" they asked.

"I don't," said Cassander, "but you might. She's not the type you want to get near; she's a *Horseman*."

The Spartan mercenary mulled it over. He peered at Kayana from the front of the window, and then spat. He moved away from the van and stopped twenty meters away to make a phone call through his earpiece. He came back to the van and spat again.

"By Charon's orders, we'll let the van in," said the mercenary, "but if you've smuggled in any contraband or migrants, *intentionally or not*, your life is forfeit."

"I have no hitchhikers," said Cassander. "Nothing could survive that ride."

The mercenary gave a nod and the gates started to open. *The Hellenica I remember was open and free. A city on a hill perhaps, but welcome to all*, thought Kayana, *and now they have thick gates and spitting guards who fear migrants. All this came about after I was in the institution for only a few short years.*

Kayana also wondered what Cassander meant by *Horseman*. She'd noticed that he had not called her a *god*, and she'd never felt that she was a god. Gods were petty, and only acted in their own self-interest. *But everyone here seems to understand the power of Horsemen,* she thought. *Whatever we are, people open gates for us, and keep their distance from us too.*

The van went through. Hellenica spread out before Kayana and she couldn't believe what she saw. Long walls protected the city, each with turrets of guns, and each with a Spartan mercenary in the tower. The interior of Hellenica was still the same; there were broad streets, single-story buildings with Doric columns, and doors open to the public. But it felt oppressive, quiet.

Hellenica is a city of ideas, not mistrust for the outside, thought Kayana, *and they don't depend so heavily on Spartan mercenaries.*

"Quite a bit has changed since you went away," said Cassander, "and don't think we're unaware of our flaws. Not pretty anymore, am I right?"

"Hellenica is not as it should be," said Kayana.

"By *Ninkharsag*, you're right," said Cassander, his Sumerian accent thickening just a bit. He pulled out his necklace and kissed the small tablet attached to it. Kayana noticed that the tablet was covered in cuneiform.

/***/

Cassander told Kayana to keep her distance from all passersby, and they walked through the streets of Hellenica freely. As they walked, Kayana sensed Hellenica still held a bit of its old self. She heard citizens freely squabbling about philosophy, art and the gods. She was pleased that the coliseum was hosting theater and not war games, and that there were still foreigners walking about. Hellenica had not yet fallen towards complete provincialism and xenophobia.

They passed through an open market that was selling fruits and vegetables from across the conurbation. Kayana saw meter-wide giant mushrooms from the Manitou, honey mead from Little Asgaard, and sushi straight from Dagon's markets. She also saw a bull about two meters high at the shoulder; a man in a white coat claimed that this was an Aurochs he'd brought back from extinction through genetic modification.

She saw a Mesopotamian man and a Papuan arguing in a public forum about the nature of gods in society.

"Pluralistic societies *can* exist next to one another," said the Papuan. "It simply takes a common *economy*. One never attacks a trading partner, so if the Celts ever went into business with the Apaches, they would be bound together and—"

"That's simply not true," said the Mesopotamian, interrupting. "The conurbation *has* a unified economy, and we're headed towards civil war as we speak. The gods, *if they are really gods*, gain power through strife. We'll be at each other's throats for the next thousand years, unified economy or not."

"There's a human desire for justice, for sanity and for dignity. Over time they will win out," said the Papuan.

"Justice, sanity and dignity are on the wane, and depravity is on the rise," said the Mesopotamian. "Many districts have resumed the practice of human sacrifice to appease their leaders. The Celts have their Wicker Men, the Aztecs their blood ceremonies, and even my people, the Mesopotamians, have resurrected their fire pits!"

"Yet we still have a free society within these walls," said the Papuan.

"And outside these walls our society is crumbling, common economy or not," said the Mesopotamian. "Our gods are so petty that I would be killed for these words, most likely as a human sacrifice. This is truth and you know it."

The Papuan nodded, defeated in rhetoric. The crowd dispersed and Kayana noticed that the Mesopotamian took no pleasure in his victory; he was deeply saddened by his own argument.

"Don't let his eloquence disturb you," said Cassander as they walked on. "All is not lost here."

"Perhaps it soon will be," said Kayana. "This is a town of poets defended by paid mercenaries. How long can this last?"

"You'd be surprised," said Cassander. "The citizens of the conurbation secretly yearn for Hellenica, even if they're too terrified of their gods to admit it. They all want the freedom to listen to men argue like that."

"Freedom alone cannot sustain a society," said Kayana.

"Are you sure about that?" said Cassander. "Look there."

Cassander pointed at the man in the white coat walking by, leading his Aurochs past them. The Aurochs was even taller than Kayana had initially thought. She looked down and saw that the added height was due to a floating pad the Aurochs was on, made weightless by a powerful electromagnet. Cassander pointed at the wheel that guided the pad; it had a full-color digital display.

"Freedom brings innovation, innovation brings *technology*," said Cassander. "Hellenica has technology and the other districts don't. That alone will maintain these city walls and pay the mercenaries for quite some time."

/***/

They walked up to the Acropolis and saw the city as a whole. The city wall was imperious and impenetrable with clean, sharp lines that wrapped around Hellenica completely. The wall was so high that even from the Acropolis, Kayana could barely see the city beyond. She saw enough though; there was a fire in Little Asgaard and pollution coming from Dagon's docks. The Yōkai district's shantytown piled upon itself and seemed like it was ready to spill over Hellenica's walls at any minute.

But still, thought Kayana, *within these walls, it is as it should be. Children still die, plagues still come, but Hellenica is as it should be.*

Kayana noticed a few more young recruits coming to the Academy with their mercenary handlers. There was a shirtless boy who looked normal at first, but she noticed that his feet were cloven hooves and his legs were covered with brown fur. She saw a thick girl almost two meters in height shrug off her guard and try to enter the Acropolis by herself. She saw another young man with green, scaly skin, sharp teeth and a long snout.

They entered the Acropolis one by one. After the thick girl entered, Kayana heard some clashes and then saw the girl burst out, followed by some Spartan mercenaries. The thick girl eventually calmed down, shrugged off one more mercenary and entered the Acropolis again.

"She's an Amazon," whispered Cassander. "Amazons and Spartans don't get along."

When it was Kayana's turn, Cassander nodded towards her to go, and they entered the Acropolis. It was enormous, dark and vacant, much as it always had been. They walked towards the far end, Spartans opened a door, and soon they were in a brightly lit interrogation room.

There was a woman sitting down at the table who had an attractive but odd face; she looked something like a cat. Behind her stood a tall, imposing man with green-shaded skin.

"You may go, Cassander," said the cat-faced woman, "and thank you."

Cassander smiled and then knelt down in front of Kayana. Though he was a Spartan, he had a strong kindness in his eyes that Kayana hadn't seen before. She wasn't certain of what he was trying to convey, but if she had to guess, she'd say that Cassander was being *fatherly*.

"Good luck, okay?" he said. "And stay out of the shadows."

Cassander left the room, and the cat-faced woman nodded at the green-skinned man.

"Please remove your gloves, Ms. Marx," said the cat-faced woman.

"I wouldn't advise that," said Kayana.

"We're well aware of your powers, Ms. Marx," said the woman, "and I assure you, ours will protect us. Remove your protective gloves."

Kayana took off the gloves and the cat-like woman took Kayana's hands in hers, analyzed them and then put them down.

"My name is Bastet," she said. "As you may have ascertained, I am a feline goddess. Behind me is Osiris. We're going to ask you some questions, and I would highly suggest you tell the truth. Osiris will be able to sense your lies before they leave your mouth."

"I do not lie," said Kayana. "You should be aware of that, as well."

"Then be sure to tell the *whole* truth. Osiris can also sense when anything has been withheld. Let me preface this by stating that you're free to go at any time; you aren't here against your will. However, the goddess Mnemosyne will erase your memory of this place if you choose to leave. Do you understand?"

"Neither Mnemosyne nor any other god will be able to erase my memory," said Kayana, "and if she dares peek into my thoughts, she will see such horrible things that it will leave her crippled."

Bastet stared at Kayana, unimpressed.

"But yes, I understand," said Kayana.

"Good," said Bastet. "Now to move forward, your past must be wiped clean. Our enemies will scour the conurbation to hurt your loved ones, so we must erase all ties. Mnemosyne will find your loved ones first and erase their memories of you. Do you accept this?"

"I have no loved ones," said Kayana, "so I accept."

"Let's be sure," said Bastet, flipping through a digital holographic tablet with her paws.

Kayana had seen technology before, but she hadn't seen anything as advanced as the display in front of Bastet. The tablet displayed a three-dimensional representation of each member of her previous families, in perfect color and detail. As the cat goddess swiped her paws over the screen, new representations of people showed up, most with the word *deceased* above their heads.

"Now, it says here you've had several foster families, most of whom perished after being exposed to your touch?"

"Yes," said Kayana. "Have Mnemosyne track any remaining living members down and take away their memories of me. You'd be doing them a favor."

"Understood," said Bastet. "Now, did you acquire any friends during your childhood?"

"None."

"No friends? Not even acquaintances?"

"Perhaps one man."

"Who's that?" asked Bastet.

"The mercenary Cassander, who drove me here," said Kayana. "And tell Mnemosyne she need not worry about erasing his memory. If any entity were to harm him, I'll know, and I'll make sure they regret it. Now please, destroy whatever you can find of my past, erase whatever you need to erase, and show me what plans you have for me, so that I might accept or reject your terms."

Bastet looked at Osiris, and he smiled with admiration.

"Put your gloves back on and proceed downward," said the cat-like woman.

Kayana did as she was told, but before she left the room, Osiris beckoned her to stop.

"I'm glad you're out of that dreadful institution," he said. His deep voice came out as a quivering whisper. "You've glimpsed but a fraction of your power. You're destined for great things."

Osiris released Kayana and gave a nod to Bastet, who pressed a button to summon two Spartan mercenaries. They took her back out to the inside of the Acropolis, and she saw a small boy in a mechanized suit walk in.

Such a soft face, such a harmless disposition, thought Kayana, *but I sense a dark power. He can kill more than I could without even knowing it.*

The two mercenaries escorted her to an escalator and they began to descend. The underground was cavernous and seemed to match the size of Hellenica above. Kayana knew that Hephaestus had designed an underworld to correspond to the city, but she hadn't imagined it would be this beautiful. Doric columns of steel supported the ceiling, and she looked up to see bas-reliefs of the past thousand years of human history. Every generation had left a mark on the ceiling, and the ceiling was large enough for ten thousand more years.

Kayana could see that the mercenaries were bringing her towards a small auditorium. The room was filled with heavy, regal chairs with thick seatbelts that would constrain both waist and shoulders. The seats were each a meter apart and laid out in concentric circles of ascending layers, and they were attached to the floor with thick steel spikes. Several of the other recruits were sitting peacefully in their chairs and some had already buckled their heavy seatbelts and were strapped in like prisoners. They looked calm and in no danger; the only one who seemed to be under stress was the Amazon girl. She refused to be restrained and was fighting the guards.

Another girl had a pet hyaena with her. The guards had anticipated this and placed it in an iron cage below her seat, and the hyaena lay with unusual calm beneath her.

Kayana allowed herself to be buckled in and counted the other recruits. There were sixteen in all in the concentric circles, with twelve on top and four at the bottom. The mercenaries allowed a grey-looking man to come into the auditorium, and then the guards closed the door and strapped themselves in on the third row above the recruits. Once the door had closed, Kayana noticed that the room wasn't as large as she'd previously thought. It was big enough to hold everyone inside, but no bigger. It had three rows, a space in the middle where the grey-looking man was standing, and circular walls that led her to believe that the room was in a tunnel. She felt her seat shake and realized the room was descending; it was then she realized that they were not in an auditorium, but a *vessel*.

The man walking on the bottom floor of the vessel wasn't old; in fact he looked quite spry and handsome, and his hair was brown. But he appeared *grey*, as if he had lived a thousand years and seen everything there was to see. He came down to the center of the auditorium and spoke with a stern voice.

"Good evening. My name is *Charon*, and I am honored to transport the first class to the Academy. We are prepared to make the journey underground," he said. He then looked at the defiant Amazon. "Though seat constraints aren't required, they're highly recommended. We have a saying here at the Academy: *technology trumps the deities.* You may have slayed a Hydra and survived a demon, but you're no match for the speed at which we'll travel, and you're no match for our ability to *stop*."

As Charon said the word *stop* he pressed a button, and the vessel came to a jarring halt. Kayana shook a bit, and the Amazon went flying forward and hit a wall. She got up, looked around with a scowl and strapped herself into her chair.

"Good," said Charon. "Now we'll begin the descent."

Charon pressed a button and the auditorium began to pick up speed. The ride was smooth, and soon it felt as if it were not moving at all.

"It's on levitating rails," said the boy with cloven feet. He was smiling, as if he was withholding a secret. "You can't feel it, but we're going *fast*. Faster than Hermes, with more range than Artemis and more agility than Apollo—"

Boom! The entire vessel shook, and they felt still once more.

"Maybe not quite as agile as Apollo," he said with a smile. "In any case, my name's *Pan*. Pleased to meet you, everyone!"

They traveled onward. Some of the young kids began talking with each other, and one of them laughed at how the Amazon girl fell out of her chair. One young man named Rowan heard this exchange and took offense on her behalf.

"Silence, all of you!" he bellowed in a thick Asgaard accent. "This Amazon will not be bound by social grace nor buckling of seat! I am the great Berserker Rowan, and I'll not tolerate the insults towards her!"

After a moment of awkward silence, the cloven-hooved boy Pan spoke up.

"We apologize for insulting her," said Pan. "We just thought it funny how she flew into a wall."

The Amazon was frowning and slightly embarrassed. She was clearly not interested in being the center of attention.

"I thank you for standing up for me, Rowan the Berserker," she said, "but I take little offense from the laughter of fauns."

"I take great offense at the laughter of a coward," said Rowan. "Are you a coward, faun?"

"Yes," said Pan, laughing, "a coward through and through."

Rowan took more offense at the cloven-hooved boy's tone and was about to unbuckle his seatbelt when a tall boy put his hand on Rowan's chest and prevented him from standing up.

"I wouldn't," said the boy.

"I've heard of you," said Rowan. "Gunnar Redstone, the cowardly Spartan dropout. Now, remove your hand from my seatbelt before I remove your hand from your arm."

The room made a violent shake and then almost turned upside down. It stopped again, and Gunnar removed his hand.

"There," said Gunnar, "stand up and attack the faun if you must. They'll sing songs of you for years to come, *Rowan the faun-slayer.*"

The room laughed and Rowan's jaw began to quiver with rage; he stared down Gunnar, muttered some words to himself and looked away in disgust. The talk amongst the students resumed, and from the din Kayana heard Pan singing a tune.

> *Rowan the faun-slayer insulted by one*
> *He will always stand up for his re-demption*
> *Rowan the faun-slayer stands in his seat*
> *A slight left turn and he'll be thrown from his feet*

Kayana scanned the room and found it a mixed crew, to say the least. Some looked more or less human, but many were clearly gods or monsters. There was a huge, brutish young man who must have been three meters tall and was covered in icy white fur. She listened to the conversations around him and learned that he was a young Frost Giant named Körr. *Frost Giants and Berserkers are blood enemies,* thought Kayana. *This Academy is bold indeed.*

She looked at the green scaly boy again and watched as he sat almost motionless, as if he were some sort of plant god. But she knew this couldn't be the case; his mouth held rows of sharp teeth. *He must be Sobek,* she thought, *the Egyptian god of crocodiles.*

There was a hawk-faced boy and a dog-faced boy; *the Egyptian gods Horus and Anubis.* She sensed an odd connection between herself and dog-faced Anubis, and when his eyes met hers, his pupils glowed red.

Pan had brought out a lute and was playing it while he sang.

> My name is Pan, and this is the PAN-theon
> Traveling to the A-CAD-e-MEE
> And if you should choose to stay in this CLAN-theon
> You'll be a god with a lowercase "g"
>
> We have falcons and dogs, a Japanese frog
> And if you want to be killed with a breath
> We have a fire demon, a Frost Giant freeman
> And beautiful, voluptuous Death
>
> We have Amazon wonders, polar bear hunters
> Crocodiles and ghouls of the night
> And if you were to tell that we're all straight from Hel
> I'd think twice and then say that you're right
>
> And there is a man, he is a Norse-MAN-theon
> Hurt his pride and he'll have a fit
> And there are Four Horsemen, who won't like this Norseman
> And the world won't like them one bit
>
> My name is Pan, and this is the PAN-theon
> Traveling to the A-CAD-e-MEE
> And if you should choose to stay in this CLAN-theon

You'll be a god with a lowercase "g"

The crowd clapped in wonder; even the Amazon cracked a smile. Rowan muttered another curse but was drowned out by cheering as the students asked Pan for another song.

Kayana stared back at the dog-faced boy and his eyes continued to glow. *Anubis is a death god,* thought Kayana. *You have a connection to all death gods.* Kayana sensed the same connection between herself and another girl; a girl who looked half-alive. This girl's hair grew in ashen-grey clumps and her skin was falling off, and she didn't seem to be aware of her surroundings. Kayana heard a murmur from the group that this girl was a *ghoul* from Little Riyadh named *Asra*. The other kids whispered complaints about Asra's pungent smell, but Kayana thought the girl smelled divine. *She has no agenda, no malice and no hatred in her heart*, thought Kayana. *Asra is pure.*

Kayana's eyes scanned the room and landed on the warrior Gunnar, the girl with the hyaena and the sick boy with the suit. She couldn't explain it, but these three were familiar to her. She'd not seen their faces before today, but she sensed a connection with all of them, as if they'd known each other a thousand lifetimes ago, or in a nightmare long forgotten. Gunnar looked tense, as if he was steeling for a confrontation with Rowan; the sick boy sat meekly in his suit, and the girl with the hyaena sat imperiously and stared straight ahead. *I feel a dark power from them,* thought Kayana, *and they aren't gods. Though they sit amongst gods, these three aren't the same.*

The kids spoke to each other, gossiping, bonding and forming groups, but Kayana maintained her silence. Charon also showed the indifference of an elder chaperone and seemed to be lost in thought, but when the vessel came to a stop he unbuckled and sprang into action.

"We're here," he said. "Now follow me into the next room."

They all unbuckled their seats except for Asra, who was in a stupor. The mercenaries had expected this and cautiously took off her restraints. One of the mercenaries was struck by the ghoul's odor and ran off to get sick in a corner. His comrades guffawed at his expense, but Asra snapped awake and cut them off mid-laugh. They jumped back quickly, and one of them screamed. They calmed down and approached her again, and one kissed an amulet around his neck. *They fear her,* thought Kayana, *but it's more than that. The ghoul seems to drain emotions of all those in her vicinity.*

The students filed into the next room, which was a small amphitheater with two tiers of seats. Each chair was labeled, and they all sat down. Charon was the last to arrive and stood in the middle of the theater. This room was compact, but larger than the previous vessel. There were no straps on the seats, and the walls were made of heavy stones. It was dark and cold, but clean, and the acoustics were so good that she could hear Charon's breath as he approached a podium.

"Welcome to the Academy," he said. "I introduce Headmaster Indra, and Heracles, dean of the school."

Indra was a tall, golden man with a long overcoat covering a suit and tie. His body bulged unnaturally in the middle; he was clearly hiding an extra set of arms. Heracles was more humbly dressed and a bit shorter, but much thicker and hairier. The two gods commanded quite a presence and all the students were in awe, including the Amazon girl. Rowan broke the silence by kneeling before them.

"Please be seated, Berserker," said Indra. "Blind fealty is one of the reasons we're here in the first place."

Rowan reluctantly stood up, bowed one more time and then sat down. Tears of joy filled his sparkling-blue eyes, and he grinned nervously in Indra's presence. Kayana noticed that Rowan was almost as tall as Gunnar, and his muscles were nearly as well-developed. His clear, clean face was without scars, but his jaw held a quivering fierceness and

Kayana saw a reckless streak within him. *He's not yet seen a battle,* thought Kayana, *but if he hears one, he'll run towards it and pick a side on a whim. He's a fool cloaked in courage and honor, but I should be wary, because fools such as he can kill friend and foe just the same.*

"As of today," said Indra, "your past is gone. You have no family, and no friends outside of this room. If you are to perish, no one will mourn for you. There will be no temples built in your honor, no scores of worshippers currying favor, no idolaters begging you to do a magic trick in their self-interest.

"You were selected for the Academy because you don't care about this, or at least you can be *taught* not to care. You are young, malleable and still yearn for something greater than your own interest.

"The conurbation, and the world as we know it, is dying. The gods will make sure of this; they're growing out of control, and if we fail to act now, they'll pass the threshold and the world will lay in a state of permanent war. We need a police force to bring the world back to sanity, to bring the gods back under control. We have tried to do this with diplomacy, technology and sheer warfare, but to no avail. So we have called upon you: the first class of young gods at the Academy.

"Not all of you will make it. Some will quit, some won't pass our training, some will succumb to the temptations of pettiness and disappear back into the conurbation. Some of you will fall in the line of duty and die."

There was a hush in the room. Asra seemed not to notice and Rowan smiled, but the rest of the gods were now rapt in attention.

"Oh yes," said Indra, "though you're not mortals, our enemies have found ways to kill gods. Don't take this calling lightly; you may perish."

The group was tense and quiet. *These students have never contemplated death before*, thought Kayana. *It's as foreign to them as flight is to a mole.*

81

"Do not overworry about death," interjected Heracles with a smile. "You're at the Academy, and we'll teach you to defend yourself. Whatever powers you have will be magnified a hundredfold by the time we're done with you. Dagon, Lugh, the Yōkai and even great Poseidon will take notice when you approach. They'll tremble and know that you're part of a powerful force, a force that can't be fooled, co-opted or bought off."

Heracles looked directly at Rowan.

"We're not in the business of dying here at the Academy," said Heracles. "Even if it means great honor."

Indra got up to speak again. His golden skin pulsed as he talked, and his voice was clear and calm. He and Heracles resembled giants rather than gods, with Indra nearly three meters in height, and Heracles seemingly that in breadth.

"There are sixteen of you," said Indra. "You'll be grouped into one of four Classes: the Elements, Death, War, and Nature. There will be four teams, each team with one member of each Class. You will train within your Class, and both live and fight within your team.

"All necessary information will be found underneath your chair. Read it and then go to the mess hall immediately and sit with your team. Training will begin within the hour."

Indra left the room. After a few moments, the Amazon was the first to look under her chair. She took out a bit of granite with some carvings on it and read it. She smirked, smashed the granite over her knee and then stared at Heracles. The others began pulling their granite tablets from under their chairs and erupted into various reactions. Soon Kayana and Asra were the only students who didn't know where they were going, so Kayana pulled her piece of granite from under the chair and it read:

KAYANA MARX

CLASS = DEATH

QUARTERS = KAZBEK

TEAM = HORSEMEN

"You'll survive this training," said Heracles. "We'll make sure of it. But you may end up grievously injured, so be very, very careful. Now rest up and get something to eat."

TRAINING

Gunnar walked to the mess hall to meet his new team, the Horsemen. *Two girls and a boy who can't walk*, he thought. *I should be fighting* for *them, not* with *them.*

They sat down at four tables, each with four chairs hewn of ironwood. The chairs had their names engraved upon them: Tommy Alderon, Kayana Marx, Gunnar Redstone and Saoirse Frost.

Hestia, goddess of the hearth and home, had cooked a large pot of ambrosia and placed it in the middle.

"Watch out," said Hestia, "this will make you strong, but it's not for the weak of stomach."

Hestia left and Tommy poked his ambrosia and smiled. His helmet's shield retracted slightly so that he could eat, but he didn't take any food in yet. His face was small and gentle, with straight black hair and light brown skin that had been flushed pale by a childhood spent inside a suit. In the ride down to the Academy, Gunnar had heard the guards whispering that Tommy held virulent diseases in his body, but Gunnar sensed that Tommy would sooner die than let those sicknesses out. Tommy wasn't a killer, and he reminded Gunnar of *Tōfu-Kozō,* a comical Yōkai spirit who befriended the bullied and was often bullied himself.

"Ambrosia requires the power of a god to make it taste good," said Tommy. "It's a mental thing; you have to willfully *make* this substance into something edible. They gave us this on Lepros. I never got the hang of making it edible, but it's good. It cures whatever ails you."

Tommy dropped his face shield down and took a mouthful of the blackened mush. He grimaced, but continued to eat. Gunnar followed suit; the food tasted worse than ashes. But Gunnar ate heartily; the hunger from the Agoge taught Spartans to eat anything short of human waste.

As Gunnar ate, he felt stronger.

"I cannot eat this," said Saoirse.

"You should," said Gunnar. "I heard Heracles's tone of voice. He speaks the truth; our training will be dangerous."

"I know I should," said Saoirse, "I just can't stomach it."

"I learned a trick on Lepros," said Tommy. "Just wait a moment."

Tommy went to the far corner of the hall and gathered several condiments. He grabbed a bowl of Nahuatl chia seeds, a bottle of Hellenic fish-intestine *garum* and one Indian ghost pepper. He brought them back to the table and began to mush them into Saoirse's food.

"The key is to make the ambrosia wretched, but wretched in a way we can handle," said Tommy. "This will be intense, perhaps too much to bear, so eat quickly before it gets too hot."

Saoirse ate it quickly, and then laughed as the spice took over. Tears came from her eyes, and she drank an entire pitcher of water.

"Drink milk instead," said Tommy. "And drink it slowly."

Soon the whole hall took notice and was mixing spice into their food; everyone except for Asra the ghoul and Rowan the Berserker.

Asra preferred to eat it plain, and Rowan refused Tommy's help on principle.

"You should do as he says," Anubis said to Rowan. "Fire is easier to stomach than ash."

Rowan refused to acknowledge the gesture and ate in silence. After a few moments he turned over his plate and exploded in rage.

"I'll not accept *wisdom* from Children of the Apocalypse," said Rowan, "let alone from *Pestilence*."

Rowan stared right at Tommy. *Tommy has no idea what Rowan's saying,* thought Gunnar, *nor do I.* Gunnar steeled himself in case Rowan attacked.

"You heard me," said Rowan. "You *all* heard me. There is good and bad in this world, the noble and the ignoble. Gods fall on one side only; never in the middle. And the likes of Frost Giants and Horsemen know naught else but destruction. Like the scorpion riding the frog across the river, they'll sting us even if it means they drown as well. It's in their nature."

"I think you're mistaken," said Tommy. His voice shook; he seemed unfamiliar with confrontation.

"I am not," said Rowan, "and by Thor's own hammer, I'll stop you before you can use that suit to destroy us."

Tommy had no response; instead his jaw began to quiver and a tear rolled down his cheek. Gunnar got up in a flash and pounced on Rowan. The young Berserker unsheathed a small axe from his armor and swung at Gunnar. Gunnar dodged the axe and punched the Berserker's breastplate, denting it. *It must be some strange alloy, strong yet flexible,* thought Gunnar. *That punch would have shattered Spartan armor.* Rowan shoved Gunnar off, and the other students instinctively spread out around the periphery. Rowan pushed over the tables to clear some space and prepared himself.

"Come at me, War," said Rowan. "You've no armies to protect you."

We are pit-fighting now, thought Gunnar, *and no one short of Heracles can best me.*

Gunnar crouched on the ground and lowered his center of gravity.

"You've seen many foes, but not a Berserker rage and—"

In a flash, Gunnar blasted into Rowan's legs. Rowan tried to jump over Gunnar, but Gunnar was too quick. He grabbed Rowan's armored leg and used gravity to push the Norseman's momentum downward, slamming the Berserker's face into the ground. Gunnar locked Rowan's legs and put his knees on Rowan's shoulder blades. Gunnar used his free hand to lock Rowan's arm, and instantly the Norseman was helpless.

"I suggest you apologize to my teammate, Berserker," whispered Gunnar. Gunnar twisted his opponent's arm just to show that he could break it if he desired.

"I will apologize to neither your teammate nor anyone else," said Rowan. "Break both my arms if you wish, but I won't apologize."

Gunnar twisted Rowan's arm. Rowan spat and snarled, but he didn't yell.

"Look upon these four!" yelled Rowan, addressing the rest of the students. "Death and destruction is in their nature. The cripple will bring plagues, and the brute above me will one day foment genocide. Laugh at me for the prideful warrior I am, but hear my message. These four will hasten the end of Hellenica, then soon thereafter the conurbation, and then one day the world."

Heracles burst into the room in a rage, followed by Charon. Heracles picked Gunnar up as if he were a rag doll and threw him against the far wall. *Heracles was hiding his strength during our initial fight*, thought Gunnar. *No one has ever thrown me like that.*

"What's the meaning of this?" screamed Heracles.

Gunnar remained silent, but Rowan spoke up.

"I was ridding the Academy of these destructive creatures from Hell and—"

"Quiet, you!" yelled Heracles.

Heracles turned red and picked Rowan up by his neck. Rowan's tan, muscular arms grabbed onto the hairy shoulders of Heracles, but Rowan was like a child in the strong man's grip and could only flail about helplessly. Heracles looked as if he were about to crush the Berserker in his fists, but after a moment dropped Rowan, who fell with dead weight onto the ground.

"This is *precisely* what's killing our society, creating *blood feuds* when there are none," said Heracles. "In-fighting will not be tolerated. Any more blows, deserved or not, will warrant both parties being sent to Tartarus. For now, we'll let you off with a warning; your first test is punishment enough. Charon will escort you to the training center. Now go!"

"Follow me," said Charon. "A brutal lesson awaits."

Charon went out of the room and each student soon followed him, sticking to their own groups. Gunnar got up to follow too, but Heracles stopped him and held him by the arm. Once again, Gunnar felt that he could be broken at any moment.

"The Berserker Rowan is a fool; we know this," said Heracles. "But we still took him in because of the value that he brings. One day you'll lead him into battle and his Berserker rage will accomplish more than ten squadrons. Until then, you'll not take his bait, you'll not take his feuds, and you'll *not* best him in combat.

"I said your days of pit-fighting were over, Redstone, and I meant it. You're a General, not a petty brawler. Any more comeuppance from you and I'll *personally* ensure that your punishment is harder than it should be. Is that understood?"

Gunnar nodded yes.

"Good," said Heracles, "now concentrate on your first day of training. It's up to you to keep your teammates alive."

"I thought you said we couldn't die this day," said Gunnar.

"We're protecting you, this is true," said Heracles, "but a god can die any day."

/***/

Charon walked the students out of the lunch hall, across a courtyard and up to an ominous building that looked like a windowless gladiator's coliseum. Though the underground floor was cavernous, Gunnar looked around and knew that this was just the beginning of the Academy. *This is an underground world, with architecture so profound that it must have been designed by Hephaestus himself,* thought Gunnar. *And Hephaestus is known to dig deep. There must be floors below this, so many that this Academy might be connected to Hades itself.*

Charon motioned the students towards the windowless building, and Gunnar noticed that there were four rooms, each engraved with names of the four teams: Power, Stealth, the Scalpel and the Horsemen.

"Teams, go into your rooms right now," said Charon.

Rowan immediately strode into his room; he was on the Power team. The rest of the groups gradually followed suit and went into their rooms, leaving Gunnar and his Horsemen alone. "Shall we go in?" Gunnar asked. He got no response, so he just said, "Follow me."

Gunnar strode into the room and was followed by Tommy and then Saoirse. He'd never seen a girl like Saoirse before, and thought that the blonde hair laying against her dark skin was one of the most beautiful sights he'd ever seen. Her hyaena hugged her leg as she walked past, and Gunnar averted his gaze for fear that she'd belittle him like the Agoge girls had been taught to do. She simply smiled and walked by though, and was soon followed by Kayana, who disappeared into the darkness of the room.

Once they were all inside, the door shut behind them with a thud. It was completely quiet. After a moment, Gunnar pulled on the door, but it wouldn't budge. They were alone, just the four of them and a hyaena. It was quite dark, but Gunnar had excellent night vision. He saw the far end of the room was the entrance to what looked like a maze. He listened closely and heard an eerie snapping from the depths beyond.

"What's that?" asked Tommy.

"Something dangerous," said Saoirse.

"It makes no sense," said Tommy. "They just threw us in here."

"It makes perfect sense," said Gunnar. "They did this all the time during the Agoge. When training a team, start by dropping them in a hostile environment. It'll help us bond and work together."

There was another snapping sound and then a large *splash*. Some water came out of the maze's dark entrance.

"I'd rather bond another way," said Tommy, "perhaps through conversation."

"We'll have time to do that," said Gunnar, "but for now we have a task before us. There's a maze in front of us, and most likely a few dangerous creatures lurking in its shadows. If we come across one of these creatures we need to work together, and that starts with knowing our abilities. So let's discuss our powers. Tommy, you first."

"Powers?" asked Tommy. "I don't know. As of yesterday I was just a contagious boy from Lepros."

"What can that suit do?" asked Gunnar.

"Quite a bit," said Tommy. "It gives me strength, protection, sight. It can go in most every environment. But I built it mainly to protect others. If I opened the face shield, you'd get infected."

"Does it have night vision?"

"Yes," said Tommy.

"Perfect," said Gunnar, "you'll be our eyes. Saoirse, what can you do?"

"I don't know," she said. "Other than charm, I don't believe I have any abilities."

Gunnar found it odd that a girl like Saoirse would self-deprecate like that. She wasn't athletic and sinewy like the girls in the Agoge, but her square jaw and gently curving body suggested a sort of nobility, and regal girls always had hidden powers. She was the kind of girl who would either fight in a war or have a war fought over her, but whatever the case, she'd always have a role to play.

"They didn't bring you here for your charm," said Gunnar. "What's your power? You have one."

"Then my power is as yet unknown," she said. Her hyaena growled and then nuzzled against her leg, whining.

Gunnar gave up on deducing Saoirse's abilities, but made a note to keep an eye out for them whenever they showed themselves.

"And you?" he asked Kayana. "What can you do?"

"Whatever my power is, it's not helping us now," she said. "How about you, General? What's *your* power?"

"Strength," he said. "Fighting, endurance, something like that."

"The fool called you *War*," said Kayana.

"Then he's indeed a fool," said Gunnar. "I fight in pits, lunch halls and back alleys. My time for the battlefield is over."

"But it appears we're Horsemen," said Tommy. "They call us *Horsemen*."

"Indeed," said Gunnar. "Do any of you know what gods *Horsemen* were? Or *are*?"

There was a silence until the hyaena made a high-pitched bark.

"I know," said Saoirse. "They taught us this at Elysia. The Horsemen were ancient gods—well, not really *gods*, but supernatural beings from the monotheistic times. They were to bring about the end of humanity. War, Death, Pestilence, and the White Knight."

"Perhaps you are indeed War, General," said Kayana.

"Then you, Death," said Gunnar. "Tommy, perhaps you're Pestilence?"

"Perhaps I am," said Tommy. "Perhaps I am."

Tommy checked his mask again and then sat in the corner, dejected and motionless. *Tommy's suit is amazing,* thought Gunnar, *but he doesn't want to fight. If some monster were to come from the maze, he'd be helpless.*

"And what of you, Saoirse?" he asked. "What does this White Knight do?"

"I don't know," she said. "It's unclear what the White Knight does."

"What about your dog?" he asked.

"It's a hyaena," said Saoirse. "A striped hyaena, and I don't know what it can do."

Saoirse remained silent, and the hyaena's hair stood up straight until its size was almost doubled. They looked into the darkness and at the entrance to the maze was a small, stout man.

"We don't know what the hyaena can do," said the man, "and for that matter, we don't know what any of you can do."

The man came out and he had smooth brown skin, short arms and legs; he looked to be a dwarf.

"My name is Bes," said the man. "I'm an Egyptian god, but in the Academy I'd be considered your *advisor*. So for the time being, our interest is one and the same. That interest is you making it through the next hour without having your bones crushed."

Bes came near them; he might not have been a meter in height. Gunnar knew Bes to be a powerful god so he paid him respect and gestured towards his group to stand at attention.

"Relax, Redstone," said Bes, "I care nothing for your deference. In fact, this whole school can go to Hades as far as I'm concerned."

Bes is the god who defends the weak, the old and the infirm, thought Gunnar. *He's good, but detests authority. It's a miracle he agreed to come to the Academy in the first place.*

"We thank you for coming to our aid," said Gunnar, "and we ask your advice how to manage the maze ahead."

"First of all, it's not a maze," said Bes with a smile. "It's a *labyrinth*. Mazes are built for recreation; labyrinths are built to punish."

"It's a labyrinth without light, too," said Tommy.

"You'll survive it," said Bes. "It's the creature inside that concerns me. We placed this creature, a *monster*, if you will, to lie in the depths for you. It's young, just barely hatched, but still quite deadly in this environment. You'll all use your powers to navigate the labyrinth and get past the monster."

"Get past him?" asked Gunnar. "Shouldn't we fight him?"

"You're no match for this creature; don't fight him," said Bes. "I'll be watching to make sure that no fatal injuries occur, but should this creature decide to shatter your collarbone, even I won't be fast enough to defend you.

"Now, your task is simple: make it through the labyrinth," he said. "Do you still wish to go forward?"

The team was quiet, and then Tommy broke the silence.

"Yes," he said, "let's do it."

Tommy got up, walked through the entrance to the chamber, and disappeared.

"I suggest you follow him," said Bes. "It's dark in there, and easy to become separated."

They all followed Tommy in, but Bes stopped Saoirse at the last minute.

"Leave your pet behind and I'll let him out the way you came in," he said. "Hyaenas aren't fond of cold water."

/***/

They entered the labyrinth, and yet another door shut them in. *This whole Academy is a series of rooms and locking doors,* thought Gunnar. *This* whole place *is a labyrinth.*

Gunnar had good night vision and so did the rest of the crew.

Tommy seemed to have the best vision; his helmet allowed him to see in the dark. Kayana didn't let on how well she could see but said that she was *comfortable in complete darkness*, before going her own way.

Something scurried above them, crawling across the ceiling.

"What was that?" asked Gunnar.

"I'm tracking him," said Tommy.

Tommy peered through his helmet and then turned to Gunnar.

"It's Bes," said Tommy. "He's staying a hundred meters or so in front of us."

They moved forward through a tunnel and found little glowing larvae on the walls. It was enough to let them see where they were going, but the labyrinth was beginning to spread out, and water on the ground was getting deeper.

"We'll be swimming shortly," said Tommy.

The labyrinth soon turned into a canal. It was a bit cold, but Gunnar didn't mind; he'd spent many winters in the Agoge on one frozen lake or another. He worried about his companions; Saoirse in particular was shivering.

"Water strips heat away from your body," said Gunnar. "Not everyone can take it."

"My suit can generate external heat," said Tommy. "Check this out."

Tommy pressed a button and a light came on under water. Soon the water around his suit was tolerable. *Not warm*, thought Gunnar, *but tolerable*. A few glowing swimming creatures were attracted to the heat and darted around Tommy's suit. Saoirse walked closely behind Tommy, and after a minute she stopped shivering.

They walked further and came to a fork in the tunnel.

"Both forks lead to two more forks," said Tommy.

"This is indeed a labyrinth. Tommy, can you see Bes?" asked Gunnar. "Perhaps he's leading the way."

Tommy looked both ways but couldn't find their advisor.

"My suit can record where we've been," said Tommy. "It'll make a map of sorts. I can also use sonar to see dead ends ahead."

"Good," said Gunnar. "Please do that, and lead the way."

Tommy looked both ways, took a look at some images on the inside of his face shield and then went left. He took another left at a turn, then a right, and then another left. Gunnar took notice of how the team navigated this maze. He saw that though Tommy had been shy above ground, he was quite comfortable walking through the dark depths of this labyrinth. And Saoirse, though she held a regality befitting a princess, also strode through the black, cold water without complaint. If she was indeed a princess, she was one that didn't mind getting her feet dirty. Gunnar tried to observe Kayana, but just as he would take note of her, the dark-haired girl with pale skin would disappear from his line of sight.

They walked for half an hour like this, backtracking only once. It got even darker, and soon the only light was Tommy's suit and the glowing creatures that followed them. Tommy increased the light he gave out, but it was still too dark. After a moment they heard a little splash, and soon all the glowing creatures around them were gone.

Gunnar motioned them to be quiet; he could hear something ahead swimming towards them.

"I hear it, but I also sense it," said Saoirse. "Ahead, just around the corner."

Tommy looked at the internal display in his suit.

"It's about four meters long, and it's coming at us pretty quickly," said Tommy.

Tommy shone his light ahead and they saw a ripple in the water moving forward. It disappeared for a moment and then reappeared. It was quite thin and wriggling back and forth. The creature disappeared under the water, and Gunnar felt something glide against his leg. It was swimming between them, over and over again. Saoirse shrieked.

"What is it?" said Gunnar.

"It's thin, like a ribbon," said Tommy. "It looks like a snake, perhaps a meter long."

"Virtually every swimming snake is venomous," said Saoirse. "I get a bad feeling from this one too."

"Stay together," said Gunnar. "We must appear bigger than it is."

"No," said Kayana from the darkness. "Creatures kill when they're frightened. This one isn't frightened, not yet at least."

Gunnar thought for a moment. He wasn't in the Agoge any more, and he definitely wasn't in the pit. He was underwater, cold, lost and confronted with something that could swim a lot better than he could. He followed his instinct and took Kayana's advice.

"Split apart," said Gunnar, "but just a bit. Lie very still."

They split about a meter apart and stayed quiet, but their eyes were rapt on the water. They could see the snake swimming about. It would disappear and reappear again. Each time it seemed to be getting closer to Tommy. Tommy turned his light and his heat off and on, but it didn't matter; the creature seemed to like him.

"He's going to bite one of us," said Saoirse. "He's determined."

Tommy waded apart from the group, luring the snake.

"What are you doing, Tommy?" whispered Gunnar. "Get back here!"

Tommy wouldn't listen and continued to walk away from the group. Gunnar kept whispering at him to stop, but Tommy couldn't be controlled. Tommy then took the glove off his suit and dipped his bare arm in the water. The sea snake reared its head. It had a thin snout and followed Tommy's arm as he raised it above the water.

"Tommy," said Gunnar, "don't do this!"

Gunnar waded forward to take the snake's attention. *The snake's head is exposed right now,* thought Gunnar. *If I can just grab his neck I will—*

Boom! Without taking its eyes off Tommy, the snake swiped its small, powerful tail and took Gunnar's legs out from under him. Gunnar fell into the cold water and became disoriented. He finally managed to get up, gasping for air. He turned around, and after his eyes adjusted he saw the serpent's jaws on Tommy's bare arm. Tommy seemed to be in a little pain, but was allowing the snake to continue biting him.

And just like that, the snake loosened his fangs, fell into the water and swam away.

"Tommy," said Gunnar, "are you okay?"

"Completely," said Tommy, still focused on the snake

Gunnar rushed toward Tommy to examine the wound; he could see at a glance that there were two bite marks with poison oozing from the holes. Before Gunnar could grab Tommy's arm to administer any first aid, Tommy drew back from him.

"You need to stay calm and put your arm below your heart level to minimize blood flow and—" said Gunnar, but Tommy interrupted.

"The bite won't hurt me," said Tommy. "I'm immune."

Tommy put the arm of his suit back on and looked at Gunnar.

"All my life I've made others sick, but never gotten sick myself," said Tommy. "It's the same with toxins, poisons. They have no effect on me."

"The snake sensed that and left us alone," said Saoirse. "And now he's going to his master."

"His master?" asked Gunnar.

It was quiet, and then they heard a large splash in the distance. Then another splash, and some snapping like they'd heard when they were outside of the labyrinth.

"What is it?" asked Gunnar.

The team was silent.

"Saoirse," he asked, "what do you *sense* it is?"

"I don't know," she said, "but it's large. It's angry; all I sense is hatred towards us and bitterness towards those who have put it down here. It's powerful; it won't be cowed so easily like the sea snake."

"What else?" asked Gunnar. "Listen to it."

"It's not where it belongs. It should be in the deep, deep ocean. It's too big to be here."

A small wave of water hit them. They heard another gigantic splash in the distance, and twenty seconds later another wave of water lapped across their legs.

"Whatever it is, we can find it," said Tommy. "Just walk *towards* the waves."

They walked into the ripples of water cautiously. The glow-in-the-dark creatures came to surround them once again. Every time they came to a fork in the labyrinth, a wave came from one path, and they followed it. The splashes became louder each time; it was clear that this creature was enormous. But the clicking was still relatively quiet. *Large sea creatures don't make sounds on land,* thought Gunnar, *they communicate under the water. Their clicks and squeaks traverse oceans and find others of their kind.*

"Saoirse," he said, "please put your ears under the water. Perhaps you can intuit something else from this creature."

Saoirse dunked her head under the water. *She's a beautiful girl, a fragile, rare gem,* thought Gunnar, *yet she feels at ease with dangerous animals.*

Saoirse brought her head up; her wet blonde hair shone brightly in Tommy's light and she spoke calmly, as if in an oracle's trance.

"It knows not where it is," said Saoirse. "It senses our presence and wants to kill us. It wants to ..."

Saoirse put her ear to the water once more and listened for a moment, and her eyes soon widened with fear.

"It wants to wrap its arms around us and smash us to bits. But it can't unless we come to it; it cannot move in this shallow water."

"Can we approach it in safety?"

Saoirse listened to the water.

"Yes," said Saoirse, "but it won't let us pass."

They went into the waves, around turn after turn, through fork after fork. Soon it was clear that the creature was around the corner, and the waves had them almost submerged.

"Saoirse," said Gunnar, whispering, "does it sense our presence?

That we are here?"

"It senses us," said Saoirse, "but doesn't know where we are. It can see quite well though."

"Tommy," said Gunnar, "can you look around the wall's edge with that suit somehow? See it without it seeing you?"

Tommy smiled, glad to be an asset to the team, and then crept to the corner. The water was thrashing him now, but his heavy suit held steady in the current. He latched on with his right hand to the wall, and extended his left hand around the corner.

"I have a camera," he whispered.

After holding his hand there for a few moments, he crept back towards the team. He pointed at his mask and showed a grainy black-and-white projection of the creature.

It looked like a giant squid stranded in shallow water. Each picture was blurry; its long tentacles were in constant motion. Its eyes were enormous and shone in the darkness. It seemed helpless, but its arms were so long that it had a range of at least fifteen meters.

"It's a Kraken," said Gunnar. "A Norse sea monster."

Gunnar paused a moment. He remembered the Agoge's sea training; they'd taught them to do *anything* in the ocean. Gunnar could hold off a tanker with a small, lightly armed boat; he could live for a month on open water with no food. But his Spartan teachers only taught him how to *avoid* Krakens. *They'd teach us the signs that a Kraken was near: abundant fish, roiling water and moonless nights,* thought Gunnar, *but they wouldn't teach us to fight Krakens, because neither god nor technology can defeat these creatures.*

Gunnar looked at the Kraken and started formulating a strategy. *Not even a god can capture a live Kraken,* thought Gunnar. *This one must be weak, or perhaps ...*

"This one's a juvenile," Gunnar said to the crew, "probably only a few decades old; but it'll still be strong. They can see quite well, especially in the dark; as soon as we go around the corner it will see us. Now, look here ..."

Gunnar pointed at the images. It looked like there was a small doll sitting behind the creature. Tommy zoomed in on it, and it was clear that it was Bes. He was sitting near a door with light pouring from it.

"That's our exit," said Gunnar. "That's our goal."

"Can we get around this Kraken?" asked Tommy.

"No," said Gunnar. "His range is too big. Once he sees us, he'll get ahold of us with his tentacles, and then we're done."

"I've got a suit," said Tommy. "I made it out of titanium alloy—"

"That clicking sound is his beak," said Gunnar. "It can put a hole in a steel ship. Even if he can't break your suit, he'll hold you under the water for a few days and try."

Gunnar studied the pictures again. The exit was clearly behind this creature, but unfortunately there was no way past it. *I only know how avoid Krakens, not to get past them,* thought Gunnar. *Four unarmed kids in cold water won't be able to escape its tentacles. There's got to be another passageway around it.*

"Tommy, can you see another path?" said Gunnar. "A tunnel, another route, anything ...?"

"I can't see anything," said Tommy. "But maybe if we—"

"There's no other way," said Saoirse. "The Kraken knows this, and I sense it. He's blocking the only exit."

"Can we lure him away?" asked Tommy.

That could be it, thought Gunnar with a smile.

"Legend has it that Krakens are extremely protective of their young," said Gunnar, "even young not their own. Exposed Kraken eggs send an electrical signal through the water and can lure them from far away, even a juvenile."

"True," said Saoirse. "I've heard this legend too."

"We don't have Kraken eggs," said Gunnar, "but Tommy, can you *simulate* the signal from a Kraken egg?"

Tommy shook his head no.

"We learned much on Lepros," said Tommy, "but we didn't learn about sea creatures."

Gunnar paused to think. *This isn't the pit, this isn't the Agoge. Though this is training, this is real. The Kraken is real, and if it grabs hold of one of us with a tentacle, Bes won't be able to help.*

"Then we go back the way we came," said Gunnar. "We fail, live to fight another day, and—"

"I'll go," said Kayana.

The team looked back at her. She'd found a ledge above the water and was perched in the darkness, looking off to an odd angle.

"Go where?" asked Gunnar.

"Let me talk to this Kraken," said Kayana. "Not like Saoirse would communicate, but like I would. I'll enter into dialogue with this creature, and we will pass."

"Enter into *dialogue* with a Kraken? I can't allow you to do this," said Gunnar. "This Kraken will—"

"I'm not yours to allow, General," said Kayana. "I will talk to it, and then we will pass because I wish it."

She's determined, thought Gunnar, *but she knows not what she's about to do. Death or not; the Kraken will rip her head off.*

"Shine the light, Alderon, so that I can sneak past this creature," said Kayana.

"Shine the light?" asked Tommy. "That will tip it off to our—"

"One of my powers is that I disappear into shadows. A Kraken's eye is strong, but it cannot see what's invisible. I require a light."

"Please tell us your plan, Kayana," said Gunnar. "We beg of you."

"Shine the light, Alderon," she said, "or this creature will rip me apart."

And in a heartbeat, Kayana disappeared around the corner. Tommy hurried to shine a light from his suit, and the pale girl immediately flickered and then disappeared. The Kraken was disturbed by the brightness, but didn't notice Kayana.

They heard her wade through the water, just barely. Tommy crept up to the corner and stuck another hand around. He pressed a button and they saw a live video feed of the Kraken. They could see a ripple where Kayana was walking and even a faint outline when she went into direct light. The poisonous snakes encircled the Kraken, sending roils and ripples through the water. But they parted ways when Kayana went through.

Kayana reappeared right in front of the Kraken's eye. The Kraken quivered, clicked and shook in surprise. It tried to grasp at Kayana, but she was too close to it; it started to beat itself with its own tentacles. It started clicking more and more furiously, but couldn't grab hold of her; she was right by its ear, whispering something. The Kraken slowly stopped thrashing about, as if listening to her words. It secreted a black substance into the water, and soon it was still.

"She made it calm," said Tommy.

"It's not calm," said Saoirse, "it's terrified. That black substance in the water is ink."

Kraken's ink, thought Gunnar. *The Norsemen believe it to be a legendary substance. I never thought I'd see it with my own eyes.*

Kayana walked behind the Kraken and climbed up the perch next to Bes. She was at the entrance.

"Hurry," she said, "it won't be still for long."

Gunnar took one more look at the creature. Its eyes were dull and vacant, and its limbs were quivering slightly. *A Kraken can do many things,* thought Gunnar, *but it doesn't give ink unless its world is about to end.* Gunnar signaled them to move forward. All the sea serpents seemed to have vanished, and the team trudged quickly by the giant monster.

It smelled horrendous. Gunnar pushed Tommy and Saoirse up the ledge to safety, but couldn't help but to stay there for a moment. He examined the juvenile Kraken up close; its giant eyes, its tentacles, and its enormous head sagged with gravity. From an angle he could even see its pale beak. *A thousand generations of Norse marines have come and gone,* he thought, *but not one of them have been this close and lived to tell the tale.*

Gunnar crawled up to the ledge and was joined by Bes.

"Congratulations," he said. "You've passed the test, unharmed as well. I cannot say the same for the other teams."

Bes went out the door, followed by Saoirse and Tommy. Kayana was about to leave, but Gunnar held her back.

"What did you say to the Kraken?"

Kayana laughed.

"I didn't say anything; Krakens don't speak," she said.

"What did you say?" he asked again. "Please tell me."

Kayana sighed deeply, and then looked up at Gunnar.

"No one, not even a god, can capture a living Kraken, even a juvenile," said Kayana, "so this Kraken must have come from an egg brought to this place. This world is all he's ever known, and so far his life has been only darkness and hatred, nothing more.

"He sensed me, and for the first time in his life he understood that he would one day *die*. He then sensed that he'd most likely die here, alone in this artificial dungeon. He became afraid, and since he's never felt fear before, it overwhelmed him."

Kayana pointed at the Kraken quivering on the floor beneath them. The water was now almost completely black with ink.

"Krakens have no language, but they experience emotion on a deep level, deeper than we," said Kayana. "He's more afraid than we could ever understand."

THE PLEDGE

Saoirse's hyaena met her at the door a few moments after she walked out of the labyrinth. He wasn't brought by Bes or anyone else; he'd navigated around the Kraken's maze by himself. Bes didn't seem to have any problem with this and barely paid it any notice. *Why are they so comfortable with a free-running hyaena?* Saoirse wondered. She looked into the creature's eyes as he laughed twice and began to whine. *This hyaena was worried about me*, she thought. *I should give it a name soon.* Saoirse pet the hyaena twice more and walked forward; the animal quickly fell into step with her.

Saoirse was still shaken by the experience with the Kraken. She was no fool; she knew the Kraken would have gladly torn her in two if given the chance. But still, she'd never felt an emotion that deep before; it was the fear of a child, magnified a hundredfold.

Saoirse also wondered what her power was. Occasionally Elysia would host monotheists, so she had studied the scriptures that contained the Horsemen. But if she was the White Knight, what was her gift? To speak with animals? And was she to harbinger the Apocalypse? She looked up at Gunnar and felt that he fit the mold quite well. He'd shown her compassion, but he was a boy who would clearly *do what needed to be done* when necessary.

The group followed Bes back to their quarters. On the way, they saw the other teams' doors. The team with the Amazon was celebrating in the halls after their victory. Her teammate Pan joined with a Yōkai and tried to put her on their shoulders. But the Amazon and her armor were too heavy and they collapsed with a thud. The girl got up, laughed, then hugged the faun to her breastplate; clearly she had adjusted to life here.

Gunnar still eyed the Amazon warily, and then walked on. *Spartans and Amazons have done horrible things to each other,* thought Saoirse. *Their history is too deep for reconciliation, even for a young Amazon and an ex-Spartan.*

The team with the ghoul was still struggling in their labyrinth. Saoirse listened closely and heard some whinnies and thuds from inside the room, but Bes informed them that the team inside was going to be fine.

"They're fighting a Minotaur calf," said Bes, "and they're winning."

But Bes became concerned when he walked by the final labyrinth. He told the team to be quiet and listened intently. Saoirse heard some clashing of armor, some yelling, and an ungodly shrieking.

"Go back to your quarters and wait for me there," he told the Horsemen. "Now!"

Bes disappeared into the last labyrinth, and Gunnar nodded at them to leave. As soon as the door shut, Gunnar winked at Tommy, and Tommy hid beyond a corner. Tommy stuck out his hand and pulled a recording device from his suit's forearm. He discreetly planted it on the wall and then gave another wink. Gunnar looked at it out of the corner of his eye; no one would notice it, not even a god.

"Let's leave," said Gunnar.

Kayana had already disappeared, so Gunnar, Tommy, Saoirse and her hyaena went back to their dormitory.

/*** /

Later in the common room of their quarters, Tommy projected the scene onto the wall. The picture and audio were quite clear.

Bes burst out of the labyrinth door dragging Rowan, who looked like he'd been hit by a boulder. Soon after that, Heracles came bursting out in a rage. Bes dodged him easily, so Heracles charged again. Heracles moved fast, but Bes moved faster. It was like the bigger man was chasing air.

"Calm yourself, brute," said Bes.

Heracles took a moment to compose himself. After a few seconds, Heracles put up his hands to say that he no longer wanted a fight. Bes's brown skin, pug nose and hairy shoulders made him look like a squirrel in the shadow of Heracles's enormous girth, but the big god kept his distance.

"This boy needs medical attention," said Bes.

"This isn't your worry, Bes," interrupted Heracles, still angry. "Rowan's team is under my purview."

"You had him fight a *Banshee*," said Bes. "This boy is no match for a young warlock, let alone a *Banshee*."

"And your team is a match for a Kraken?"

"My Horsemen escaped *unscathed*," said Bes. "And your Berserker has his femur broken in three places."

Heracles frowned.

"Rowan's a fool, but fights with honor," said Heracles. "When he recovers from these injuries, we'll teach him how to fight smarter, *with his team. We will teach him his limits*. But *his honor* will help clean this city. He won't be bought by Dagon or sold a bill of goods by Loki. I understand that the concept of *honor* is foreign to you, Bes, but it has tremendous value."

"I know *precisely* what honor is, Heracles," said Bes. "*Honor* is the artifice kings sell the peasants' sons so that they may fight and die without pay. *Honor* is what drives a peaceful man to bloody vengeance. *Honor* is what drove the Celts to behead the children of the Apache Courts."

Bes pointed towards Rowan's broken body.

"Honor makes a boy fight a Banshee, even if it leaves him crippled," said Bes, walking out. "Now get this boy medical assistance, *real medical attention* from a licensed doctor. If you fail to do this, I'll know, and I'll find you."

Bes walked closely to Heracles and stood like a figurine at Heracles's sandaled foot. Bes stepped forward, as if to charge at the great Heracles, and the big man flinched. Then with one last scathing look, Bes walked out in a huff. Heracles mulled everything over, and then spoke to two Spartan mercenaries outside of the screen.

"Do precisely as he says," said Heracles.

The Spartan mercenaries brought out a stretcher and carefully put Rowan on it. They took him off the screen, and soon everyone was gone. Gunnar nodded at Tommy, who turned off the screen.

"I don't want to take sides in their quarrel," said Gunnar, "but this much is clear: we can't trust them."

"But Bes has faith in us," said Tommy. "He's the protector of the weak. All the kids on Lepros prayed to him."

"It doesn't matter if he has faith in us," said Gunnar. "He doesn't care to be here. He doesn't believe in this Academy. We survived the Kraken on our wits alone; if we get between him and Heracles we may not be so fortunate."

Gunnar thought for a moment and then looked at Saoirse.

"What's your feeling on this?" he asked. "What do you *sense* from them?"

Saoirse was at a loss for words. Elysia had taught her to intuit men's carnal wishes, but these were not men; Bes and Heracles were full-grown gods.

"I don't know," she said.

"This is a school," said Tommy. "They'll care for us. They may argue from time to time, but they'll care for us."

"This is a school, perhaps," said Gunnar, "but it's *young*. As of a year ago, this place didn't exist; there's no precedent. That means things can go wrong, and it's not to be trusted."

"So what do we do?" asked Tommy. "We can't leave."

"I'm not asking us to leave," said Gunnar. "Though one day I may. What I am asking is that we treat this place with wariness. What trust we have, we place in each other."

Gunnar got up and caught his breath.

"Now, I know we just met," said Gunnar, "and I don't know what truly drives you. But this is a hostile situation, a hostile school. We've been ripped from the world, threatened repeatedly and fed to monsters, and this is *our first day*. So I want to know: can we in this room, *the Horsemen*, put our faith in one another?"

They were silent for a moment.

"I know the trust isn't earned," said Gunnar, "but we're somehow bonded; you all sense that. I ask for nothing but a small show of faith. And from what I saw in the labyrinth, I can put my faith in you."

"I still believe in this school," said Tommy with a smile, "but I believe in you too, and in us. I'm in."

Saoirse paused for a moment. Back on Elysia, the Emetor taught her to be wary of men. *You can love your Danna*, he would say, *but you cannot be friends with a man, let alone a group of men. A group of men will absorb you in the spirit of camaraderie and then spit you out when they're bored of you.*

But these were not Danna, and they didn't want her for her charm. *Tommy is young and trusting,* she thought. *He's lived a life of safety despite his condition and has never known a reason to cheat. Gunnar is fierce and a killer. He wouldn't shed a tear at my funeral, but I don't notice him leering at me either.*

She looked at Kayana and drew a blank. *I sense nothing from her,* thought Saoirse. *My intuition, my thoughts, my first glance all tell me nothing about this dark-haired girl; this Kayana Marx may as well be a stone. But she bears no malice towards me or anyone else.*

"I'm in," said Saoirse. "You can count on me."

"How about you, Kayana?" asked Gunnar.

Kayana was silent, looking off in the distance. She was seemingly lost in her own world, disinterested at best.

"Kayana?" asked Gunnar.

"I hear you, Redstone," she said.

She turned her eyes towards Gunnar; they were almost completely white. Gunnar was unnerved by Kayana's stare and averted his gaze. He noticed that Saoirse was uncomfortable too, but Tommy was fascinated, and he smiled at Kayana.

"She's meditating," Tommy explained with a grin.

"So be it, then," said Gunnar. "But I need to know if you're with us, Kayana. Just let us know—"

"I have no faith in you, in our team, or in anyone else," she interrupted. "This whole place is an artifice, a stopgap placed against a growing ocean of corruption in this world. Our teachers are just as self-interested as the gods we're to police, so no, I don't trust anyone yet."

There was a moment of silence, and then Tommy gave a little laugh. He smiled at Kayana, but her eyes turned black again, and Tommy started to wring his gloved hands. He took a deep breath and again focused on her.

"You haven't answered the question," said Tommy. "Are you with us?"

Kayana mulled it over and then began to nod.

"I don't *distrust* you three," she said, "and I do actively *distrust* the others I have met here."

"Good enough for now," said Gunnar, forcing a smile. "We're the *Horsemen*. Right now we have each other, and nothing else."

/***/

Saoirse woke to find her hyaena gone. He had cozied up next to her but had vanished sometime in the night. She heard faint whimpering coming from the window and saw him there outside of her balcony.

The hyaena was pacing back and forth in the underground courtyard, occasionally looking back to meet her eyes. Saoirse wanted to call him but realized she had yet to give him a name. *Only things with names return to you when called*, she thought. But the hyaena seemed to know exactly where she was, pacing back and forth, and then staring right at her window. *He wants me to come down*, she thought.

Saoirse felt that despite her Elysian training, she was growing attached to the hyaena. The Emetor had taught her to *never become attached to anyone but your Danna, for your Danna is the only soulmate that you'll ever have. Love is fleeting, so don't give your emotions away lightly, for a Hetaera with a trampled heart is worthless.*

But she sensed something different between her and this hyaena. This was the first creature that didn't see her as a means to an end, and he never wanted anything from her. This creature loved her without hope of recompense; she rarely even brought him food.

Saoirse decided to follow the hyaena outside and first walked from her cell to the common room of their quarters. Their housing unit was sparsely furnished and symmetrical; there was one square sitting room surrounded by four private, rectangular bedrooms. Tommy's and Gunnar's doors were closed, but Kayana's door was open. Kayana was staring out the window, not at the hyaena, but at something else.

"Kayana," said Saoirse, hoping to get her attention gently.

Kayana had no response. Saoirse came closer and it appeared that Kayana was in a trance. *She sleeps with her eyes open,* thought Saoirse, *but only the whites are visible.* Saoirse looked out the window from Kayana's vantage point and saw nothing. She left Kayana alone and shut the door.

Saoirse left her quarters and went out into the night. *The "night,"* she thought. *This place is completely underground, yet still they make it night.*

The lights in the high ceiling were dimmed, and the courtyard was dark. Saoirse crept past the teachers' quarters to where her hyaena lay in wait. She felt the strange plants and looked up at the ceiling and saw the trees stretch a hundred meters into the sky. She thought it to be magic, but Tommy had told her computers on the ceiling analyzed the foliage below and put out the right amount of water and artificial sunlight. *Science is powerful,* she thought, *perhaps more powerful than the gods.*

She came within a few meters of her hyaena, but he bristled his fur, whimpered and crept backwards.

"What's wrong?" she asked.

The hyaena gave her a high-pitched whine and then looked into her eyes and winked.

Just follow me, he seemed to say. *Follow me.*

And in a flurry, the hyaena burst off into the darkness. Saoirse froze for a moment and then realized that he wasn't going to slow down for her. So she sprinted after him through the tall trees.

They ran through the artificial forest, the courtyard, and onto the tiled floors. The hyaena slowed down even more, but Saoirse could still barely keep up. They sprinted past the elevator from whence they all arrived, and they went by several lecture halls. They hurried beyond the labyrinths, and she could still hear the echoes of the strange creatures within.

They ran past the labyrinths through a door and opened it to find a staircase. She jumped down the stairs, four steps at a time. The hyaena had a hard time navigating the staircase, yet still he was faster than Saoirse. She followed him down the steps, around and around. *Each floor has ceilings a kilometer high*, she thought, *so the stairs are endless.*

The hyaena bounded by a large door. When Saoirse passed it, she couldn't help but peek through. She saw a long trimmed field, with stars in the moonlit sky. The stars and moon were artificial of course, but it looked real. *This is the field where they train the warriors,* she thought. *Gunnar will know this place soon.*

She slammed the door shut and continued to follow the hyaena. Down, down, down he went, so far down that she could no longer see him. He let out a high-pitched laugh: *I'm here.*

She went to the sound of the laugh and it was another door,

smaller than the one that led to the field. She opened the door and they were in another room with high ceilings. It wasn't endless like the room above, but it was still vast; a contained hangar. It was bright, white and sterile.

The hyaena was just inside, waiting for her. He came up to her waist, nuzzled her arm, and began to gently gnaw on her leg. She looked into his eyes. *No more running,* she thought, *just let me follow you.* The hyaena looked her in the eyes for a moment and then turned around. He walked elegantly through the hangar.

She ascertained that they were in some sort of lab, or rather a *group* of labs. Each room was connected to the ceiling, but self-contained, like giant metal yurts. Some were five meters in diameter, and some were the size of castles. Some had their windows sealed shut, and some were completely exposed to the air.

She peered in one window and saw two well-muscled men, both mercenaries, strapped into gurneys and covered with monitor wires, jerking as if in spasm. One of the men burst out of his wires and then started screaming. He relaxed a bit, saw where he was, and then voluntarily strapped himself back into the chair. From the darkness came a tall, hairless being, too tall to be a human. The tall creature put his hands over the mercenary, and the mercenary fell asleep once again, and soon began to shake. The tall creature turned around, and Saoirse noticed that his eyes were completely black. He was completely hairless and his arms were like pale sticks as he put his hands on the mercenary. Behind him was another god, even taller. This god was larger than Gunnar, and Saoirse noticed that he was floating several centimeters above the ground. His eyes glowed red, he had a thick mane of grey-black hair, and his body was cloaked in shadows.

This hairless creature is Phobetor, god of dark dreams, she thought. *Behind him, the god Mantus. These mercenaries are doing voluntary research on nightmares.*

She passed another room filled with pools that contained large, flat translucent eggs, illuminated with UV light. She looked closely and saw the outline of small squid. *Kraken eggs,* she thought. *This is a nursery. They cannot breed these creatures in an open-ocean tank; adult Krakens will sense them and come from the depths to violently take them away. So they breed them down here.*

Other rooms held other infant monsters: there were Minotaur calves, young salamanders crawling through fire, and juvenile Aurochs, still two meters tall at the shoulder. *These creatures can't all be for our training labyrinths,* thought Saoirse, *but what are they growing them for? What other purpose can monsters serve?*

She passed by a section of laboratories where they were doing simple materials testing. She saw a mercenary wearing a strange thin armor, and another mercenary was shooting the armor with some sort of high-powered rifle. The mercenary saw her peering in and didn't seem to mind; he winked at her, pointed to his armor, and mouthed the word *adamantine.*

I'm not trespassing, thought Saoirse. *With Mnemosyne here to erase our memories, there are many open doors in this place.*

When she turned around, her hyaena was ten meters ahead of her, heading around a corner. She rushed forward to catch up and when she did, he was sitting by the door of a large, windowless laboratory. He squeaked once and she opened the door.

It was dark inside, humid and just a bit foul-smelling, though she couldn't quite identify the odor. She saw the outlines of cages; her hyaena was sniffing them.

What is this scent? she thought. It was wet, musty, and stale, but tolerable. Her eyes were adjusting to the dark, and she could see that there were animals in these cages. She could hear them breathing, asleep; whatever they were, she and her hyaena were either unnoticed or ignored. Her hyaena gave the slightest chirp, and she followed the noise. She felt the wall and noticed a light switch.

Should I awaken these creatures? she thought. *What if there's a baby Minotaur running about, or a hive of poisonous asps? What if these cages aren't locked?* She felt her hyaena and he bit her leg playfully again, and then gave a small whine.

Turn on the lights, he seemed to say. *Nothing will harm you here.*

She turned on the lights, and saw the cages were filled with dogs. Upon closer inspection, they looked a bit different than dogs: they had larger heads; strange-looking necks; and odd, thick tongues. As they woke up, they sniffed at her intelligently and then exchanged glances with each other. They didn't explode into a sea of barks like kennel dogs normally do; it was more akin to if she had walked into a troop's barracks at night.

They began to make some whispered noises, until a dog in the middle gave a giant bark, and then they were all quiet. He seemed to beckon Saoirse forth.

"*Ari-khana, ntaka,*" he seemed to say.

Saoirse came to his cage and looked at him. He was sleek, regal, and clearly the alpha of the group. His thick tongue looked odd on a dog, and he looked at her straight in the eyes as he spoke.

"*Tange, ngane Kaiser,*" the dog said.

Saoirse couldn't understand, but this dog was speaking real, tangible *words*.

"I'm sorry," she said, "I don't follow you."

The dog seemed to understand her words, or at least her tone. He paused to think and then motioned to her hyaena.

"*Ntaka,*" he said. "*Yoye.*"

Saoirse's hyaena was calm, as if he understood the dogs and was one of them. Saoirse looked around the room and observed all the other dogs; there were all shapes and sizes, from lapdogs to Bull Mastiffs.

"*Ntaka Kaiser,*" repeated the alpha dog, pointing at the hyaena with his nose. "*Oonda yoye.*"

She stared at the dog uncomprehendingly, and then heard a voice come in through the door.

"He's saying that his name is Kaiser," said the voice, "and that the hyaena is yours."

It was Indra, the headmaster of the school. He strode in, glowing and tall, his same overcoat covering a different suit. Though Indra was golden and nearly twice the height of most of the students, he made an effort to appear normal, and if you ignored his size and color, he looked almost human. Saoirse noticed that his tailored overcoat was perfectly sized for him and hid his extra arms quite discreetly. Still, Indra commanded a presence, and when he came near, all the dogs bowed to him in unison.

"*Ahaa-le,*" he said. "*Kara. Tangi.*"

The dogs all sat at ease, and Indra shifted his attention to Saoirse. The hyaena came up and sniffed him. Indra knelt down and held out his palm; the hyaena sniffed his giant hand and then sat, looking like a housecat next to Indra's large frame. After a moment the hyaena came back to Saoirse and knelt by her side again.

"There's a strong connection between you and the hyaena," said Indra. "He's smart too; that's why he led you here."

"He likes me," said Saoirse.

"No, it's deeper than that," said Indra. "The average *pet* likes his owner but will abandon him as soon as the food runs out. This hyaena sees you as an extension of himself, and him of you."

"Perhaps," said Saoirse.

Saoirse looked at the hyaena and noticed that he stood between her and Indra, his eyes trained on the golden god. Though Indra was no threat, Saoirse felt that the hyaena would protect her if need be, even from a foe four times her size. *The hyaena shows no fear, even when facing a god,* thought Saoirse. *He's more than just a pet.*

Indra stood up and walked around the room, deep in thought.

"You're a mystery to us, Saoirse, and your powers are too. Gunnar fights, Tommy infects, and Kayana kills. But you? What's your ability, Saoirse?"

"I don't know," she said.

"We accept this. Of the Four Horsemen, you're the White Knight. And the White Knight's always been a mystery," said Indra. "The other Horsemen's abilities are clear, but you seem to be able to communicate with animals, with nature. But to what end?"

"I don't know," said Saoirse.

"Once again, nor do we," said Indra. "We understand War, Death, the Elements, but know little of your Class. We know the *power* of nature, as evidenced by Poseidon's ocean, the Ragnarok, and the endless Manitou to our northwest. It could be our salvation, or perhaps our destruction. What say you to this?"

"I've no say over the storms," said Saoirse, "nor the ocean, nor the Ragnarok, nor anything else. I listen, that's all."

"Precisely," said Indra. "You listen, you intuit, you translate what nature tells us. You and your Class are our link to our natural surroundings. But that's not enough to fight our enemies outside Hellenica.

"We're but a handful of gods here, outnumbered by the conurbation's deities a hundred to one, outnumbered in population a hundred *thousand* to one. And our enemies aren't burdened by any semblance of morality. So after maximizing your powers and teaching you to work together, we'll give you the one thing our enemies lack: *technology.*

"Look around you," he said. "These dogs aren't from the gods. They're from *science* and nothing more. We augmented the neurons in their brains and gave them thicker tongues. We couldn't give them lips though, so we invented a language for them, one with no *Ps, Ms, Ws* and so on."

Saoirse didn't know what to say in response.

"The White Knight's power is to communicate with the natural world, and we will use science to magnify your abilities a hundredfold. You'll learn these dogs' tongue and communicate as coherently as you are speaking with me."

Saoirse peered at the hyaena that was apparently *hers*, and then looked at the alpha dog, who seemed to have understood the whole conversation. Indra let the dog out and gave it some instructions in its sibilant tongue.

"This dog Kaiser will take you back to your quarters," said Indra. "With your permission, we would like to keep your hyaena."

"Keep my hyaena?"

"Yes," said Indra. "Striped hyaenas are quite intelligent, and we feel we can augment their abilities, perhaps moreso than dogs. We're going to thicken his tongue and increase his brain size until he can talk. With your permission, of course."

Saoirse looked at all the other dogs; they had unnaturally big heads but were otherwise beautiful.

"Granted," she said.

"Good," said Indra. "Among other things, you'll learn the language of these creatures."

The dog Kaiser came down from his cage and sat by Saoirse. He was large, perhaps weighing fifty kilograms. Saoirse came down and gave her hyaena a hug. She sensed a deep anxiety within him, as if he was worried that she might never come back. *He won't hesitate to attack a god to defend me,* thought Saoirse, *but he's not without fear. He fears abandonment and worries that I might die.*

"I'll return, but I must go," said Saoirse. "I have a long day tomorrow."

Saoirse got up to leave, but then knelt back down again and looked her hyaena in the eye.

"When I come back, you must have a name, so I'll give you one now," she said. "With your permission, I'd like to call you *Kross*."

"*Kraa-suh,*" repeated Kaiser behind her. "*Kraa-suh.*"

THE BANSHEE

Kayana couldn't sleep, which was rare. She had a nightmare that disturbed her deeply, which was rarer still; she dreamt the Spartan mercenary Cassander was meeting a brutal end at the hands of a demon. The dark spirit was doing vicious, unspeakable things to Cassander and there was nothing Kayana could do to stop it. She couldn't move, and Cassander screamed endlessly while the demon had his fun.

The demon was cruel, she thought upon waking, *so cruel that Cassander must have somehow felt it in his own dreams. That should not be.*

She was trying to get back in the dream to free him from the demon, or at least avenge him. But she couldn't fall asleep; she was too consumed with feeling. The emotion of *vengeance* was new to her, and she soon realized that she liked it quite a bit. It felt good; clean. She knew vengeance to be a pitiable, puerile emotion, but she found it simplified the world and brought it into focus.

I'll fall asleep later, she thought, *and I'll find this demon. I'll bring it such torment that it will never bother Cassander again, in my dreams or anywhere else.*

She heard a quiet yell outside her window. It was faint but powerful, like an echo from a girl who died screaming a century ago. Kayana opened her window to the courtyard, but couldn't see anything. She felt a strong breeze blowing in her face, and her black hair flew backwards, exposing the pale skin on the sides of her head. She sensed something was coming for her, and in the next moment the ghost of a woman wearing a flowing dress crashed through the window and came within inches of her face.

The spirit looked sickly and appeared to be in agony; her eyes were bleeding and her skin was a translucent white. The ghost threw Kayana to the top of the room. Kayana slammed into the ceiling, leaving a broken crack in the concrete. The wraith drove Kayana down to the ground and wrapped her hands around Kayana's neck. Kayana felt this woman's superhuman strength; she knew in the next few moments she could die.

But it's not my time, she thought, *not here and not now.*

Kayana put her bare hands over the ghost's face, and the ghost collapsed to the ground with a thud, motionless. Kayana straddled the spirit and stared into its eyes; she saw anguish and little else.

"Speak your intentions now, wraith," said Kayana, "or I'll take the life from you. Even if you have no more life to give, I'll find a way to take more."

"If only you could take my life," said the ghostly woman, black blood pouring from her eyes, "I'd want nothing else."

The spirit relaxed her grip and hinted that she was going to behave now. Kayana relaxed her grip too, and the specter flew up to the ceiling. The ghost turned around to talk; drops of blood were dripping from her eyes onto the ground, but she was no longer a threat.

"I apologize for the altercation," said the ghostly woman. "I can't help it. My anger comes out through my voice and I must stifle it, lest I kill someone. I am a Banshee."

This is the Banshee that broke Rowan in half, thought Kayana. *Her shriek can fell an army, so Rowan is lucky to be alive. Perhaps I'm even luckier to survive her throwing me against the ceiling.*

"Why didn't you kill the fool Rowan?" said Kayana. "The world would have been a better place."

"Were it not for your guardian Bes, I would have," said the Banshee.

"It would have been right for you to kill him," said Kayana. "A youthful death for his kind *should be*."

The Banshee flew at Kayana, picked her up and threw her at the ceiling once more, and then dropped her. The spirit then flew against the opposite wall herself and started to tear out her hair and gnash her teeth. *She's trying to control her anger,* thought Kayana. *Don't upset her anymore or she'll scream and you'll be destroyed.*

The Banshee eventually calmed down and turned around to face Kayana. There was a pool of blood on the floor where her eyes had bled.

"Nothing here is as it *should be*, child," said the Banshee. "Not in this school, not in this world. Everything is wrong. There are no rules, no meaning underlying our existence. So do not speak to me of how it *should be*."

"I won't," said Kayana. "I assure you of that."

The Banshee calmed down again and floated to the ground. She sat in the pool of blood until her dress was soaked.

"Come here, child," said the Banshee.

Kayana came nearer, and the Banshee drew her in within a

whisper's distance. *It's like peering into the barrel of a loaded gun,* thought Kayana. Kayana couldn't help but smile; this was the first time in her life she had experienced the emotion *fear.*

"Have you any idea of what you can do?" asked the Banshee.

"My touch makes people die, and I disappear in shadows."

The Banshee laughed, and it sounded like metal being torn in half.

"Those things are mere *powers*," said the Banshee, "and mere *powers* are things that the gods have."

"Am I not a god?" asked Kayana.

"You and your Horsemen are *deities*," said the Banshee. "There's a difference."

"What is this difference?"

"Powers like incredible speed and superhuman strength are parlor tricks, nothing more," said the Banshee. "The Horsemen don't engage in parlor tricks. Your *powers* cannot be defined by a single sentence, nor are you bound by the number of worshippers you have.

"And of the Four Horsemen, it is you, Kayana, whose powers are the deepest and the most opaque. Gunnar can fight, Tommy can infect, and Saoirse can tell her animals to run through the forest. But your powers are deeper, so deep that even *I* don't know their full extent."

"I bring death," said Kayana. "That seems quite simple to me."

"It's not; every culture has a death god, and none of them are simple. Hades: What exactly can he do? Is he strong? Can he fly? Can he disappear? No one knows, because no one *cares to know.* Each culture prefers not to think of the afterworld; they tuck death away into a dark temple hidden in the bowels of the city. No one prays to a death god, and no one curries favor from one; they just accept our kind and forget about us."

"*Our* kind?" asked Kayana.

The Banshee rose upwards and Kayana feared she was about to yell, but the wraith stopped at the ceiling and spoke in an imperious voice.

"You really have no idea of *who you are*, do you, child?" asked the Banshee. "Myself, Hades, Hel, Shinigami; we're merely caretakers of dead souls, nothing more. But you *are* Death. *Death!* Do you know what that means? You transcend our worlds and are the one link that binds us. We have *all* known you since the day you were born."

"Then why did you let me grow up with human adoptive families, knowing that I'd bring them to their end?" said Kayana. "Why wasn't I sent to Hades, or Hel, or raised by Shinigami? Why did you place me where I was neither wanted nor needed?"

"We placed you with doomed families to hide you in plain sight," said the Banshee. "Hades foretold that this was the only way to keep you from your enemies. When you imposed yourself to an institution, you put yourself at risk. I assure you if you'd stayed there, your enemies would have destroyed the whole place just to get at you."

"My enemies?" asked Kayana. "I have neither friend nor enemy."

"Rowan despises you, and he won't be the first. Though you'll travel through this world in the shadows, largely unseen, there will be those who want nothing more than your end. They'll attempt to immolate you, tear out your heart and bury you alive. They'll proclaim to the world their intent to kill you, or they'll come in silence. They'll bring an army, or they'll send a single assassin. This is your lot; this is all of our kind's lot."

"Then what shall I do?" asked Kayana.

"Trust in your Horsemen. Do you care for them?"

"No," said Kayana. "If they were to perish, I wouldn't feel anything. But I recognize that they should—"

"That they should *be*. I've heard this before," said the Banshee. "Learn to care for them. This is difficult for our kind, nigh impossible for you. But learn, for they're the only ones that care *for you*. They're your only protection against the Rowans of the world, and I assure you he is the least skilled of your enemies.

"And though this Academy is merely an artifice, this place will teach you to defend yourself. As of now, you can only exercise the simplest of your powers. If Lugh knew of your whereabouts, he'd send an army and you'd be defenseless."

"I'll keep that in mind next time I'm in Éire," said Kayana.

The Banshee took Kayana and threw her up against the ceiling, causing more cracks. Kayana tried to escape her grasp but couldn't; she was pinned.

"Do *not* take this lightly, child," said the Banshee, hissing. "Learn your powers and you'll be able to *take down* Lugh's army. Your Horsemen have a destiny that transcends this Academy, and *your* destiny transcends *even the Horsemen*. If you fail to realize your potential out of indifference, it won't be an army, an assassin, or even Lugh who brings you to your end. It will be me."

The Banshee dropped Kayana and crashed through the window again. Kayana fell to the floor with a thud and heard a scream as the ghost faded into the distance. Kayana got up slowly, and then looked out the window. She could still hear the Banshee screaming as she flew away, but the wraith was gone.

THE FIRST CLASS

Gunnar got up in the morning well before dawn to do exercises and was surprised by Saoirse, who was sitting in a chair in the common room, strumming a lute. She was playing it quietly so she wouldn't wake up her team, and Gunnar marveled at the deftness of her fingers as they flew over the strings, sweeping through scales and grabbing chord after chord.

"What are you doing up so early?" she asked.

"I was about to ask you the same thing," he said.

"I'm up because I can't sleep. My hyaena is having surgery and I'm worried. But you, I've known you for several days and haven't seen you rest, not ever. How is that?"

Gunnar never revealed himself to anyone, but he felt different around Saoirse. Perhaps it was the way she spoke; perhaps it was part of her powers to be able to get others to trust her. *Perhaps you're lonely*, thought Gunnar. *Perhaps you've been lonely all your life.*

"It's an old habit from the Agoge," said Gunnar. "I sleep, but no one sees me do it. Older Spartans would burst into our barracks early in the morning and steal our food, and sometimes torment us for hours afterwards."

"What did you do about it?" asked Saoirse.

"I slept in hidden places," said Gunnar, "but ..."

Gunnar had no more words, but Saoirse helped him.

"But you can't sleep in hidden places for an entire childhood," said Saoirse. "They'll find you."

Her intuition is incisive, but she doesn't use it to gain advantage over me, thought Gunnar. *This isn't a girl from the Agoge.* For the first time in his life, Gunnar wanted to reveal his past and the bad things that were done to him. He even felt like he could tell Saoirse the dark parts of his history, the times where he did bad things to others.

"Yes," he said, "they found me; they found all of us. I remember once some older Spartans uncovered our troop's hiding place one evening and took our clothes, our food ... everything. It was freezing, so we went over to their barracks and I begged for our clothes back on bended knee. I was eight years old.

"Their leader was a bully named Lysander and he returned a few blankets soaked in urine, nothing more. We took the blankets and survived that evening, but it was tough. Some of my troop began to cry and I yelled at them, *'Don't shed a single tear; we'll take everything back! Follow me and we'll have our revenge.'*"

"Revenge," asked Saoirse. "How do you feel about that?"

"It's a weakness. Revenge is a base, useless emotion that enemies can use to defeat you," said Gunnar. "But at the time I could think of nothing else. I had our group lay low for eight days, feigning defeat. On the last day I had us all drink water before bed, and the first to awake would wake us all.

"We woke three hours before dawn. We snuck into Lysander's

132

barracks, locked them in and barred all the exits. Then we doused their building with gasoline. I built a fire on the periphery and then wafted the smoke into the quarters. When the older Spartans awoke, I let them scream for a few minutes and figure out what a mess they were in. I wanted them to find out for themselves that we could kill them all if we so chose.

"'Well played, Spartan!' one of them yelled from within the garrison. 'We'll give you back your clothes, your food and more.'

"'Keep your clothes and food, we'll steal all we need elsewhere,' I said. 'Give Lysander to us and we'll let you go unscathed.'"

Gunnar took a breath and frowned. He noticed Saoirse frowning too; like him, she took no joy in this tale of revenge.

"They brought Lysander to the roof," said Gunnar. "That was the only way out, but it was three stories in height. They threw him off and he broke both his legs. We beat him savagely for another hour after that."

"An hour is a long time to be beaten," said Saoirse, "even for a Spartan."

"Even from an eight-year-old," said Gunnar. "He was never the same again. More importantly he had lost the respect of his troop, so who knows what happened to him."

"But I'm sure your legend grew," said Saoirse. "And I'm sure you were never quite comfortable with that."

"Indeed," said Gunnar, "I became troop leader and spent the next years excelling in just about everything. But I can't forget how Lysander looked at me when he was taken away. He *smiled*, as if he was proud of my brutality. Perhaps he was just happy to leave, but nonetheless as he left he said, 'Well played, Spartan. Soon you'll do this to a Helot.'"

"I've heard of this practice," said Saoirse. "To graduate the Agoge, the Spartan must murder a Helot in the middle of the night. Helots are—"

"Not like Lysander," said Gunnar. "They're innocent, often supporting a family, and bound and gagged when you see them."

"Did you kill a Helot?" asked Saoirse.

Gunnar looked at her, ashamed. *I cannot reveal the truth too soon,* he thought, *but neither can I lie.*

"It's complicated," he said.

Saoirse thought a minute and then looked into his eyes.

"Now you're at the Academy, another school for warriors, filled with arcane rules," she said.

"Indeed," he said. "Perhaps this is my calling: to forever be trapped in a warrior's school."

"This isn't the Agoge," said Saoirse. "I don't know their goals here, and I know not if we can trust them. But the Academy is not cruel. They might ask us to do brutal things, but they value our trust in one another. Rowan will not urinate on your clothes, nor will they ask you to kill a Helot."

"If they throw us into battle, the Helots of the world always find a way to die," said Gunnar. "But yes; the Academy's intent is noble, if not pure."

Saoirse gave him a kiss on the cheek.

"My intent is pure," she said, "and I don't kill Helots, whether I'm a Horseman or not."

Saoirse left Gunnar, and soon he began walking towards his first class, still an hour before anyone else awoke. It was going to be a lesson filled with intense physical training, and Gunnar wanted to get to the warriors' field on the floor beneath them and warm up. He noticed that he was alone and decided to scout out the floor they were on, just in case he and his team would ever need to escape the Academy.

/***/

Gunnar walked outside his quarters and explored the area, first passing the courtyard and then walking by the teachers' quarters. *These people aren't your enemies,* thought Gunnar, *and there is no need to set fire to their barracks.* He walked by the main elevator, the one that had brought them down to the Academy. It was currently up on the surface, and the hole was loosely guarded by a few structural bars; anyone could fall through it in the dead of night. The walls of the shaft were made of hollowed-out stone, but the bars that supported it were made of long steel rods, and when Gunnar peered in the tunnel he could see neither the top nor the bottom. *It seems to go on forever in both directions,* he thought, *but that cannot be. This hole is clean, structured and built. Perhaps it's a millennium old, but it was built by men. And all things built by men end somewhere.*

"Watch your back, someone might push you in," said a voice coming from behind him. It was Heracles.

Gunnar turned around and saw the large god in front of him, pinning Gunnar in against the elevator shaft. Gunnar tried to walk away from the hole, but couldn't; Heracles was just too wide. Gunnar stood his ground against the bearded god and showed no fear, because he had none. He was wedged against an endless drop, but Gunnar had faced both Heracles and death before, and he'd most likely face them again.

"Your Agoge training has served you well," said Heracles. "I was hoping to surprise the Class of Warriors with an early-morning intrusion, but it appears that the Spartans never sleep."

"I am no Spartan, and you're wrong about the Agoge," said Gunnar. "The Agoge teaches a Spartan to sleep *always*. We can sleep with hunger, under the rain, and surrounded by enemies. I woke because of curiosity, nothing more."

"Then be aware, sleepy non-Spartan, that there will be hardships in your training here," said Heracles. "Some easy in comparison to the Agoge, some much more difficult, some nigh impossible."

"I welcome the challenge," said Gunnar, "and if I fail, so be it."

"I like the attitude, Redstone," said Heracles, "but you must understand the role for which you're being trained. There will be no ending line, no ranking against your comrades, no promotion to commander of your troop. There is no failure here, no success; there is only survival."

"Then I still welcome the challenge," said Gunnar, "and if I fail, so be it."

Heracles smiled and bowed to Gunnar, bested in rhetoric, and Gunnar smiled in return. In a flash Heracles burst towards Gunnar, and quickly had Gunnar's hands bound. Heracles pushed Gunnar over the edge of the tunnel, and soon Gunnar was leaning over, facing the endless drop. Gunnar's arms were bent behind his back awkwardly and felt like they were about to come out of their sockets. *It hurts,* thought Gunnar, *but if I wriggle out, it will mean my death.*

"*If you fail, so be it*?" asked Heracles. "Is this still your sentiment? Your code of ethos?"

Gunnar couldn't get out of Heracles's grasp; he considered his other options, and there were none.

"No," said Gunnar, "this isn't my code of ethos."

"Survive, Gunnar," said Heracles. "That's all I ask of you."

Gunnar laid still; Heracles held him facing the darkness, unmoving.

"I don't want this, Heracles," said Gunnar, his voice shaking slightly. "I beg of you, take me away from this tunnel."

Heracles took Gunnar and shoved him away from the elevator shaft. Gunnar landed in a crouching position, and momentarily thought to run towards Heracles and have them both fall down to their deaths. But in another burst of speed Heracles had moved away, and was now behind Gunnar.

"Watch for the elevator shafts, the bridges, the cliffs, and anywhere else you might be vulnerable," said Heracles. "The strong often meet their end by the quiet and the shameless. And there are those on the surface who want nothing more than to push you down into the darkness, to destroy you before you raise your army. There are those who would kill you even if it means they die as well. One day, a shameless man will try to push you to your death. When that time comes, will your mantra still be *'if I fail, so be it'*?"

"I will not fail," said Gunnar.

"You won't," said Heracles with a smile, "because I won't let you."

/***/

Gunnar's Class of Warriors started the day with a run around the field. The Academy had many floors, and the floor below their quarters was a city unto itself. Technically, it was a city, a field, a weapons-testing range, a laboratory, and a gladiatorial arena. It was enormous.

The simulated city was for urban training, the gladiatorial arena was for one-on-one combat, and the seemingly endless grounds were for open-range fighting. They were running laps around the field under brutal conditions. Indra had turned up the heat and put two artificial suns in the sky so Gunnar was always blinded by the oncoming light.

"The enemy will always come from the sun to attack you!" yelled golden Indra. "They'll come when you're tired, grieving or sick. They'll come when you're sleeping. They'll incinerate a hospital full of your loved ones in order to get a better shot at you."

Gunnar was struggling with the run; the pit had taken away his long-term endurance. In the pit, victory depended on the quick strike, and most fighters had a thick layer of fat to absorb blows. Gunnar was not yet thick but had still lost most of his long-distance training he developed in the Agoge. After the second hour of running, he started lagging behind, and soon he was last.

The three other members of the Warrior Class began to lap Gunnar, one by one. Alkippe the Amazon passed him, and her presence sent a small chill up Gunnar's spine. She was tall and thick, and for this exercise she kept most of her brown hair in a braided bun, which was now soaked with sweat. Her appearance didn't unnerve Gunnar so much, but he felt uncomfortable being this close to an Amazon and considered attacking her preemptively. *Amazons do bad things to Spartans,* thought Gunnar, *but I must admit that this Alkippe is impressive. She'd be in first place were it not for the fact that she refuses to remove her armor while she runs.*

Horus, the falcon-faced Egyptian god of hunting, was doing pretty well too; he started out fast and then seemed to coast the rest of the way. His large eyes and beaked nose resembled that of a bird, but his body was that of a human, and his long, brown legs ran with effortless strides. *He runs as the falcon flies,* thought Gunnar. *He has a burst of speed, but he can also glide.*

At the front was Rowan, heavily bruised and running on a broken femur. Rowan had somehow recovered from the fight with the Banshee and had lapped Gunnar twice. Gunnar wanted to be impressed, but Rowan treated him with such disdain that it was difficult. Rowan had supporting words for both the Amazon and Horus, but when he passed Gunnar, he said nothing.

The fool heals from injury quickly, thought Gunnar. *Clearly he's not quite mortal. He's grievously wounded and still besting us all. Perhaps I should offer an olive branch; if not for peace, then for an ally.*

"You impress me, Berserker," said Gunnar as Rowan limped by.

Rowan said nothing in return. The Norseman patted Horus on the back and even lifted Alkippe as she fell, yet he refrained from giving Gunnar words. He didn't even lodge an insult; he just silently ran by.

After the third hour, Gunnar could run no more. He knelt down in the middle of the field, his head down but his eyes open. It was his training from the Agoge: *you can be spent, but never close your eyes.* Soon Alkippe joined him in the middle, and then Horus. Rowan was still going, but Indra stopped him. Indra brought the sun down and had the mercenaries bring out glasses of grey liquid. It was a liquid form of the ambrosia and tasted of ash, but its effects came soon. Gunnar was still tired, but his body no longer felt sore.

The other members of his Class felt the same effects and drank glass after glass, grimacing as the liquid ambrosia went down.

"It cures everything, but you never get used to it," said Heracles with a laugh. "It makes even Hephaestus himself vomit. And vomit from Hephaestus isn't something I'd care to see again."

Rowan refused to drink the ambrosia, but he soon passed out and started to seize. Alkippe held him down and forced the liquid into him. Rowan stopped seizing, and soon thereafter arose. He leered at Gunnar and then put his attention towards Indra and Heracles.

"What is strength?" asked Indra. "Countless millennia ago, Heracles moved a river with his bare hands. Is that strength?"

There was silence until Rowan answered.

"Yes, that's strength," said Rowan. "If moving a river with your bare hands is not strength, what is?"

"You're partially correct, Berserker," said Indra, "but not entirely. That *was* strength, but now? Now it's only legend. Heracles, can you still divert a river with your bare hands?"

"Perhaps," said Heracles with a laugh, "but by the time I'd be done, a score more rivers would be dammed elsewhere, and two canals built."

Indra smiled and stared at his students.

"Technology crushed the gods so long ago, and will continue to do so even today. Lugh may come for you, but he'll not come by himself. He'll bring fancy guns, strategy and propaganda to pull your army from under you. What can we do to fight Lugh? What do we have?"

Indra peered right at Gunnar. Gunnar didn't particularly feel like engaging in rhetoric, but he knew what answer Indra wanted.

"Technology," said Gunnar. "Or at least better technology than Lugh."

Indra smiled, looking Gunnar right in the eye.

"Gylippus," he bellowed, "to the front!"

There was a pause and then Gunnar saw a mercenary running towards them from the haze of the far end of the field. The man came to a stop right at the foot of the four Warriors. He wasn't large, perhaps sixty kilograms at most, and was barely more than a meter and a half in height. But he was wiry and had scars all over his body, particularly on the interior of his joints. He was young but had the look of a seasoned warrior to him.

"Gylippus," said Indra, "show them what you can do."

The Spartan mercenary Gylippus started doing pushups and didn't stop. After ten minutes, he started doing *handstand* pushups. Then he started doing backflips, twenty per minute for another three minutes. He then began to stretch, doing splits and bending backwards at inhuman angles. After another few minutes, Indra commanded him to rest. Gylippus did so, and his breaths were moderately quick.

"Now, who would like to fight this mortal?" asked Indra.

"It would be an honor for me to dispatch such a—" said Rowan, but he was interrupted.

"Gunnar, you're the most skilled in the pit, and I believe in ten score matches, you've lost but once," said Heracles with a smile. "You'll fight Gylippus at full strength, and not pull your punches."

Rowan sat down with a huff, and Gunnar got up reluctantly. He felt he could easily destroy this mercenary who, while in perfect shape, was still a human.

Give him a quick knockout blow, thought Gunnar. *This mortal is brave, but does not deserve a full punch and—*

Instantly, the mercenary was on him. He ran at Gunnar's legs and Gunnar jumped out of the way at the last second. Gunnar turned around to face Gylippus, but the fighter had already taken the offensive again and jumped on Gunnar's legs once more. This time the mercenary got a grip and Gunnar was pushed to the ground. Gylippus wasn't a skilled grappler, and Gunnar shook him and then kicked him in the chest. Gunnar kipped up and put some distance between them; this gave him some time to think and gauge his opponent's weaknesses. Gunnar looked to neutralize Gylippus's quickness by maintaining his distance and crouching low to the ground.

The mercenary crouched twice as low as Gunnar; he went on all fours like an animal. He burst forth and Gunnar was able to dodge, but just barely. The mercenary made two more attacks in a row and Gunnar dodged them both, but lost his cool and took a clumsy swing at his opponent. Gylippus dodged it easily, and then hit Gunnar in the gut with a right hook, knocking out his wind. Gylippus then took out Gunnar's feet and together they fell to the ground with a thud. Gylippus was on him, raining punches to the back of Gunnar's head and back. Gunnar turned over and tried to defend himself, but Gylippus was too quick. Gylippus dodged or blocked every punch, then returned a few of his own.

Gunnar was getting destroyed. He tried to get up but had no leverage. The mercenary's technique was flawed, but he was just too strong. *His fists are like hammers*, thought Gunnar, *like punches from Heracles. This isn't a battle you're supposed to win.*

Gunnar then realized what to do. He worked on blocking the mercenary's punches, and then used his full strength to push Gylippus off of him. Gylippus crouched and prepared to fight again, but Gunnar crouched to one knee and yelled at him.

"Wait," said Gunnar, his hands out. "I yield."

Gylippus attacked once more and Gunnar dodged.

"I yield!" he said.

"He yields, Gylippus," said Indra. "You have won."

Gylippus bowed to Indra and then to Gunnar. His scarred body was quivering, but he soon relaxed and was breathing normally.

"The god of War, beaten by a mortal," said Rowan under his breath.

Indra came over to Gylippus and displayed the scarred inner elbow of Gylippus to the group.

"Technology comes in many forms," said Indra. "It's not just mechanized ships and night-vision glasses; technology can also enhance the body. The average fifty-kilogram female chimpanzee would, on average, kill the toughest pit-fighter in less than two minutes. Why? Simple physics: their tendons connect their arms at a different angle, creating a fulcrum that gives them incredible power.

"The giant cat's bone structure gives them great speed, the horse has endurance, and the bird has the power of flight. We've been experimenting with our human soldiers to give them advantages until some, like Gylippus here, can come to rival the gods. Imagine what we can do with *you*.

"Augmentation will be the second part of your training. Be warned, though: it won't be a quick fix and will come at a steep price. You endured the simple pain of running well, but that's merely a taste of what's to come. Every augmentation will be a thousand daggers in your body."

"If I may, sir," said Rowan, kneeling, "I volunteer myself to be the first augmented."

"You'll all get your chance," said Indra, "but for now, you're off to the stables to earn your keep."

"I don't muck horses," said Rowan. "It's beneath me."

"Then you can muck the Wildman," said Heracles. "But he's dangerous, so beware."

Gunnar got up to take a swig of ambrosia, and by the time he looked up, Rowan had already left. The Norseman was running full-speed towards the stables and was almost halfway there.

/***/

The stables were overflowing with scat from legendary creatures. There was an adolescent Minotaur locked in an iron cage, several Aurochs, and an Erymanthian boar the size of a small shed. There were several predatory creatures too. The Aztec *ahuizotl* was dog-like, but had strange hand-like paws and kept swiping at Gunnar from afar. The creature actually got hold of Alkippe through its cage, but Horus beat him back and she escaped with only a few bruises.

The Celtic Wildman made the place truly foul; he kept hurling his waste at the Warriors. Gunnar ignored it, but Rowan took offense and had to be restrained. The Wildman was covered with hair and dirt and yelled in an incomprehensible tongue. Eventually the Wildman pointed at a bucket of slop out of his reach and Gunnar took the bucket and brought it closer. The hairy man then dropped his face into it, ate, and then dropped down into a long, snoring nap.

The team smiled as Rowan left in a huff to the far end of the stables. He was so disgusted with the work that he left to clean out the section of the menagerie with actual horses.

It was hot, dirty work, but Gunnar didn't mind. If nothing else, the Agoge taught humility; even the supreme commanders engaged in manual labor when necessary. Gunnar enjoyed the task, though judging by the size of the stable it wouldn't be done this day, if ever.

"It's fitting that Heracles gave us this work," said Horus with a smile. "He committed a grievous sin so many years ago and had to perform twelve labors as penance. The fifth was to clean stables much like these."

"The ninth labor was to steal the belt of our queen, Hippolyta," said Alkippe. "He slew many to do it. Make no mistake, Redstone, your mentor is no saint."

"I never claimed he was," said Gunnar, "and you're not one to talk of sainthood. I know what Amazons do to their male captives; older Spartans would tell us these tales to give us nightmares."

"Redstone speaks the truth," said Horus with a smile. "I met an Amazon gladiatrix while hunting; the stories she told made me ill."

"When we women fight men or even fight *alongside* them," said Alkippe, "we must be better, faster and braver than our counterparts at *every* opportunity; respect means more to us than it means to you."

"Yet you build your reputation not on respect, but *fear*," asked

144

Gunnar. "When my cohorts told tales of your kind, they spoke not of your bravery or your speed, only your cruelty."

"We're never crueler than the prisoner we torment; that's our rule," said the Amazon. "We do bad things to captured Spartans because they *invariably* have done bad things themselves. Spartans must by rule *slaughter an innocent Helot to graduate the Agoge*, and by the time they reach our prisons they've raped and tortured endlessly; is this not true, Redstone?"

"Perhaps," said Gunnar, "but let's say you've captured not a Spartan, but a truly innocent man. What would you do to him?"

"Release him immediately; I've *personally* done this on a score of occasions," said Alkippe. "But when the *cruel* come in our clutches, we'll make an example of them."

Horus laughed loudly.

"All this talk does nothing to clean these stables," said Horus. "In fact, it's gotten worse since we arrived. I fear a Griffin has given our friend Rowan something awful."

They peered over at Rowan on the far side of the stable; a Griffin had indeed kicked his waste at the Norseman, and Rowan was cursing uncontrollably.

"What say you, Rowan?" yelled Horus. "Would you like to come back here and help us out of this mess?"

The Berserker simply sneered and went back to shoveling his own pile, and Horus laughed at Gunnar.

"Rowan would rather shovel *Griffin scat* than be near you, Gunnar," said Horus with a smile. "*That* is a man with whom to have a vendetta, not this girl. And Alkippe, Gunnar is no Spartan, and I see no Amazons coming to help you clean the stables."

Alkippe and Gunnar looked at each other; their bird-faced friend was right. *I don't need more enemies, not now,* thought Gunnar. *She's not my friend, nor do I trust her, but she can't be my enemy.*

"I see no reason to quarrel with you, Alkippe," said Gunnar.

"Nor I you," said Alkippe.

/***/

Gunnar continued to shovel the manure into a pile for another half hour. After that, they heard a crash in the distance and a great squawk, and then silence. Gunnar looked at the far edge; the Berserker and the Griffin had knocked each other out. Gunnar looked behind Rowan; the place was filthy from years of neglect and there was another three sections not yet done.

"Tell me Horus," asked Gunnar, "how did Heracles clean the stables on his fifth labor?"

"The Augean stables were much worse than this," said Horus, "and he had to clean it in a day. So he diverted both the Alpheus and Peneus rivers to wash it out."

Gunnar came up with a plan and knew even Alkippe would take part. Rowan was still unconscious, so the three of them went to work alone. They found the main water supply of the stables, and then went on a search for a hose strong enough to take the pressure. Years of stealing supplies in the Agoge had given Gunnar a sense for these things, so he broke into the materials-testing lab and eventually found a water cannon Hephaestus had made for riot control. Gunnar and his team brought it up to the stables, connected it to the water supply and turned the pressure up.

The water cannon had wheels and a long hose so they could go from stable to stable, from cage to cage, and clean each animal in a matter of minutes. The Celtic Wildman couldn't get enough of the spray. Though the pressure was enough to knock a man down, he somehow stayed in its blast and yelled incoherently when it stopped. *The Wildman is quite small when wet*, thought Gunnar with a smile. *He now looks like a lap dog in the rain.*

Gunnar couldn't help it and awoke Rowan with a blast from the hose. Rowan jumped up and demanded justice but Gunnar paid him no mind; the Griffin was squawking too loudly to hear anyway. Rowan tried to attack Gunnar, but Alkippe caught him and held him back. The Berserker stormed off in a huff, vowing something.

They cleaned the Griffin's stables and the great creature loved the water as much as the Celtic Wildman. After that, they cleaned the regular horses' stables, and they were done. The waste had all gone down into a grate, and what could not pass into the grate they decided to leave there. They put fresh straw in the stables, gave another bucket of slop to the Wildman, and they were done. They all smiled, in particular Horus.

"It appears we did it," said Horus. "The most odious of the labors is over, and only eleven more to go. Alkippe, will you join us when we steal Hippolyta's belt back from Heracles?"

Alkippe stopped smiling and her face became red.

"No need," she said. "I'll steal it back from Heracles myself."

THE LEGGED SNAKE

Tommy awoke to see a shadow jump around his room and then disappear. *It's a hallucination*, he thought. *You've got to get some rest.* He couldn't fall back asleep, and couldn't stop thinking of home; he missed it so much that he started to cry. He stopped crying, but still he missed home. He missed Kojo's pock-marked face and kind eyes. He missed High Priest Elazar and his morning rituals. He missed the structure, the safety of Lepros. But most of all, he missed having a *place*. He had no place here amongst the gods; he was simply a contagious boy who had built a suit, and nothing more.

Tommy didn't like it here. This Academy was a place of competition, of violence, of learning the skills of death. Tommy started crying again when he realized he might never leave this place. *You'll be here forever*, he thought. *Lepros is a place for the sick. If you ever get back there, Kojo will probably be dead.*

Then he saw a shadow jump across the room again, and it wasn't a hallucination. Tommy's thin jaw tightened, and he instinctively reached for his suit. He moved cautiously because he didn't want to fall in the dark without the protection of his armor. He had fallen before, and his bones had always found a way to break, and he didn't care to spend the next two months in a cast. Tommy cautiously worked his way into his suit, and then slowly put on his mask and turned the night vision on. He waited three minutes and saw the shadow again; it was under his desk. He didn't want to move, lest he scare it away, so he brought out an ultraviolet light from his belt and placed it on the bed. It illuminated the room just a bit, but Tommy turned on his UV vision and got to see everything.

The creature was small and slithery and had hidden most of its body behind Tommy's desk. Tommy couldn't quite figure out what it was; he saw countless little legs tucked underneath its body and wriggling slightly. Tommy opened his face shield and smelled the creature. *It smells like a snake*, he thought, *but not quite.*

He was going to put his visor back down, but the small creature jumped out of the darkness and pushed him over. He wrestled the creature away from him, but it was too slithery and kept hissing at him. He threw it off against the far wall and its short legs grabbed hold and it stuck. It ran to the ceiling and then crawled down the wall to hide under the bed again.

Tommy put down his face shield and locked the door. *With this suit I'm invulnerable to small, slithery creatures,* he thought, *but I can't say the same for the others. Whatever it is, I can't let it out.*

He looked under the bed and saw it scurry back up the wall and hold on to the ceiling. *It's a snake*, he thought, *a snake with many legs.*

"What are you?" he asked. "And what do you want?"

The creature looked at him and just as it did, a blunt force hit him right in his temple. He tried to move, but instead became dizzy and couldn't breathe. He fell to the ground and soon all he knew was darkness.

/***/

Tommy woke up that morning with a splitting headache and his helmet taken off. Kayana was in his doorway and in a panic he went to cover himself.

"Relax, Alderon," she said. "I don't get sick, even from a vector as strong as you. I had a dream that you were in danger, trapped deep underneath the earth, so I came to investigate."

"Thanks," he said. "How did you open the door?"

"A lesson the Death Class learned yesterday," said Kayana. "Apparently we have a gift for bypassing locked doors."

I've heard that, thought Tommy. *We left our doors unlocked back home because there were 'no criminals on Lepros but Death,' and Death was a thief that couldn't be locked out.*

Kayana came in close to Tommy to touch him and he withdrew; this was the first time a girl had gotten this close to him, and he didn't know how to react. She put her hand close to his neck and rubbed it; her fingers were cool and soft, even beneath her thick gloves.

"I ..." said Tommy.

He was struck by Kayana's beauty. Her porcelain skin was flawless against her dark hair, and the way she looked at him with pure black eyes put a lump in his throat. *She's an angel of death,* thought Tommy, *but an angel nonetheless.*

"You look dreadful, Alderon," said Kayana, before turning herself away.

Tommy was mortified. He took a deep breath and snapped himself back into reality. *A girl like Kayana doesn't fall for a broken, crippled thing like yourself,* he thought. *It's embarrassing that you'd even consider it.*

Tommy wanted to hide; he wanted to fall into a deep, dark hole, far away from pretty girls like Kayana. He wanted to be swallowed deep into the earth and find his place with the ugly gods like Hephaestus. He wanted to pound coal into diamonds and then send them to the surface, so Kayana could see his love without having to see his small, crooked body.

He thought Kayana was going to leave the room in disgust, but instead she looked around, found a hand mirror and brought it to him. She showed him his neck and Tommy's heart rose back up again. *She didn't mean I look dreadful,* thought Tommy, *she was referring to these bites.*

His neck was covered with small bumps, and each one had a pair of puncture marks. They were red and scabbed over, but Kayana didn't seem to mind; she was even closer than she was before.

"What are they?" she asked.

"I was attacked by a creature last night," he said. "I think."

"You think?"

"It looked at me and I blacked out," he said. "It was like a legged snake. It must have opened my helmet."

"Snakes bite like this," said Kayana, "but they don't open helmets. How do you feel?"

"My neck itches," he said. "It's annoying."

Kayana narrowed her eyes and thought for a moment.

"I'm going to try something," she said. "If you feel any pain, let me know."

Kayana took off her right glove and then breathed in deeply. She put her finger on one of Tommy's bite marks and it felt cool.

"How does this feel?" she asked.

"Good," he said. "It's stopped itching."

She put her whole hand on Tommy's neck and it felt even better. Her hands were smooth and gentle; it was like nothing he'd felt before. But before he could catch his breath, she removed her hand and put it back in her glove.

"My touch is death to most," she said, "but my teacher says that the Horsemen and a few other gods are immune to it."

"It felt like it healed me," said Tommy.

"Perhaps," she said. "Perhaps I killed an infection inside of you. Regardless, no snake can unscrew a helmet, let alone knock you out with a look."

"What was it?"

"I don't know, but there will be more; we'll see more of these creatures before our schooling is through," said Kayana. "This Academy is buried in a strange, deep place, so deep that it's the domain of neither gods nor men. There will be many creatures that come in and pinch us in the neck while we sleep."

"I don't like that," he said. "On Lepros there were no creatures that—"

"You need not fear neck-pinchers," she said, interrupting. "You're immune to both poison *and* disease. You need to fear the creatures that will come in here and rip your neck *open*."

Tommy rubbed his neck and worried; he wasn't used to creatures biting him in his sleep, let alone creatures that ripped necks. He felt vulnerable, even in his suit. He wanted to go back to Lepros, or at least to a place so deep in the earth that the neck-rippers couldn't find him. *But she dreamt that I was trapped under the earth,* he thought. *Perhaps neck-rippers are waiting down there to eat me alive.*

Tommy looked up to ask Kayana about her dream, but she was gone.

/***/

Tommy had a hard time concentrating in his class later that day. He was grouped with the Elements: a Djinn, who represented fire; Körr the Frost Giant, who represented ice; and a Japanese goddess named Mazu, who represented water. Their teacher, Professor Verminus, was lecturing endlessly about their *importance*, but all Tommy could think about was the next creature that would come in through his window.

"There are many Classes at this Academy," said Verminus. "We have a group of Warriors led by Heracles; a Class of Death; and a Class of Nature. They're impressive, but they aren't the Elements. They aren't you: fire, ice, water, and poison."

Verminus, though he droned on and on, snapped Tommy to attention with his odor each time he walked by. The decaying professor smelled odd, like old, sweet cheese. The other students thought Verminus to be mean and ugly, but Tommy liked him. Verminus's scarred face and sad eyes reminded him of Kojo.

"Yes, Thomas, though they call you Pestilence, here we call you poison," said Verminus. "For at the Elemental level, Pestilence is merely an evolving and self-replicating poison. You are both, and you are just as strong as your classmates. Now I ask you, what makes our Class so great? Why are we superior to the others?"

There was silence, and then the Djinn put up his smoldering hand.

"It's *control*," he said. "Men can choose not to fight, and they can pave over nature. But they cannot control the Elements. When we come, there is nothing they can do."

"True," said Verminus, "but what of Death? Can men control Death?"

"No, but they can ignore it," said the Djinn. "Death comes for all men, yet still they build cities. When our kind comes, they can't ignore us."

Verminus took a deep breath and then exhaled. He smiled to reveal yellowed teeth with blackened roots.

"Very good," said Verminus. "Wars, Nature and Death may hinder mankind, but they cannot *stop mankind* like we can. Humanity might have a hundred generations of peace and progress, but if we send an Ice Age on the hundred and first, they'll eventually starve, fight and become cannibals."

Körr the Frost Giant laughed under his breath, but it came out with a *boom* and soon the other classmates joined in. *They're laughing at Körr*, thought Tommy, *but he's laughing at humans becoming cannibals. It's not right.*

"The Elements can do more than destroy," said Tommy. "They ...*we* ... we can also build."

"Precisely," said Verminus. "*That's* why we're *truly* superior to the other Classes. So tell me, what can we build?"

Tommy thought, but had no answer; Mazu soon picked up her hand. She was a thickly built girl with smooth, pale skin and dark hair. She wore long, flowing , bright red robes that were made to be seen by fishing boats, and she wore a flat-topped, bejeweled hat that was covered with hanging beads.

"Water builds cities," she said. "The rain feeds crops and the river brings trade. When Poseidon looses the ocean currents, a thousand of Dagon's boats harvest the fish."

"Brilliant example," said Verminus. "Poseidon and Dagon are mortal enemies, yet their Elemental battles have only served to build! Poseidon's anger keeps his ocean pristine, and Dagon's machinations keep his docks thriving! What else?"

"Fire separates man from the animals," said the Djinn.

"Another great example," said Verminus. "For though fire is destructive, Prometheus's gift brought warmth to the tent and illumination to the night. Where would humanity be without fire? Thomas, what of your Pestilence; can it build?"

"Yes," said Tommy, "but I don't know how."

Verminus laughed.

"Neither does humanity," said Verminus. "This I know. Perhaps sickness is a bit more arcane in its benefits than a warm fire and an ocean full of fish. But humanity has grown with vermin and unseen bacteria since its inception, and yes, Thomas, those harmless bacteria that live in man's intestines: those are under your purview as well.

"And perhaps their less savory cousins, the bacteria that eat the dead—those creatures are under *my* purview. Without them, humanity would be in a bind, would it not?"

Verminus looked at the Frost Giant and was about to ask him to talk, but the creature cut him off.

"Not make me speak," said the Frost Giant.

"Surely you feel the concept of *ice* has been used to build," said Verminus. "From food preservation to—"

"Not make me speak!" yelled Körr again. "Say you that the humans need us! But how they show?"

Körr pounded his fist into the desk, shattering it. Though his strength was unquestionable, Tommy didn't find him threatening. The Frost Giant wasn't showing anger; he was only showing his own pain.

"I, Körr, I am hunted my whole life," said the creature. "They hunted my family. Killed them, were heroes. I come here yet still I am hunted, by the Norseman Rowan. If he kills me, he will be hero, have songs. Tell me, if humans need me, why they hunt me?"

Verminus thought for a moment and frowned; he then shook his head in understanding. Tommy could see small insects running in and out of Verminus's coat, and when he walked by, his odor was overpowering.

"Sadly, Körr speaks the truth, and what's more, he speaks the truth for all of us. We will always be hunted, and we will always be reviled," said Verminus. "Perhaps none of you so much as myself, the Lord of the Worms. Though we build, the world *will* curse us. They'll bring out their finest warriors to hunt us and mothers will use us to threaten their ill behaved children. This is our plight.

"But that is my point; though the world knows it not, they *need* us. We burn their refuse and eat their dead. We clean their battlefields and save them from overpopulation. We keep areas of this earth pristine, and bleach the land when it needs to be cleansed."

Verminus put his hand on Körr's shoulder. Though some liquid oozed out onto the Frost Giant, Körr didn't seem to mind, and instead listened intently to Verminus.

"Do not expect to be loved; do not expect to be prayed to. Expect to be reviled and hunted. But though they know it not, the world needs your powers. Let me give you a glimpse of what you all can do."

/***/

They took a small break and then started their first lesson. Verminus had the mercenaries roll in a thirty-meter-long terrarium filled with countless snakes, lizards and insects.

"Within this box are a thousand creatures that can kill a man, or even a god, within twenty seconds. You'll use your powers to walk from one end to another unscathed."

Tommy studied the terrarium. The floor was a nest of snakes, some with poison and some that would strangle. The ceiling was a cluster of webs and flying things, and the walls were covered with lizards and tiny, brightly colored frogs.

"The first to walk through this terrarium will be the Djinn."

The Djinn was taken aback. He snarled, and a small outline of smoke burst from his body and spread outwards. His eyes turned red and he growled. Though he looked fearsome, Tommy knew him to be shy and mostly unaware of his own powers. The Academy had picked him up from a juvenile prison in Little Riyadh after he had burned his school down.

"I can't do this," said the Djinn in a quiet, but deep and grating voice. "I'm just an ordinary boy. I have no powers."

"Really?" said Verminus.

"Really," said the Djinn. "I'm a young student unjustly accused."

"Ah yes," said Verminus, remembering. "Arson."

"I'm no arsonist," said the Djinn.

"The police saw it differently."

"The police were wrong," said the Djinn, now glowing red.

"We don't know that," said Verminus.

"I was innocent!" said the Djinn.

The Djinn pounded a flaming fist into his desk and cleaved it in two. Both halves were set on fire with the punch, and Verminus called in the mercenaries to extinguish the flames. The mercenaries couldn't control the fire, so Körr stepped in and smothered the flame with his body.

When the class calmed down, Verminus continued his lesson.

"The legend of the Djinn has been corrupted so that people think of them as *genies*, living in bottles, granting three wishes, and so forth," said Verminus. "But the Djinns at their core are beings with *fire* in their hearts. A Djinn who knows his powers can knock down an army by himself. A Djinn who doesn't know his powers commits arson."

"Fine," said the Djinn, "but I still can't walk through the gauntlet of snakes. They scare me."

"*They* scare *you*?" asked Verminus.

Verminus pointed at the terrarium. The creatures had huddled to one edge, terrified of the Djinn's flames. The Djinn relaxed a bit, and after some prodding, timidly entered the terrarium. The creatures made a path for him as they scurried out of his way. When the Djinn got through, he grinned.

"Every creature is terrified of fire, even the creatures who are themselves terrifying," said Verminus. "Your task, young Djinn, is to learn to control your inflamed anger, and unleash it at the appropriate times."

Verminus tapped the Frost Giant to go next. At four meters in height, Körr was perhaps the largest creature in the Academy, and dwarfed both Indra and Heracles. He was covered with thick white fur, and his fangs jutted out of his mouth at awkward angles. But Tommy sensed a sadness in him, and felt that Körr, like so many Frost Giants, just wanted to be left alone. The Norsemen had banished them to a reserve in the North, and used them to practice their hunting skills. Tommy had heard tales of these hunts on Lepros, many of them coming in the form of epic poems, but he'd always found them sad. Though they described the Frost Giants as hideous and dangerous, the Frost Giants never seemed to strike first.

Regardless, Körr had a good grasp of his own abilities but still needed Verminus's advice to navigate the terrarium. Verminus told him to use his powers of cold rather than just his brute strength, and Körr gave a knowing smile. The Frost Giant put his hands on the terrarium and frosted the cage, then breathed in to cool the air inside. The spiders hid from the cold and the snakes and lizards couldn't move. Körr walked through without a hitch, and then smiled. *Few have seen a Frost Giant smile,* thought Tommy.

Mazu the water goddess was a bit out of her element. She needed big spaces, oceans and winds to work, but Verminus taught her how to work in a small environment. She made eight small water tornadoes, and they formed a barrier as she walked through the terrarium.

"These creatures have been burnt, frozen and now soaked," said Verminus. "They're undoubtedly looking to take their revenge out on you, Thomas."

Tommy was at a loss. He had powers to be sure, but he couldn't *do* anything. *But my suit leaves me invulnerable to these small creatures,* thought Tommy. *The legged snake pinched my neck, but these creatures can't pierce metal, and they can't unscrew helmets.*

Tommy walked forward with his suit and opened the door to the terrarium, but Verminus stopped him.

"Your powers aren't so easy to define, Thomas," said Verminus. "But remove your suit and you'll see a glimpse of what you can do. You needn't worry about getting us sick; the Elements are immune to your diseases, and you may walk freely among us."

"I'd gladly do this," said Tommy, "but I can't walk without my suit."

"Then crawl, Thomas," said Verminus.

Tommy was insecure about taking off his armor, and looked back at his classmates. *I see a boy drenched in fire, a mist-covered water spirit, and a frozen giant,* thought Tommy. *They won't make fun of me.*

Tommy took off his suit and immediately collapsed to the ground. Körr stood up in response and rushed over to help Tommy, but Verminus got in the path of the Frost Giant's clumsy, four-meter frame. The snakes in the terrarium sensed Tommy's weak position and slithered towards him and snapped at the glass. The Djinn's back began smoldering and he ran to the terrarium with muscles glowing orange, ready to smash through the thin wall and put the crawling creatures back in their place. But Verminus pushed himself off Körr and stopped the Djinn as well.

"Your camaraderie is both noble and right, but this is Thomas's battle," said Verminus to the class. "Though he'll not emerge unscathed, stay back and I assure you he'll emerge stronger."

Tommy saw both Körr and the Djinn back down, and even saw that Mazu's beaded headdress and red robes were soaked; she'd been preparing to flood the terrarium, and perhaps the entire classroom.

"You've always been quick to gain friends, and your classmates look out for you, Thomas," said Verminus. "But you must do this yourself. No help from anyone, and no help from your suit."

The terrarium looked even larger from ground level, and each crawling creature inside looked ready to bite him.

"Now go forward," said Verminus.

Verminus put his hand on Tommy's shoulder. Several mealworms fell out of his sleeve onto Tommy; one was pulled back in by another insect and eaten. Körr growled in the background.

Without thinking, Tommy crawled into the terrarium. There were Indian cobras and a boomslang at the front, and a Komodo dragon behind them. Insects were flying in the air, and Tommy saw that spiders were coming from the ceiling to land on him.

He moved forward and the creatures didn't part. Two cobras

splayed their neck hoods and began to hiss at Tommy. Another snake from far off spat blinding liquid into Tommy's eye, and though he was immune to it, the liquid stung a bit. The Komodo dragon was hissing as well and inspected Tommy from afar. Tommy crawled forward and he heard a rattle from the distance, and then some small stings as spiders on his back bit into him. The Komodo dragon let loose one more rumbling hiss, and then burst through the snakes towards Tommy. Tommy held up his hand and blocked the Komodo dragon's bite with his forearm. The Komodo dragon let out a strange high-pitched whine and then retreated.

Tommy started scurrying forward in a panic, and the two Indian cobras bit his neck and held on. He pulled them off and one of the smaller lizards bit him. He pulled that creature off and crawled forward. There was a clear path to the exit, blocked only by the black mamba. Tommy looked around and saw that all the other creatures were now away from him, purposely keeping their distance.

Tommy looked forward and the black mamba was now crawling towards him. It stopped at his head and then slithered around him like an affectionate cat. Tommy stayed still, and then felt a pinch as the black mamba bit his shoulder. Tommy winced and then turned around; the black mamba released its bite and then stared at Tommy for a moment. After another moment the black mamba was off, scurrying towards the other creatures. The path was clear and Tommy exited the container. Verminus picked him up and brought him to his suit. Tommy strapped his legs in, and then brushed off the mealworms that came from Verminus's cloak. After he stood again, his classmates applauded him.

"Your classmates' powers are less esoteric than yours," said Verminus. "Körr freezes, the Djinn burns and Mazu drenches, but what do you *do*? You're immune to both poison and disease, and can spread both. But what can you do?"

Tommy had no answer.

"You've always protected the weak, the ugly children, those that are crippled, broken and shunned," said Verminus. "But now you'll also be a friend to the terrifying, the reviled, the creatures with eight dull eyes, foul odors, caustic breath and rough scales. We will set the creatures in this terrarium loose, and they'll spread the word with their own forked tongues and silken webs of who you are.

"So when you're in the forest and feel something pinch your neck, or when you're in the sewer and feel something slither by your leg, know that this is your friend."

Tommy wondered if the unseen creature that attacked him earlier in the day felt the same way.

"Elemental powers are neither cute, nor sweet, nor clean," said Verminus, now addressing the class. "Our powers are terrifying, ugly and cruel. But when the beautiful gods fail in their heroic gambits, society will rely on us to do our dirty work to save them. And when that time comes, we will not fail. We cannot."

THE AMAZON DEMON

Kayana's fifth class of the day started late at night; it was a class on dream manipulation. Her professor, an Etruscan god named *Mantus,* had brought in a Spartan mercenary named Dion. Mantus was at the front of the room with his hands spread across a gurney where Dion was laying. Dion wasn't small, but Mantus was a tall god and dwarfed the Spartan like a father in front of his sick child. Mantus had a large, broad face and a thick mane of black hair that was short on top and long in the back. Mantus's eyes were a single color, with neither white nor iris, and they glowed brightly, shifting in color depending upon his mood. He was staring at Dion and speaking calmly, and his eyes were presently a shade of dark blue.

"You will sleep, young man, strongly but not deeply," said Mantus. "You will stay on the light edges of rest, where words become thoughts, and thoughts become dreams. If pain comes, you'll not feel it, and if death comes, you'll awake."

"I will do this, Praetor," said Dion, addressing the god by his title.

Dion relaxed into the gurney and two of his Spartan cohorts strapped him in like a condemned prisoner. The assistant teacher and Praetor Mantus's wife, a goddess named *Mania,* administered an IV into

Dion's arm and then injected a dark fluid into his body. Dion became woozy, moved his head, and then fell asleep.

"It is done," said Mania. "He will dream the rest of his life, if we so desire."

She stepped away from the gurney while wringing her fingers. Mania's pale face twitched twice, and she started nervously tugging at her dry, straw-like hair.

Praetor Mantus stood in front of the sleeping mercenary to address the class. Kayana had three other classmates, and except for the ghoul, they looked surprisingly alive. Dog-faced Anubis was there, alert and hanging on to Praetor Mantus's every word. There was also Ereshkigal, a young Mesopotamian goddess. Though death was her domain, she looked like a fertility goddess; her skin was a pale yellow, and her body was voluptuous and supple. Her black hair fell perfectly over her shoulders, and Kayana found her quite beautiful.

Kayana's third classmate was the Arabian ghoul Asra, and she appeared to be sleeping. *I wonder if she can understand our words*, thought Kayana. *Perhaps a ghoul doesn't need to.*

They were all standing in a semicircle around Dion, and the students had their own gurneys behind them. Mantus sat in front of his own gurney, which resembled a stone sarcophagus.

"Every culture has a death god that they fail to worship," said Praetor Mantus. "The Norse don't kill in Hel's name, nor do the Greeks build temples for Hades. We're not hated, loved or even *feared*. Death just *is*. This is our plight, and this is our advantage. Let the other gods negotiate promises and petty arguments from their constituents; we'll wait for them at the end of their life."

Praetor Mantus smiled.

"Perhaps that's why they don't build temples to us, because that is all we do: *wait for them at the end of their life*. We greet them after their desires are met, after their cards have been played out; we act when they're old, withered and useless. We are essentially powerless."

"I disagree completely," said Anubis, raising his hand.

"You do?" said Praetor Mantus. "Please tell me then of your great powers."

"Death gods are the final judges," said Anubis. "We place souls in their final resting spot for eternity. Society gathers its morality from us, and from this morality, empires are built."

Praetor Mantus let out a laugh—a low, grating laugh.

"Then tell me, dog," said Praetor Mantus, "If Lugh's army were to amass outside the Academy's gate, what could we do?"

Anubis had no answer.

"Kayana would kill a few with her bare hands, perhaps the ghoul would scare three away," said Praetor Mantus condescendingly, "and you would *judge them* as they marched through our gates and destroyed everything we own."

Anubis looked down in momentary defeat. Praetor Mantus walked over to Dion and placed his hands on the mercenary's forehead.

"This is where we can influence humanity," said Praetor Mantus. "Man spends a third of his life living here, in dreams. Though we're not gods of sleep, sleep is the cousin of death, and dreams easily become our domain."

Anubis picked up his head and sneered.

"So if Lugh's army were to attack our gates," said Anubis, "we'd wait for them to fall asleep and visit their dreams?"

"No," said Praetor Mantus. "We'd have visited their dreams long ago and they wouldn't be attacking us in the first place. We'd have given them *fear*."

"We already give them fear," said Anubis. "All men fear final judgment."

"If only that were true, there would be no sin," laughed Praetor Mantus. "But tell me, class, what does *true fear* mean to you?"

"The unknown," said Ereshkigal. "Humanity fears it like no other. Distant lands, deep water, or even a small insect with a frightening face brings fear."

"This is partially true," said Praetor Mantus. "I've seen a warrior slay ten men in the morning, and then fail to approach a young girl at a dance in the evening. Why? The girl's reaction to him is *unknown*."

Praetor Mantus paused to take a sip from a bronze goblet at his side; it held a steaming, dark liquid that smelled thick. Kayana wondered if it was blood.

"But though individuals fear the unknown, *societies* do not," said Praetor Mantus. "Societies seek out new land, new ventures, risk and unknown reward. Societies will pay a great price for intrepid spelunkers and cruel conquerors; anyone who can make the unknown *known*. So tell me, what *else* is fear?"

Praetor Mantus walked by Asra the ghoul, and looked at Kayana.

"Ms. Marx," said Praetor Mantus, "what is fear?"

"Fear cannot be defined," said Kayana. "It's not an on/off switch. A masked assailant is terrifying to a woman, but exciting for a gladiator. Snakes, spiders and even large predators are pets to some. Even death itself may not cause fear; it scares many, yet young males instinctively seek it."

"You've eloquently stated what fear is *not*," said Praetor Mantus, "but what *is* it, Kayana? What *is* fear?"

"You answered that just now," said Kayana. "Fear just *is*. It's a state unto itself, nothing more."

Praetor Mantus took another drink and exhaled deeply. His breath was so cold that Kayana felt it from ten meters away.

"That's it," he said. "Fear is a neurochemical state, nothing more. Take the bravest Spartan ever and flood his system with adrenaline and cortisol; he'll soil himself each and every time you do so."

Praetor Mantus pointed at the Spartan on the table and looked at him admiringly.

"Dion is one such man without fear. He's not only volunteered to let you four enter his dreams, he's allowed us to bring a nightmare."

Mania got up and spoke in clipped tones. Her voice was quick and brittle and she couldn't make eye contact.

"You must be careful," said Mania. "Think of yourself as the surgeon and Dion the patient. Any missteps you make while you're in his dreams can have drastic ramifications elsewhere. So do exactly as my husband Mantus tells you, and nothing else."

Praetor Mantus scanned the class, but soon focused directly on Kayana.

"You may feel powerful in his dream, like the god that you always wanted to be. But you're not a god whilst in Dion's head; you're a student. Treat him with respect and do exactly as I tell you. If you fail in this, I'll know, and there will be consequences."

Praetor Mantus swallowed his blood-red concoction and Mania refilled his goblet. She then poured four more glasses and gave them to the students. Mantus prodded them to drink, and Kayana downed her glass. It was thick but it wasn't blood; it tasted like liquid smoke. She soon felt light and airy, and felt connected with the world, and especially with Dion.

"Now," said Praetor Mantus, "we're ready for our first lesson."

/***/

All four of them laid on gurneys next to Dion, and Mania gave them another glass of the thick liquid; she called it *smokewine*. Praetor Mantus explained that they would learn to enter dreams by themselves later on, but for now this substance would help them make the leap.

"I repeat," said Praetor Mantus, "if you do anything outside of my purview, there will be dire consequences when you awake."

Mania put a mask on Kayana, and then put some electrodes on her forehead. Kayana took a look left and right and noticed that all of her classmates were laying down in the same manner, including the ghoul. Kayana closed her eyes and her connection to Dion became overpowering. She forgot where she was until Praetor Mantus's booming voice woke her up.

"Pay attention," he said. "It's all too easy to become lost in the dream yourself."

Kayana shook her eyes open and she was no longer lying on the table, nor was she in the Academy. She was in Dion's dream, flying above land coated with darkened mist.

"The trick is to maintain your lucidity," said Praetor Mantus, still unseen. "If you lose focus, stop what you're doing and *concentrate on the moment*. You're not in control here; you're a small visitor to the dreamer's land, under the dreamer's rules."

Kayana focused on the land around her; she was only ten meters above the earth, and the mist was simply fog covering the ground. She looked through the haze and saw dead bodies all around, mostly soldiers, but some young boys as well.

She looked to the left and right and saw little flying balls of light circling around her. One was flickering and would just barely turn into the shape of a woman before turning back into a ball of light. Kayana concentrated and noticed that it was the body of Ereshkigal.

"You can look like yourself if you choose to," said Praetor Mantus. "It's best to stay as something else. If you want to control someone through their dreams, it's best to come in and out unnoticed, or at least unremembered. But Dion isn't focusing on us, not now, so concentrate on your old self."

Kayana jumped from the ground again and looked at her feet to see nothing; she was also a ball of light. She focused on her legs, and then her arms, and envisioned them growing. They sprouted out of her torso, but then she looked down and realized she had no torso. She concentrated on growing her whole body; she visualized that it would just come into existence and *be*.

Her body came, and she bounded over a dirty pool of water and blood in the battlefield. She skimmed above it and waited until she could see a reflection; her head was not quite made, so she envisioned it, and it too came to life.

She looked at her classmates. Ereshkigal had morphed into her own voluptuous body, and Anubis was struggling. She skimmed next to Anubis and whispered into his ear, *"You are who you are, just be."* The ball flickered, and then he emerged whole. She looked to the left and the ghoul had managed to turn into her normal self and was running across the land on all fours, like a wolf.

Praetor Mantus then showed up in the middle of them; she could only see the outline of his body. He was barely visible, as if he was trying to be unnoticed, but not unseen. Kayana concentrated on just leaving the edges of her body in existence, and soon she was just like Praetor Mantus.

"You can be anything you want here," he said, "but the rules of

Earth don't apply; there is no advantage to being a giant or a terrifying monster, though there may be some advantage in becoming a hidden imp. Strength, ferocity and courage don't exist; secrecy and hiding do."

"We're approaching Dion," continued Praetor Mantus. "Lose your body and become small, lest we be noticed."

Anubis and Ereshkigal flickered into an outline, and Asra the ghoul vanished into nothingness while still running on all fours. She left footprints on the ground and splashes in the pools of blood when she ran, but was otherwise invisible.

We think of the ghoul as mindless, thought Kayana, *yet she understands every word the Praetor says, and grasps his instructions faster than we.*

Kayana turned herself into a shadow and then shrunk herself down to the size of a fly. She maintained her speed so her tiny size made the ground below fly a lot faster. She skimmed over the giant dead bodies of the battlefield, mostly soldiers. She soon noticed women standing in the battlefield, alive and snarling.

This is an Amazon raid, she thought. *The women are looting the men for captives and female children.*

"Praetor Mantus," she whispered, "it appears we're too late. Someone has already put fear in Dion's mind."

"It's a dream, Kayana," said Praetor Mantus. "Hush before you're noticed."

"Spartans don't have dreams of Amazons," said Kayana, "they have nightmares."

Kayana didn't like Amazons herself. She understood they had to do what they had to do to instill fear in male armies; but still, *they did things to their prisoners that should not be done.*

Kayana flew by a small, wiry Amazon who was checking for survivors. This woman had no face; her helmet cast a deep shadow, leaving only glowing green eyes. Kayana looked around and saw that none of the Amazons had faces either; they were just helmets, bodies and glowing eyes. Kayana still focused on the wiry Amazon and saw her pick up a baby and check to see if it was a female. It was, so the Amazon put her in a basket. Kayana noticed that many of the other Amazons had baskets and forks; they were collecting all female children and sticking males with their forks.

Kayana saw a man struggling in the distance and as they approached noticed that it was Dion. He and several other Spartans had been captured alive, untouched and whole, and he was now struggling with the women as they took him away.

Kayana felt Dion's emotions; they were *deep and real*. She listened to his screams and they didn't seem like yells from a dream. *Terror from a nightmare is muted and compressed,* she thought. *This is genuine fear to him.*

The Amazons seemed real too. Creatures in dreams lurked in shadows or behind doors; they rarely dragged you away in full view. The way they moved seemed calculated and planned. Their dark faces communicated with each other to move, even when Dion wasn't looking.

"We have indeed fallen into Dion's nightmare," said Praetor Mantus. "So we'll simply observe; if we add more fear, the emotion could kill him. So close your eyes and *feel* what's happening to him. Asra, ghouls are incapable of feeling fear, but try to sense the intensity of his emotion. Try."

Asra closed her eyes, grunted and then bashed her head on the ground in chagrin. She shook her body, flashed an angry scowl, and then morphed back into a ball of glowing light.

The Amazons took Dion to a tree in the distance and tied him up.

His hands were bound backwards around the trunk, and they stood him up and tied his feet. They tied a tourniquet around his eyes then and then slapped him twice. The largest Amazon, perhaps two meters in height, walked in front of Dion and spoke, her eyes glowing green.

"They're all out to destroy you," said the Amazon. "When you awake you shall know this."

A large moon arose from behind the Amazon. The small, wiry, green-eyed Amazon who was clearing the battlefield stopped by with her basket of female babies. She laid the basket on the ground and the babies morphed into scaled, scarred women with glowing eyes. They crawled out of the basket and dragged their claws across Dion's shoulder. He screamed in agony.

"He's in trouble," said Kayana. "We must intervene."

"He'll be in bigger trouble if we intervene," said Mantus. "His heart could stop from the change; we must let the dream play its course."

"Those screams aren't the sounds of a dream, nor even a nightmare," said Kayana. "He's in danger."

"And how would *you* know?" asked Praetor Mantus.

Because I've brought nightmares to people before, thought Kayana, *and they don't sound like this.*

Kayana decided to hold her tongue, and the small, wiry Amazon got in front of Dion.

"You won't remember this when you awake, but you'll know who did this to you," she whispered. "It was them, those whom you serve."

The Amazon took a metal gauntlet and put it on her fist; it was covered with sharp edges and hooks pointing in every direction. Another Amazon brought out a pit of molten liquid and the Amazon dipped the gauntlet in it until it glowed.

She punched Dion in the abdomen and her fist went through slowly. He screamed so loudly that the ghoul rematerialized and bashed her head on the ground in frustration. The Amazon continued to push her fist into his gut and he screamed even more. The Amazon appeared to open her hand inside him and then clutch at something in his rib cage. He yelled even louder and was trying to cry but couldn't because of his rapid breathing.

"This should not be, Praetor," said Kayana. "End this."

"It's his nightmare; we can't interfere."

"This is no nightmare. Listen to Dion's screams; those are screams of pain, and you can't feel pain in a dream."

"How would you *know* you can't feel pain in a dream, Kayana?"

"Because I've tried to give it, many times," said Kayana. "And if you don't end this, I will."

The moon shone on Dion and he whimpered as the Amazon pulled her arm out. A glut of black blood flowed out of him and he coughed more up as she stood up and looked away.

"Mercy ..." he begged.

"A Spartan warrior doesn't even know the word *mercy*," said the Amazon in return. "Look what they've done to you; they've turned you into a coward."

The Amazon snapped her fingers and four horses appeared from the mist behind her and came to a stop at Dion's tree.

"Tie his hands and feet," she said.

The other Amazons followed her instructions and tied his arms to two horses, then splayed him out and tied his feet to two others. Black blood continued to pour out of the wound in his midsection and soaked the dirt beneath. The Amazons tightened the rope until he was suspended, but held it loose so that his body still bounced a bit, and Dion writhed in agony as he swayed.

Kayana peered over at her classmates. They were quite affected by the scene; Anubis was looking away. Praetor Mantus had an air of disinterest to him and stayed as an outline, barely visible.

"Do you know how far you've fallen?" asked the Amazon of Dion. "How weak they've made you? You're an embarrassment."

"Mercy ..." whimpered Dion.

"You won't find it here, Spartan," said the Amazon.

The horses were lined up to go in four directions and quarter him. They walked forward and tightened the rope and he screamed some more. The Amazon gave a nod to her fellow demons and they hit each horse on the back of its haunches. The horses went forward, Dion screamed, but then the horses stopped and there was silence.

"Go!" yelled the Amazon.

She went over to Dion and he was no longer screaming; he seemed to be in a trance and couldn't feel pain. The horses backed up out of fear and he slammed to the ground.

"Someone's here," said the Amazon, looking around.

"We must leave this place," whispered Praetor Mantus.

Praetor Mantus turned around and bid the class to follow him, but Kayana wouldn't leave.

"You must come with us," said Praetor Mantus.

"You may go," said Kayana. "I'd like to have a chat with these Amazons."

"This is not your place," said Praetor Mantus, "and you cannot wage a war within another man's—"

It was too late; Kayana had already turned into a ball of light and was flying towards the Amazons. She flew towards Dion, but slowed before the demons saw her. *Don't just rush in there*, she warned herself, *you'll only get one chance to surprise them.*

Praetor Mantus flew forward to block her path. Kayana looked through Praetor Mantus's outline and saw the Amazon preparing to let the horses run again.

"Don't do this, Kayana," he said. "This isn't real."

"Then it matters not what I do," said Kayana as she flew through the outline of Mantus's body.

She materialized behind the biggest Amazon guard and ripped off her head in a single movement. The other Amazons took notice and crowded around her. Kayana visualized vines, and soon plants sprouted from the grounds and wrapped around the four Amazons, slamming them to the ground and immobilizing them.

Praetor Mantus had turned into himself and was rushing towards Kayana. She imagined a barrier, and soon a small dome separated her, Dion and the demon Amazons from the outside. She heard a *thud* as Praetor Mantus bumped into the wall, then heard him yelling from the outside.

"You know not what you're doing, Kayana!" said Praetor Mantus. "Tear down this wall at once and …"

Kayana visualized silence, and soon all was quiet within the dome. The horses, the other Amazons and Kayana's classmates were gone, leaving only Kayana and a single Amazon about to put a knife into Dion. The demon turned to look at Kayana to show that she was the small, wiry Amazon with glowing green eyes and a shadowed face. The demon took off her helmet to reveal a hairless head that was a mass of knife scars. Her eyes glowed deeper green and her jaw quivered to reveal a row of black gums and yellowed teeth.

"Pray, tell what you're doing here, girl," said the Amazon, "and tell me who you are."

"This is none of your concern," said Kayana. "I promise a quick end without pain if you leave the Spartan alone."

"Look upon me, girl," said the Amazon, pointing to her scarred face. "Do you think *I* fear pain?"

"I will make sure that you do," said Kayana.

The Amazon's eyes glowed and she got up to face Kayana. Kayana visualized Dion whole again and instantly his wounds healed, leaving only blood on his body. He scurried backwards against the edge of the dome, still too terrified to speak. Kayana visualized a protective shell around him so that the Amazon could do no more harm.

The Amazon flew at Kayana and Kayana jumped and then floated above her. The Amazon grabbed Kayana's ankle and slammed her to the ground, but right before impact Kayana morphed back into a ball of light and disappeared. She flew upwards to the roof of the dome, materialized back into herself and then called more vines from the ground to engulf the Amazon. The Amazon pulled two knives from her leg armor and hacked at the vines.

Kayana used that moment to fly down at the Amazon and shove her further into the ground. The Amazon was on her back, trying to stab Kayana through the sides. She would have been successful, but Kayana dematerialized her own torso just at the right moments so that the Amazon kept stabbing air. Kayana pushed herself off the ground and flew up to the top of the dome and then had more vines grow to capture the Amazon. The demon struggled, but soon she was completely bound. The Amazon's eyes burned green and her scarred head pulsed with rage as she spat angrily at Kayana.

"You think yourself strong with these thorned shackles?"

Kayana visualized the vines growing tighter and their thorns growing longer. The demon screamed in defiance.

"Strong enough," said Kayana. "Now, I promised you a quick death had you left the Spartan alone. You failed at that, so perhaps I'll start with your midsection ..."

"Do what you will," said the Amazon. "I'm the head of this little group, but still a mere foot soldier. There will be more; there are already more."

"More who?" asked Kayana.

"More of us," said the Amazon with a smile.

Kayana heard a rumbling and made part of the dome clear. She saw a storm on the horizon and then looked closer; there were thousands of demons coming towards them on horses.

"Not just the ones you see there, child," said the Amazon demon. "There's an army coming for every Spartan and god in the Academy. So make my torment long if you want; by the time you're done half of your school's minds will be annexed."

"Tell me who you are," said Kayana. "And why you've invaded this boy's dreams."

"My name is irrelevant. Tell me *your* name, so that I might invade *your* dreams next," said the Amazon.

"My name is *Death*," replied Kayana. "And if you dare enter my dreams, I'll sleep forever so that I may punish you eternally."

Kayana plunged her hand through the Amazon's chest plate and ripped out her heart. She heard a scream; but it wasn't from the

Amazon. It was from Dion and it was real; he was awake and so was the entire class. Kayana awoke too; they were back in the Academy.

Dion kept screaming until Mania came over and put her hands on him. He calmed down a bit but kept yelling, and his eyes were extremely dilated. Mania tried talking to him calmly, but it was no use; part of him was still in a nightmare. She gave him an injection, and he soon fell back asleep.

"More dreams are the last things he needs," said Kayana. "You're sending him back to Hell."

It was quiet now except for Asra the ghoul's grunts; the rest of Kayana's classmates were sitting upright and staring at her. Praetor Mantus grimaced, stood up and then glowered at the class.

"You're all dismissed," said Praetor Mantus. "But not you, Kayana. Walk with me."

/***/

They walked through the courtyard, down the stairs, and into the artificial city where the Warriors practiced their maneuvers. It was completely empty and lit by an artificial moon. Praetor Mantus took Kayana down a dark grotto and into an abandoned building at the end. He opened a room, pushed Kayana in and closed the door. There were no windows in this room; only a single lamp in the middle and two chairs. This building was modeled after a run-down Yōkai tenement, so the room was spare, dirty, and the light flickered erratically.

"Sit," he commanded.

Kayana didn't sit. Praetor Mantus put his hand out towards her and a force pressed her into the seat and kept her there.

"What you did down there was reckless, ignorant and foolish," he said.

"Why?" she asked.

"You don't know the power of artificially altering someone else's dreams."

"We entered a nightmare *already altered*," said Kayana, "and you sent him back to it."

"Artificially altered by whom?" asked Praetor Mantus.

"I have no idea," said Kayana, "but something."

"How do you know?"

"I know nightmares," said Kayana. "They have unseen creatures and dread lurking beyond, but not that. That was too real."

"You think you know everything, Kayana, but you're a student and—"

"I know what should be, and what should not," said Kayana. "And I know a man's screams. This wasn't a nightmare; those creatures were *from* somewhere."

Praetor Mantus stood up and then faced the wall as if he were looking out a window. His head nearly touched the ceiling and Kayana could barely see his body in the darkness. Kayana tried to get up so that she could disappear into a shadow, but couldn't stand; Mantus's force was still keeping her in the chair. He turned around to speak to her and his voice was calm, but had dropped an octave.

"Let's say they were demons," said Praetor Mantus. "An invading force set to destroy us, and you're the first to see them. You have two options: the first is to go in there with guns blazing, kill one of their foot soldiers, then let their entire army know that you're on to them before disappearing. Or the second option: you sneak away and bring the information to us. We figure out who they are and who is behind the invasion, *if indeed it is an invasion at all*. We could then mount a sneak attack together, using the full force of the Academy. Which option would you choose, Kayana? Which option *should be*?"

"The option that doesn't allow an innocent man to be tortured to death in front of my eyes," said Kayana. "There is no other choice."

Praetor Mantus laughed; his breath hit Kayana in the face, and it was so cold that she shivered.

"Perhaps it wasn't a nightmare," said Praetor Mantus. "But you still have so much to learn."

"Perhaps I do," said Kayana. "But I don't learn by fleeing from demons."

"I don't know what that was, if it was a dream, an army or perhaps even a solitary creature," said Praetor Mantus, "but you've done Dion a great disservice. Demons that come in nightmares don't follow the rules of fair play or nobility, and you've just humiliated them. They'll not come after you immediately; you're too strong. They'll come after Dion, perhaps other mercenaries; Spartans are strong physically but they don't have the *powers* of gods."

"Then it's now my duty to protect Dion," Kayana said. "I'll protect anyone else who comes under attack of these demons too. I'll visit their dreams every night and punish these demons until they leave us—"

"You're strong, but not an army," said Praetor Mantus. "One night you'll be away and they'll visit Dion. Or they could be visiting him now, or perhaps someone else, just because they can."

Kayana had nothing to say; Praetor Mantus was right. For the first time in her life, she felt *remorse*, though not fully. She felt neither guilt nor a hole in her conscience; she only recognized that her actions were incorrect. *I must make this right,* she thought, *but not just by entering Dion's dreams and tearing out another demon's heart. I must get to the root of this "invasion," and make it right.*

"I'm taking you to your quarters," said Praetor Mantus. "Upon your return you'll stay there. Until we can figure out what to do with you, and how to save Dion, you're officially in detention."

THE MANITOU

Tommy brought Kayana her meal and all four ate in the common room, sitting around a small stone table. Gunnar was pacing around the room, deep in thought, and Kayana was looking out the window onto the courtyard. The meal was more ambrosia, and she was ignoring it.

"It's odd that Mantus sent Kayana here," said Gunnar. "You don't discipline a cadet by detaining them with their team. They have a small prison here called *Tartarus*; if he really wanted to punish Kayana, he'd have sent her there."

"They probably sent her here on purpose," said Tommy. "They probably want us to bond."

"I don't think *they* want anything," said Gunnar. "This place seems to make up the rules as they go. But perhaps he wants us to come up with a plan. Mantus himself admitted the possibility that Kayana was right, and that means she's on to something."

Gunnar looked at Kayana; she was staring at her food with white eyes. *What's she thinking when she's in that state?* he thought. *Is this her version of sleep?* In a moment she looked up at him and her eyes were were jet-black once again.

"I'm not on to anything," said Kayana. "I saw a man being tortured in a dream and made his situation worse."

"What's your sense, Saoirse?" he asked.

Saoirse was playing with her ambrosia and thought for a moment. She was wearing a silk kimono that she had sewn earlier that day. The white cloth highlighted her blonde hair and accentuated her dark skin perfectly, but Gunnar pretended not to notice.

"I don't know," said Saoirse, "but I have Kross run free at night, and he's reported creatures much like the one Tommy described."

Kross growled and whined at Saoirse, and she spoke in sharp, clipped tones back to the hyaena. His surgery had gone well, and both were apparently glad to be able to communicate with each other so clearly, though Gunnar was left out of the conversation completely. Gunnar had been taught by the Agoge to at least decipher *intent* from the languages he couldn't understand, but he was absolutely clueless in regards to the strange tongue Saoirse shared with her pet. Though he dared not show it in front of his team, for this and a host of other reasons, Gunnar was lost, disheartened and didn't know what to do. *I was trained to fight in wars and brawl in pits,* he thought. *I'm not built for mysteries.*

"Continue to have Kross run free, and have him report to you only. He can't even share his knowledge with the dogs. But tell me," he said, now looking at Kayana, "what do *you* think is happening?"

"I don't know," said Kayana, "but there's something wrong here, and right now it's wrong on a very small level. The creature that attacked Tommy and the beings that infected Dion's dream are all connected somehow. I cannot prove it, but I *know*. Our teachers are oblivious to this and will continue to be so. It's up to us."

"*Up to us* to do what?" asked Gunnar.

"To be aware," said Kayana. "That's all we can do now."

/***/

Gunnar found the match invigorating. He and his Class of Warriors were playing *lacrosse* on the field below in the fashion of the Iroquois. The pitch was two kilometers long and there was no rule other than *first goal wins*.

Gunnar had an edge; he had played and studied lacrosse for years in the Agoge. *It's a beautiful concept*, he thought. *Instead of engaging in endless bloodshed, have warriors settle disputes with the most violent game imaginable. There will be pain and death to be sure, but there will be no genocide, no rape and no prisoners of war.*

Indra had split their class into two teams: Gunnar and Horus on one side, Rowan and Alkippe the Amazon on the other. Indra supplemented the teams with ten Spartan mercenaries apiece, and the game was working on its second hour. The losers would have a pit-fight against a Spartan enhanced with strength and speed, and the winner would get to see it from the front row.

Gunnar had lost Rowan's team in the fray and was by himself behind an artificial hill. It was silent; Rowan's team had the ball on their end and was formulating a strategy of attack. *This game is beautiful*, thought Gunnar, *but it's not real. For though it is war in its purest, most heroic form, societies that settle scores by lacrosse will inevitably be conquered by a society that does not. The army who fights unfairly will always win.*

A scout mercenary on Gunnar's side jumped over the hill and lay down, out of breath.

"They're coming," said the mercenary. "Alkippe is without the ball but she's in the lead, slashing at us viciously; she already broken one of our warrior's knees."

Gunnar looked over the hill and saw Rowan's pack of Spartans running towards them, five hundred meters ahead in the artificial forest that was now growing. *It's Manitou, the god of the forest,* thought Gunnar. *Indra let Manitou loose in here to grow a real terrain, and now it's growing out of control. Rowan's surprisingly using it to his advantage; we can barely see him hiding behind the trees.* Gunnar gathered his team together and first spoke to the Spartans on his team.

"Avoid Alkippe's blows, but don't *fear* her," said Gunnar. "She's not an Amazon anymore; she's just a ferocious girl, and Spartans don't fear girls."

The Spartans laughed, but they were still a bit nervous.

"She's just one part of their team," said Gunnar. "Focus on finding *who* has the ball and then find a way to get it from them. Once you do, give the ball to Horus; he has a plan. If we get the ball to Horus, we've won the game."

Falcon-faced Horus stared straight ahead at Rowan's team.

"They've retreated back into Manitou's forest," said Horus. "They're waiting for us."

"He's picking the battlefield we must fight upon," said Gunnar. "It's a sound strategy."

And I'm surprised the fool Rowan has chosen such a sound strategy, thought Gunnar. *What's more surprising is that he knows lacrosse.* Whether Rowan had played it before or it was simply raw athletic talent, Rowan moved well as his team passed the ball to one another. *He glides with and without the ball as if he's floating,* thought Gunnar, *and on a broken femur, no less.*

"Where is the Amazon?" asked a Spartan.

"In the skyline," said Horus. "She's perched in a tree."

Alkippe was indeed in the canopy of trees, sitting in a lookout position. She had a scowl on her face and some of the Spartans shuddered. *Give them some confidence,* thought Gunnar, *for fear of Amazons is a Spartan's only weakness.*

"She won't hurt you from up there," said Gunnar, "and if she tries, I'll rip her in half before she gets to you. Let's walk, slowly and deliberately."

They walked towards the forest, fanning out in a semicircle. Rowan continued playing with the ball and even did a few tricks with his stick to show off. He stopped playing when Gunnar's team was a hundred meters away and then held the ball in his hand. He smiled, then yelled *"Go!"* and all his Spartan mercenaries rushed out towards them.

The collision will be vicious, thought Gunnar. *The Agoge prepares Spartans to smash their friends to pieces upon command.*

The Spartans rushed out and there was a clash as the two groups collided. Rowan retreated with his ball backwards into the forest and Gunnar followed, leaving the Spartans to fight in a scrum. Rowan ran through the forest at angles, using the trees to block Gunnar's path. Whenever Gunnar got close Rowan would do an about-face and run the other way, often leaving Gunnar on the ground.

He's employing tact and restraint, thought Gunnar. *The Rowan I've come to expect would rush at me full-force in order to overpower me. What's he doing?*

Gunnar finally got traction and tackled Rowan as he rounded the corner of a tree. Rowan pushed himself off and crouched, still with the ball. Rowan took the ball and cradled it, keeping a tree in between himself and Gunnar. Gunnar whistled and three of his Spartan teammates came to his back; Rowan was surrounded.

"Give up the ball, Rowan," said Gunnar, "and we'll spare you a thrashing. I promise you."

Rowan smiled and peered into Gunnar's eyes.

"Agreed," he said.

Rowan heaved the ball forward, high in the trees. The ball went to one of his mercenaries, who caught it and jumped forward through the canopy to the perched Alkippe. She held onto the ball clumsily, then climbed down her tree quickly and landed with a *thud* on the ground. She then proceeded to run off to the goal on Gunnar's team's side. Half of Gunnar's team was stuck fighting Spartans, the other half was around Rowan; Alkippe was running off with no one to block her way.

"Stop her," said Gunnar.

Gunnar's Spartans paused and then reluctantly ran after Alkippe, leaving Rowan and Gunnar alone.

"Who are you?" asked Gunnar.

Rowan gave a smile and then his sparkling-blue eyes flashed green for an instant. After a moment he burst away in the opposite direction, towards his own goal. *He's leading me somewhere*, thought Gunnar, *but I have to know what he's up to.*

Gunnar followed Rowan through the forest. Rowan was even nimbler than before and jumped through thick patches of brush with incredible agility. Gunnar kept stumbling but plowed forward. They reached a patch of empty field and Gunnar was able to catch up a bit; Rowan's leg wasn't fully healed and he was still hobbled a bit. The Berserker ran off to the right to a patch of swamp, and then disappeared into the mist. Gunnar followed but was slowed by the mud and soon realized that he had lost Rowan. He looked around at his surroundings and couldn't see the Norseman anywhere.

Boom! Rowan emerged from behind a patch of mist and tackled Gunnar. Gunnar turned around to face Rowan and headbutted him, connecting his forehead into Rowan's nose. Gunnar pushed Rowan off and regained his footing. *Don't go in for the kill just yet*, thought Gunnar. *There are too many questions unanswered.*

Rowan's nose started to bleed profusely, but his blood looked odd. It seemed to pulse *green*, like his eyes. *It dries dark red on his face and neck*, thought Gunnar, *but as it comes out it's definitely green.* Rowan put his hand over his nose and pressed it; the blood stopped flowing and soon he was healed.

"What are you?" asked Gunnar.

"The man who has beaten you at lacrosse," said Rowan. "Your Spartans have followed her, but half-heartedly; they'd rather face a pit-monster than an Amazon. Alkippe should be scoring now."

They heard the wind rustle, and in the far distance they saw a small figure dart through the mist on the edges of the swamp.

"Hardly," said Gunnar. "My teammate Horus is a hunting god; what he lacks in strength he makes up in stealth. He can travel unseen, and I instructed him to patrol our goal. Alkippe reached it alone and Horus took the ball from her before she even knew he was there. He should be scoring any minute now."

Rowan tracked the figure as it disappeared into the far mist towards his goal, and then turned around to face Gunnar. Rowan bowed and then gave a friendly smile.

"It appears I've been defeated," said Rowan. "I congratulate you."

"The real Rowan would never congratulate me," said Gunnar, "nor would the real Rowan act as you've acted at a hundred moments over the past hour. I'll ask you one final time before I rip your head off and let that green blood pour from your veins. *Who are you?*"

Rowan smiled and his eyes flashed green again.

"A mere foot soldier in an army," said Rowan. "I'm but part of the first wave; kill me if you will, and a thousand will take my place."

Rowan ran towards Gunnar and tackled him again, but this time the Berserker had gained a lot more traction. Gunnar was pushed backwards into the swamp water and fell into a patch of mud. He sank just enough to eliminate all leverage, and now he had to focus entirely on breathing again. Rowan was keeping Gunnar's head under the water at a downward angle. He tried to push Rowan off, but the Norseman wouldn't budge. *You have but one shot to get him off you*, thought Gunnar. *Make it as vicious a hit as you've ever thrown.*

Gunnar relaxed a moment and feigned passing out. Rowan wouldn't relent his grip, so Gunnar grabbed Rowan and pulled him into the swamp water with him. Gunnar pulled his knee back and blasted it into Rowan's leg at full force. Gunnar heard a crack as Rowan's femur fractured again, and then he pushed the Berserker off. Gunnar burst above the water and took in a deep breath.

Gunnar looked around and saw Rowan floating on his back. The Norseman tried to stand up but couldn't; his leg was too badly damaged. Instead of yelling in pain though, he laughed, then swam to shore and propped himself against a rock.

"You've beaten me, Redstone," said Rowan. "Perhaps you've earned the right for us to use you, though they'll probably just want you dead. Spartans can be controlled, but a god like yourself …"

"You have five seconds to tell me what's happening," said Gunnar, "or I'll rip off your head until the green blood—"

"Pours from my veins, I got it the first time," said Rowan. "You can fight, War, but your rhetorical skills need sharpening."

Gunnar had enough and lunged towards Rowan to end him. Rowan's eyes flashed green and he put up his hands in a gesture of supplication.

"Easy, Horseman; I'll tell you everything you need to know about what we are," said Rowan. "Better yet, *I'll show you.*"

Rowan smiled and motioned behind Gunnar. Gunnar peered behind him and saw twenty strange-looking legged snakes behind him. They were quite agile but wriggling about blindly; Gunnar looked closer and found that they were all closing their eyes. Gunnar heard the *crack* of Rowan's leg and then immediately felt the Norseman's arms behind him. Gunnar lunged backwards into Rowan and pushed them both into the water. They went down with a splash and Rowan's leg floated uselessly upwards beside them. Rowan wriggled from underneath Gunnar, rose on his good knee and gave Gunnar a punch to his face. It was almost as strong as the punch of Heracles had been and left Gunnar in a daze. Rowan limped backwards and started to pull up Gunnar's left pant leg, exposing his calf.

"Don't fight them," said Rowan. "If they open their eyes, you're a dead man. You're probably still a dead man, but we'll take a chance."

Gunnar felt the creatures come over him and then felt a pinch as one of them pressed its jaws into his leg. He felt another bite, and then knew no more.

KROSS

Tommy had visited Gunnar in the infirmary and was now informing Saoirse and Kayana back in their quarters.

"He's in stable condition," said Tommy, "but he can't breathe unassisted. The doctors don't know what's happening; he just collapsed."

"He didn't just *collapse*," said Kayana. "He's the god of war. What did he look like?"

"Here," said Tommy. "See for yourself."

Tommy rested his forearm on a table and pressed a button to light up the wall in front of them with several photos he'd secretly taken of Gunnar. Saoirse turned off the lights and soon Kayana was inspecting them closely.

"Right there," said Kayana.

Tommy zoomed in on the photo she selected and saw that Gunnar's leg had swollen up slightly. He zoomed in more and saw two bite marks on his calf.

"These are just like the bites on your neck, Alderon," said Kayana.

"But Gunnar isn't immune like you, so now he depends on a machine to breathe."

"What are they?" asked Saoirse.

"I don't know," said Kayana, "but whoever bit him is smart. Biting a leg in a swamp hides your intent. What did you feel when you visited him, Alderon?"

"Nothing," he said. "I don't *sense* things like you both do. But I asked the doctors. There was no trace of poison in his system, and there was no trace of poisonous creatures in Manitou's swamp."

Kross whined at Saoirse's feet.

What's happening? he asked her in their language. *Tell me.*

I'm sorry, said Saoirse, *but I know less than you.*

"We'll do our own investigation," said Saoirse.

"Good," said Kayana.

"Kayana," said Tommy, "will Gunnar die? Is it his time?"

"It's not his time," said Kayana. "But these creatures have sent an assassin nonetheless; this should not be, but it is. And if we fail to make it right, Gunnar *will* die."

"He's a god," said Tommy.

"Everyone dies," said Kayana. "Even gods."

/***/

Saoirse visited Gunnar in the infirmary with Kross by her side. Gunnar's leg had stopped swelling, but his entire body had turned pale, with blue-green veins criss-crossing his skin. His great height and musculature were still imposing but he seemed useless now, like a great ship in a junkyard. She felt his forehead; it was cool. She then put her hands on his massive upper body and it was cold too, and covered with sweat. When she'd seen him last he was powerful enough to break a god in half, but he was now naked and helpless, covered with a thin blanket and lying prostrate on a gurney. His face was covered with an oxygen mask, and it was connected to an electronic machine that breathed for him. The machine compressed air, and Gunnar's massive chest would rise in response. Saoirse knew that if the power went out in the Academy, or if someone were to remove his mask, Gunnar wouldn't survive.

"I know not what's happening Gunnar," she whispered into his ear. "We're gods, yet we can fall lifeless with a strange creature's bite. We live in a school that protects us, yet has us face death at every turn. We live in a city filled with corrupt gods, and no one questions why we're here, and to what end we're headed. This world has many contradictions, but no answers."

She looked around the room at Gunnar's things; nothing was there save for his lacrosse stick and a pile of armor in the corner.

"Your gambit worked," she whispered into his ear. "Horus took the ball from Alkippe and snuck across the goal line. They fought for another hour before Horus came back and announced the victory. It was another hour before they found you. Rowan and Alkippe are to fight in the gladiatorial arena tomorrow even though Rowan's leg is broken."

If only you'd lost, Gunnar. You'd have ended up in the gladiatorial arena, but you wouldn't be here, she thought. *You can handle pit-fighting. It's assassins in swamps that are too much for you.*

Saoirse looked at Gunnar's armor; it was thin and lightweight but incredibly sturdy. *It's the adamantine they were developing downstairs*, she thought, *the strongest armor on Earth*. She looked at his leg and saw the faint edges of a bite mark, now healed over. She put her head against his cold, naked body and breathed in.

Gods of war are killed by assassins, she thought, *and assassins use poison.*

She looked at his blue-green veins; they had turned greener since she'd arrived. Saoirse thought for a moment and then went to his armor. She found a small knife hidden in his shoulder mount and took it over to him. She pricked a vein on his leg and green blood came out onto the blade's edge. She used her shirt to blot Gunnar's wound, and soon it scabbed over.

Smell this, said Saoirse to Kross, holding out the bloodied knife.

What is it? asked Kross.

Friend is sick because of poison here, said Saoirse in Kross's odd language.

Here? asked Kross.

Here, said Saoirse.

Saoirse let that sink in for a bit. Kross seemed to understand everything, but still had an animal's sense of intuition; he couldn't take the next logical step on his own. She would have to take that step for him.

Creature poisoned him, said Saoirse.

Creature? asked Kross.

Yes, said Saoirse. *Creature smells like poison here.*

Creature smells like poison, said Kross.

Find creature that smells like poison, said Saoirse.

I find, said Kross.

Be scared of creature, said Saoirse. *Creature has poison. Creature can poison you.*

I find, said Kross. *I find.*

Kross snuck into the shadows and disappeared out of the room. Saoirse marveled at the hyaena; Kross could be powerful but was as agile as a housecat when he wanted to be. *And he fears nothing,* thought Saoirse, *not even poisonous creatures that can kill a god with a bite.*

Left alone with Gunnar, she put her hand on his forehead and it was still cold. He started to sweat, and then his body jerked in spasm. She took a cool washcloth and set it on his forehead, but it was no use; he continued to seize. He moaned twice and then relaxed after a minute, still breathing heavily.

Saoirse sensed that he was in a great deal of pain and tried to hold him, but couldn't quite do it; he was so large it was like embracing a rock. She wrapped her arms around him as much as she could and pressed her ears to his chest. His heart was racing. *He's fighting a war within his body and mind, and this means he's in pain,* thought Saoirse. *But it also means he's still very much alive.*

/***/

Saoirse spent the next day pretending everything was normal. Kross had disappeared, but her classes revolved around rhetoric, so fortunately her animal wasn't required. The Muse Calliope had come in to teach them how to speak like a god when addressing regular humans. Though Saoirse was disinterested, Calliope brought the class into an auditorium filled with Spartans and started the lesson.

"I've instructed these Spartans to jeer," said Calliope, "and I assure you any constituents you'll face will be much worse. They may be under the auspice of Dagon, Lugh or any number of other gods, and there is nothing a human respects less than a god not his own."

Though Calliope was admonishing them, her beauty enraptured both the class and the spartan audience. The Muse's dark hair was wrapped in a loose bun, revealing a fleshy neck with flawless skin. Her voice was like spun silk, and every word she spoke sounded like part of a poem.

Saoirse had three young gods in her Nature Class: Sobek, the Egyptian crocodile god; Pan, the cloven-hooved faun; and Nanook, a northern tracker of polar bears. Sobek had the long, snouted face of a crocodile, and the body to match. Though he stood upright, his skin was thick and scaly, and it looked as if he was wearing armor of cured green leather. Nanook the hunter was the size of a polar bear himself, and thick white hair covered a calm, quiet face. Though he was built like a barrel, his feet were nimble and he barely made a sound when he walked. Pan had the legs of a goat and horns peeked out from his thick brown hair. His face was boyish and cute though, and its softness reminded Saoirse of Tommy.

"A god's power is given; you're born with the ability to fly, control elements, talk to animals, or whatever it is you can do," said Calliope. "But real power, the power of humanity, is *alienated* to you. They follow you because they *choose* to, not because you force them. You may be able to set a forest ablaze or breathe deep beneath the ocean, but when you're in front of the masses you have only the power of *persuasion*.

"Persuasion can build a nation or turn a people against their god. It's more powerful than any ability you have, but it's not so easy to master. There's no fundamental rule of oration that will work on any crowd, or turn any individual to your side. It is up to you to figure out what works best in any situation, and your first task is to develop your own style.

"Your task in this first exercise is simple: get the jeering Spartans to be quiet for thirty seconds. I've given you each a card with what I think to be your strength, and it's up to you to use it to make them quiet. It may work, it may not; only you will know your own style of persuasion."

Calliope snapped her fingers and the Spartans started to yell at the stage, booing, heckling and throwing whatever they could. She sent out Pan first; he was the most comfortable in situations like this. His strength was *merriment*, so he gave them a song and dance and the crowd started clapping along. He performed several magic tricks and the crowd became silent; when Calliope bid him off stage the Spartans wanted him back, and they started booing again and would not stop.

Nanook was sent out, and though the jeering Spartans mocked his size, he soon charmed the audience with a tale of hunting. He left the stage and once again the Spartans wanted him back and began to boo even more.

Calliope brought on Sobek the crocodile god, whose word was *anger*. His raspy, angry voice captivated the audience; though he was younger than Saoirse he lent an air of authority, like everyone was *in trouble*. The Spartans responded well to it, and soon Saoirse was up.

She opened her envelope and read her card. Her strength, according to Calliope, was *virtue*. She went on stage and heard the Spartans begin their jeers, but had no idea what to do. *Virtue?* She thought, *how can virtue tame a crowd?* She was at a loss and wanted to disappear; the men's jeers were increasing in volume, and soon she started to hear personal attacks upon her. One man said he had visited her on Elysia, and the others began to laugh. Though she knew it not to be true it hurt her deeply; she wanted to cry but swallowed her tears. *If nothing else,* thought Saoirse, *Elysia taught me to swallow tears and behave in front of men.*

Saoirse took a deep breath and chose the only option she felt remained.

"I'm leaving," she said. "You may stop jeering now."

She left the stage with dignity, shut the door behind her, and left for the mess hall.

/***/

She ate lunch alone, still thinking of Gunnar and the creature that poisoned him. The ambrosia still tasted of ashes to her, but she ate everything on her plate slowly and deliberately. The ambrosia soon began its work, and the sting of the morning's class soon faded away. She looked up to see a man, a Spartan, standing in front of her.

"May I sit?" he asked.

"Yes," she said, "but I warn you I'm about to leave …"

"I won't be long," he said.

He sat down in front of her. He was handsome, young and blond but had a mature look to him. He spoke with a slight Sumerian accent and had a necklace with an odd tablet around his neck.

"My name is Cassander," he said.

"I've heard of you," said Saoirse. "You picked Kayana up and brought her here. She speaks well of you and likes you."

"Her kind is incapable of *liking* anyone," said Cassander with a smile, "but it's good to hear that she speaks well of me."

"She's capable of more than you know," said Saoirse. "And yes, she *likes* you."

"Good," he said. "Speaking of unknown capabilities, that was some number you pulled in the auditorium today."

"I apologize," she responded, "I wasn't prepared to tame an army of—"

"They became quiet," interrupted Cassander. "After you stormed out, it took the wind out of our jeers. We had nothing to say, and you accomplished your goal. You've quite an imperious air about you."

"I'm happy to have quieted the audience," she said, "but it was inadvertent; I was not trained to be imperious."

"Of the Four Horsemen, you're the White Knight, are you not? And is the White Knight not meant to be a leader? If nothing else, does the White Knight not lead by her *virtue*?"

"Perhaps," said Saoirse, "but I wasn't meant to lead. Quieting an audience by shame is one thing, but my kind leads neither nation nor army."

"Fine, we'll argue your destiny later," said Cassander, smiling again. "For now, I wish to speak of another Horseman: the god of war."

"Gunnar," she said. "What of him?"

"I should ask you that: what of him? Why is he sick? How should we find the cure?"

"That's not your concern," said Saoirse.

"Why not?"

Be quiet, thought Saoirse. *Share as few words as possible, and no more. The Spartans may defend us out of duty, including Gunnar, but they share little love for those who failed the Agoge. Be clear with this message, but couch your words carefully.*

"I may be able to trust you, Cassander," said Saoirse, "but I can't trust the Spartan mercenaries in aggregate."

Cassander laughed and then looked around the room before bending in closer to Saoirse.

"You know so much, yet not all," he said. "You're right to distrust the Spartan nation, or any group for that matter. But though Spartans have disdain for those that fail the Agoge, their relationship with

Gunnar is mysterious. They put him on a pedestal."

"They treat him with no special respect in the Academy," said Saoirse. "And your *Little Sparta* has given him nothing but disdain."

"I can't speak for the government of Little Sparta," said Cassander, "but when no authority figure is around, the Spartan individuals speak well of him."

"Why?"

"Spartans are tough, but we hold one dirty secret," said Cassander. "We can run for three days without sleep, swim a river in full armor and fight endless battles without food. But we can't do any of this without being *ordered* to do it. Gunnar was exiled from our country only because he *thought for himself.*"

"He told me of his time," said Saoirse. "Did he kill the Helot?"

"That's for him to tell you," said Cassander. "But I'll tell you that he made a *choice*. And the Spartans admire that deeply. They won't admit it, not now, but they admire him for it."

Cassander leaned back and took a deep breath.

"When I brought Kayana to Hellenica, she said to me that '*This is a town of poets defended by paid mercenaries. How long can this last?*'

"I told her that we were stronger than she thought, because our poets brought technology and *technology* is the true power of this day and age. That wasn't entirely true; if the mercenaries on Hellenica's outer wall were to turn their guns inward, what could we do?"

"Lock the doors of the Academy and wait down here for another age," said Saoirse.

"You speak like a Horseman indeed," said Cassander. "But for now, for *this age*, I ask you ... *why is Gunnar sick?*"

"He was bitten by something," said Saoirse. "That's all I know."

"Just a small bite, two marks?" asked Cassander.

"Yes."

Cassander sighed deeply and thought for a moment.

"Though I know less than you what's causing this, I fear Gunnar isn't the first warrior to fall to these creatures, whatever they are."

"Kayana spoke of a mercenary acting strangely," said Saoirse.

"Dion, yes," said Cassander. "He was in a coma after she visited his dreams, and when he awoke he was different. It's hard to explain, but he was different."

"Tell me what this thing is that I must fight," said Saoirse, "or at least help me."

"I know not what it is, and I can't help you," said Cassander. "I'm a Spartan and I'm only built to follow orders. But I can tell you that if this Academy is a newborn, there is an *infection* spreading among us that means to kill us in our infancy. What causes it and to what end it will lead I do not know. But it seems to be starting with the Warriors: the mercenaries, Rowan, and now Gunnar."

"Has it infected you?" asked Saoirse.

"I should hope not," said Cassander, smiling again. "But if you see me tomorrow, it may."

"I shall keep that in mind," said Saoirse, "but *while you are still sane*, I need you to be more than a Spartan following orders. I need you to help me fight this."

"If the White Knight of Virtue commands me I must certainly follow," said Cassander. "So I'll tell you *this*. These creatures that bite and cause us to act strangely; they seem to lurk in the Manitou forest of the Academy. This is where your afternoon class is; so keep your eyes open."

"I shall," said Saoirse.

"To cure this infection, you must find what this creature is," said Cassander. "Once you find it, be careful to whom you show it, even me. Mercenaries and even gods may already be under its grasp."

"I will," she said, "but first I'll find a way to cure Gunnar."

"Good," said Cassander. "For the Spartans know that one day, it will be Gunnar to lead us to freedom. That's his destiny, and he can't do it lying on his back in a coma. Keep your eyes open this afternoon, and above all else, *survive*; your afternoon class is in the Manitou, and these creatures are bound to hide well within its foliage."

/***/

Saoirse went with her classmates and their dogs down to the second floor and entered the underground forest. The Manitou had grown since Gunnar's lacrosse match and was beginning to encroach upon the artificial city. Moss and grass had covered the streets on the border and large, fierce birds had taken up residence in two buildings. Saoirse saw Spartan mercenaries hacking away at vines covering a shop, but Saoirse knew the store would be covered again within a day. *The Manitou of the Academy is like its counterpart, the Manitou district to the northwest of the conurbation,* thought Saoirse. *Neither gods nor men can contain it.*

Their teacher didn't seem to mind; he was the Manitou itself, or at least an extension of it. He was over two meters tall and appeared hazy: part ghost, part man and part deer. He had a cloudy, human-like face and body, and antlers with over a hundred points rested on top of his head. He walked quietly, and when he did so, he disappeared into mist; when he stopped walking, he rematerialized . He bid them forward and they trudged for twenty minutes; the environment held no roads, and the walk was slow-going and covered with thorns. Only Pan seemed to relish the ground and chirped nonstop as they walked.

"Our teacher, Manitou, he's not an individual god," said Pan. "He's part of the forest to the northwest of the conurbation. It's also called the Manitou. *This* forest is an extension of it, and *he* of this forest. They're one."

"How do you know so much, faun?" asked the crocodile god Sobek with a sneer.

"I spent two years in the Manitou growing up," said Pan. "The real one to the northwest of the conurbation. It's like here, but has more brambles and strange creatures that bite."

Speaking of strange creatures that bite, thought Saoirse as she looked around, *I need to find these legged snakes.*

She looked around and found nothing. They traveled further through the forest and the walk got more difficult. Even the rocks were covered with thorny bushes. *But these creatures are out here somewhere,* she thought. *I wonder if Manitou senses their presence? Perhaps they've already bitten our teacher and he's just leading us to their nest.*

Pan ran ahead with his dog, already fluent in the canine tongue. After twenty minutes, Manitou bid them to stop and they looked up to see Pan in the tree, playing his lute. His small dog had somehow gotten into the branches and was barking in tune with Pan's song:

> *When Earth falls to night*
>
> *And warmth becomes rare*
>
> *When the sky loses sight*
>
> *And dreams vanish in air*

When cities collapse

And the gods disappear

You might think the world ended

But it will not end here

In the Manitou, the Manitou

The earth stays alive

The sun will shine through

'Til brambles sprout wide

In the Manitou, the Manitou

The forest lives on

It will fight, it will bite

But it will always live on

But you cannot relax

This place is no haven

The trees break your axe

And the rain's god-forsaken

You might think you can live here

And conquer it too

But it will rise out of control

'Til it grows over you

In the Manitou, the Manitou

The earth stays alive

The sun will shine through

'Til brambles sprout wide

In the Manitou, the Manitou

The forest lives on

It will fight, it will bite

But it will always live on

Manitou smiled and asked Pan to come down; the faun and his dog came down the tree gracefully.

"Cloven hooves and nailed paws make for hard climbing," said Pan. "But we climb nonetheless."

"Indeed," said Manitou, smiling. "Though you may think Pan perfectly suited for these environs, he's anything but. Nature is suited for itself, not for man and not for gods. It's in *how we approach it* that Nature lends us its power. The humble faun who climbs trees will survive while an army is swept away by a flood below."

Manitou sang a song in a language that Saoirse couldn't understand. Pan joined in, first with his lute and then with his voice. The song was peaceful and entranced the group as night fell over the land. Soon an artificial moon rose above them.

"Now your task for this lesson is simple," said Manitou. "There is an 'evil deity' hiding somewhere in this terrain. This deity is our own Heracles, of course, but you should consider him dangerous. Your job is to find him and subdue him. Have your dogs help with the former, and use your wits for the latter.

"Be warned, finding him is only half the battle. Heracles will take great relish in playing the part of a mischievous god, and will fight back through nefarious means. You have two hours to find him and make him yield. Good luck."

Manitou snapped his fingers and the moon became brighter, and then snapped his fingers again and a thousand artificial stars appeared in the sky. Saoirse and her class marveled at the change, and then realized that Manitou himself had disappeared.

"This is going to be fun," said Pan.

A moment later it began to rain, and gusts of wind blasted them with chilly air. The Class gathered around with their dogs. They shivered for a bit, and then Pan and Nanook snapped into action. Nanook knocked down several trees on the periphery of their camp and stripped them of their leaved branches. He leaned the trees up against a rock and covered the top with branches until he made a small shelter. Pan had whipped up a fire, and in a moment they were drying themselves out. Only Sobek with his scaly skin preferred to stay outside.

"Thank you so much," said Saoirse. "I'm not accustomed to the outdoors, and I'm not accustomed to the rain."

"*This* isn't rain," scoffed Nanook with a smile.

"Actually, it's *really* not rain," said Pan. "It's water from the ceiling, programmed to fall just on us. Look out twenty meters beyond our perimeter; it's dry in every direction."

Saoirse looked outside; indeed the rain only came in a circle around their little camp.

"We need to find Heracles," said Pan. "This place is large; if he's running, every moment will take him further from us."

"We don't need to find him," said Nanook, "we need to *hunt* him."

"*Hunt* Heracles?" asked Pan with a smile. "You don't hunt a god as powerful as he."

"He's strong, but we are four—eight if you consider our animals," said Nanook. "We'll fashion some simple weaponry, then corner him. He will be ours."

"He'll destroy us if we do that," said Sobek, speaking from just outside the shelter. "We must lay in wait for him, and then ambush him while he is unaware."

Pan smiled and then laughed.

"Hunt Heracles or ambush Heracles, both ill-fated quests!" said Pan with a smile. "It's impossible what they ask of us!"

"Then do you suggest we do nothing?" asked Sobek.

"No, just that we think outside the box a bit," said Pan, now looking at Saoirse. "So tell me, Horsewoman, what should we do?"

The White Knight can lead, thought Saoirse, *but for right now, lead as they taught you on Elysia. Start with praise and bring your idea as a suggestion.*

"Nanook, your idea of hunting Heracles is indeed noble," said Saoirse, "but it won't work with any weapons found in this artificial forest. Heracles is invulnerable to bullets, and shan't be deterred by sharp sticks.

"Sobek, your idea of setting a trap might work, but remember that we only have two hours. I have an alternative."

"It'd better be a good idea, girl," said Sobek, "because I'm getting hungry."

"I say instead of hunting Heracles," said Saoirse, "we have Heracles *come to us."*

As Saoirse told them her plan Nanook smiled, Sobek let out a hoarse, grating laugh, and Pan started to dance. As they focused on the task ahead, Kross let out a whine and then came close to her ear.

It's here, he said. *Poison is here now.*

While Pan danced Saoirse saw a creature run by on the periphery. She looked closer, and it appeared to be a legged snake.

/***/

Pan's little dog found Heracles half a kilometer away.

Strong man in tree, said the little dog. *High in tree, throwing pain.*

"Throwing pain?" asked Nanook.

"He means some sort of weapon," said Pan. "Heracles has perched himself up there and will probably be heaving things at us."

"He can't hurt us from a tree," said Sobek.

"You'd be surprised," said Nanook with a laugh. "He's like a bear. They're always dangerous."

"All right," said Pan, "let's put the Horsewoman's idea into action."

They came within two hundred meters of Heracles's tree and set up another camp. The rain followed them so they moved quickly. Nanook augmented this camp and gave it a better roof and a bigger fireplace. Saoirse gathered some big leaves and weaved them into a fan. Pan and his dog collected several armfuls of herbs, nuts and berries and warmed them on a rock by the fire. Nanook took the fan and started wafting the scent towards Heracles's tree.

"Keep pushing it towards him," said Saoirse. "We need the smell to cut through the rain."

Then Sobek walked out and sat by the tree. The artificial rain followed him and the dogs soon followed, barking and causing distractions. They heard Heracles laugh, and he started throwing pinecones at the dogs but couldn't quite reach them. He switched his aim towards Sobek, but the pinecones bounced off Sobek's thick skin. Sobek got up and started cursing at Heracles, but Saoirse ran out and calmed him down.

"We can't make him yield if we're his enemy," said Saoirse.

Sobek sat back down and buried himself beneath some sticks on the ground. Soon, Heracles had run out of things to throw and just sat in the rain. For good measure, Pan climbed the tree and ripped some of the upper branches down. Heracles was getting soaked, and Saoirse knew it was just a matter of time before he gave up. *Even a god as mighty as Heracles is miserable in cold rain*, she thought.

"Heracles!" she yelled. "We have you cornered."

"I can run, girl!" he said.

"Then we'll hug your heels and bring this rain with us," said Saoirse. "Would you like to come out of the rain?"

"Of course," said Heracles.

"Then surrender peacefully to us," said Saoirse. "A dry den and hot food await."

There was a moment of silence, then an earth-shaking *thump* as Heracles jumped down and hit the ground, splashing mud and leaves all over the place. He stood above them in the pouring rain, as wide as he was tall, bearded and angry. Even Sobek shirked from his presence. But then Heracles laughed and pushed Saoirse aside.

"I yield, surrender and give up," he said. "And I regret I ever volunteered for this gods-forsaken exercise. Next time I'll send Bes in my stead, or the Banshee."

/***/

Moments later they were drying off next to the campfire, eating baked nuts and some strange steamed delicacies that Manitou had brought. The rain was shut off, but most of them were still wet, including Pan's dog, who kept shaking water on them. Kross kept looking at the periphery of the camp, and then shared a knowing glance with Saoirse. Saoirse ruffled Kross's head, and he nuzzled in close and whined quietly into her ear in return, as if he were whispering a secret.

Kross knows those creatures are out there, stalking us as we speak, thought Saoirse, *but he's keeping it between us.*

"The power of Nature is arcane, to say the least," said Manitou. "You must ask Nature to come to your will, and find a way to do so. But let's say something bigger than Heracles was threatening you, something bigger than a single god. Imagine that Lugh had an army waiting outside the doors of the Academy right now; what would you do?"

"I'd have already built a moat," said Sobek, "and filled it with the fiercest crocodiles I have."

"All well intentioned, Sobek," said Manitou, "but Lugh's army has guns, flamethrowers and poison. Your army of crocodiles wouldn't stand a chance."

"You've not seen my crocodiles," said Sobek.

"I wouldn't care to see his crocodiles either, Manitou," said Heracles with a laugh. "All men fear those creatures, and most gods do too."

"Pan, what would you do when faced with an army?" said Manitou, ignoring the quip.

"I'd make it rain," said Pan, "just as we did now. I'd send colder rain, flooding rain perhaps."

"It would slow them down, but Éire rains nine days of ten; Lugh is accustomed to downpours. Nanook?"

"I'd bring the cold," said Nanook. "Éire rains, but his people aren't accustomed to icebound winters."

"Better idea," said Manitou, "but that would only work for an extended engagement, and Lugh prefers short campaigns. How about you, Elysian? Your idea brought down the mighty Heracles; what would you do to bring down an army?"

Kross whined and looked at Saoirse once more. *He's motioning to me that the creatures are on the periphery,* thought Saoirse. *Answer Manitou and end this class. Do not appease, do not persuade, tell them what is needed to be done and then have them gone. Think like a Horsewoman, not a deferential Hetaera.*

"I'd tell my hyaena to run into the forest and talk to every animal he can," said Saoirse. "He'd spread a message throughout the land that any creature that comes to our aid will be rewarded, even the unlovely. We'll bring rabid pigs, malarial flies, snakes, spiders and choleric rats to bite the army in their sleep. And just as we did with Heracles, we'd tell Lugh that we'll call off the animals as soon as he surrenders."

Manitou thought for a minute, then looked at Heracles and they both laughed.

"Hetaerae always seem to have both softer and harder edges than the rest of us. This plan would work, though there is one fatal weakness."

"Please tell me what it is, teacher," said Saoirse, falling back on her Elysian tone of appeasement. "Please tell me what it is so that I may learn from you."

"The first step involves sending out your hyaena," said Manitou, "and your hyaena seems to have run off."

/***/

Manitou sent the class home, but allowed Saoirse to find her hyaena by herself. He left it nighttime and she listened patiently for any sound from Kross. She heard him laughing in the distance from beyond the woods. She ran over branches and soggy mud until she was on the edges of the forest, and still Kross was further away. She caught up with him around a small artificial cave; he was growling at something inside.

It is here, said Kross, *in the hole.*

What is it? asked Saoirse.

Poison, said Kross. *Poison in there.*

Let's wait, said Saoirse. *Wait for friends.*

No, said Kross, *find it now.*

She peered into the dark hole; the moon illuminated her surroundings but wasn't strong enough to light up the cave. *My night vision is good,* she thought, *but I see almost nothing in here, just blackness and faint edges. I hope Kross can see more.*

It was a shallow cave made half of imported rock, half of substance made by the Manitou. Kross was ahead of her, growling. Saoirse felt along the edges and heard a hiss in the distance about ten meters ahead of her. *I'm out of my element,* thought Saoirse. *I have to place my faith in Kross.*

Be careful, said Saoirse.

I found the poison, said Kross back to her. *The poison is here.*

Saoirse heard Kross burst forward and snarl. She heard several hisses and smashes, and then felt something scurry by her leg. Kross soon followed, bursting out of the cave. Saoirse ran out to see her hyaena with a small, dying creature in its mouth. The snake-like creature had many legs and large eyes; it opened its mouth in one last death gasp to reveal two fangs dripping with green liquid.

You've found it, said Saoirse.

We leave now, said Kross. *More.*

More what? asked Saoirse.

More poison, more creatures all around us, said Kross. *They're coming for us here, now. We leave. We leave now.*

THE NORSEMAN'S BANQUET

Kayana was meditating when the Banshee visited her again, flying in through the window and smashing Kayana's bed to pieces.

"You needn't feel obligated to blow everything about," said Kayana. "A simple knock at the window would do."

The Banshee ignored the comment, but refrained from pushing Kayana up into the ceiling this time. The wraith's face had deteriorated since she'd last visited Kayana, and her pale skin was now covered with black, necrotic sores. The Banshee's hair was matted into clumps and smelled like a dying pig, and she stared at Kayana with bleeding eyes full of accusation.

"You've been flying in dreams, Death, skimming the battlefield, nipping at the heels of demons and thrashing one soundly."

"You've heard of my nighttime adventures no doubt," said Kayana with a wry smile, "but I fear I've made things worse."

"You've not made things worse, for it's not possible to make a demon *worse*," said the Banshee. "The demons are coming in droves whether you thrash them or not."

"Who are these demons?" asked Kayana.

"I don't know," said the Banshee. "All I know is that they're coming. I heard of your dreamtime exploits not from Praetor Mantus, but from the depths."

"The depths?"

"Aye," said the Banshee. "Hel, Hades and even Mictlan heard how you beat that Amazon she-demon; they found it humorous. Hel herself told me that *'though the demon army shall surely destroy the Academy, one poor foot soldier took on Death and paid the ultimate price.'*"

Kayana felt a strange feeling; she felt no pride that the Lords of the underworld were speaking her name, but she did feel the weight of the moment. *If Hel is speaking my name, they're surely watching the events that are about to transpire. And if they're watching, something big is about to happen.*

"I don't like this," said Kayana. "The demons, whoever they may be, aren't right to come here. Though this Academy is a foolish venture and the gods here are misguided, they're trying to make things *right*. The Academy sees the conurbation for the abomination that it is, and the Academy *acts*. Though we may fail to correct the wrongs of our surrounding districts, I can't sit idly by while an invading force of demons comes to stop us before we can even begin. Hel, Hades and Mictlan are weak to sit on their thrones and jeer at us as we get run over."

The Banshee laughed and the sound blew Kayana to the back of the room. The Banshee covered her mouth and thrashed her own head until she stopped cackling.

"This is not their *domain*, child, nor is it yours," said the Banshee. "These demons are attacking the living only."

"The demons attacked an acquaintance of mine, a fellow

Horseman," said Kayana, "and now he lies in the infirmary, a power outage away from suffocation. Whatever they are, they're in my domain as of now."

The Banshee frowned and then slowly nodded her head. Blood dripped from her eyes and fell onto the floor.

"Then so be it," said the Banshee. "But how are you to fight an army when you know not from where they came? When you know not what they are?"

"I'll fly back into Dion's dream and find one more demon," said Kayana. "I'll plunge my hands into the demon's chest and wring the truth from it."

"And that demon's friends will gladly lie in wait for you there," said the Banshee. "Once you get this 'truth' they'll wrap you in a suit of thorns and drag you down to their home deep beneath the earth. They'll destroy the Academy and keep Death herself as a prisoner."

Kayana realized that the Banshee was right. *Going it alone* wasn't prudent, nor was pursuing any act of vengeance.

"Then perhaps I need help," said Kayana. "Perhaps I need *your* help. In real life strange creatures bite us in the neck, and then demons torment us in dreams soon afterwards. I know not the first thing of what's happening, nor how to rectify it. All I know is that it must be rectified, so I beg you to help me."

"I never thought Death could beg, let alone of me. I'll help guide you," said the Banshee. "That's all I can do. I know not what the neck-biters are, nor where the dreamtime demons are from. I know not how to beat them; all I know is that this requires secrecy, which is a skill you have and I don't."

"Thank you," said Kayana.

"I'll teach you how to enter dreams yourself, so that you can spy on these creatures," said the Banshee, "but I would advise you not to enter Gunnar's or Dion's minds; the demons will surely be waiting to take you prisoner there."

Kayana looked outside her broken window at the artificial night. In the morning, Praetor Mantus would see her broken room and realize something was awry. If there was a time to act, it would be now.

"I'll go with you into dreams and then find what the demons are," said Kayana. "I'll not enter Gunnar's nor Dion's head; I'll enter another possessed soul's dream and study the demons under the cover of shadows."

"Good," said the Banshee. "Do you know whose dream you would like to enter?"

"Yes, I have someone in mind; a fool surely possessed," said Kayana. "His name is Rowan."

/***/

Kayana meditated with the Banshee for twenty minutes before she began to feel herself float away from her body. She saw herself cross-legged on the floor with white eyes next to the Banshee, who was floating face-down as if drowned in a lake.

"We can see everyone's dreams from here," said the Banshee in a calm, clear voice.

Kayana looked up and saw the Banshee in her dream form; the spirit was whole and beautiful, as she once was. The Banshee had red flowing hair, porcelain skin and beautiful, dark eyes. She sang softly as she floated above Kayana, and the wraith's clean, white dress floated gently and exuded an inviting warmth.

"You must help me pick which dream to enter," said the Banshee. "I can guide you, but you must choose."

Kayana flew from her window and saw the sleeping Academy and the dreams that spilled out of their quarters. She was surrounded by an endless array of images and sounds, and soon became overwhelmed. She saw Heracles wrestling with a large boar, and his dream was soon pushed out by a Spartan mercenary whom she'd not seen before; he was kissing a young girl. She saw nightmares in the distance; it appeared many Spartans were succumbing to the demons that had attacked Gunnar. She saw Tommy on the island of Lepros, speaking with a tall, dark man with a pockmarked face. The tall, dark man morphed into a girl; it was an image of Kayana herself! Tommy started to glow and soon both he and Kayana's image turned into lights that began to dance and intertwine with one another.

"He fancies you," said the Banshee with a smile.

Kayana didn't know how to respond.

"He's dreaming of you," she explained. "And his brain is filling itself with the pleasure chemicals dopamine and seratonin to their maximum amount. Be warned; you might not be able to bring him to that level in real life."

"I've been so warned," said Kayana, still unsure how to respond.

Kayana flew through Tommy's dream and saw the dreams of the rest of the Academy. They avoided the nightmares on the periphery, but flew through dreams of anxiety, love and some odd images that made no sense at all. Kayana saw a Viking longship floating around a moat of a castle. There was a celebration going on inside, and Rowan was behind a curtain, kneeling to a man with his head bowed.

"There," said Kayana. "That's Rowan's dream."

"Are you sure?" said the Banshee. "Perhaps the dreamer is the one to whom Rowan kneels."

"It's Rowan," said Kayana. "Even in his dreams he kneels before a greater man."

The Banshee laughed and it felt like silk on Kayana's ears. The red-haired woman spread her arms out and all the other dreams went to the side, leaving the castle in front of them.

"I cannot enter with you, Kayana," said the Banshee. "Someone will recognize me. They may recognize you too if you're not careful, so be sure to disappear into the shadows and if you must materialize, come across as someone else."

"I will," said Kayana.

"And do not underestimate the dreamer nor the demons that attack him. Though you may call him a fool while he is awake, his dream is his own and you're a mere visitor. If any part of him should spot you for who you are, the demons will come and take you to a very dark place."

"I understand," said Kayana.

The Banshee flew away and the castle came at her quickly. Kayana looked around and saw that all the other dreams had disappeared. She was now facing the moat and behind her was rural Scandinavia. She saw a dark cloud on the horizon and dematerialized quickly, leaving only a shadow. *This may be what a man's subconscious looks like when his thoughts have already been annexed.*

Kayana's shadow walked across the moat and saw creatures swimming in the water below. Upon a closer look, the creatures appeared to be Mermaids, laughing and swimming about. They were singing a strange, giggling song:

> *The Bazer-elk, the Bazer-elk,*
>
> *The Bazer-elk, in night*
>
> *The Bazer-elk, now pretty*

Yet still, he'll sure bite

Kayana was tempted to sit and listen to these creatures until she could decipher their song, but thought against it. *Mermaids are put on earth to distract, to lead you astray with their charm*, she thought. *They do this even when in another man's dream.*

Kayana walked across the moat into the castle to join a banquet underway. The foreground was filled with a hundred members of royalty, and in the head of the hall there were ten Norse warriors kneeling by the empty throne. The royalty's eyes glowed green, but other than that they acted just like royalty did, eating, laughing stiffly and keeping one eye on the king's seat at all times. After a few moments, a small man came from behind a curtain and made an announcement.

"Ladies and Princes," said the small man, "Viceroys and Barons, may I present to you *Cnut the Great*!"

A great cheer went among the crowd, and the ten Vikings bowed their heads in unison. The king came from behind the curtain proudly, stout-chested and somewhat fat, and held his hands out to his people. His hair was grey, his skin was ruddy; he looked every bit the king save for the fact that his eyes glowed as green as his subjects'. He snapped his fingers once, and soon everyone was quiet.

"Thank you, thank you," he said. "Welcome to the feast of victory; a *small victory* perhaps, but the first of many, I assure you."

The crowd cheered again, and the king bid them be quiet once more. Before he spoke again, Kayana heard the sound of whimpering beneath the floor.

"We'll move forward from this battle and expand outward, ever outward," said the king. "We'll do this relentlessly, for there is no other way! To lead this conquest I've gathered the greatest, bravest men in all the land. May I present to you, the *Húskarlar!*"

The warriors stood in unison and the crowd once again cheered. The king bid his people silence and once again, Kayana heard whimpering from the floor beneath. *It's the sound of pain,* thought Kayana, *the sound I heard from Dion when he was himself tormented by demons.*

"And to lead them, I've brought in the fiercest, most noble, and most loyal man in all the land. Please pay homage to Rowan the Berserker!"

Rowan stood up in front of the audience and plunged his sword down into the ground; it lodged within the stone in front of him. The crowd cheered, and Kayana noticed that Rowan was bearded and a bit taller than he was in real life. His eyes flashed green like the rest of them and he beamed with pride.

The answers I seek aren't here, thought Kayana, and she slipped unseen through the dining royalty to the curtain behind the king. She went through the curtain and saw stairs leading downwards, and listened carefully to hear the whimpering coming from their depths. She floated down the spiraling stairs, going round and round until she reached a basement. The basement was dark, but illuminated with the green faerie-light that came from torches along the wall.

It was a dungeon, and there were hideous goblins holding several innocent-looking villagers behind bars. The goblins had glowing green eyes, and the villagers whimpered each time the creatures hit them with a whip. Kayana breathed deeply and concentrated on what was before her. After the larger of the goblins hit the villagers with a whip for the third time, she knew what was happening.

These are the last bits of Rowan's subconscious that the demons have yet to subjugate, thought Kayana. *These are the last bits of his free will.*

Kayana decided that her strategy with Dion would not work here; she could not make a dome and fight these creatures one at a time. *Besides*, she thought, *I'm not here to exorcise these demons from Rowan. I'm here for answers.*

Kayana materialized into a goblin and then lit her eyes green for good measure. She walked in front of the bar doors and looked at her fellow demons.

"Leave," she said with a growl. "It's my turn."

The goblins squealed and ran off. Kayana looked at the villagers and they cried in horror.

"Keep whimpering," she said, "but only so those above don't suspect that I'm not one of these dungeon-goblins. I won't hurt you."

Kayana dropped her whip to the ground and materialized back into her normal self. A small grimy-faced boy rushed to prison bars and looked up at Kayana. Though he appeared to only be eight, he had a gravelly whispering voice, like a defeated old man.

"Have you come to free us?" asked the boy.

"I'll try," said Kayana, "but even if I eliminate these demons, Rowan's kind never have free thoughts. Get used to these bars."

The boy looked down and started to sulk.

"But in the meantime, yes," said Kayana, "I hope to destroy the goblins who whip you. I hope to once again let you roam freely with Rowan's thoughts, however limited they may be."

"What do you need from us?" said a woman in the back. Her voice was quivering and soft.

"I need you to tell me everything," said Kayana. "Hold nothing back."

She nodded at two young men, who in turn went into the shadows. They brought out an armored soldier and placed him at Kayana's feet. The soldier was heavily injured, but Kayana recognized him by his armor. *This is Rowan before the demons came*, she thought, *or at least what's left of him.*

"Hello, Rowan," she said, "I've come to save you."

"I need no saving," he said, spitting up blood.

"Then I've come for your story," she said. "Tell me everything, even if you find it shameful."

"There is no shame to what I've done," said Rowan. "I fought honorably at every chance, and I'll continue to fight these invaders until I draw no more breath."

I should tread lightly, thought Kayana, *for if this is Rowan's last shred of dignity and independent thought, it's surely small and weak. Bury any disdain for this Berserker; now is not the time to expose his shortcomings.*

"Tell me your tale, I beg of you," said Kayana. "Tell me so that I might follow you in battle to vanquish these trespassers."

Rowan got up and propped himself up on a chair. He put his head back against the wall, smiled and coughed up some more blood.

"It all started the night before the game," he said. "I was scouting our lacrosse pitch by myself so that I could best Gunnar. I'd come up with this grand plan to give Alkippe the ball in the trees, when seven snakes surrounded me, *snakes with legs*. I tried to fight them, but my kind is equipped for fighting bears and men, not small snakes.

"The creatures would have jumped on me sooner were it not for the fact that they were fighting me with their eyes *closed*. They were still agile, and my heavy sword and armor were useless against their speed. One of them burst between my legs as I parried, felling me. They jumped on top of me and bared their fangs; I tried to dodge them, but one bit my neck and I could not move.

"I was still conscious and I heard them *talking* to each other in a strange tongue, still with their eyes closed. Though I didn't understand their meaning, it was clear they were deciding what to do with me.

"They let me alone and disappeared into the forest, and after an hour I was able to move again. I went back to my quarters thinking nothing of it, but that night I had a horrible nightmare, with many of the characters you see in the room above. They took over the castle and kept me hostage down here; they wanted me to surrender and had me beaten. But I refused to succumb to their demands; I'll never give in."

Your green-eyed kneeling counterpart upstairs begs to disagree, thought Kayana.

"Do you remember any of your consciousness though?" asked Kayana. "When you're awake?"

"Yes," said Rowan, "but it's like I'm no longer in control of my body. Though I can see and hear everything, those upstairs decide what I do. The next day they had me *lose to Gunnar* in lacrosse."

"What else?" asked Kayana. "What else did they make you do?"

"I led him far from his team; if they'd let me run against him in fair play I'd surely have gotten the ball across the goal. But they had me perform an odd strategy to separate him from the pack, and once in the swamp my body wrestled him to the ground. It cracked my femur further, but once again I could have bested him if they had let me! Instead they had me hold Redstone down while these vile legged snakes bit him. They bit him in the leg to hide the wound."

"Tell me more of these creatures that bit you. Are they here?"

"No," said Rowan, "they aren't *here*. Do you see slimy snakes running around biting people's calves? These creatures merely *opened the door for the invasion."*

"Not all have been invaded," said Kayana. "Gunnar fails to act strangely, but instead lies comatose."

"That is how it lies," said Rowan. "Some subjects are invaded, some are killed. I guess Gunnar was weak."

You're the weak one, Rowan, thought Kayana. *Gunnar was too strong to be controlled, so they sent him to a coma and used you as a puppet.*

"If we're to defeat these creatures and take back what's rightfully yours," said Kayana, "you must tell me more. What are these legged snakes? What have you seen *here*? What have you—"

Kayana was interrupted by a clashing of armor and rumblings from upstairs. Two more goblin prison guards came down with more weapons of torment. Kayana transformed back into a goblin just in time.

"We shall pick up where you left off," said the larger goblin, grabbing a metal scabbard. "You're relieved, soldier."

The larger goblin was about to slash Rowan with the scabbard, but Kayana stopped him.

"Leave him be," she said, flashing her eyes green.

"Why is that?"

"Because I've already beaten him mercilessly, and then I gnawed his liver."

Kayana visualized Rowan with the appearance of more bruises and a disemboweled midsection, but made sure it was just an artifice and that Rowan was in no pain.

"He needs time to heal before he can be questioned again," said

Kayana.

"You've strange methods, soldier," said the goblin with a laugh. "I shall let him heal, then begin my beatings again. But I don't know if I can eat his liver."

I'll poison it beforehand in case you do, thought Kayana. *No man deserves this prison, not even Rowan.*

Kayana left up the stairs and then disappeared back into the shadows. She floated through the hall and saw the nobility laughing gaily as Rowan's green-eyed doppelgänger beat a poor peasant senseless. *Rowan was ignoble before he was bitten,* thought Kayana, *but he has only a few days before he becomes irreparably worse.*

She flew out of the hall and across the moat. Before she flew upwards and out of Rowan's dream, she took one more look at the dark clouds on the horizon. She flew closer and saw that there were no clouds at all. It was just an array of countless creatures: demons, goblins, ghosts and flying trolls. They surrounded the castle completely, but seemed eager to fly outwards to new lands and new dreams.

I know not what they are, thought Kayana, *but they own their subjects' thoughts completely. There may be no cure, and if there is none I must visit every infected subject in the real world and give them a quick, peaceful death. Every mercenary and every god who has been touched by these demons must die in his or her sleep. I must even deliver death to Gunnar if fate necessitates it; there is no other way.*

THE CURE

Tommy nodded in recognition when Saoirse put the small creature on the table in their common room; it was definitely the thing that had bitten his neck. It was the size of a small dog, but was scaled and slippery, and had legs like a centipede. It had the jaws of a snake but held a mouthful of sharp teeth behind two prominent fangs. Its two red eyes pointed forward and its face was like that of a bat's, pug-nosed and slimy. It had the most terrifying appearance Tommy had ever seen, but he felt an odd sort of kinship with it. *Now you will also be a friend to the terrifying, the reviled,* he remembered Verminus saying, *the creatures with eight dull eyes, foul odors, caustic breath and rough scales.*

"It's still poisonous," said Tommy.

Tommy took off his gloves and grabbed the creature with his bare hands. He held it up to his eyes and examined it thoroughly. He smelled it and looked into its glaring, dead eyes. *It's a dangerous creature when alive,* he thought, *and mean too. But it knows not what it does; it only kills when told to.*

"It's not harmful anymore, just handle it with gloves and don't touch its mouth," he said. "But yes, this is the same type of creature that attacked me. We should tell Heracles."

"No," said Kayana, "we shouldn't."

"Why not?" he asked. "He's trustworthy."

"That's yet to be seen," said Kayana, "but still, let's assume he is. This creature bites, and then people become possessed, controlled. What if Heracles has been bitten?"

"His skin is like adamantine," said Tommy, "stronger even. He's just as immune to their bite as I am."

"Perhaps," said Kayana, "but he's part of the Academy, and intelligence isn't his strong suit. He'll inevitably show this creature to an infected colleague who'll most likely kill us before morning."

Tommy examined the creature once more; it was fearsome to be sure, but small. *This creature's not fighting a war against us*, he thought. *Even if a hundred lurk in the forest, creatures like this don't fight wars.*

"I don't sense anything from it," said Saoirse, "not even when it was alive. I can always sense something from an animal, but not this."

"We need some help," said Kayana. "A leader, perhaps."

"Agreed," said Tommy, "but our leader is currently lying comatose in the infirmary."

"I have someone else in mind," said Kayana. "One of our teachers."

"Our teachers?" asked Tommy, with surprise. "I thought you distrusted them all."

"I do, completely," said Kayana, "but there is one here who might be able to help us. These creatures only attack those that can be controlled, and this teacher rebels against any authority. Furthermore, he wouldn't be able to tell his friends here of this creature, because he has no friends here."

"Are you speaking of Praetor Mantus?" asked Tommy.

"Not him, he's most likely in league with the demons already," said Kayana. "The god I speak of is our advisor, Bes."

/***/

"It's a basilisk," said Bes, examining the creature with his short arms. "You're lucky you found it in the dark; they're so poisonous even their gaze can kill you. Even luckier they found Tommy first; he's probably the one being on Earth who could survive their attack. They're dangerous, but not too smart."

"They've brought your Academy to the verge of collapse," said Kayana. "They sound smart to me."

"They're not smart," said Bes, "they're great at taking orders; there's a difference. Someone ordered the basilisks to come down here to wreak havoc, probably starting with you guys."

Bes walked around the common room with a concerned look on his face, lost in thought. He was less than half Tommy's height, but still had an intimidating presence. Though he wobbled as he walked, his gait had a subtle grace to it, and his short brown arms flexed with power. Bes went through several scenarios mentally, shaking his head *no* each time.

"It's brilliant, you know," he said. "You can't fight basilisks; not even with gods. You try to root them out and they hide; you find them and they kill you with their stare. Basilisks aren't smart, but whoever sent them is *really* smart."

"I don't understand the connection," said Tommy. "These creatures bring poison, to be sure, but poison kills. No one's being killed by these bites; they're either being brought to coma or insanity."

Bes smiled, picked up the basilisk, and put it down.

"Truth is, I don't understand the connection either," said Bes.

"These creatures are so dangerous that anyone who went to study them wound up dead. This is the first time I've heard of anyone *surviving* a basilisk bite, let alone having their thoughts flooded with demons afterwards."

Saoirse looked up at Bes.

"While we debate this, Gunnar's life flows from him," said Saoirse, "and if we fail to act, he'll die. We need answers now, so tell us Bes, what do we do?"

Bes thought for a moment, and then nodded his head.

"All these basilisks live under the purview of a single King Basilisk who lives deep within the ground, deeper than even this Academy. He holds antivenom that can cure your friend Gunnar."

"Perfect," said Saoirse. "I'll talk with him."

"No," said Bes. "If you do, you'll soon be lying comatose next to Gunnar. The king is surrounded by darkness, filth, and a thousand of his children, any one of which would kill you with a bite. Tommy is the only one who can go; he's immune."

Tommy smiled. He didn't mind the idea of descending into darkness and filth; it felt right.

"Tommy," said Bes, "the King Basilisk didn't conceive of this attack; it's not in his nature. But perhaps someone forced his hand; ask him who did it once you get the antivenom. I know of a vehicle that can take you there tonight and have you back by morning."

"Great," said Tommy.

"One more thing," said Bes. "A warning. The King Basilisk is hideous. He has eight dark eyes, a noxious odor and a fanged, hairy mouth. A basilisk's gaze is poisonous, but the King Basilisk is so terrifying that even a portrait of him can make a man's heart stop."

"I'll be fine," said Tommy.

"You will," said Bes, "but don't shrink from his gaze; he's sensitive about his appearance."

Tommy had no problem talking to a hideous creature, though he was scared of leaving for this journey alone.

/***/

Bes took Tommy down, down, down to the lower depths of the Academy, and then down some more. Tommy had heard that there was a crypt down here to house the undead gods, but all he saw now was stairs. Tommy thought he was five levels below the main floor but couldn't tell for sure. *Some floors have ceilings two hundred meters high*, he thought, *and there are some areas no bigger than crawl spaces.*

Bes hurried down, jumping over stairs gracefully and silently.

"I have one question, Bes," said Tommy.

"Make it quick."

"Perhaps we should tell Heracles of this basilisk," said Tommy. "Or someone else? This sneaking about is—"

"You trust everyone," said Bes, cutting Tommy off. "That's not necessarily a bad thing; though I don't care for Heracles, the brute is nothing if not trustworthy. But you cannot trust an institution; institutions take care of themselves, nothing else, and they act *slowly*. If we inform the Academy of this, Gunnar will be dead and cold for a month before they act."

After ten more minutes of stairs, ladders and tubes, Bes brought Tommy into a large, incredibly hot room. It contained several odd-looking vehicles and a few large holes in the floor. Bes rushed over to one vehicle and pulled a latch on its side; it opened to reveal a small cabin and some electronic equipment.

Tommy had never seen vehicles like this before; their dull black armor was almost clumsily thick, and there were neither windows nor wheels. They were each the size of a small tank, but most of their volume was made up of their bulky outer shell. Tommy looked down and saw that they were all attached to rails that led into the holes. *They're meant to be vehicles, but they only look like slabs,* thought Tommy, *slabs on rails.*

"You're going to the basilisk's lair through a volcanic tributary," said Bes, "an underground river of lava. I've programmed the coordinates already; it will take you there and back. You'll survive, but I warn you: it won't be comfortable."

"I'll be fine," said Tommy, clinking his suit.

"Good," said Bes. "Now, don't take too long. If you're not back by morning call, I'll have to concoct some strange tale as to your whereabouts, and I don't lie too well. Still, don't come back without the antivenom."

"I won't fail you," said Tommy.

"Don't worry about me," said Bes. "Worry about your friend Gunnar. He'll be dead within forty-eight hours if you fail."

Tommy got in the vehicle and Bes shut the door; it closed with a blunt *thud*, and then he heard several *clicks* and *whirrs* as the door's seal clamped tighter and tighter. Tommy felt the air click on, but he was already sweating. For the first time in his life he felt *cramped in* and took off his helmet.

He felt the vehicle move forward and the displays showed that it was doing just that: rolling over on the rails. The vehicle tipped down and the dashboard showed the temperature increasing until it was 800 degrees Celsius and climbing. It was getting so hot that he thought about putting his air-conditioned helmet back on, but chose not to. He felt free without it, driving a vehicle for a job, just like a normal person.

He then sensed a strange presence and turned around into the darkness and felt the space behind his seat. Someone was hiding there!

"Relax, Alderon," said a voice from the darkness. "It's me."

It was Kayana. She had disappeared into the shadows and stowed away on board with him. Tommy scrambled to put his helmet back on, but Kayana put her hand out and stopped him.

"It's okay," she said. "You can't make me sick, remember? Besides, I need to come to the front seat; it's getting too hot back there. I need some more space up front; can you take off your whole suit?"

"I don't think it's wise to ..." said Tommy.

"Just do it," said Kayana.

It took a while to take off his suit. The ride was bumpy, the space was cramped, and perhaps most importantly, Tommy was ashamed. He didn't want to show his bent limbs to Kayana, let alone have her sit next to them. But he finally took off the lower part of his suit and revealed his thin, crippled legs and Kayana jumped into the front seat with him, pushing his armor to the back of the vehicle.

"This is better," she said. "I'm equipped for shadows, not small spaces."

Kayana cozied up next to him, and though it was uncomfortably hot, Tommy's heart started to race. He'd never felt anything like this before in his life; Kayana was so near to him. *This is what it's like to be close to a girl*, he thought. *Kojo had told me of this, but I'm actually doing it.* Her icy skin cooled him off a bit and he stopped sweating, but his heart was still beating incredibly loudly.

Though she stared straight ahead, Kayana's body seemed to get closer to him with every passing turn. *She can't be feeling what I'm feeling*, he thought. *She's beautiful and could never love a crippled thing like me.* But she was with him, closer than anyone had ever been in his entire life.

"Your heart's beating quickly, Alderon," she asked. "Is there something you fear down here?"

"No," he said.

They drove in silence and Tommy's heart continued to race.

"Perhaps this is the first time you've touched someone without your suit," said Kayana, "and you fear they might die."

"Yes," he said, lying once more.

"You're not the first person *I've* touched," said Kayana, "but everyone I've touched *has* died. It's good to be near someone who's immune to my skin."

They cruised through the underground tributaries at a quick clip. They were flowing through lava but were still on rails. Tommy had studied these rails years ago and thought for a few minutes to remember a fact that wouldn't bore her.

"Hephaestus put these rails here himself," he said. "He built them of adamantine so they wouldn't melt."

"Interesting," said Kayana. "Tell me more of these rails."

"Well," said Tommy, "they're all over the world; only Hephaestus knows where they all lead. Supposedly you can enter a volcano and come out on the other end of the Earth."

He dared to look over at Kayana and she was looking back at him, concentrating intensely. *Her eyes are beautiful when they're black,* he thought, *and even more beautiful when they're white.*

"You know I've never ...," he said. "What I meant to say is that I've never *felt* ..."

"We're here," interrupted Kayana as the vehicle came to a halt. "The King Basilisk's cave."

/***/

They opened the vehicle to absolute blackness. Tommy put his suit back on and turned on his night vision, but he still couldn't see anything.

"There's no light here," said Tommy. "None. Do your powers allow you to see down here?"

"No," said Kayana, "but I'm quite comfortable in darkness. I have a good sense of where we are and what's around us."

"What do you sense?"

Kayana breathed in for a second and then exhaled.

"Millions of creatures live here," she said, "and not only basilisks. Living things are all around us, reviled and sad, forced to live here because the world above finds them hideous."

Tommy sensed it too, but he liked it down here. *There is some safety in being cast out,* thought Tommy, *because you cannot be cast out again.* He pressed a button on his forearm, and his suit let off a low-level glow in all directions. It was still dark with his naked eye, but when he turned on his night vision, the place became illuminated.

The cavern was enormous and mostly empty, but he could see a number of creatures lying about. They were several basilisks that hissed and ran back into their holes, but there were other creatures there too, many of them unaware of Tommy and Kayana's presence.

There were pale, eyeless spiders that glowed brilliantly in his light. There were snakes that hung from the ceiling, attached with some sort of adhesive secretion. There were centipedes that seemed to have a thousand legs and millipedes that seemed to have a million. There were odd plant bulbs that were oozing a pale grey liquid; small insects gathered around the liquid and seemed to be eating it.

Tommy projected his display onto his face shield so that Kayana could see, and once again she came close to him. He showed her the pale grey oozing plants and she smiled.

"What are these plants?" she asked. "I like them."

Tommy remembered the plants from his studies on Lepros.

"They go all the way to the surface," said Tommy. "Their roots reach down here and become the center of this ecosystem. They're carnivorous."

"Carnivorous plants?" asked Kayana. "How do they kill?"

"They don't, really," said Tommy with a laugh. "They mostly eat the dead on the surface. What they can't digest they excrete down here."

"Are the plants a threat to us, Alderon?" asked Kayana in a flat voice.

Tommy looked at the puddle of ooze coming from the bulbs; he'd hate to be deposited down here like that, dead or alive. But still, he felt safe in the cave. The creatures could be dangerous, but not here. Tommy and Kayana were walking amongst the blind and disinterested.

"There's no threat to us now," he said.

"I sense danger still," said Kayana. "From where or what I know not. But I'd like to follow you closely."

"Of course," said Tommy.

"Stay close so I can see the projection in your face shield," said Kayana. "You illuminate this place well."

Kayana walked behind him so nearly that he could feel her

presence through his suit. *If she uses me only for visibility, so be it,* thought Tommy. *It feels right to be of use to her.*

There were many turns in the cave, but it was pretty clear where the King Basilisk stayed. At each turn there was one path with a hundred basilisks that peeked out from the darkness with closed eyes and then scurried backwards.

"They're leaving their eyes shut in the dark," said Tommy. "They do it to protect each other."

"They're doing it for you, Tommy," said Kayana.

"For me?"

"They revere you," said Kayana. "I sense it."

Tommy looked at Kayana; she was still following him, but her eyes were white again.

The basilisks form a collective intelligence, led by their king, thought Tommy, *or at least that's what Bes said. But if they revere me, they don't seem to show it. They're ignoring me, which is good enough for now.*

"Their king is near; around the corner," said Kayana. "I sense that too."

"What do you sense from him?" asked Tommy. "Is he dangerous?"

"He's not dangerous," said Kayana. "I sense shame and nothing else."

The king has eight dark eyes, a noxious odor and a fanged, hairy mouth, thought Tommy. *Perhaps that's why he feels shame.*

They turned the corner and Tommy saw the hulking body of the King Basilisk ahead, looking away. He was about the size of a rhinoceros and was swarming with smaller basilisks running over him and grooming his fur. Tommy found it odd that a basilisk would have fur, and then looked closer; the King Basilisk's fur was golden, shiny and smooth! Tommy turned up his suit's illumination and then released his helmet and breathed in the air; it smelled nice, like the ocean.

"You have come," said the King Basilisk in a deep, calming voice.

I didn't know that basilisks could talk, thought Tommy, *let alone talk beautifully*. He took a look at Kayana, and she was just as surprised as he.

"Yes," said Tommy.

"You withstood our bite," said the King Basilisk. "Is this true?"

"Yes," said Tommy. "I'm immune to most sicknesses and most poisons, including …"

Before Tommy could complete the thought, the King Basilisk turned around to face them. He didn't have *eight dark eyes and a fanged, hairy mouth*. His face was noble, with two large, clear eyes, the hooked beak of a falcon and a gloriously flowing mane. The King Basilisk turned around and sat on his haunches, much as a lion would when surveying his pride.

"You're like the weasel, but perhaps stronger," said the King Basilisk. "Weasels can dodge our bites, yet you can withstand them."

"I know that in nature the only match for a basilisk is the weasel," said Tommy with a smile. "Perhaps I'm the King Weasel."

"Weasels tear us out of our holes so that our bodies can be sent to Oracles," said the King Basilisk. "So tell me, *King Weasel*, have you and your queen come to rip me out of *my* hole?"

"No," said Tommy. "We come seeking knowledge."

Tommy looked over at Kayana and her face was blank, showing

neither fear nor compassion. *She's my queen*, thought Tommy, *and she stays by my side.*

The King Basilisk took a deep breath and then relaxed, sitting on all fours much as a cat would do on his owner's bed.

"Come closer, Lord and Lady Weasel," said the King Basilisk. "And bring some illumination so you can see us."

Tommy inched closer with Kayana behind him. He came within ten meters of the King Basilisk and then knelt. He took out a portable light from his forearm, turned it on, and rolled it out to the King Basilisk's feet.

"What do you think of my appearance, weasels?" asked the King Basilisk. "Be honest. I can sense if you're lying."

"You look ...," said Tommy, unable to complete the sentence.

"You look magnificent, King," said Kayana. "You know this to be true. It's also a surprise that you speak so well, or even at all."

The King Basilisk stared at them, trying to see if they were truthful or not. Tommy noticed that several small basilisks at the king's feet were coming to resemble his noble appearance. They didn't yet have his gloriously flowing mane, but each was sprouting a tuft of yellow hair, and two had begun to develop beaks.

The King Basilisk took in a deep breath, and then let out a small laugh.

"Pardon my insecurity," he said, "but my kind has been hunted and reviled for millennia; I have never seen two before that didn't recoil in horror."

"You're not horrifying," said Kayana. "This surprises us. Every legend, every warning states that a glimpse of your portrait alone can—"

"Make a man's heart stop," said the King Basilisk. "That holds truth, or at least *held* it."

"But it holds no truth now," said Kayana.

"Not now," said the King Basilisk with a sad laugh. "But this only means men will now hunt me, perhaps; to use my noble looks as a stuffed ornament in their trophy room. Is this what you want?"

"No," said Tommy. "We don't wish to harm, let alone *hunt* you."

"Then why have you come here?" said the King Basilisk. "To make fun of me?"

"We don't wish to make fun of you, King," said Kayana. "We come because you've sent your children to our Academy, and they're currently killing us. Your assassination attempt on Tommy failed, but the other basilisks have brought insanity to our mercenaries. They've also bitten one of our friends, and he now lies in a coma."

The King Basilisk stared at them, and then looked down sadly. He started to cry and his tears came down in glistening, sparkling drops.

"I didn't mean to do it," he said. "Though I'm responsible, perhaps; my children can't bite without my consent. I am sorry."

"We didn't come here seeking *mea culpas*, King," said Kayana. "Our comatose friend will surely die by this time tomorrow if he doesn't receive your antivenom. We desire this above all else."

"Antivenom you shall have," he said. "Give me a vessel and bring it near."

Tommy pressed a button on his belt and procured a small jar. He opened it and brought it to the King Basilisk. The King Basilisk took a furry paw and pressed a bulge in his neck. A glob of dark fluid came out of his mouth, filled up the jar and drenched the sides.

"Inject this into his blood and he'll survive," said the King Basilisk. "Now take it and be gone. I'll call my children back and you will be hurt no more."

"We won't leave—not yet," said Kayana. "We came here not just for antivenom, but for truth. Why did you attack us, and who told you to do so?"

"Be gone," repeated the king. "Do not return."

The king growled, spat, and cried some more, but Kayana wouldn't budge. He shrunk from Kayana, but she came closer. He thought for a moment, laughed slightly, and then sat down.

"That's one thing I miss about my old appearance," he said. "I can't even scare anymore, let alone make a man's heart stop. Come near and I'll tell you my tale."

/***/

An army of slithering, ant-like bugs crawled into the room, carrying some of their largest brethren on their back. The carried insects had small heads and torsos, but had grossly distended abdomens, about three centimeters in diameter. The King Basilisk instructed Tommy to take out two more jars, and the bugs held their engorged comrades above them. The large insects pumped their abdomens until liquid came out. Soon the jars were overflowing with a milky white paste. The King Basilisk ordered Tommy and Kayana to drink and they did so; the paste was sweet and somewhat crunchy.

"I'm getting used to normal society," said the King Basilisk. "Your light will serve as a campfire. That substance is nothing more than sugar paste, so it will serve as tea."

"Thank you," said Tommy.

He drank the sugar paste; it wasn't bad, but it was too crunchy to feel like tea. Kayana drank nothing; she just stared at the King Basilisk.

"I'm hoping to join normal society, to *be normal*," said the King Basilisk. "And this is how this fiasco started; a Mermaid promised to give me normality, in exchange for sending my children to the Academy."

"A *Mermaid*?" asked Tommy. "So they exist?"

"Aye," said the King Basilisk, "they're goddesses indeed, and their power is beauty. I met one while scavenging in my previous form, which was fanged, hairy and eight-eyed as you know. I was surprised when she didn't die after seeing my face, and even more surprised when she kissed me! I never thought another creature could do that to me."

I know the feeling, thought Tommy.

"She made me a promise," said the King Basilisk. "She would give me beauty if I agreed to send my children to the Academy. She wanted them to poison the gods there, starting with the Horsemen."

"That doesn't sound like a Mermaid," said Kayana. "Mermaids neither scheme nor conspire, and they don't murder."

"Indeed," said the King Basilisk, "from her tone it was clear that *someone else* was forcing her hand. I cared not who and I jumped at the chance. She gave me this beautiful form, and I sent my basilisks to poison you."

"And a failed job of that you did," said Kayana.

"Yes," he said, "I fear I've poisoned a few—an undeserving, innocent few at that."

"Poisoning is your mildest sin," said Kayana. "You've brought demons."

"Demons?" said the King Basilisk.

"Demons that invade dreams," said Kayana, "and then bend a man to their will. Your children bite, but they don't kill; not directly at least.

They bite, and soon thereafter their victims succumb to bad dreams, dreams that drive them to either insanity or coma!"

"What?" asked the King Basilisk.

Kayana walked up to him and stared him directly in the eye.

"Your children have caused little death," said Kayana, "but much suffering. I've seen men tortured indefinitely, all because a basilisk wanted to be beautiful."

"I know not of what you speak," said the King Basilisk, choking back tears.

"Your beauty comes at a price," said Kayana. "A price of men disemboweled, drawn and quartered. They're tormented only in dreams perhaps, but when they awake they're under the control of something, of someone not in your purview. Why? Because a Mermaid made you pretty. Tell me who this *Mermaid* is, and whom she works for."

"I don't know," said the King Basilisk. "I don't know."

"You sent the most poisonous creatures in the history of the world to our Academy," said Kayana, "and you *don't know* for whom you work?"

The King Basilisk's eyes quivered and more tears began to flow.

"Don't judge me!" he screamed. "Have *you* spent the last thousand years being synonymous with hideousness? Have mothers warned their children that if they don't behave, they'll see *you* in the mirror? Have you come to meet a man as a friend, only to see him squeal as his heart stopped because of your face?"

"Yes," said Kayana. "I've seen such things happen every day of my life."

"Then you understand my predicament! When someone offers you the one thing you wanted for the last millennium, *you take it*. You don't ask their motives, you don't ask who will get hurt. You *take it*."

The King Basilisk moved to the corner with surprising agility and buried his head in his paws. The smaller basilisks swarmed him and he talked to them in his own odd tongue. Tommy moved forward to talk to him, but Kayana held out an arm.

"Wait," she said. "Let him think of what he's done and come to his own conclusions."

After ten minutes, the King Basilisk came back and faced them. His face sparkled with his dried tears.

"I've called off my children; they'll attack your Academy no more. Give your friend this antivenom; it will work on him, but don't use it on any of the Spartans. This substance is strong and will kill mortals; you'll have to find another way to clear the Spartans of their demons.

"And as far as these demons go, I know neither their purpose nor from whence they came. Perhaps you should take it up with the Mermaid."

"Where is this Mermaid?" asked Kayana.

"I know not where she is nor what her motives are," said the King Basilisk. "Now please make haste and leave me in the darkness. The antivenom breaks down within a few hours, and your light is irritating me."

/***/

They made it back to the Academy an hour before morning call. Tommy and Kayana brought the antivenom to Bes and he rushed it into Gunnar's room in the infirmary. Saoirse was there putting a cool cloth on Gunnar's head while he jerked, seized and foamed at the mouth. *If this substance heals him,* thought Tommy, *I wonder if his recovery will be full.* Tommy thought back to his time on Lepros; though most people eventually dealt with handicaps, warriors had a hard time with lessened abilities. Impairment of strength and agility seemed to take their identities away.

Bes took a syringe and drew in some antivenom. He waited for Gunnar to stop seizing, then jabbed it into Gunnar's forearm. Gunnar seized some more, then seized violently, and then relaxed.

"It's working," said Bes. "The King Basilisk's antivenom is effective. Your friend Gunnar is going to be fine."

Kayana didn't smile, but gained a slight look of satisfaction on her face. Saoirse beamed and hugged Bes, and then kissed Gunnar. Tommy smiled too; Gunnar was already beginning to gain some of his color back.

"Save some of that enthusiasm," said Bes. "When Gunnar heals 'on his own' later today, you need to look surprised. We don't know who else is infected."

Kayana nodded and made her face blank again. Saoirse gave Gunnar one more hug and then tried to hug Kayana, but Kayana held up her hand to stop her.

"Now get back to your quarters before morning call," said Bes. "And remember that if anyone asks, you've *been sleeping the whole night.*"

Saoirse nodded once more and went to open the door of the infirmary. When she did, the door burst open to reveal Rowan, followed by Praetor Mantus, Heracles and two more Spartan mercenaries. Rowan had an angry look on his face. He pushed Saoirse aside and pointed his finger at Kayana.

"Her," said Rowan. "She was the one who invaded my dreams."

Praetor Mantus came up to Kayana and his eyes went completely black as he scanned her. Kayana didn't flinch and stared right back. Praetor Mantus's eyes went back to normal, and he slapped Kayana. Still, Kayana didn't flinch.

"She's guilty," said Praetor Mantus. "This is the second time she's disobeyed my direct order. Until we figure out how to punish her for this dangerous action, I command that she be placed deep beneath these floors. Spartans, bring her to Tartarus."

"You don't understand," said Bes.

"Perhaps I don't," said Praetor Mantus. "And until I do, she'll be imprisoned."

"She can still invade dreams," said Rowan.

"Not from Tartarus," said Praetor Mantus. "It's too deep and too dark."

"She'll find a way to hurt," said Rowan. "That's in her nature. I should ask to cut off her head, right now, before she does any damage to anyone else in the Academy."

"You'll not cut off her head," said Tommy. "To do so, you'll have to go through me—"

Rowan shoved Tommy aside easily. Tommy flew into the wall and his face hit the inside of his visor. Blood came out of his nose and Rowan yanked him from behind, and then slammed him onto the floor. He saw Rowan's eyes flash green, and then he saw the Norseman's blade held high, preparing to decapitate.

"Leave him be!" yelled Kayana.

In a flash she jumped at Rowan, pushed him to the ground, and then put her knee on his chest. Kayana ungloved her left hand and put her little finger on Rowan's neck, which caused his skin to turn white. He was still alive, but couldn't move. Her right hand was also ungloved, and she placed it near his face and stared the teachers down. The teachers yelled and moved toward her, but Kayana's eyes flashed white and they instinctively shrunk back, even Praetor Mantus.

"Come closer and I'll take the rest of his life away," she said.

The teachers kept their distance.

"Rowan is under the spell of demons," said Kayana. "Perhaps you all are, perhaps not. Either way, I fear for this Academy."

"Tell me, child," asked Praetor Mantus, laughing nervously, "Why would *you* fear for this Academy?"

"Because you're weak-minded," said Kayana, motioning towards Rowan. "You follow the likes of *him* and imprison the only ones who can save you."

"And I take it," said Praetor Mantus, "that you *Horsemen* are the only ones who can save us?"

"Perhaps not," said Kayana. "I don't know if you're worth saving."

Praetor Mantus's eyes flashed black and stared at Kayana.

"Kill Rowan if you wish, Kayana, but we will not—"

"I will not *kill* him," said Kayana. "Someone else will do that. Be it on the battlefield, in joust for a king, or in duel for a perceived slight, his destiny is *to die*. *That* is all he's good for, at least to the likes of Praetor Mantus."

Kayana got up close to Rowan's ear and spoke to him while he still seized.

"I've been in your dreams, Rowan, and I've seen your demons," said Kayana. "And I want them to listen to me now."

Kayana's eyes turned white and she drew even closer to Rowan's ear.

"I don't care for the boy whom you inhabit, this is true, but I won't punish him," said Kayana. "He was a fool before, *perhaps*, but you've made him a puppet who knows not what he does. So listen to me; when I return to your dreamscape castle I won't hide this time, nor will I come under the protection of disguise. I'll come with an army one score bigger than yours and ten score fiercer. I'll shred your soldiers in moments and then chain you in the dungeons that you have built yourself. Once you're there I'll spare no effort in getting every answer out of you that I wish. So hear my warning: *when I come you should surrender and tell me your secrets immediately, or your last moments will be filled with torments you have not thought possible.*"

Kayana took her finger off Rowan and he spasmed back to life and began gasping for breath. Kayana put her gloves back on, placed her hands behind her back and turned to the gods around her.

"Now shackle my wrists and take me to Tartarus," she said. "I need time to think, and right now the silence of prison appeals to me."

/***/

Back in their quarters, Gunnar was walking around the common room and getting used to his healed body. Tommy explained the last few days to Gunnar, and Gunnar frowned.

"We have to act now," said Gunnar. "We have to break her out of prison soon, before they take the next step."

"What are they going to do?" asked Tommy.

"I don't know," said Gunnar. "But Kayana is in a vulnerable spot, and if just one of her jailors has been infected by the demons, we might never see her again. They may be flooding into Tartarus to kill her as we speak."

Gunnar opened the door.

"I'll be back in half an hour," he said. "Don't go anywhere."

/***/

Thirty minutes later he was back, reached into his pocket and pulled out a small blueprint of the Academy's floors.

"I stole this," said Gunnar, pointing to the map. "Tartarus is right there, on the second floor, far away from the Manitou and warriors' fields."

Gunnar studied the map for a minute and then looked out the window.

"Tommy, I need you to rescue Kayana from Tartarus," said Gunnar. "Can you do it?"

Tommy looked up and nodded. Gunnar went back to the blueprint.

"Tartarus is built for punishment, not for security," said Gunnar. "You'll be able to get her out. All you need to do is follow my instructions and get back to this floor; I'll take the plan from there. Just get us to the meeting point *here*."

Gunnar pointed to an area right outside the main lecture hall. *Hardly a discreet place to regroup,* thought Tommy.

"Trust me on this Tommy," said Gunnar. "Follow my instructions, and you'll be fine."

"What are you going to do?" asked Tommy.

"You bring Kayana here," said Gunnar, "and I'll take care of the rest."

/***/

Tommy waited for the lights to go off, turned on his night vision and descended the stairs in darkness. Gunnar knew where the

Academy's power was, and where the backup power was. He cut both. *They can reroute the power in thirty minutes*, Gunnar had said, *so be back here in twenty. Once you open her cell, Kayana will be able to take care of herself.*

Tommy descended the stairs quietly. He snuck by four Spartan guards mulling about in the stairwell, and then entered the second floor where Kayana was held.

He couldn't fully see the prison's setup; it was too dark to see farther than a few meters, but he could tell the prison was large. It seemed to be endless, like most of the places in the Academy. *They modeled it after the real Tartarus*, Gunnar had told him, *but this is a school, so they don't have prisoners. It's mostly empty now, save for some predatory animals they keep.*

Tommy didn't want to see any *predatory animals*; even some of the *forgotten, ugly creatures* that now worshipped him. He heard some growls, then looked around and saw a cage holding the Celtic Wildman that Gunnar had told him about. He saw a Spartan guard in front of the cage, completely unaware of Tommy's presence in the dark. Tommy looked into the cage and found that the Wildman wasn't growling; he was snoring. He was sleeping nude behind the Spartan guard, and for some reason he'd been completely shaved.

Tommy sneaked on from cell to cell, hoping each time that he'd see Kayana so that he could leave more quickly. He found her in the third cell; she was meditating, with only the whites of her eyes visible. She saw him instantly, even in complete darkness. Her eyes regained their color, and she pointed to the iron bars on the door in front of her.

Tommy looked around and saw that no one was guarding her cell, save for a Spartan guard in the distance who couldn't see them. Tommy carefully took out a metal bolt-cutter from his forearm's armor and placed it on the bars. He cut the metal bars slowly so as not to make a sound, and after cutting placed each piece carefully on the ground.

After ten minutes he'd made a space big enough for Kayana to crawl out. When she squeezed out of the space she stumbled into his arms; he caught her and she brushed him off, but still stayed close to him.

"Thank you," she whispered.

"Gunnar has a plan for us," Tommy whispered in return. "Follow me."

They turned to leave, and bypassed the Spartan guards; they had eight minutes before the light turned on again. They walked past the Wildman and he was awake. He sniffed them and started yelling, but still none of the Spartan guards noticed.

They were about to leave Tartarus when they ran into a solid being who seemed to materialize out of thin air. At first Tommy thought it was Heracles, but when he saw the glowing red eyes, he knew it to be Kayana's teacher, Praetor Mantus.

"The innocent don't break out of prison at their first chance," said Praetor Mantus.

"The *unjustly* imprisoned will always break out," said Kayana. "You know this to be true."

Kayana pushed Tommy aside and stood in front of Praetor Mantus.

"I don't like you, Praetor, but I know you aren't a fool," said Kayana. "You know as well as I do that we aren't guilty of any wrongdoing. And you know that the only thing that will keep this Academy from destruction is us."

Praetor Mantus floated back and forth, gliding on air and contemplating what Kayana had said. His dark robe swayed outward and seemed as if it would swallow them both, and his fiercely glowing eyes suggested that he could turn them to dust if he so chose. He came in close to examine them, and then exhaled his icy-cold breath against Tommy's helmet.

"If you should reach the surface, keep your suit on, Alderon," said Praetor Mantus. "Your intentions are noble, but you can still cause plagues."

Tommy nodded and then Praetor Mantus got out of the way and pointed to the exit.

"You're both expelled," he said. "Now go. Leave this place before they turn on the lights."

"Expelled?" asked Tommy. "We cannot be …"

Tears began to well up in Tommy's eyes, but Kayana dug her uncovered fingers into his left glove and grabbed hold of his bare hand. The emotion seemed to fall from him, and his tears dried up.

"It's fine," said Kayana.

"Now go!" screamed Praetor Mantus.

Both Tommy and Kayana ran.

/***/

They bounded up the stairs, quickly but quietly. The Spartan guards had been called to alert and they were amassing everywhere. The guards had brought weapons too; guns and lances that would certainly cut through Tommy's suit.

Though he was still thinking of Praetor Mantus's expulsion, the adrenaline was kicking in and all he wanted to do was get to Gunnar's meeting point. They tiptoed through the stairs quietly, barely grazing the guards. Kayana took the lead and gracefully jumped from step to step, holding Tommy back when a mass of guards shuffled past. Tommy was glad to see that Kayana had put her gloves back on; he just wanted to leave quietly and didn't want anyone to get hurt.

Tommy got to the first floor and opened the door to the main courtyard. They were a hundred meters from their goal; Tommy had set Gunnar's meeting point on his forearm's monitor. Kayana held him back again; he heard the din of another mass of Spartans between them and the goal. Tommy and Kayana were plotting their path when the generator whirred and the lights turned on, all at once.

There were a hundred Spartan mercenaries in the room, as well as Heracles, Verminus, and Charon. After a moment of confusion, the Spartans turned their weapons on Tommy, and Heracles walked up to him. He stood above Tommy, nearly twice his height and three times his breadth.

"Where's Kayana, Tommy?" asked Heracles.

"What?" asked Tommy.

"Where's Kayana?"

Tommy looked around and she was gone. *The lights turned on and she disappeared into the shadows,* thought Tommy.

"Follow me," whispered Kayana.

"Where?" he whispered, under his breath.

"Just follow me."

Heracles came closer to Tommy, and Tommy backed away.

"Tommy, we have to know what's been happening," said Heracles.

"Do as he says, Thomas, and we can work this all out," said Verminus in a calm voice.

"I've been ... expelled," said Tommy.

"What?" asked Verminus.

"We've all been expelled," said Kayana, appearing from his

shadow. "Now leave us be."

Kayana took her gloves off and put her hands out; she then disappeared again.

"Leave us be," she said, cloaked in invisibility. "Clear a path for Tommy to rejoin his comrades or I'll start killing at random, touching necks until the life is drained from all of you."

Heracles thought for a moment, and then smiled.

"Stand down, Spartans," he said. "Do as she says."

The Spartans cleared a path towards Gunnar, Saoirse and Kross. They were standing by the elevator. Tommy walked towards Gunnar, rejoined them, and turned around. Heracles looked at Gunnar and spoke.

"You have nowhere to go," said Heracles.

"Precisely," said Gunnar.

Gunnar motioned for his team to go inside. After the team was in, Gunnar took a weapon out from his back pocket. He pressed the button and the elevator door began to close. He opened up the elevator's control board and pressed a few buttons.

"It's on manual override right now," whispered Gunnar. "They can't stop us."

"You won't get far!" yelled a voice as the door shut.

Tommy wanted to go back to the Academy and talk; he still felt the situation could be resolved if they just explained everything. But it was too late; the elevator was moving upwards and they were headed towards the surface.

The ride was bumpy, but during a lull Gunnar addressed the group.

"We had no choice but to leave this place," said Gunnar. "And after we reach Hellenica, we must leave its walls and hide."

"Hide where?" asked Tommy.

"I don't know," said Gunnar, "but it must be somewhere deep within the conurbation. Whoever has infected the Academy knows our intentions now, and will spare no expense in hunting us."

PART III

DAGON AND THE MERMAID

THE TRIAL

Saoirse looked out the window from their hiding place in the Yōkai district. The room was filthy and sparse, with a table, four chairs, a mattress that smelled of sweat, and not much else. They were on the seventh floor of a muggy, dilapidated tenement, the third of seven on that block alone. *They'll find us here,* she thought, *but not soon.*

Tommy and Gunnar were standing over the dirty table, poring over the information that Bes had sent them. Bes knew little more than they did, so he sent them all that he knew about the conurbation, and all he knew about the possible whereabouts and motives of the Mermaid. Kayana isolated herself into the corner to meditate, and when Gunnar asked her to help them she disagreed.

"What do I have to do with a Mermaid?" she said. "Why should I care about saving an Academy which has spurned us out?"

"You said yourself you want to defeat the demons," said Gunnar.

"I can do this without solving this little mystery," said Kayana.

"No you can't," said Gunnar. "You might clear one Spartan's head of demons, perhaps two. But sooner or later they'll get you. You can win a battle, but to win the war we need to know the root of our problems."

Kayana thought for a moment and then let her eyes turn white. She stared back at the corner and resumed her meditation.

"That's her way of agreeing with you," said Tommy.

"Good," said Gunnar. "Now, the Mermaid is the root of this struggle. She told the King Basilisk to attack us; we need to find her, and find out *why*. She may not be our enemy, but she's the key to understanding why the demons have invaded the Academy."

Gunnar thought for a moment, and then looked at Saoirse.

"What do you know of Mermaids?" he asked. "Anything, anything at all?"

"Every once in a while one came to Elysia," said Saoirse. "There's more than one of them, so we have to find out which one spoke to the King Basilisk."

"True," said Gunnar. "What else?"

"They're charming," said Saoirse. "They have their own language; the average mortal can kind of understand it, but kind of not. It brings a mystique and an intimacy to whomever they speak with."

"Could one of them want to destroy us?" asked Gunnar. "Or want to destroy anything?"

"No," said Saoirse, "they're not built for that."

Gunnar studied the sheets Bes sent, and then brought out an article.

"Here," he said, pointing to a clipping, "Bes told me to look at this. Two gods, Dagon and Poseidon, are currently at war with each other over a clutch of Mermaids found in a disputed territory; I don't know anything about it, but it looks promising. I'll stay here and study the conurbation; Saoirse, you need to investigate it."

"Me?" asked Saoirse.

"Yes," said Gunnar. "Hellenica has sent Spartans to look for us, and Tommy, myself and Kayana stick out too much. But if you dye your hair and leave your hyaena with us, you'll look like just another girl from Elysia."

"All right," said Saoirse, "but you're sending me to a *war*? I'm not suited for bloodshed—"

"Not *that* kind of war," said Gunnar with a laugh. "Dagon and Poseidon are blood enemies to be sure, but their battlefield in this matter takes a different shape."

Gunnar put an article in front of Saoirse. It spoke of Dagon, the god of the docks, and Poseidon, the god of the ocean. Their latest skirmish was indeed over a clutch of Mermaids, but their war wasn't with weapons. They had been waging an ongoing war *in court*.

/***/

Saoirse sat in the courtroom with dyed black hair, feeling like a new woman. For good measure she had tinted her skin pale and wore thick glasses that their Yōkai landlord had given her, but she still felt a bit naked without her friends and her hyaena. As she listened to Dagon's counsel speak, she realized that this was the first time in her life that she'd ever been alone.

Dagon, Babylonian god of the docks, dressed in a soft-shouldered suit to lessen the impact of his enormous height. He had green scales, a small bony fin that ran over the top of his head like a Mohawk, and the face of a water lizard. His enormous frame and scaly appearance reminded Saoirse of a cross between Heracles and Sobek, but Dagon was clearly doing everything he could to look like a normal member of society. His tailored suit and good posture made him less of a monster and more of a man, and he smiled quite a bit, making him look almost friendly. He had an army of lawyers whispering into his ear at every moment, and no matter what they said he grinned and nodded his head in quiet agreement. On the other side of the aisle sat but a single court-appointed lawyer; Poseidon was not even there.

Dagon's head lawyer, a woman named Omarosa, was the first to present her closing argument. She had the tanned skin and lean frame of a Babylonian dock-worker, but she was dressed professionally in a grey business suit, wire-rimmed glasses and thin black hair pulled up into a tight bun. Saoirse leaned in to listen as Dagon's counsel faced the judge.

"Your Honor," said Omarosa, "I would first like to reiterate my client's *absolute commitment and reverence* to the law of the conurbation. First and foremost, my client Dagon is present, whereas the defendant Poseidon has chosen *not to attend* after no less than *twenty-seven* court orders.

"But my client has more than a respect for the law on his side. He has the best interest of the conurbation at heart. His fisheries already provide 15 percent of the conurbation's economy, he's built twelve schools, and has an all-inclusive open-border policy that allows anyone citizenship in his district, regardless of their creed. And yes, this citizenship extends to *Mermaids* when they voluntarily swim into his waters to escape Poseidon's persecution.

"This progressive, open policy has made my client's district the jewel of our megacity. Crime in my client's district is the second lowest in the conurbation, trailing only Hellenica! And in regards to employment, my client's district is number one by far. If someone in the conurbation wants a job, my client takes it upon himself to *personally guarantee* that they'll find one if they migrate to his district. This promise is good even if the migrant is old, infirm or perhaps *even a Mermaid*.

"My client has signed every document you've asked him to sign, and made every payment necessary. You've asked my client more, and he's given you more; more tax revenue, more jobs, and more openness. And now only one thing stands in the way of his principles: a single god named Poseidon, a god who doesn't even bother to show up to defend his case. This is a god who mocks progress, who disdains the conurbation, who refutes the very legitimacy of *this court* with his repeated absence!"

Omarosa looked over at the lone public defender's desk on the other end of the aisle.

"But if he were here, I would ascertain that all Poseidon would say would be *No*. *No* to progress, *no* to freedom, and *no* to allowing his Mermaids to move wherever they wish. *No* to the conurbation whenever they need food, and *no* to showing up to this court to defend whatever principles he has.

"It's up to this court to decide what we want for our society, for our children. Do we want a more open economy, more schools and easier migration? Or do we want to say *no*, just because?

"The choice is clear, and we ask this court to allow Councilman Dagon's proposed *and completely transparent* request to allow the refugee Mermaids to stay in his district. Don't say *no*. Say *yes*."

Omarosa sat down and whispered into Dagon's ear, and Dagon smiled once more. The sharp teeth behind his scaled lips were perfectly white.

Poseidon's public defender, an overweight man named Geno Kardel, stood up, already sweating as he got out of his chair. He breathed heavily a few times, leaned against the chair, and then faced the judge.

"Your Honor," said Counselor Kardel, his face looking like a grey ham, "I don't apologize for my client's absence, but I do offer an explanation. As I've said before, he lives outside of the conurbation's jurisdiction. This has been documented time and time again; Poseidon lives in the open ocean and belongs to no one but himself. If *you* were sent a fabricated traffic ticket from a country not your own, would you honor it? Would you show up at the court that had issued it? No you wouldn't, for doing so would lend the ticket legitimacy.

"This is Poseidon's viewpoint. He asks for no more territory and doesn't expand, asks for no help and receives none; all he asks is to be left alone, to leave his oceans untouched and fertile. He has never asked for anything more, and never will.

"Dagon's counsel tells a tale of the openness, but what of the openness of Poseidon? Anyone is free to come and go on Poseidon's ocean, provided they don't claim any sea for themselves. Travel to Dagon's docks and you're expected to pay a 40 percent tax on everything you own before you can even rent an apartment! And true, any creed can live in Dagon's district, provided they don't pray to one of his many enemies. Poseidon allows all; he even gives safe passage to Dagon's ships on a regular basis.

"It just so happened that one of these ships wasn't just looking for fish one day; they were looking for Mermaids—"

"Objection!" yelled Omarosa. "My client isn't on trial here, especially not with hearsay."

"Sustained," said the judge. "Make your point without accusations, Counselor."

"Then Dagon's counsel fails to mention," said Counselor Kardel, "that he sent his fishermen to Poseidon's waters to take a clutch of Mermaids by force."

"Objection!" yelled Omarosa again. "These Mermaids *escaped* to our waters. This is proven."

"Sustained," said the judge. "You're on thin ice, Counselor Kardel."

"Understood," said Poseidon's lawyer. He drank a glass of water, and then wheezed a bit to catch his breath. "Then although we don't believe that the Mermaids fled Poseidon's grasp, we do understand that the court believes this. All we ask is that Councilman Dagon make good on his policy of openness, and drop the Mermaids into the open water, under a neutral third party's observance. Wherever they choose to swim, Poseidon will accept as their final home."

The court became quiet as the judge took the weight of deciding what to do.

"Would Dagon's counsel accept this proposal?" asked the judge.

Dagon and his lawyers commiserated for a moment, and then Omarosa spoke.

"We do not accept," said Omarosa. "For all we know, Poseidon could fill the water with sharks."

"They don't accept, Counselor Kardel," said the judge.

"My client's history would not suggest he would send *sharks*," said Poseidon's lawyer with a laugh. "That's ridiculous. And we don't understand why we can't let the Mermaids decide for themselves, with an independent arbiter."

"Will Dagon's counsel address the query?" asked the judge.

"Poseidon owns the ocean," said Omarosa. "As soon as we drop the Mermaids in there, if not sharks, he could send currents to sweep them down into his depths, or anything else. We have an independent arbiter in this court in *you*, Judge, and we will respect your decision."

"Then that's it," said the judge. "I'll decide in one hour's time."

/***/

Saoirse figured the verdict from the look on Dagon's face as he exited the courtroom. Reporters swarmed him and though his counsel tried to lead him away, Dagon stopped and spoke to the press.

"Justice has been served today," said Dagon. "Some Mermaids escaped the clutches of Poseidon and I gave them safe refuge, nothing more, and the court saw to respect their rights as free beings able to go where they wish. This isn't just a victory for me, but for the conurbation. Our society is falling apart, but *not my district*. Our whole world is factionalizing, but *not my district*. Crime and unemployment are on the rise, but come to *my district* and I'll give you a job and make sure no one messes with you while you're doing it. Good day, and I'll be at the docks!"

Dagon and his entourage left in a flurry to the waiting car at the bottom of the stairs. The reporters clamored for one more soundbite, but his car sped off and soon everyone began to disappear. Saoirse was about to walk away when she heard a craggly voice yell at her.

"I know who you are!" said the voice. "You're undercover."

She looked behind her and saw an incredibly old man, perhaps ninety. She didn't recognize him. *Am I that easy to spot?* she thought. *Could he be a Spartan guard under disguise?*

"Come here," he said.

Saoirse came near, keeping some distance in case someone sprang at her.

"You're a worshipper of Poseidon, just like me," said the old man. "Undercover."

Saoirse could tell that he was genuinely mistaken and didn't see her as a god.

"I'm not," she said with a smile.

"Ahhh, you and I are the only ones in the courtroom not wearing

Babylonian clothes, so I thought you were with me," he said. "Still, just the fact that you're not one of Dagon's henchmen gives us kinship. My name is Melicertes; *Mel* for short."

"I'm Saoirse," she said.

"Pleased to meet you," said the old man. "Yeah, it was a real show in there all right. Everyone in the court was on Dagon's payroll, including the judge; probably the court-appointed lawyer too!"

The old man coughed, and then spat on the courthouse steps.

"Dagon's public relations machine will always win out. They say his docks represent *progress*, but at what cost? His district brings the conurbation food, but puts more pollution into the air than all the other districts combined! There's no crime in his district, but that's because if you do anything to get in the way of his money, one of his goons will make you disappear in the middle of the night. There *are* murders there, don't you worry about that. Miss a tax payment and you've got a one-way ticket to the sea, and you won't return.

"I don't blame anyone for not following Poseidon; there's no profit in it. I've followed him my whole life and he's never helped me once."

"With all due respect Mr. Melicertes," asked Saoirse, "if he does—"

"Call me Mel," he said.

"Of course," said Saoirse. "So *Mel*, if your god doesn't help you, why *do* you follow Poseidon?"

"I wish I didn't have to," said the old man with a laugh, "but I must, for the conurbation. Dagon's council is right; our society is falling apart, but it's not Dagon that's keeping us from collapse, it's my god, Poseidon, though not even *he* knows it. Dagon sells the conurbation food, but the fish come from Poseidon's ocean. Poseidon sends rain, and his plankton cleanse the air of pollutants. If Poseidon were to disappear, we'd be in big trouble. It's my job to make sure he stays where he is; I've dedicated my life to it."

Saoirse paused for a moment and contemplated whether she could trust the old man Melicertes. Understanding animals came naturally to her, but humans took work. *Humans are simply sentient animals,* her teacher Manitou once told her. *Read them just as you'd read a wolf.*

She sensed she could trust Melicertes. He seemed genuine, and more, he seemed lonely. *If he wanted to tell my secrets,* thought Saoirse, *he'd have no one to whom to tell them. Couch your query so he does not think you insane, and see what he tells you.*

"Mr. Melicertes?" she asked.

"Mel," he said. "That's what I like to be called."

"Forgive me," said Saoirse. "Use of formal names is due to my training; I'm a reporter."

"A reporter!" he laughed. "Doing a story on *show trials*, I take it?"

"No," she said, "I'm investigating a rumor, a bizarre rumor that I don't fully understand. I'd love your thoughts on it."

"I've got nowhere else to go, darling," said the old man with a smile.

"There's a theory that Dagon captured the Mermaids to control them. One Mermaid made a deal with the King Basilisk to give him beauty in exchange for sending his basilisk children out to attack a certain ... district. After the basilisks bit members of that district, demons invaded their victims' dreams, causing some to go insane, and some to be controlled by an external force."

Saoirse thought that chain of events silly as it came out of her mouth, but noticed that Melicertes was nodding in agreement.

"Sounds like Dagon," he said.

"Really?" asked Saoirse.

She smiled but tempered her excitement and regained her reporter's composure.

"Go on," she said.

"Dagon pulls convoluted maneuvers like this all the time," said Melicertes. "He'll send gods to bribe mortals to build a labyrinth to trap a rival. He'll blackmail a nymph to lure an ordinary man away from his wife so that she'll miss a minor council vote. To the world he's just a thug, but he achieves his agenda through *schemes*. These schemes have so many steps that they're talked about by conspiracy nuts perhaps, but they're never traced back to him. And Dagon's strange plans always seem to end up working."

"What does he hope to achieve by sending demons into dreams?" asked Saoirse. "Demons tend not to be so controllable."

"Listen to me closely, child," said Melicertes, leaning in. "Whether he sends a tame Mermaid or a wild demon, Dagon has but one goal: *more*. More land, more ocean, more rights, more money, more worshippers and just ... *more*. When you get to the bottom of this rumor and find yourself tied to a chair, being interrogated by his Babylonian goons, remember that though his schemes are complicated he wants only one thing. His only agenda is *more*."

/***/

Saoirse draped a cloth over her head, put on her oversized dark glasses and crept back quietly through the Yōkai district. She looked odd, but in this district of Japanese spirits she was just another castout.

Gunnar was the one who had decided to hide them in the Yōkai. They could have gone to the Manitou or even fled the conurbation altogether, but Gunnar liked the central location of the Yōkai slums. It was close enough to explore the mystery wherever it led them, but bizarre enough for them to avoid notice.

Saoirse looked up at a half-decayed flophouse and saw some graffiti on the side, written in crude Yōkai pictographs. She understood a little of it from Elysia's language training.

Powerful gods never suffer, it said, *someone else always pays.*

Saoirse laughed; it was true. Powerful gods had struggles, to be sure, but they never seemed to bear the consequences. Poseidon might lose a rigged trial here and there, but he wouldn't *suffer* like the Yōkai. The Japanese Yōkai were gods, but weak gods, so weak that mortals often employed them. *They're esoteric forest sprites with unclear powers,* thought Saoirse. *They'll never escape this broken-down district.*

Saoirse realized that the only entity that had an interest in protecting these creatures was the Academy. *They saved me from a life as a Hetaera,* thought Saoirse. *Perhaps if I save the Academy, it will one day help save these Yōkai.*

Saoirse stopped at the stoop of their tenement; it rose upwards endlessly into the grey haze. She entered the building and the Tanuki landlady came out with some cookies and smiled at her, pointing cheerfully towards the attic where the other Horsemen were housed. She was a raccoon-like Yōkai, but her fur was mottled, filthy, and smelled of urine; she was cheerful but oblivious to the ways of modern life. The Tanuki landlady smiled and said *"Up there,"* as if it were news that the Horsemen were in the attic. Saoirse felt warmth from the Tanuki landlady, but knew warmth wouldn't conceal them. If Spartan guards came searching for them, the Tanuki landlady would simply smile, offer cookies, and say *"Up there."*

Saoirse went upstairs to their safe house, and then went upstairs once more to reach the attic. She gave a coded knock and Gunnar let her in, soon followed by Kross, who jumped on her and started to whine. She imagined his anxiety; what would it be like to be thrown into a world where no one but your master shares your language? She pet

Kross and hugged him.

Don't leave more, he said. *Don't leave more.*

She told Gunnar of the trial and then of the old man. Gunnar shot a knowing glance to Tommy and then sat at the table in the middle of the room. Gunnar spread out a map of the conurbation and pointed to a far corner of Dagon's docks.

"Dagon keeps his Mermaids here, in his aquarium," said Gunnar. "We're going to break into it and question them. My responsibility is to get us in and out, but Saoirse, can you speak their language?"

"With time," she said. "Mermaids don't have a hidden agenda, but they always seem to speak in riddles and metaphors. It will just take time."

"We'll get you there, but we might not have time," said Gunnar. "Dagon loves his aquarium, and most of all his Mermaids. Some alarm somewhere might go off."

"It will take time," said Saoirse. "Mermaids are odd …"

"If she needs more time, Gunnar," said Tommy, "we can give her more time."

Gunnar nodded at Tommy; they had a secret plan in case everything went badly.

Gunnar got Kayana to stop meditating and brought her over to the table. He pointed to Dagon's docks and then looked at the team.

"We'll enter Dagon's district in the cover of night; Spartan mercenaries aren't allowed there, so we won't need disguises. We'll find our way to the aquarium, break in, and the Mermaids will tell us what's happening, and perhaps even clear our name."

"What about my hyaena, Kross?" asked Saoirse. "Can we bring

him?"

"Dagon's district is a bizarre place; pet hyaenas patrolling the streets are not uncommon. He can come with us," said Gunnar. "As long as he can swim."

/***/

They left their tenement at sundown; the Tanuki landlady arranged a ride for them. It was a covered, half-broken rickshaw with a boy driver who looked to be twelve years old, but it concealed them well. Citizens of the other districts were so accustomed to ignoring Yōkai rickshaws that Saoirse and her group were all but invisible.

The rickshaw driver called back to them and said that they were going on one of the long-distance trains. Saoirse peeked outside and saw that workers were loading the entire rickshaw on the back of the train. *They ignore the Yōkai so much that we could travel a thousand kilometers without them pulling back this curtain. We're beyond invisible.*

They rode on the train for an hour. Kross kept asking Saoirse where they were going, but Gunnar bid the hyaena to be quiet.

"We'll be able to speak freely once we're in Dagon's district," said Gunnar. "Dagon's greedy, but if you aren't hurting his bottom line, you can say whatever you want."

They eventually got off the train and were ordered by Dagon's border patrol to exit the rickshaw.

"It's okay," said Gunnar, "they'll let us through; do everything they say."

Two of Dagon's patrolmen chattered in Babylonian with each other, one with an Algonquin accent and one with the accent of Hellenica. They inspected Tommy's suit and allowed him through without making him take it off. They gave Saoirse's hyaena a once-over and let him through. Kross actually said *Thanks* in his tongue, and though the guards did a double-take, they simply found it funny. Kayana and Saoirse went through easily, and after finding that Gunnar had brought eight weapons, they let him through and gave him the weapons back without even registering them.

"Punishment is severe in Dagon's district, so severe that he doesn't care what you bring in as long as you don't use it," said Gunnar. "Even Zeus would be afraid to let his lightning loose here."

They walked through the gates and saw that Dagon's district was bustling with a continuous stream of activity, from the train station on to the horizon. *It's midnight,* thought Saoirse, *and still the streets are filled.*

"Dagon's docks run continuously," said Tommy. "We studied them on Lepros. Fishermen come in at every hour, and the fish are processed and sent out within five hours of landing. The cannery has three shifts of workers."

Saoirse looked around and saw workers just starting their day and outgoing workers headed to the pubs. *The pubs are probably owned by Dagon too,* she thought.

They walked by shops owned by ex-Celts, Spartans, Apaches, and even immigrants from the Yōkai district. There were tea-houses, bakeries, medicine-huts and shops that seemed to sell just about everything. Every shop prominently displayed a picture of Dagon in the window.

This place is odd, to be sure, thought Saoirse, *but all come here willingly, and then stay. The Yōkai shopkeepers are clean, without mottled hair. This place is disquieting, but Dagon's society isn't without its draw. Everyone who comes here will have a "place."*

They came to the edge of the main business district and then got in a line for water taxis. Dagon had flooded some streets to make canals and the quickest way to get around was by boat, even if you were going inland.

They got on their water taxi and asked the driver to take them to the aquarium.

"It's closed," he said.

"We know," said Saoirse. "We just want to see what it looks like at night."

The driver smiled and sped off with them. They cut through the canals quickly and noisily; the motor ran on a crude diesel and pumped grey smoke into the night sky. The water beneath had a sharp smell, like sulfur and meat, and was blacker than the night around them.

Their water taxi drove on for twenty minutes and soon they were far from the main docks. They passed by the shipyard where goods were imported and exported; the port was gargantuan, with hundreds of vessels, none of them idle. They were docking, unloading, loading or leaving. *This city is a machine that runs forever,* thought Saoirse.

"You guys are visitors, no?" said the water-taxi driver in a thick Elysian accent.

Saoirse recognized him; he was a driver from her home island. She knew he wouldn't identify her, for without the makeup, silken clothes and deferential smile of the Hetaerae, she was unrecognizable. But her heart still went out to him. *He must have lost everything when Elysia burned,* she thought. *It's good that he's found a home here.*

"The fisheries and canneries make money here, to be sure," said the driver, "but the ports are the *real* moneymakers. They built this city. Anything we buy from foreign lands comes through there. Your shirt, my shoes, and probably this water taxi were boxed in a ship there at one time or another."

The port is why Dagon doesn't need Hellenica, thought Saoirse. *The port is why the courts will always say yes to him.*

Saoirse looked at the water-taxi driver and tried to get a sense of him. She felt that he was indeed trustworthy. *But still*, she thought, *look at the pictures of Dagon on the dashboard. Look at the way he talks of this place; he has the zeal of a convert. The denizens here either love or fear Dagon, but ultimately their allegiance is to him. We have limited time here before someone reports us for some sort of "crime" here.*

They made the water taxi come to a stop a kilometer away from the aquarium. Like the rest of the district, the aquarium was massive and brightly lit. Unlike the rest of the docks, it was *clean*. Half of it was inland and the other half was built into the ocean, with nets containing the creatures that lived in the saltwater.

"Fisheries, canneries, ports, they make the money," said the driver, "but the aquarium is Dagon's first love. It's the one place that closes here; he likes his creatures to rest."

Gunnar paid the water-taxi driver with some money that Bes had sent them, and the driver sped off. Gunnar waited until the driver was far away, and then talked.

"The aquarium will be closed, but there's a way in. It's near the ocean side," he said. "It's a little dangerous, but if we hurry we'll be okay."

Ten minutes later, they were near the ocean and saw what Gunnar was talking about. One of the tanks led out to the sea, and though the giant nets would hold whatever creature was inside, they were easy to climb for humans, even for Kross. They could hop the nets, swim in the tank and then reach the interior.

"Pretty easy to get in," said Tommy.

"No one would want to go in the tank; there's a predatory fish in there," said Gunnar.

"What kind of fish?" asked Saoirse.

"A big, primitive one," said Gunnar. "I don't know its name. All I know is that it's so primitive that your communication is largely useless, Saoirse, and though it lives in the deep its mind is too dull to befriend you, Tommy. If we go one at a time though, we'll be fine. The creature only recognizes large prey."

Gunnar was the first to jump in the water, and swam to the other side in less than a minute. He motioned them forward and Kayana reluctantly went on, with Tommy closely behind her. They motioned Saoirse to go forward, but she was having a difficult time getting Kross to go in the water.

Come on, she said, *we must go forward.*

There is whale, said Kross.

Saoirse looked in the distance and saw that he was right; there was something that looked like a whale in this tank. It was hanging at the far edge, oblivious to them.

It's far away and sleeping, said Saoirse. *It won't wake if we're quiet.*

They jumped in the water quietly and started to shiver immediately; it was cold. She swam through the water quickly, and heard strange sounds while she was under. They weren't whale sounds though; just odd snapping noises that cut through the water. Saoirse was then hit by a massive wave and was pressed against the nets. The nets were made of rope and steel, and she was stunned for a moment under the water, not knowing which way was up. She felt a bite in her shoulder, but it didn't break the skin; she opened her eyes to see it was Kross bringing her to the surface.

Hurry, he said, *whale is coming.*

They swam harder and soon made it to the edge. Gunnar pulled them onto the surface and then directed them away from the water.

"Maintain a space of fifteen meters from this tank's edge at all times," said Gunnar.

They went twice that distance, and Saoirse saw the whale-like creature swim near the water's edge. She couldn't see what it was, but it was massive and incredibly fast.

"What is it?" asked Saoirse.

Gunnar motioned Tommy to speak.

"It's a Megalodon," said Tommy. "An extinct species of shark, several times bigger than the sharks today."

"That makes no sense," said Saoirse. "If it's extinct …"

"Then Dagon's been experimenting with genetic engineering," said Gunnar.

Saoirse saw the creature bolt back towards the far end of its tank; its massive back skimmed the surface and she saw the dorsal fin cut through the air, as tall as a man. *Whether he's been experimenting with genetic engineering or not, he's succeeding at whatever he's done*, said Saoirse. *He's truly a god to rival Hellenica.*

/***/

They walked through Dagon's aquarium in awe. It seemed to hold every type of water creature there was: salmon swimming in freshwater streams, translucent jellyfish glowing behind illuminated glass, and even killer whales swimming in huge, circular tanks.

There was marine life that Saoirse thought to be extinct like the Megalodon; she saw sea scorpions almost three meters long and giant turtles the size of vans. There were tanks dedicated to very small fish; some appeared almost empty. And there were enclosures that held large creatures and extended deep into the ocean. Saoirse saw that one of these long tanks had several monitors attached showing that it housed blue whales, most of them a hundred kilometers out.

"Don't get too lost in here," whispered Gunnar. "We have a mission to do."

They wandered for thirty minutes. Saoirse heard the chatter of Mermaids and followed it; she eventually came to a large, empty tank.

"They're on top," said Kayana. "Up there."

Saoirse looked up and saw the shadow of three Mermaids swimming concentric circles around a reef, twenty meters above. They climbed stairs to the top and saw two more Mermaids lounging on the land Dagon had made for them. It was immaculately constructed, with a rocky jetty and even an abandoned boat moored nearby. When they saw Saoirse's group, the other three Mermaids came swimming to the top and started to giggle. They were all beautiful, with scaled tails that reflected brilliant colors, even in the moonlight. The Mermaids each had silken hair that came out of the water flowing and dry, and their faces, though not quite human, were stunningly attractive. Their inordinately large eyes were built to see under the water, and their dainty fingers were connected by webbing. The skin on their upper bodies was smooth and shiny, like that of dolphins. One of the Mermaids had shells tied into her hair.

"Your turn, Saoirse," said Gunnar. "Tell them what we want."

Saoirse walked forward and bowed. The Mermaids giggled some more.

"Hello," said Saoirse.

"Why're ye here?" asked the Mermaid with shells in her hair.

"Excuse me?" asked Saoirse.

"Why're ye here," said the Mermaid. "Why're ye come? Ye come t'save us? Or ye come t'hold us more?"

The Mermaids then clicked, squeaked and laughed amongst themselves some more. *They speak in their own language of clicks, mostly underwater,* thought Saoirse, *but to our kind they make up a language as they go along.*

"We come t'save," said Saoirse. "We're the Horsemen."

"The Horsemen—aye!" squealed one, and then the rest giggled in harmony.

"The tall, he's the stallion," said another Mermaid. "And the cute boy in the suit, he's the plow-pony."

Gunnar and Tommy blushed, and the Mermaids laughed more at that.

"Ye're the show horse, and the pale girl is the mare, the *night-mare*," said another Mermaid. "The Horsemen, come t'save, come t'save us! Four Horsemen of the poco-, the pahkko—"

"The pocky-lips!" squealed one. "Four Horsemen of the *pocky-lips*, come t'save us!"

They laughed at the word *pocky-lips* for awhile, and then Saoirse spoke again. *Speak calmly,* she thought, *or they'll break into hysterics once more.*

"One of ye has spoken with a basilisk," said Saoirse, "and the basilisk 'as given us harm. Much harm."

"Harrrm," said a Mermaid, "From the *bazer-elk*."

"Yes," said Saoirse, "one of ye gave the bazer-elk beauty, and in exchange he attacked our school. Tried t'have us killed."

The Mermaids chattered amongst themselves once again. They

started clacking incessantly, and then one of them made a noise like a dolphin. Soon they all joined in. *They're not laughing, at least,* thought Saoirse.

"Our sis-tarr talked to this bazer-elk," said a Mermaid. "Dagon sent our sis-tarr to talk to this bazer-elk."

"The bazer-elks mayhaps be mean," said the another Mermaid, "but he not hurt our sis-tarr, she mak'him beautiful."

"Is she with ye now?" asked Saoirse.

"Nay," said another Mermaid, "she nay with us now."

"Where is she?"

The Mermaids spoke quietly amongst themselves, and then one stopped and pointed at the ocean beyond the glass.

"She 'scaped," said the Mermaid, "to island far yonder. After our sis-tarr talked to this bazer-elk, Dagon wanted her *kilt*."

"This island," said Gunnar, interrupting, "can you show us where it is? Can you take us there?"

"Yes, stallion," said another Mermaid, "if ye free us. Dagon put us in this prizin."

Kross nuzzled Saoirse's arm and then whined a bit to get her full attention.

What is it? she said. *And make it quick because—*

Wolves here, said Kross.

Wolves? she asked.

Wolves.

"What's he saying?" asked Gunnar.

"He says there are wolves around here," said Saoirse.

"Wolves?" said Gunnar.

"The animal means *guards*," said Kayana. "I sense them too. They don't know where we are just yet, but they know there's been a break-in."

Gunnar looked around, and then motioned everyone to be quiet. He looked to the floors beneath and Saoirse followed suit. She saw a man swinging his flashlight and then looked through the aquarium to see several more men patrolling outside.

"We're trapped," whispered Gunnar. "Kayana, is there any way out that you can see?"

Kayana meditated for a moment and then looked at Gunnar.

"We're surrounded, and they have more guns than we," said Kayana. "The only way out is for me to hide in the shadows and take the guards' lives, one by one. I warn you, that option should not be."

"Agreed," said Gunnar. "That's not our way. That *will never* be our way."

Gunnar thought for a bit, and then jumped in the tank with the Mermaids. They giggled a bit, but he quieted them with a finger to his lips. He checked out the surroundings, then came back and hid with Saoirse. He spoke to one of them, and she nodded. He soon came back to the group.

"We're going to free them," whispered Gunnar. "And they're going to take us far away from here, to the island where their sister is held. Follow me, and Tommy ... take out the glass-cutter that I know you have in your suit."

They all jumped into the tank, and then snuck into the boat placed on the rocks. It was small and wooden, but its hull was wide and could hold them all comfortably. Though Dagon had built it only for show, with two oars and a shallow hull, it floated. Gunnar unmoored it and then brought it close to the glass. Tommy took out a small knife from his forearm and used it to etch a large hole in the glass. The glass didn't break, but it started to leak water. The Mermaids giggled one last time and then disappeared underneath the surface. After a few moments there was a *thump* from underneath the boat, and it started to move towards the hole in the glass. Gunnar pushed the hole out until water flooded out into the sea outside. They pushed the boat out smoothly; though the tank was three stories high, the top of the water was at sea level.

The Mermaids continued to push the boat out into the ocean, and Gunnar had the team lie flat on the bottom; there were a few guards on the docks with flashlights, still oblivious to their presence. The Mermaids picked up speed, and soon their boat was cruising at a decent clip. It wasn't that fast, but it was quiet, and when they cut through the aquarium's outer nets, they barely made a sound.

/***/

Dagon's crew noticed the missing Mermaids twenty minutes later. The lighthouses on the coast lit up and they heard the faint whine of an alarm signal. They saw several speedboats travel from the coast and even saw a few helicopters travel from the island.

"We have no power, no radio and no lights," said Gunnar, "so we'll be able to hide a little bit more."

"What will happen when they catch up to us?" asked Tommy.

"We fight," said Gunnar.

"There's hundreds of them," said Tommy. "Perhaps we should—"

"We're gods, they're mortals," interrupted Gunnar. "We fight."

Saoirse peeked above the boat's edge and saw the speedboats

searching a few kilometers from them. The Mermaids were pushing their boat surprisingly fast, but it was nothing compared to one of the Dagon's cruisers. If they were spotted they'd be surrounded in a matter of minutes. Saoirse put her head down and tried to be quiet, but couldn't resist looking back. Every time she peeked over the edge, the helicopter got closer and another speedboat had been launched into the water.

"We've got a few minutes left," said Gunnar. "When they come we've got to board one of their vessels, and then take it over. Kayana, you touch people, just enough to stun them. Tommy, you use your suit, and Saoirse, have your hyaena attack them. We'll take the boat and then—"

They saw a blinding light and felt a blast of air from above; they looked up to see the helicopter hovering above them. They looked back to see five speedboats now surrounded them, slowed to the Mermaids' pace. Each speedboat had five armed guards with their weapons out, and the wind blasted them as the helicopter sank down until it was a few meters above the boat.

Gunnar tried to bark out instructions, but it was just too loud. The helicopter extended a ramp down to their boat, and several armed men prepared themselves to board. Gunnar had pulled out several weapons, Kross was growling and Kayana had removed her gloves. *If we take out these men, then what?* thought Saoirse. *This is not our way.*

One of the men was listening to something on his headset, nodded, and then went back into the helicopter. The helicopter closed its hatch flew back into the sky. The men in the boats holstered their guns and decreased their speed. The helicopter started flying away, and soon all the boats were headed back to the island. Dagon's lighthouse relaxed its alarm and dimmed its lights. Soon it was completely quiet again.

"What happened?" said Tommy with a laugh.

"I have no idea," said Gunnar with a smile.

"We're near the island that holds the Mermaid," said Kayana, "and we're no longer in Dagon's territory."

"But they just left without a fight," asked Gunnar.

"I sensed fear in them," said Kayana. "They fear the members of this island."

Saoirse looked around and saw the surrounding sea littered with the island's own boats; their vessels were modernly built, with powerful electric engines and heavy weaponry on each bow. She then looked at the land ahead; it looked familiar. Gunnar turned pale and looked at her for confirmation.

"This is where our Mermaid is being kept," said Saoirse. "And they'll give us safe harbor; *all* of us. They know me well here; this is the island of the Amazons."

THE BOMB

Gunnar looked for a way out, but there was none. The Mermaids powering the boat were now lounging on the beach, and even if he had a working vessel, the Amazon ships behind them had already made a blockade. His pulse quickened and he tried to quash the deep sense of dread that grew within his chest. He made a mental inventory of the weapons he had on him, not to fight the Amazons per se, but to use on himself. *Don't find yourself captive by Amazons*, his Spartan teachers would say. *Die nobly, or die like a coward if need be. But don't find yourself alive and in their clutches, for they do horrible things.*

"We must leave this place," said Gunnar under his breath as the Amazons started to surround them.

"We should not," said Kayana. "We should be here."

"We need to leave," said Gunnar.

"No," said Kayana. "This is our place to be."

Gunnar saw that he was the only one amongst his group that was visibly frightened; the rest of his team was glad to be saved, and the Amazons grinned in return with weapons undrawn. *I can't abandon my team*, he thought, *but if the Amazons corner me, I'll not hesitate to do what needs to be done.*

Gunnar could see a small building in the forest ahead, and beyond that, several paved roads. The Amazons had clearly embraced modernization. *But they still keep to their old ways,* thought Gunnar. *Deep in their prisons, they're just as cruel as they've been for centuries.*

Two Amazon speedboats came up to the shore behind them and landed on the beach. They shined their light on the Horsemen from behind and two soldiers came out of each boat and pointed their weapons at Gunnar. From the building ahead, three more Amazons came out. The lead one was a large, muscular girl, taller and broader than even Alkippe back at the Academy.

"My name is *Orithia*," said the Amazon. "State who you are, and why these Mermaids have brought you to our shores."

The group was quiet; they were used to Gunnar leading, but he couldn't open his mouth. *Silence is on my side,* he thought. *If I speak, they'll recognize my accent.* He nodded towards Saoirse and she stepped forward.

"We're from the Academy," said Saoirse. "The Amazon nation took me from Elysia and sent me there, with President Hippolyta personally arranging it. We're seeking a sister of these Mermaids who is taking refuge here. She's brought a course of action that may lead to the destruction of the Academy that you yourselves have helped build. We don't believe the Mermaid to be at fault; we just want to know who has tricked her into doing such a nefarious deed."

Orithia went up close to them and looked them up and down. She had two guards with her; one was short and athletic, the other was even taller and broader than Orithia and had yellow, broken teeth that looked like they belonged in a dying ape. Orithia had the guards frisk them for weapons. The short one frisked Saoirse, finding nothing, and then frisked Tommy, not knowing what to do with his suit. Orithia waved her on.

The tall one started to frisk Kayana, but Kayana blocked her before she reached exposed skin.

"I wouldn't advise you to touch me, ogress," said Kayana. "If you do so, you'll die within a fortnight."

Orithia nodded to the tall Amazon and she left Kayana alone. *They know exactly who we are*, thought Gunnar.

The big girl with bad teeth proceeded to frisk Gunnar. She was taller than he was, and though not as muscular, she was bulkier. Her yellowed mouth snarled as she frisked him, and her breath was atrocious. She found weapon after weapon in attachments on his pants, and soon there was a pile of guns, knives and sharp objects on the sand below.

"Is this all you have, warrior?" asked Orithia.

"Yes," said Gunnar, trying to hide his Spartan accent.

The big girl snarled once more.

"I know he has more," said the Amazon through her rotten teeth. "Beware this one."

Her voice was rough, lower than Gunnar's.

"No," said Orithia, "if they're from the Academy, we should give them the benefit of the doubt. We'll bring them in for questioning."

The hulking girl spat and walked away. The Amazons behind them kept their guns down but still surrounded them, and they all started to march deep into the island. Soon they were on paved roads, walking through the capital city that the Amazons had built. It was clean, modern and mostly uniform. *Ostentatious houses and displays of wealth were rare here*, thought Gunnar. *Being the alpha female holds little importance in Amazon society.* Women stared from their windows as they walked past, and little girls approached before running away giggling. Some of the younger girls cried in horror at the sight of Gunnar and Tommy.

"Apologies," said Orithia. "They've never seen a man before."

They've seen a man before, thought Gunnar. *When they were young they saw you kill their brothers and fathers in front of them.*

They walked out of the town and back into a forested area, but they were still on a paved road. The island was a lot more civilized than Gunnar thought it would be, but he still kept up his guard.

They walked deeper and deeper into the forest until they reached a small grey building; it was clearly the entrance to an underground bunker. Saoirse, Kayana, Kross and Tommy entered the building and went down the stairs without hesitation, but Gunnar balked. He'd heard about these bunkers in the Agoge. *Once you go in, you won't see the sun again,* his teachers told him. *You'll die in prison or end up in an "Amazon marriage." So don't go in.*

The concept of the *Amazon marriage* could have been myth, but it still scared Gunnar. If the Amazons caught a particularly strong, handsome or brave Spartan warrior, they'd keep him for breeding purposes. The Amazons didn't want their enemies to think of their island as a pleasure palace, so after they were done with the warrior they'd execute him in a particularly cruel way, and then send his body back to his homeland as proof.

"Go in," said the tall Amazon, her breath smelling of meat. "We have some questions for you."

She smiled, and her teeth glistened with yellow spittle. After he balked, she gave him a shove. He still didn't go into the bunker, and when she went to shove him again he pushed her aside and then threw her towards her comrades. They raised their weapons and started to yell. He knew their weapons were most effective at distance, so he came in close to them and disarmed the nearest one with a single move.

He used the guard as a shield, and then backed up.

"I'm not going to hurt anyone," said Gunnar, forgetting to hide his Spartan accent.

He shoved his hostage at the group and ran the other way, deeper into the forest. He heard some yells, and then some laughter. Then he heard quiet. It was dark in the woods, but still well lit; the island was so well developed that the city's glow cast light everywhere. He thought about his next move; he'd have to get to the beach and capture one of their boats. But where would he go? Dagon most likely wanted him dead, as did the Academy.

Then die on your feet, he thought. *Just do not die here.*

He heard a rustling behind him and was surprised to see the massive Amazon giving chase. She seemed too bulky to have stamina, but there she was, matching him stride for stride. She seemed to know the woods better than he did, so every turn he made, she seemed to gain ground.

After five minutes of running, he realized he wouldn't be able to shake her. *You'll have to fight*, he thought, *but don't kill her. If you kill an Amazon on their own island, they'll do such bad things that your legend of suffering will become a warning for centuries to come.* He reached into a hidden compartment on his upper thigh and got platinum knuckles. One punch would knock her out, and he'd pull it to make sure he did no further damage.

He turned around to face her, but instead of stopping she ran full speed into him, tackling him against a tree. He felt the wood crack with the impact of her force. She pushed him down, grappling with skill that he'd never seen before, not even in the pit. She left him prostrate on the floor and started punching him. He held up his hands to block, but it was no use; her punches found a way to hit his face and body, and when they didn't they pushed his hands into his face.

He finally managed to dodge a punch, and used the momentary momentum to punch her in the stomach with his platinum knuckles. She fell off a bit and he pushed her away, and then got to his feet. She coughed a bit and then smiled.

"I've waited my whole life to fight a Spartan one on one," she said. "Please give me everything you have."

Gunnar stood his ground and she attacked him low, trying to grapple once more. He dodged her dive, and then tried to punch her in the back of the head, but missed. She moved her feet around and tripped him up, then jumped on his back and put him in a choke hold. He tried to get out, but her technique was flawless; she leveraged her body against his so that he couldn't move. He struggled and struggled, but couldn't gain any traction. He was beginning to black out and put everything he had into one last move; he would push her to his left and throw her off.

He tried the move, but she fell under him, still gripping his neck. He felt his arms go weak for a moment, and then he blacked out.

/***/

Gunnar woke up to a sharp kick into his midsection. He went to protect himself, but soon realized that he was shackled. He looked up to see the yellow-toothed girl towering over him and wearing his platinum knuckles.

"Never thought I'd capture my own Spartan, let alone *the* Gunnar Redstone," she said. "My name's Pyrgomache. Time to go underground; we've been waiting for you for a long time."

Pyrgomache punched him in the temple, and once again all he knew was darkness.

/***/

Gunnar woke up, bound to a chair and naked except for a cloth across his waist. He was in a modern-looking room with a flat-screen monitor at one end and a commode at the other. *This is a holding cell at least*, he thought, *not a place of torture.* Still, he remembered that Amazons would do horrible things to unconscious Spartans. He looked at his toes and then felt for pains in his body. Except for a throbbing headache in his temple, he seemed to be all there.

He felt the ropes around his wrists; they weren't rope. They were handcuffs made of some odd flexible alloy. He wasn't uncomfortable; there was a mirror against the far wall and he could see that his wound had been dressed appropriately. *Still,* he thought, *Amazons are known to treat their victims well before they make an example out of them.*

He jiggled the chain slightly to test the chair; it was expertly bound and there was nothing he could do. He wondered where his compatriots were. If Pyrgomache came back, could they mount a rescue? *Would they mount a rescue?*

The door opened and another retinue of Amazon guards came in, including Pyrgomache. Gunnar stared her down and even managed to smile, but inside he was terrified. Strangely though, Pygromache didn't look at him, let alone try to intimidate him further. Instead, she stood up straight with the rest of the guards and surrounded Gunnar.

"Attention!" yelled an Amazon from outside. "May I present President Hippolyta!"

All the guards stood up even straighter and stared away from the door. President Hippolyta walked in with two more armed guards, and Gunnar tried not to look at her. He'd heard grand and horrible legends of her, that she'd slayed a thousand men in battle and oversaw all Amazon torture sessions personally. But from the corner of his eye, she simply looked like a well-dressed old woman.

"At ease," President Hippolyta commanded.

The guards relaxed and put their eyes back on Gunnar once more.

297

President Hippolyta took a key from her pocket and showed Gunnar. Without telling him what it was, she unbuckled his constraints and soon he was free. He shook off the shackles then went to the far wall to put some distance in between them. His loin cloth fell off, and President Hippolyta nodded at an assistant to get a replacement. Soon the assistant came back in with a shirt and some pants.

"Trust," said Hippolyta, holding the key. "It's lacking in our society, don't you agree?"

Gunnar didn't answer. He knew the head captor would always befriend him; it was an old psychological trick.

"The Spartans taught you well," she said, "but I'm not playing a game here, nor am I your enemy. It's true, the Amazons and the Spartans have been quite cruel to each other over the years, but this is a different time now."

"Is it?" asked Gunnar. "You still hold Spartan prisoners to this day, if you haven't killed them."

Hippolyta smiled and then nodded her head. Her eyes were heavy from days spent in meetings and negotiations, and her old skin looked soft. If Gunnar hadn't known her bloody, torturous past, he'd have thought her a trusted statesman.

"True," said Hippolyta, "we still hold many Spartans in our jails. But the Spartans hold many of our Amazons prisoner, and we treat our Spartans as guests provided they treat ours well."

"I guess you're right," said Gunnar, "trust is indeed lacking nowadays."

"I won't engage in a war of words with you, Redstone," said Hippolyta. "All I'll tell you is this: the Amazons are a friend of the Horsemen and a friend of the Academy. And though we may still be at war with the Spartan district, remember that you *are not* a Spartan."

Gunnar thought and then relaxed a bit. The Amazons were cruel to their enemies but perhaps they were fair to noncombatants and even defectors like himself. President Hippolyta turned on the flat-screen monitor in the far corner and it showed Saoirse, Kayana and Tommy in full color, sitting and talking with a Mermaid in another room.

"We're not your enemy," said President Hippolyta.

"Perhaps you're a friend of both the Academy and the Horsemen," said Gunnar, "but the Academy does not currently share your friendship with us."

"The Academy is currently ... *misinformed*," said Hippolyta with a smile.

President Hippolyta beckoned Gunnar towards the monitor. He saw his friends talking jovially with the Mermaid from a variety of camera angles; Gunnar could tell that it wasn't a fake tape.

"Now, you attacked Pyrgomache, and she fought back," said Hippolyta. "There will be no more of this behavior. What we are dealing with in Dagon and the Academy is too important to be sublimated by personal prejudice. Do you understand?"

Gunnar looked back at Pyrgomache; she was staring in another direction, as if he was the furthest thing from her mind.

"I understand," said Gunnar.

"Good," said President Hippolyta. "Now the Mermaid is telling your friends what really happened."

Gunnar looked at the monitor; there was some audio of the Mermaid speaking, but he couldn't decipher her sing-song tongue.

"Would you like me to summarize?" asked President Hippolyta.

"Of course," said Gunnar.

President Hippolyta nodded at her second-in-command, and the woman snapped her fingers. Two more Amazons came in with a formal presidential chair made of dark wood and black leather. President Hippolyta sat in the chair gingerly, and her face winced as her arthritic joints creaked into place. *Her past may have been filled with legend and cruelty,* thought Gunnar, *but she's now just an old woman.*

"Dagon, of course, is largely behind this," said Hippolyta. "His district was set to take over the conurbation, but then came along our idea of an *Academy* that would help police us so that we could all live together. We don't know if it will work, but Dagon is threatened nonetheless. So he captured some of Poseidon's Mermaids, and promised one of them her sisters' freedom if she'd convince the King Basilisk to send his children into your Academy."

President Hippolyta shook her head and smirked a bit.

"Dagon's power lies in these roundabout plots," said President Hippolyta. "He puts forth several of these obscure plans at once, and one of them inevitably achieves his goals. The successful plan is, of course, so bizarre that it would never get traced back to him. Sending basilisks is a brilliant touch; the best way to quash a revolution is to poison it from within."

"Basilisks bring poison," said Gunnar, "yet those that they bit in the Academy have demons flood their head, and then are controlled."

President Hippolyta sighed, and then nodded her head.

"This is what I meant when I said that Dagon is *largely* behind this," said President Hippolyta. "You see, basilisk poison doesn't kill by itself. The best way I'd describe it is that a basilisk bite, *or even stare*, simply strips the protection from its victim's soul. So if a basilisk were to attack you in the wild, its bite would really allow *everything else* to attack your body and kill you.

"Something, perhaps a god, perhaps something else, found out that the Academy was going to be attacked by basilisks. They sent their demons there and instructed them to wait for the bite, then attack the victim's soul, and try to control him from within."

"And this isn't Dagon's doing?" asked Gunnar. "He likes *control*, and this sounds—"

"Dagon controls through money, and failing that, he'll eliminate his enemies," said Hippolyta. "Relying on demons to *control* isn't his style. We've looked into it extensively; he unknowingly opened the gate for something, but ultimately the end result was not his intent."

"I was bitten," said Gunnar. "I was in a coma."

"Perhaps the bite overloaded your system, perhaps these demons wanted to see what they could do with you," said Hippolyta. "I understand you remember nothing from when you were under?"

"Nothing," said Gunnar.

"As far as we can tell, it appears you've been cured by the King Basilisk's antivenom," said Hippolyta. "And if you're not cured later on down the road, Kayana has made it clear that she will take care of you."

Kayana "taking care" of me, thought Gunnar. *I don't like the sound of that.*

"So there we have it," said Hippolyta. "We're on your side—the just side."

"Agreed," said Gunnar.

"But we still have a problem," said Hippolyta. "Though *just* sides are ultimately vindicated by history, *for the moment* we have a major problem."

"Speak," said Gunnar.

"Dagon still wants the Horsemen dead," said Hippolyta. "And he's made an embargo around our island, and will only lift it when we turn you over."

"Hellenica would not allow this," said Gunnar.

"No," said Hippolyta. "But Hellenica's strong in principle, and Dagon's strong in force."

"Can we wait him out?"

"Perhaps," said Hippolyta, "but we need to sneak you back to Hellenica *now*, to clear your name and then have Kayana cleanse the victims down there of the infestation. She can enter the dreams where the demons live, and with help she will be able to save the Academy before they collapse upon themselves."

"Okay," said Gunnar. "How will you sneak us past this barricade?"

"We're going to give you up," said Hippolyta, "but you'll carry something that will take a bite out of Dagon's empire and allow you to escape. In simple terms, it could be considered a *bomb*."

Hippolyta snapped her fingers, and Pyrgomache left the room. Moments later, the large Amazon came back with an oblong-shaped grey casing, which was flat and about the size of Gunnar's outstretched hands. It was light and cold to the touch, but solid, and Gunnar wondered if it was bulletproof. Pyrgomache placed the casing on Gunnar's back, frowned, and then brought it around to his stomach. She smiled, strapped it onto his waist, and then another set of guards put a shirt on him. It was hard to move with this odd casing on him, but it was more or less hidden underneath his clothes.

"You'll turn us over to Dagon?" said Gunnar in a mistrusting voice. "And then I'll let loose a *bomb* strapped to my midsection that will allow me and my friends to escape unharmed? This does not sound like a plan so much as a ruse to—"

"It's not a *bomb* in the conventional sense," said Hippolyta. "It's a gift from Poseidon. Needless to say, he's quite upset with Dagon for kidnapping his Mermaids, and Poseidon will take great pleasure when this goes off. We'll teach you when and how to use it, and if you use it correctly it will allow you to escape unharmed."

Gunnar looked at Hippolyta with distrust.

"We'll tell you and only you what this bomb is and what it can do," said Hipployta. "And we'll not turn The Horsemen over to Dagon without your approval."

"Fair enough," said Gunnar.

"It *is* fair," said Hippolyta. "Like I said, trust is lacking in our society, and now is a good time to bring it back. Perhaps this gesture will even begin a peace between the Amazon and Spartan nations."

"I doubt it," said Gunnar, "especially because as you said, I'm not a Spartan. I failed the Agoge and subsequently, I'm reviled by them."

"I disagree," said Hippolyta. "The Spartan district has officially disavowed you, perhaps, but you're not reviled. The Spartan infantry speaks highly of you; legend has it that you'll come back and lead them one day. If you bring this bomb from the Amazon nation into the heart of Dagon's district, your legend will only grow."

Gunnar felt the casing around his stomach. It seemed innocuous; smuggled contraband, perhaps, but not anything dangerous.

"The reunification of the Amazons, Spartans, Hellenica and the Academy starts now, Gunnar," said Hippolyta. "Right here, with you. I promise you that if you use this device properly, it will get you home safely."

Gunnar felt the casing one last time, then looked up at President Hippolyta, who stared back at Gunnar with rheumy, calm eyes. She wasn't lying.

"And if you use this gift from Poseidon at just the right time," she said, "it will tear Dagon's entire world in half."

/***/

"We yield the captives," said Pyrgomache.

"And we have already begun lifting the blockade around your island," said the General in Dagon's speedboat. "We want no quarrel with the Amazons."

Yet you would keep the blockade forever if it profited you, thought Gunnar.

Gunnar and the rest of the Horsemen had been shackled in heavy chains, and they were led onto Dagon's boats and ordered to sit in chairs built into the vessel's wall. Dagon's guards locked the chains to their chairs, and they were secured, though not uncomfortably and not tightly. Gunnar looked back to see the Amazons downcast; this was humiliating for them. *They can't stand to give ground,* thought Gunnar, *even if they're doing it on purpose. Even Pyrgomache looks sad, and perhaps more surprisingly, I'm sad to see her go.*

Dagon's boats sped away with them, and soon the island of the Amazons was just a small speck in the night's water. *No wonder the Amazons retain their cruelty,* thought Gunnar. *They have an island, but Dagon has a nation. Fear is the only thing keeping his soldiers from running them over.*

Though he no longer felt any fear himself, Gunnar feared for his team. They had given control of themselves and there were just too many variables now. Gunnar felt confident in his mission, but couldn't guarantee his team's safety; Dagon was in control now. Still, as the boats sped towards Dagon's docks, Gunnar gave each of his Horsemen a look that said *We'll be fine. No matter how dire the circumstances, we'll be fine.*

Once on the docks, they were led back to the aquarium and then put in a cavernous, empty room several floors underground. The room had ten thick chains dangling above a large, above-ground crocodile tank. The crocodiles swam freely and could even escape the tank if they wanted; the only thing preventing them from doing so was the five-foot drop onto the ground.

The guards bound Gunnar's hands and feet and then attached them to one of the chains dangling above the tank, and they did the same with Saoirse, Tommy and Kayana. The group stood shackled in front of the tank, but could be pulled backwards and then dangled stomach-first over the crocodiles on a whim. Gunnar had heard that this was one of Dagon's tricks; the Babylonian god would deal with rivals by bringing them to this room and pulling them backwards with every answer that displeased him.

Dagon's men clearly knew who they were dealing with; they had a cage for Kross and wore gloves while handling Kayana. Dagon walked by the tank, showing no fear of the crocodiles, and frowned in front of Gunnar. He was taller than Gunnar, and almost as broad as Heracles. He swallowed his anger and then forced a grin.

"Remove their armor," said Dagon.

The guards tried, but couldn't; it was a brand of armor that Hippolyta had instructed them to wear to conceal Gunnar's bomb. The guards struggled and struggled, but couldn't unclasp the linking plates.

"Armor won't come off sir," said Dagon's underling. "But we scanned them; no weapons."

"Amazon armor," said Dagon with a laugh. "Can't be taken off; helps prevent assault after capture."

Dagon circled his captives slowly, and then reached into his pocket. He pulled out a hunk of meat and threw it in the crocodile tank. The crocodiles snapped at each other while devouring it, and then all was quiet again.

"You've heard the legend of *Horatius Cocles*?" asked Dagon.

The group was quiet. Gunnar had heard that legend every day of the Agoge, but chose to remain silent.

"This guy Horatius was a Roman soldier," said Dagon. "One day, this rival king from Etrusca sends an army to Rome, begins attacking the outskirts of the city. Everyone goes into a panic and tries to flee into the walled portion of the city, just across the Tiber River. Problem is, there's only one bridge. Cut the bridge, you screw the people in the countryside fleeing inwards; keep the bridge, and the rival king is gonna send his soldiers too, and the walled city becomes useless.

"So three guys take it upon themselves to sit at the front of the bridge and let any Roman country bumpkin by, but fight off any Etruscan soldiers they see. Just three of 'em, defending this bridge. Two of them are big time commanders from noble families, and Horatius is the third. Horatius wasn't famous, wasn't from a big family; he was this cocky little one-eyed soldier who would give anything for Rome.

"So the Roman peasants go by, and then some Etruscan soldiers come to fight, and Horatius and company fight them off. Then some more Roman peasants and a few fleeing Roman military guys who were too scared to fight. Then some more Etruscans, and more Etruscans, and more and more. And these three guys are holding the bridge!

"This Horatius is a scrappy little fellow, so when he sees that he's outnumbered, he gives a little ground and fights, and then gives a little more ground. He then tells the Romans behind him to destroy the bridge. They don't want to do it, because it'll surely kill him, but he yells at them to just do what he says. They destroy the bridge, and Horatius ends up in the water. Rome is safe, but Horatius's armor is so heavy that he drowns."

Gunnar tried not to show any reaction; he'd heard many different versions of that story with many different endings. Sometimes Horatius lived and sometimes he died, but he always saved Rome.

"Horatius is a hero," said Dagon. "Is he not?"

Dagon hit Tommy in the back of his suit, shoving his face against his helmet shield.

"Simple question; do you think Horatius is a hero?" asked Dagon. "Someone answer me or I'll hit this boy again."

Dagon raised his hand once more and Gunnar stopped him.

"Stop it, Dagon," said Gunnar. "Yes, I believe Horatius is a hero. I've always believed that."

"Good answer," said Dagon. "I've spied on the Academy quite a bit, and this Horatius reminds me of someone in your class; what's his name?"

Gunnar stared back at Dagon angrily, and Dagon grinned patronizingly in return.

"Oh yeah!" said Dagon in a mocking tone. "Rowan! That's who Horatius is like! Rowan—you must like him, right? You must think Rowan's a hero, right?"

Gunnar was once again silent.

"Wrong," said Dagon. "What I know of your Rowan is that he's an idiot, and what I know of Horatius is that he never existed. They made him up so they can tell stories that convince your kind to go out and defend the bridge while the cowards live another day. You want to be a hero and drown in your armor?"

Dagon clinked the Amazon armor on Gunnar's chest.

"They'll sing songs about you," said Dagon in a mocking voice. "Just say the word and I'll throw you in the water. You'll die, but who knows, they might make you the next Horatius."

Dagon let the silence linger a bit.

"No takers?" said Dagon. "All right."

Dagon snapped his fingers and his guards brought him a chair and a remote control device with a grid of buttons. The remote control was thick and waterproof, and Gunnar knew what it was for. It could pull any one of them backwards until they hung above the tank, and then drop them into the water whenever Dagon wished. The green god caressed his scaly fingers over the device and smiled at it as a father would look at his newborn child. Dagon then sat down in the chair and stared at the Horsemen.

"My society is successful because I do away with all that stuff of nobility and honor," said Dagon. "You work for me, I pay you. No honor, no medals; I give you *money*, and that money buys you a place in my district. Use the money for a house, a business, a family, whatever you want. Don't worry about defending the bridge; we'll pay someone else to do that. That's my philosophy.

"And that's my proposal to you four Horsemen: work for me and I'll not only let you live, I'll pay you, and pay you well. Vehicles, technology, houses, whatever you want. I'll have you do some crazy things, but I won't ask you to jump off a bridge in full armor. That's my offer; no nobility, just a job and respect."

Kayana started to laugh.

"Is something funny?" said Dagon, smiling. "Tell me! I want to laugh too."

"You speak of giving us *respect*," said Kayana, "and yet you negotiate with us in front of a crocodile tank."

Dagon frowned, and then laughed again.

"It's true," he said. "That's the other half of my style. You work for me and I pay you; *disobey me and I punish you*. It's that simple, and I'll be the first to admit I'm not a paragon of virtue. But look around you, little girl; our world's in pieces, and everyone's out for themselves. This world needs someone tough like me, someone who's willing to do what it takes to get everyone in line. A few generations from now, the conurbation won't need a strong man like myself. But at this stage of history, if you want to get order, you've got to get your hands dirty.

"So yeah, that's it, Horsemen, a straight-up proposal. Work for me and I'll make it worth your while; you won't be fighting for country, honor or any of that nonsense. You'll be fighting for the mansion I'll provide each of you, and the twenty or so servants that'll do everything you say. On the other hand, say *no*, and you're going in the tank."

The group was quiet and Kayana snapped back from a moment of white-eyed meditation.

"So what'll it be, little girl?" asked Dagon. "You havin' visions of a world under me? Half of it under *you* perhaps?"

"My vision was indeed of your world," said Kayana, "but as your world will be in the future: crumbled and broken."

"Interesting," said Dagon. "My district looks pretty strong now if you ask me."

"It's not strong now," said Kayana. "It runs on bribery and fear, little else."

"They say the best leaders are both feared and loved," said Dagon. "And if a leader has to choose one, choose fear."

"That's good advice for battle or for fleeting endeavors," said Kayana, "but not for building a *society*. Your people fear you, but they don't *respect* you. A society needs respect and pride to move forward. People can't look back at their founder from a century ago and think *this man was a petty thug who fed his enemies to crocodiles.* You fill your constituents with fear, and when you're gone that fear will turn to shame and your society will collapse."

"Your flaw lies in your conception of me, little girl," said Dagon, getting angry. "I'm not just a leader; I'm a god. My society won't collapse after I'm gone, because I *won't be gone*; I'll live on and on. Am I wrong about that?"

"You're wrong about two things," said Kayana. "The first thing wrong is the idea that you'll *live on*. I had a vision about your life and see you dying a year from now, in your sleep. They'll find you cowed in fear and soiled. The word will get out about this and *that's* how they'll remember you: the god who soiled himself before he died. You're also wrong about my title; I'm not a little girl. To the world I'm Kayana, and to you I'm *Death*, and you'll address me as nothing else."

Dagon got up, breathed deeply and then smiled. He snapped his fingers and the guards gave him a glove. Dagon hovered over Kayana, nearly four times her size, and then smacked her with the back of his gloved hand.

"Perhaps it's time to get my hands dirty," said Dagon. "I'm not talking to you now, *little girl*; I'm talking to your friends. Watch what happens to those who don't work for me."

Dagon sat back in his chair and took his remote control device out. He punched some buttons into the device and Kayana's chains lifted her up until she dangled above the tank. The crocodiles all made a frenzy around the surface, but still, Kayana showed no fear.

"A year from now," she said. "In your sleep."

Dagon mashed another button, the chains loosened, and Kayana went crashing down into the water. Both Tommy and Saoirse yelled and struggled against their constraints, but it was no use; Kayana was on her own. The crocodiles thrashed around Kayana and one of them dragged her under the water. The creature had clamped around her armor and was shaking her about furiously. He brought her into a death spin, and the creatures above jockeyed for territory.

The water stopped roiling and Saoirse cried out once more. The crocodiles on top stopped their frenzy and disbanded. After a minute, Kayana floated to the top, her chain wrapped around the floating body of the attacking crocodile. The creature was now dead and bloated from her touch.

"This little girl is hard to kill," said Dagon with a smile.

Kayana spit water out of her mouth. She was breathing heavily.

"But not impossible," said Dagon.

Dagon pressed another button and Kayana's chain tightened up and she went flying upwards until she slammed into the ceiling. He dropped her back down into the tank and she sunk to the bottom immediately; her arms were too tightly bound to tread water, and her armor was too heavy to float.

"I need you, but I don't need you that much," said Dagon. "If you aren't loyal to me, I'll use you to add to my legend; I'll be the god who fed the Four Horsemen to his crocodiles. So while your friend drowns, realize that you're going in next. You have until she stops moving to decide; I honestly hope you refuse my offer. Killing you all will just be less risk for me."

Kayana was thrashing about under the water, and Gunnar's mind raced desperately as he tried to find ways to save her. Was there any way to grab a guard hostage? To break these chains? To get into the tank? *There are no options*, thought Gunnar, *and there is no time*.

"We yield!" said Gunnar. "We yield; just let her go."

Dagon thought about it, smiled, and then shook his head and pointed at Kayana.

"I'll accept your surrender, but not hers."

"We yield! Now bring her up!"

"Sorry, Horseman, that girl will kill me first chance she gets. Just give her a few minutes, and then we'll talk."

Kayana had stopped thrashing now. She opened her eyes; they were white, and they were staring right at Tommy through the side of the tank. Tommy whispered something to Saoirse, and she spoke.

"Im-kōtep, kōtep-ma," said Saoirse.

"What's she saying?" asked Dagon.

"Im-kōtep, kōtep-ma," said Saoirse, looking at the crocodiles.

"Oh," said Dagon, "you're talking the crocodile's language. That's your skill, *talking to the animals*, got it. Well I've got news for you, crocodiles don't listen to *anyone*."

The crocodiles disappeared under the water, and soon brought up both Kayana and her chains. They pushed her over the edge of the pool and she slammed to the ground, coughing and spitting out water. The crocodiles began snapping their jaws in unison, and then made high-pitched barking sounds with their throats. Dagon fumbled for his remote control, and was about to reel Kayana to the ceiling again, but he paused and put the device down before walking up to Kayana and kneeling in front of her.

"How did you do that?" asked Dagon.

No one said a word. Dagon took out a gun from his pocket and pointed it at Kayana's head.

"How did you do that?"

"The crocodiles don't listen to anyone," said Tommy, "except for me. I have power over all the ugly things, things of the deep, things with fangs and poison; basically about half the creatures in this aquarium. Saoirse told them who I was, and the crocodiles obeyed. Hear that sound they're making? They're letting your aquarium know who I am."

Dagon smiled and then slammed his fist into his remote control. There was silence, and then a strange sound of the creatures on floors above erupting in various noises.

"You guys win this round," he said, "but I can't just shoot you and be done with it. I've got to do something epic now, something that will make my legend stronger, and send a message to both Hellenica and the Amazons."

Dagon thought a bit, and then smiled.

"I've got one creature that doesn't listen to anyone, and he won't be killed by your touch."

Dagon stopped smiling, and then looked at his guards. *I know where he's going to take us,* thought Gunnar, *and it's the perfect place to deliver the bomb. Perhaps too perfect; I don't know if we'll be able to get out alive.*

"Bring them upstairs," said Dagon. "Feed them to the Megalodon."

/***/

The air was cold by the tank, and the giant shark was nowhere to be seen.

But it's out there somewhere, thought Gunnar.

"This is the beginning of a new era," said Dagon. "The chaos of the conurbation is going to fade away, to be replaced by order. And it will begin at this point, when I dispose of the Academy's strongest children."

Gunnar's team was standing by the giant tank, surrounded by a score of Dagon's armed guards. Gunnar looked at the water, which was calm and reflected the moonlit sky.

"This is a monstrous act," said Saoirse. "History finds a way to dispose of its monsters."

"True and *truer*, Hetaera," said Dagon. "But I'm not thinking of history, I'm thinking of *now*. *Now*, in the chaos, society *needs me* to bring the conurbation out of the muck. Now is *my* time."

Dagon nodded at his guards and they attached chains to their captives' shackles. The chains were tied to posts in the middle of the water. *Dagon is using the same method of torment that he used downstairs*, thought Gunnar, *but we'll be dragged into the water instead of dangled above, and rather than a score of crocodiles, we'll face only one creature, but it's more deadly than anything we've faced before.*

Dagon pressed a button and the posts drew the chains in, and they soon brought Gunnar and his friends into the water. The team began kicking their legs desperately to stay above the surface; their hands were still shackled behind their backs. Kross was tied to Saoirse and he was having a hard time staying afloat. He panicked and whined, and Saoirse whispered unintelligible words into his ears until he calmed. The chains then drew back and tightened them against the poles; they were trapped, but at least they could stay above water. Gunnar looked around; the Megalodon was still nowhere to be seen.

"Drop some blood in the water," said Dagon. "Let her know dinner's ready."

Gunnar secretly dropped his wrists below his feet and brought his shackles in front of him. He ground the shackles against a secret blade in his breastplate; it was made of adamantine and cut the metal quite easily. He looked around and saw that Dagon had erected a barrier around the water's edge; he didn't want the Megalodon to jump out and do any damage. *You'll find a way to escape later*, thought Gunnar. *The bomb will take a few minutes to "go off." It's best to release it now.*

Gunnar put his hands forward, opened his breastplate and took out the case. He opened it just as Dagon's assistants started to pour blood in the water. Gunnar dunked the thin, leathery bomb into the water but didn't let it float away. *It's a matter of time before this takes out Dagon's aquarium,* thought Gunnar, *but if we're to survive the Megalodon, I'm going to have to do something very difficult.*

"Use your suit to free the others, Tommy," said Gunnar.

Tommy had already been working on his own chains and soon was swimming freely. He swam towards Kayana and brought an electric knife from his forearm and cut through her chains.

"Go ahead, swim around," said Dagon. "The shark will get you. Look, there she is."

Gunnar saw the huge dorsal fin in the distance.

"Hurry, Tommy," said Gunnar.

Tommy had freed Kayana and was now working on Saoirse. Gunnar held the bomb close to him and then looked at the approaching shark. *Poseidon's children are coming,* thought Gunnar. *I just need to time this perfectly.*

Tommy soon freed Saoirse, and the group was now swimming towards Gunnar.

"Swim away from me," said Gunnar, pointing his friends away from the aquarium to a patch towards the ocean nets.

They swam towards the shore, but Gunnar soon heard Saoirse barking orders at Kross. The hyaena whined and then spoke back to her; she yelled back and the creature left her side. Gunnar looked over and saw that Saoirse was now apart from the group and swimming towards him. She got near him and he yelled at her.

"Go away!" he said. "There's no need for both of us to risk our lives."

"I can talk to the Megalodon," said Saoirse. "At least I can send it a few simple messages. I'll help us escape after you deliver the bomb, whatever it is."

Gunnar nodded and looked around; the Megalodon had disappeared and it was completely quiet. Wherever it was, it was too late to send Saoirse back.

"Don't look down," said Dagon.

Gunnar felt an immense rush of water as the shark swam under him; it was so large that they were pulled under. Gunnar grabbed Saoirse underwater and then brought her upwards. They came through a thin layer of blood on the water; Dagon's men were pouring a steady stream into the tank. The Megalodon was still under the surface, but the roiling water showed that she was clearly in a frenzy.

"She's having a hard time locating us," said Gunnar. "We're just too small. Now, I know this creature can't talk, but can you send a message to attract her to a point, to get her to eat something?"

"Yes," said Saoirse, "I can make a sound imitating prey."

"Good," said Gunnar. "When I say *now*, get under the water and do just that."

Saoirse nodded yes.

"Good," said Gunnar. "After that, come to the surface and hold onto me while I swim away."

The Megalodon's dorsal fin appeared twenty-five meters away, and it was tracing a circle around them. The fin was the size of a man and got closer with each lap, until Gunnar could see the Megalodon's enormous head cutting through the water. It went twice more around Gunnar and Saoirse, and the third time it cut a hard left and blew by them. It scraped Gunnar's side and tore him away from Saoirse.

"No!" she yelled.

Gunnar stayed above water, and once again it was quiet. He saw that he had accidentally let go of the bomb and it was now floating by Saoirse, leathery and flat. He then heard the cry of Poseidon's children as they breached the outer nets.

"*Now*, Saoirse!" he yelled. "Become prey!"

Saoirse went underwater and Gunnar went with her. He heard her make strange noises and swam towards the sound. He then heard a snapping and the rush of bubbles as the Megalodon changed course. *No time to think*, Gunnar calculated. *All you need is a few meters' distance.*

Gunnar hit Saoirse in the midsection, bringing her to the surface. He kicked them both a few more meters away, and moments later the Megaladon swam straight up through the surface, its jaws fully open, and swallowed the bomb whole.

It swam down into the water again, preparing for another hit, and then arose two hundred meters away towards the ocean. Gunnar felt a warm splash as Dagon's men threw a vat of blood upon them. It was unnecessary; the Megalodon had already figured out where they were and was now swimming right for them. Gunnar held Saoirse and kicked away, but it was no use; the Megalodon changed course slightly and kept on them. It opened its mouth wide and showed three rows of teeth, many of them bigger than Gunnar's head.

Gunnar held onto Saoirse tightly as the shark's open jaws began to engulf them, but just before they did, a Kraken's tentacle attached to its nose and made it change course. *Poseidon's children are here*, thought Gunnar as he smiled contently.

The Megalodon dove down with the Kraken, and two more Krakens appeared behind it; they were frightening but ignored Gunnar and Saoirse and focused solely on the Megalodon.

"That's what the *bomb* was," said Saoirse. "A Kraken egg."

"Even Poseidon can't control these creatures," said Gunnar. "All we know is that they're extremely protective of their eggs."

"And their eggs send an electric signal through the water," said Saoirse.

The Megalodon breached the surface three hundred meters away, taking two of the gigantic squid with it. The Krakens had wrapped their tentacles around the shark, and when they sunk together another time, Gunnar saw two more Krakens coming in from the sea and heading for the shore.

"They know that the Megalodon ate their egg," said Saoirse. "They want to destroy it and its home."

"We need to go to the others," said Gunnar. "Amazons are waiting for us."

Gunnar swam to the nets and saw that Tommy, Kayana and Kross were already in a small speedboat. Gunnar and Saoirse swam to the edge of the boat and were helped in by the strong hands of the Amazon driver. The boat was so small they could barely fit inside, and it disappeared through the waves as it sped away, unheard and unseen.

"Nice delivery," said the Amazon driving the boat. "The Kraken egg was my idea."

Gunnar looked up and saw that the driver of the boat was Pyrgomache.

"We make quite a team, then," said Gunnar.

Pyrgomache spat black juice into the water and smiled at Gunnar. "Indeed," she said. "We brought the squid here, and now we've given them a vendetta against Dagon. They'll start attacking his trawlers next, and after that his constituents will flee his district in droves."

Perhaps it's better to be feared than loved, thought Gunnar, *but feared leaders lose all power when a greater danger arises.* Gunnar looked to shore and saw that three more Krakens had now joined the fight; one particularly large one was focusing solely on destroying the aquarium. It swung its tentacles into the side of the building, and several tanks were now pouring into the sea. The ocean nets were cut through, and another part of the building was on fire.

"It's beautiful, isn't it?" said Pyrgomache. "One of the squid probably ate him whole."

"He's alive," said Kayana. "He still dies a year from this date; I'll be there to make sure It happens."

Pyrgomache spat again and then let out a loud laugh. It was so loud that Gunnar wondered if Dagon could hear it over the destruction of his aquarium. It didn't matter anyway; three other Amazon speedboats were now escorting them safely to their shores.

"This black-haired girl's more vengeful than I am," said Pyrgomache, still laughing. "But you'll have to wait for vengeance, Reaper; we need to get you to Hellenica immediately. The Horsemen's names might be cleared, but your Academy is currently a madhouse."

THE RETURN

There was a knock on their door three hours before morning call; It was Bes. Kayana was already up meditating with white eyes, but she chose to ignore the knocks until Tommy came out and opened the door.

"Go back to bed, Alderon," said Bes. "I need to speak to Kayana alone."

"Be my guest," said Tommy with a yawn. He went back to his room and shut his door.

"Kayana, we need your help," said Bes.

Kayana chose not to answer, but stopped meditating and returned her eyes to normal.

"Headmaster Indra has made a memo to the teachers exculpating you Horsemen of any wrongdoing," said Bes. "In fact, he stated that you're heroes for uncovering the truth. Except for the fact that Heracles is now enraged because someone stole one of his belts, everything seems back to normal."

Kayana still chose to be silent; the words meant little to her, other than the fact that she need not run from the Academy anymore.

"But we still have a problem," said Bes. "Many of our men are infected with these demons, and though we could lock them up, we can't keep them locked up forever. Praetor Mantus tried to clear a soldier of his demons, but failed in that regard. I know you hate Praetor Mantus—"

"I haven't yet learned the emotional state of *hating* anyone," interrupted Kayana. "Though when I do, Praetor Mantus will be near the top of the list."

"Fine," said Bes. "Praetor Mantus needs your help driving the demons out from the Academy."

"And you shall have my help whenever you wish," said Kayana. "Line up all infected soldiers, one by one, and I'll enter their dreams; they'll be clear within a fortnight. All I ask is that Mantus or anyone else refrains from throwing me in Tartarus afterwards."

"We can do that," said Bes, "but Praetor Mantus wants to go with you; to supervise."

"To supervise?" asked Kayana. "I'd sooner take mentorship from Pan the faun."

"You're quite powerful, Kayana," said Bes. "You are what we would call a *prodigy*, and Mantus recognizes this. But you're unskilled; if you were to enter the soldiers' dreams tonight, you'd fail. Allow Mantus to chaperone and together you'll be successful. And though you're not fond of him, he'll teach you to do things in dreams you can't imagine."

Kayana meditated on this for ten minutes, and Bes didn't disturb her.

"I'll go," said Kayana, "upon one condition, which will be a secret between you and me."

"Speak," said Bes.

"I did much dream-flying this evening and know who's infected," said Kayana. "I'll accompany Mantus and clear all the demons from everyone's head, except for one remaining Spartan. He was the last to be bitten, and the bite was weak. His infection is in its infancy and he acts quite normal. I must clear his head, alone."

"Why would you want to cure one Spartan alone?"

"I cannot reveal my motives," said Kayana.

"Fine," said Bes. "Then tell me the name of this last Spartan."

"I'll reveal it after Mantus and I are done," said Kayana. "For now, let's just say that there are only two beings on this earth that I would consider true friends of the Horsemen. You are one, and he is the other."

/***/

It took the Academy a day to contain the infected Spartans. The insane and comatose ones were easily controlled, but the lucid ones took some time. The demons inside their heads knew what was happening externally, and each afflicted subject reacted differently. Some became violent, some hid, and some tried to argue their way out of a cure. Some worked together and some tried to escape to the surface. The gods worked together though, and sooner or later Heracles brought them all down to Praetor Mantus's laboratory.

"We'll bring you Rowan by the time you've cleared these Spartans," said Heracles. "He's somewhere in the Manitou. He injured four mercenaries in his escape, but didn't kill them. I'll have him ready for you by the time you're done with these men."

If you don't, thought Kayana, *I'll find him, subdue him, and he'll never harm anyone again.*

Mantus's wife Mania injected the Spartans with a dark substance and soon they were laid out in a row, thirty in all.

"They're ready," said Mania. "As always, they'll sleep forever if need be."

Praetor Mantus drank his dark liquid and poured Kayana a glass.

"Drink deeply and we'll soon be in their dreams," he said.

"I don't require your substance," she said. "I'll enter their dreams on my own and you'll meet me there."

Kayana's eyes turned white and she began to meditate.

/***/

The dreams of the soldiers were varied, and so were their actions. Some required assassination, some required chicanery, and some required Praetor Mantus raising an army with Kayana's help. *Though I learn his tricks quite easily,* thought Kayana, *I must admit he has a lot to teach me.* One by one they cleared the Spartans' head of demons, until they flew in the world between dreams and all their subjects were sleeping in peace.

"There," said Praetor Mantus, pointing at a Viking castle. "Heracles has subdued Rowan; we must enter soon."

Praetor Mantus and Kayana entered Rowan's head and set up a camp ten kilometers from his castle, in the grey, lifeless marsh that surrounded it. The demons had built an entire town around the palace since she had left, and the castle itself was now better armed.

"It's going to take some time," said Praetor Mantus, "but we must free his mind in this go-around. If we fail, he'll soon be beyond repair."

Praetor Mantus and Kayana raised an army of ten thousand soldiers. As their army encircled the Viking citadel, they flew over the castle and found it densely packed; their army was outnumbered ten to one.

"The demons must have dug barracks deep into the earth," said Praetor Mantus. "They have an endless supply, like ants from a hill. It's a miracle that Rowan's still sane. But nonetheless, the size of his army doesn't matter, nor even the fierceness; we just have to make sure ours is smarter."

/***/

Their siege lasted three days. They took and gave ground, captured enemy soldiers, and recaptured some of their own. Kayana went down into her soldiers' makeshift prison to see some of the demons firsthand. They were fierce, ugly and seemed to be enjoying her soldiers' taunts. When the soldiers beat them, the demons laughed maniacally—even as their heads were being cut off.

These creatures don't respond to violence, thought Kayana. *I won't get what I want from them with threats or torment.*

Kayana looked around; they were winning the battle, but she needed to do more than *win* when Bes would bring her the last subject.

These creatures don't cow to violence, she thought, *but there have been three days of fighting. This siege is on its third day.*

Kayana's army soon broke through the demon's ranks and freed Rowan's subconscious from the dungeon. All aspects of his soul had been taken over by the demons, save for one child near death, the child with the gravelly voice. Praetor Mantus blew life into him, and the child grew strong.

"We have garrisoned the castle," said one of Praetor Mantus's generals.

"Burn it to the ground," said Praetor Mantus. "We can't risk any demons holing away in hidden nooks."

Praetor Mantus took the child and split him into four beings: a woman, a soldier, a dog and another child.

"Multiply further," he said. "Build another castle over the ashes of this one. And if you should ever see these demons in the future, kill them without a second thought."

/***/

"Looks like you were successful," whispered Bes, back in the real world. "Rowan is a bit dazed, perhaps, but he'll be okay."

They were in the forest under an artificially moonlit sky. It was the only place they knew they could meet in secret; the Manitou had been growing out of control and the security cameras were out.

"I brought your subject in," said Bes. "Now, would you care to tell the two friends of the Horsemen what this is about?"

Kayana looked at Cassander; he looked normal, hale and hearty, and he was shaking his head *no*.

"Let Kayana clear me of these demons first," said Cassander. "I feel okay now, but perhaps I'm not. There could be something inside me, listening."

"Agreed," said Bes. "And I must be leaving; Kayana, you'll be good here?"

Kayana was already meditating and peering into Cassander's thoughts.

"She's all yours," said Bes.

"Thanks," said Cassander.

Ten minutes later, Kayana felt Cassander tapping at her shoulder and stopped meditating.

"Speak," she said.

"You have a lot to learn about human interaction, Kayana," said

Cassander with a smile.

Kayana looked at Cassander and tried to understand what he was feeling. She didn't sense fear; just the dull sense of duty that Spartans felt when faced with unpleasant tasks. But she did sense a *melancholy* in him, a longing for something that would never be again.

"I do have a lot to learn," said Kayana.

"You do," he said while lying down in the grass. "But your lessons will come later. For now, exorcise me."

Cassander closed his eyes, and ten minutes later he was snoring. Kayana began to meditate and within moments she was entering his dream.

/***/

Cassander was dreaming of his wife and young son; Kayana could immediately tell that they were both gone. She couldn't see Cassander's family, but she sensed their presence in the same way he was sensing them: through *loss*.

I'm not feeling their presence at all, thought Kayana, *I'm feeling their absence.*

Cassander was sitting alone in a dark room, and she sat next to him. He had a depth of emotion denied to most Spartans, including Gunnar, and Kayana felt his emotions flow into her. She felt his pain and from that, extrapolated what had happened to him in *his* life.

"Your wife bore you a son that was also training to be a Spartan, and he died in the Agoge," she whispered into his ear, unseen. "Is this true?"

Cassander nodded.

Kayana sat next to him a bit longer and absorbed a little more of his pain. She felt his longing, his regret and his anger. She felt it as he was feeling it, and found it fascinating. *This is what it's like to suffer emotionally*, she thought. She couldn't contain herself any longer and materialized next to him.

"A Spartan woman's only duty is to raise warriors to die for their country," said Kayana. "And when she felt no pain over your son's death, you could no longer bear the sight of her, so you left, is this true?"

Cassander nodded. Kayana turned her emotions off and dematerialized. *These emotions are fascinating, even if I can only feel them by proxy*, she thought. *But I can't dwell on this now. I have a demon to catch.*

/***/

Kayana flew over his dreamscape, but couldn't find anything out of the ordinary, let alone any sort of demon. Cassander's dream held dark, cold land and plenty of emotion, but there was nothing that caught her eye. She flew high in the atmosphere and looked at the dreamscape as a whole, and had to scan it three times before she saw it. *There is a fire in the far distance,* she thought, *and demons do not like the cold.*

Kayana flew towards the flame and was soon over the demon. He was a small little thing with charred skin and a scrunched-up face; perhaps one day he'd become an army and drive Cassander to insanity, but for now he was just a spirit in the woods. She could have easily torn out his heart and sent him back to Hell, but instead she chose to materialize a dome around them.

"What's this?" squealed the demon. "Speak, or fight!"

Kayana thought once more of what to do. *Demons don't cow under threat of violence, and seem to cherish death,* she thought, *but a three-day siege …*

She materialized at the far end of the dome, cross-legged, floating, and white-eyed. The demon rushed towards her with claws out, but hit an invisible barrier she'd constructed around herself.

"What is *this*?" asked the demon, clawing at the barrier. "Speak, or fight!"

Kayana didn't speak or fight, but instead slowed time down to a crawl inside the dome.

"So it's a waiting game you want, aye?" said the demon. "You don't know who you're dealing with, sister."

Kayana meditated more … and more. She waited a day, and then a month. The demon paced around the dome, smashed its head against the wall and tried to penetrate her barrier again, but she wouldn't let it out. She waited another year, and then slowed time even further so she could wait a decade. The demon tried to kill itself hundreds of times, of course, but she placed a barrier around its body so it could do itself no harm.

The demon gave up just as she was about to start the second decade of waiting.

"Stop," it cried. "I beg you, stop! I'll do anything you wish, just stop!"

Kayana stopped meditating and then floated towards the demon.

"I'll only stop if you tell me your kind's origins, leader and purpose," said Kayana. "If you refuse, you'll be trapped here for eternity with me."

"You can't ask me that," said the demon. "If I tell of my leaders, they'll do far worse to me than what you're doing now."

"If you tell me truth I'll make sure your death is quick and painless," said Kayana.

"All I ask of you is *death*," said the demon. "A slow, painful death at your hands will still be better than—"

"I promise you death," said Kayana. "Now, tell me where you're from and what your kind's purpose is before I slow time even further."

"All right," said the demon, "I'll tell you my tale. Cease your floating and sit with me; my name is *Yaotl*."

/***/

The demon lit a fire and reverted back into what Kayana assumed to be its original form. It kept the shape of a man but its flesh disappeared into smoke. Kayana sensed fear from it; not fear of her, but fear of what would happen if it were to return to its master as a traitor.

"Your Academy is destined for things, you know," said Yaotl. "All gods know this in the back of their minds. Powerful gods like Dagon take action, not for what it is now, but for what it might be. Its potential is extraordinary."

"How so?" asked Kayana.

"The Academy will bring the world truth," said Yaotl.

"What is this truth?" asked Kayana.

"I don't know," said Yaotl, "but the world will follow you. Gods, people, spirits and even demons will follow the Academy in time."

Kayana meditated on that for two weeks; the demon waited patiently and when she came to, he spoke again.

"But the Academy by itself does not anger my god. His name is *Quetzalcoatl*," said the demon. "It's the Horsemen. The Academy is simply setting the stage for you to come to your destiny, perhaps the world's destiny."

"I've heard much talk of our *destiny*," said Kayana. "We're to end the world, even though none of us have the power or desire to do such a thing."

"Destiny is a funny thing," said Yaotl. "It involves a long, circuitous path out of its owners' control. Oftentimes two destinies collide, and there is only room for one."

"And your Quetzalcoatl's destiny is opposed to ours?"

"Indeed," said the demon. "There is only room for one."

Kayana slowed time down only with herself and thought upon that for a week. To the demon it was a mere second.

"We are to end the world," said Kayana, "and from what I understand of the god Quetzalcoatl, his destiny is to return at world's end and save it. From what I've heard, he is a good god, and our destinies are not incompatible."

"It's not that simple," said Yaotl. "The Horsemen have been feared since the dawn of time, but the world needs you, not to help end itself, but to help itself *start over*. You'll wipe the slate clean so the world may be born again. Quetzalcoatl wants the world *as it is now*, to dominate it. Not the domination of Dagon—control through money and fear—but the domination of the soul. He wants to unify the world under one god and teach us how to live together."

"It sounds noble," said Kayana, "but no plan that starts with sending demons into dreams can be noble. He dominates through fear; at least Dagon dominated through fear *and* a paycheck."

"I assure you Quetzalcoatl's intentions are noble in the long run," said the demon. "But for now, he does what he must; destiny is a dark business."

"Dagon also claimed to do what he *must*," said Kayana. "He called it *getting his hands dirty*, and promised a better tomorrow in exchange for torment today."

"Fine," said the demon, "you win this round of rhetoric; I can't tell you what the world will look like in a century, or even tomorrow. Quetzalcoatl's Utopia or the Horsemen's Armageddon, which is better? I don't care, all I ask is that you kill me now; when word gets out that I've spoken with you, they'll begin their hunt for me in earnest. So kill me thoroughly; if any part of my soul survives they'll find it, and you'll hear my screams whenever you close your eyes."

Kayana looked at the demon; he was telling the truth, and had nothing more to tell her. She floated above him and then made her right hand sharp and hot. She ripped out his heart and burned it to cinders, and watched him closely as he faded into nothingness. The creature thanked her with a gasping breath, gave her a respectful nod, and was gone.

Kayana dispersed the dome and turned time back to normal. She then flew towards the sky and looked for a way back into reality; she'd had enough dreaming for one night.

/***/

Kayana refrained from speaking of the demon, but told Cassander of his own dream, and he nodded in silence.

"I don't remember my dreams," he said, "but I suppose it makes sense. Spartan life teaches you how to survive and how to kill, but it doesn't teach you how to deal with matters like that."

"Was the dream true?"

"Yes," said Cassander. "But in reality, somehow it's still worse."

"I felt your grief," said Kayana. "It was educational."

Cassander laughed.

"Would you like another lesson in human emotion?" he asked.

"Of course," said Kayana.

"Then stay right here," he said with a smile and walked off.

/***/

Tommy showed up ten minutes later with two odorous plants in his hand; his suit also looked strange. Kayana chose not to look at him, and instead stared forward. After a few moments of silence, Tommy spoke.

"Cassander said you'd be here," said Tommy. "I brought some flowers."

Kayana still didn't answer, but she took the dying plants with her gloved fingers and put them at her feet. She recognized his presence with a brief glance.

"I made some clothes for us, for our team," said Tommy. "Saoirse and I made them, actually."

Tommy handed Kayana a dark, form-fitting suit.

"The primary color is black, but mine is lined with green," said Tommy. "Yours is lined with black; notice how it's even darker."

Kayana examined the material; it was like nothing she'd ever seen. Her material was thinner than anything she'd ever felt before.

"Saoirse designed our clothes to match our abilities," said Tommy. "Mine wraps around my suit, but I also have clothes I wear on the inside. It protects others if take off my helmet. Yours is thin but solid, so it allows you to feel things without killing them."

"Thank you," said Kayana. "Is this all?"

"One more thing," said Tommy. "Look at me."

Kayana looked at Tommy. She stared back at him and tried to deduce his intent, but couldn't quite grasp his feelings. His heart was beating rapidly and she could smell the sweat coming from his hands. *It's a fight-or-flight response,* she thought. *Perhaps there's hidden danger down here in the Manitou.*

"I like you," he said.

"Understood," said Kayana. "Anything else?"

"No," he said, removing his helmet and looking at her, "I really like you. Cassander told me that you don't experience emotions the same way we do, and I need to describe precisely how I feel for you. So here goes …

"I've always had friends, but I've never felt about anyone the way I feel for you. I feel deeply for you, in the way that couples have felt for each other since time immemorial. I can't expect you to understand how I feel, but I know you can understand the *depth* of what I'm experiencing. You sense emotion and analyze it; all I ask is that you take in how I feel now and know that it's for you."

"Your heart's beating quite heavily," said Kayana, "as if you're in danger."

"I am in danger," said Tommy.

"Do you fear me?"

"Yes … no," said Tommy. "Yes, but in a good way. Do you understand?"

"No," said Kayana. "Not in the slightest."

Tommy smiled and then looked at the artificial moon. Tommy reached out and grabbed her hand; his palms were still sweating, but her cold skin soothed him a bit.

"I'd like to be with you," said Tommy, speaking as if he had rehearsed it. "To be with you—just you. To hold hands like this, and talk with each other. I want to elevate our relationship to a new, exclusive level. Do you understand that?"

"Somewhat," said Kayana.

"Cassander said that you might," said Tommy with a smile.

They sat hand-in-hand, silently, for another ten minutes.

"He also said that you had patience like no other," said Tommy. "But tell me, how do you feel about me?"

Kayana thought for a moment on this.

"I cannot say that I have feelings for you, Alderon," said Kayana. "If you died right now in front of me, I wouldn't shed a tear; I'm not equipped to feel such emotions, for you or for anyone. The emotions of which you speak are foreign to me; it would be akin to explaining fear to an inflamed Berserker, or bloodlust to an innocent child."

Tommy held on to her hand, but she noticed that his heart began to race again, and his eyes welled up with tears. He didn't cry, but he did grit his jaw and nod in acceptance.

"However," said Kayana, "I am interested in learning of these emotions. Cassander cared for two people much as you desire to care for me, and the mere loss of those people has wounded him so deeply that he all but lives in Purgatory.

"I would like to attempt to experience that depth of emotion," said Kayana. "And I would like to try experiencing it with you, Thomas."

"Good," he said, smiling.

An alarm on his wrist went off; it was time for morning call. Kayana got up, but Tommy pulled her back down gently.

"Can I walk you through these woods? Have this moment last a little longer?"

"It makes no difference to me whether you do or not," she said. "I have no feelings and—"

"I would like to," said Tommy, interrupting. "Please let me walk with you through these woods."

"You may," said Kayana.

Tommy took off his helmet and left it on the ground. He walked with her through the Manitou underneath the artificial starlight as the artificial sun peeked through the forest. They mainly walked in circles; Tommy told her that some dangerous creatures were growing in the Manitou now, so they didn't walk too deep into the woods.

Twenty minutes into their walk, Tommy held Kayana's hand. He was sweating, but calmed down and stepped onto a small rock to match her in height. He put his lips on hers for a moment, and then put them back there for a moment longer.

"How was that?" he asked.

"It feels," said Kayana, "like it *should be*."

/***/

They got back to their quarters an hour after breakfast. No one missed them at morning call; the Academy officially gave the Horsemen the day off to make sure that all the Spartans were clear of demons.

Saoirse was wearing her suit already; it was black with white stripes. Kayana then put her suit on and it fit well.

"Are you sure it's safe?" she asked. "I can feel everything as if it was touching my bare skin."

"Tommy made the fiber so that you won't harm anyone with your touch," said Saoirse. "But I added a hidden design element, just in case. Do as I do."

Saoirse balled up her hands and expanded them outwards in a quick motion. Kayana did the same and bits of material on her gloves loosened to expose the insides of her fingertips. With another hand movement the material covered her hands again.

"Just in case," said Saoirse.

Gunnar came out, and his suit was the most impressive of all. It was lined with red stripes and held countless pockets and compartments. It was sleek, and Gunnar had them feel his muscles. They were hard to the touch, even harder than Gunnar's muscles usually were.

"It's lined with adamantine," said Tommy. *"Just in case."*

Kross whined, and then spoke to Saoirse. She spoke back to him, and then addressed the group.

"He wants a suit too," said Saoirse. "I told him: *soon*."

"I agree," said Gunnar. "The Four Horsemen need a scout."

Gunnar pet Kross, who laughed in appreciation; this was his pack. Saoirse and Gunnar smiled, but Tommy did not.

"I don't quite understand it," said Tommy. "We're the Four Horsemen of the Apocalypse? I mean, aren't those guys bad? I don't want to hurt anyone."

"You have deadly powers whether you like it or not," said Gunnar.

"Yet I don't use them," said Tommy. "I've spent my life preventing others from getting my sickness. Saoirse doesn't hurt anyone, and I've only seen you attack bullies, Gunnar. Kayana is Death and she perhaps has the greatest sense of justice of us all. The Four Horsemen's destiny is to end the world? I don't know if any of us will want to do that."

"He has a point," said Gunnar. "What do you think, Saoirse?"

"I don't know my own powers," said Saoirse, "let alone our destiny."

They all stared at Kayana. She paused for minute to gather her thoughts and then spoke.

"I don't claim to know our destiny," said Kayana, "but I've seen a glimpse of it. It's neither good nor bad, fair nor unjust. It just *is*. We were brought here for a reason; not to end the world per se, but to guide it through a *rebirth*. The rebirth we're destined to harbring will be painful, and will tear every god in this realm into a thousand shards.

"That's why we'll gain enemies in the conurbation and beyond; all gods will soon realize that our destiny doesn't allow space for them and their petty desires."

Kayana stretched out her body and then moved her head back and forth.

"Though it's our destiny to bring the world's rebirth, our immediate responsibility is to protect the world until that time comes," said Kayana. "And we live in a corrupt time filled with gods Hell-bent on ending everything prematurely. It's up to us to stand up to these gods and tell them the world will not end on their terms."

Kayana paused another moment and her eyes turned white.

"Above all else we must realize that whatever shape it may take, the true future of the world is ours to protect. The Apocalypse belongs to us," said Kayana, *"and no one else."*

Photo courtesy of Dustin Hamano

ABOUT THE AUTHOR

Jon Maas is a writer living in Los Angeles. He writes during his bus ride to and from work, and owes much of this novel to the traffic on Laurel Canyon. He is a fan of all types of literature, with his favorite writers being John Updike, Bernard Malamud, George R.R. Martin and Larry McMurtry.

This book was edited by Patty Smith. You can find her at www.foolproofcopyedit.com.

The cover art is by LNC Art Studios.

Made in the USA
Lexington, KY
26 November 2014